Clubhouse Lawyer

Clubhouse Lawyer

The Sports Fan's Guide to Life and the Law

Frederick J. Day

Writer's Showcase
New York Lincoln Shanghai

Clubhouse Lawyer
The Sports Fan's Guide to Life and the Law

Writer's Showcase
an imprint of iUniverse, Inc.

For information address:
iUniverse
2021 Pine Lake Road, Suite 100
Lincoln, NE 68512
www.iuniverse.com

The purpose of this book is to highlight selected legal principles and court decisions of general applicability in the field of sports and recreational activities. This volume is not intended to be a comprehensive review of all legal principles relevant to sports and recreational activities. Nor is it intended to be a substitute for competent legal advice or original research into the law. The author assumes no liability of any kind resulting from the use of or reliance upon the contents of this book.

ISBN: 0-595-24092-5

Printed in the United States of America

This book is dedicated to the memory of Timothy Donovan and Alan Fleishman, avid sports fans and saintly men both, who never tired of talking sports and the law.

Let us run with determination the particular race that God has set before us.

Hebrews 12:1

Contents

Foreword xi

Introduction xv

Chapter 1 Sports Rely Upon Precedent 1

Chapter 2 Contracts in the Field of Play 8

Chapter 3 Assumption of the Risk 46

Chapter 4 Intentional Torts and the Perils of Pitching 70

Chapter 5 Criminal Law and Sports 84

Chapter 6 Women in Sports: From the Tunnel to the Clubhouse ..109

Chapter 7 Privacy in the Field of Play 125

Chapter 8 Misrepresentation: Tall Tales On and Off the Playing
        Field 142

Chapter 9 Sports Agents 167

Chapter 10 The Trading of Professional Athletes 176

Chapter 11 Baseball's Antitrust Exemption and the Road to Free
        Agency 192

Chapter 12 Baseball and the National Labor Relations Board 211

Chapter 13 Relocation and Contraction of Professional Sports
        Franchises 228

Chapter 14 Sports-Related Injuries 236

Chapter 15 Equal Opportunity in Sports 249

Chapter 16 Asylum and Other Immigration Issues Facing Foreign
        Athletes 276

Chapter 17 Locker Room Secrets, Defamation and the "Mendoza
        Line" 293

Chapter 18 Property: Partitioning the "Field of Dreams" 306

Chapter 19 Copyrights, Trademarks and Patents in Sports 320

Chapter 20 Shoeless Joe's Will and Related Points of Law 337
Chapter 21 Violations of the Rules of Sport 348
Chapter 22 Litigation: Lousy Food and Lawsuits 372
About the Author 397
Principles of Sports, Law and Life 399
Table of Cases Cited 411
Bibliography: Books 415
Bibliography: Magazine and Newspaper Articles 421
Index of Athletes and Other Sports Figures 437
Index of Terms 461

Foreword

Curious circumstances compel professional athletes to learn the law. In 1957, after three seasons with the Athletics, I was traded to the New York Yankees. It was the dream of many major league ballplayers to play for the Yankees. It was not necessarily mine. I had enjoyed some measure of success with the Athletics. I was comfortable playing in Kansas City. New York was faster paced and more demanding on a ballplayer's time and talents.

Days before the trade, I had verbally agreed to play the 1957 season with the Athletics for a salary of $14,500. I had not yet signed the contract. A $14,500 salary was good for Kansas City. I thought, however, that the Yankees, playing in a larger market and being perennial American League champs, could do better.

When I arrived in New York, I immediately encountered the business side of baseball. When talk turned to my salary, Yankee general manager George Weiss was well aware that I had verbally agreed with the Athletics to play for $14,500. Mr. Weiss expected me to play for the Yankees at the same salary. "Not fair," I thought.

Unlike today's ballplayers, professional athletes in the 1950s did not have agents to rely upon for advice. I called my dad. He told me, "don't rock the boat." So I played the 1957 season in New York, not Kansas City, for the salary to which I had agreed in Kansas City.

In later years, the Yankees were good to me. George Weiss and Casey Stengel saw to it that I was one of the highest paid pitchers on the team, second in salary only to future Hall-of-Famer Whitey Ford. However, the circumstances of how I came to play for the 1957 Yankees for $14,500 linger in memory. Was I legally bound to play for the Yankees at the same

salary the Athletics had agreed to pay me? Did I have the law on my side?
I wasn't sure. What is clear is that I didn't have much leverage in the discussions. It was one of my first lessons in sports law.

There were, of course, other lessons. I pitched for the Yankees in the
1960 World Series against the Pittsburgh Pirates. Many will remember the
seventh game of that Series for Bill Mazeroski's dramatic game-winning
home run in the bottom of the ninth inning. Some fans will remember
that announcer Chuck Thompson, who handled the play-by-play on
radio, identified me as the pitcher who gave up Mazeroski's clout. It was-
n't me. I was warming up in the bullpen.

Years later, Budweiser Beer used Thompson's call of the Mazeroski
home run in one of its television commercials. Budweiser knew that I was-
n't on the mound for Mazeroski's homer. It ran the commercial anyway. I
thought that was a reckless disregard for the truth. I thought it was wrong.
I sued Budweiser. I assumed the law would be on my side. It wasn't. The
judge concluded that "throwing a home run ball was not that big a deal."
She threw the case out.

I think the judge had it wrong. If you earn your living trying to prevent
opposing teams from winning baseball games, as I did for several years,
home runs are very important.

Like a ninth-inning home run, *Clubhouse Lawyer* is both timely and
memorable. The book provides a useful discussion of topics that will
surely be of interest to sports fans and athletes alike. It is a solid hit that
touches all the bases.

Art Ditmar
Philadelphia Athletics, 1954
Kansas City Athletics, 1955-1956,
1961-1962
New York Yankees, 1957-1961

Acknowledgements

I extend my gratitude to four individuals for their help in putting this book together. Melissa A. Keefer, a dedicated student of the law, spent considerable effort researching sports law cases, verifying sources and improving the content. John B. (Jack) Richards, a former colleague, provided very helpful suggestions for organizing the material, improving the flow and adding a touch of sparkle. My son, Minh Day, a budding sports lawyer, offered insightful comments and criticism throughout the preparation of the book. Finally, former Kansas City Athletics and New York Yankees pitcher Art Ditmar patiently related anecdotes from his playing days and willingly reviewed portions of the book prior to publication. I thank them all.

Introduction

In the 1960s, baseball historian Lawrence S. Ritter traveled 75,000 miles across the United States and Canada in search of baseball players who had played professionally in what he termed baseball's "bygone era." Ritter interviewed many ballplayers who had played the game in the late 1800s and early 1900s. One of the players whom he interviewed was reclusive former Detroit Tigers outfielder Wahoo Sam Crawford. Crawford, a native of Wahoo, Nebraska, played major league ball from 1899 to 1917. After considerable effort, Ritter tracked Crawford down in a laundromat in the small town of Baywood Park, California, located halfway between Los Angeles and San Francisco. Crawford was curious. He suggested that the past was best left alone and asked Ritter why he was spending so much time investigating the old days of baseball. Then Crawford proceeded to answer his own question. "Santayana said 'those who forget the past are condemned to repeat it,' " Crawford concluded, "so maybe there are two sides to this matter."

Precedent forms the building blocks for the law. The outcome of a legal case turns on the facts of the case—but also on the relevant precedents. And precedent, at its fundamental level, is simply the store of legal cases that have been decided in the past. In December 1959, Louisiana State University football player Billy Cannon signed a contract to play professionally for the Los Angeles Rams of the National Football League. A few weeks later, Cannon signed another contract, this time with the Houston Oilers of the rival American Football League. Cannon's motivation was simple: the Oilers offered more money than did the Rams. It was not simply a case of Cannon being mercenary, however. According to the judge who presided over *Los Angeles Rams v. Cannon*, the All-American halfback was "a provincial lad… untutored and unwise." Cannon did not know the law, and he did not know precedent.

One way or another, the law renders all of us "untutored and unwise." There is no shortcut in the learning process. We either learn the law through our own experiences, as did Billy Cannon, or through the experiences of others. Wahoo Sam had it right. With respect to so many aspects of life, and particularly with respect to the law, those who forget the past are often condemned to repeat it.

This book is intended to use cases and situations arising in sports to explain the law and relevant legal principles. The aim is to give sports fans and athletes alike an understanding of the law in a way that will be instructive and interesting. From a broader perspective, however, the hope is that individuals who are not necessarily ardent sports fans may also benefit from reading about the law as it relates to sports.

Former New York Yankee catcher Yogi Berra once said "when you come to a fork in the road, take it." When it comes to the law, we all encounter, from time to time, the proverbial fork in the road. Like the nuggets of wisdom from Yogi, this book may help to make the legal situations we face—and the decisions we make in those situations—easier.

Chapter 1

Sports Rely Upon Precedent

The law relies upon precedent. So does the world of sports. The evening of June 5, 1998 is a case in point. The Atlanta Braves were playing the Baltimore Orioles. In the seventh inning, Orioles second baseman Roberto Alomar hit a long drive to right and eased, prematurely, into his home run trot. To Alomar's chagrin, the ball hit off the right field fence and bounced back into play. Braves outfielder Andruw Jones retrieved it on one hop and threw on a line to second base. The umpire called Alomar out. Alomar erupted.

In the broadcast booth, TV announcer and Hall-of-Fame pitcher Jim Palmer faulted Alomar for not running hard. "If he'd been running all the way, it wouldn't even have been close," Palmer told the television audience. The replay confirmed that, after driving the ball, Alomar jogged to first base. Jim Palmer called upon precedent. He told a story about former Orioles outfielder Frank Robinson. Robinson, also a Hall-of-Famer, once placed a $100 bill on manager Earl Weaver's desk after a ball game. Robinson left a hand-written note with the bill. The note read, "I embarrassed you, I embarrassed the team, I embarrassed baseball and, most of all, I embarrassed myself."

Robinson had been thrown out at second base on a hit he assumed would clear the outfield wall. Like Alomar, Robinson had failed to run hard.

1

Baseball is a game of precedents. Jim Palmer knows. If Roberto Alomar were to follow the precedent set by Frank Robinson, he should have left a $100 bill on the manager's desk. However, Alomar, unmistakably a standout ballplayer, is sometimes not a very apt student of precedent. In a game in 1996, during a dispute over a called third strike, Alomar spit in the face of home plate umpire John Hirschbeck. Alomar was vilified in sports pages across the country. The American League suspended him for five games. There are precedents.

Stanley "Frenchy" Bordagaray, a colorful performer for several major league teams from 1934 to 1945, also made the mistake of spitting on an umpire.[1] Bordagaray was fined and suspended for his conduct. Before Frenchy Bordagaray, there was George Stovall, a twelve-year major league veteran, who spit on an umpire during the 1913 season. American League president Ban Johnson suspended Stovall for three weeks and fined him $100. "There isn't room in the American League for players who commit offenses against public decency," Johnson declared when announcing Stovall's suspension.[2] So, if the book of good manners did not deter Alomar from spitting, the Bordagaray and Stovall precedents should have. More recent precedents were available to Alomar as well. In 1980, three-time National League batting champ Bill Madlock brushed his baseball glove into the face of home plate umpire Gerry Crawford. The National League suspended Madlock for 15 games and fined him $5,000.

---

[1] Like Alomar, Bordagaray adhered to the view that spitting on an umpire was not a particularly egregious offense. Bordagaray was surprised by the severity of his punishment. "The penalty," he said, "is a little more than I expectorated." Neal McCabe and Constance McCabe, *Baseball's Golden Age: The Photographs of Charles Conlon* (New York: Harry N. Abrams, Inc., 1997), 102.

[2] *Spit's Long Trajectory: Back to 1913*, THE WASH. POST, October 5, 1996, D5.

The Ban Johnson Principles of Spitting on Umpires

1. There isn't room in the game for players who spit on umpires.
2. Players who do spit on umpires will be fined and suspended.

The actions that umpires consider offensive form a lengthy list. Legendary National League umpire Bill Klem detested being called "Catfish," a nickname bestowed upon him by ballplayers because of the prominence of his lips. Klem would toss players out of a game merely for uttering the nickname.[3] Frank "Noodles" Zupo, a catcher who saw limited action with the Baltimore Orioles in the late 1950s, discovered a more novel way to get tossed. While warming up a pitcher before the start of one contest, Zupo began faking throws in the direction of Ed Hurley and the other umpires working the game. Hurley was not amused. He warned Zupo to stop. Feeling a bit frisky, Zupo ignored the warning and resumed his antics. Hurley promptly ejected him from the field.[4]

Occasionally, even umpires ignore established precedent. Yogi Berra caught 1,696 games in the major leagues and, by his recollection, "got thrown out only three or four times." It should have been "four or five times." In one game, Berra tried his best to antagonize umpire Cal Hubbard, a former professional football player and a very large man. The Yankees were playing the Red Sox in Boston. It was, Berra recalled, "a brutally hot day." Berra was tired. Hoping to get sent to the showers, he heaped one insult after another upon Hubbard. Hubbard, wise to Berra's

---

[3] Lawrence S. Ritter, *The Glory of Their Times: The Story of the Early Days of Baseball Told by the Men Who Played It* (New York: William Morrow and Company, Inc., 1992), 175.

[4] Rich Marazzi and Len Fiorito, *Aaron to Zuverink: A Nostalgic Look At The Baseball Players Of The Fifties* (New York: Stein and Day, 1982), 266.

motive, refused to eject him. "Berra, if I'm gonna be out here in this heat," Hubbard informed the catcher, "you're gonna stay right here with me."[5]

Like the law, the lessons of sports are built one case at a time. In the summer of 1976, a football fan, young enough to be excited by an athlete's autograph yet old enough to be embarrassed about collecting autographs, visited the St. Louis neighborhood of former NFL running back Johnny Roland. Roland, then a coach with the Philadelphia Eagles, was away at the Eagles' training camp. A hand-written note on Roland's mailbox confirmed he was out of town. The note read, "Do Not Deliver Mail!! Please Forward Per Instructions. John Roland."

> Do Not Deliver Mail !! Please Forward Per Instructions.
>
> John Roland

Roland had gained fame in the 1960s as a running back with the St. Louis Cardinals and, briefly, with the New York Giants. The fan, ever alert to the opportunities for an autograph, removed the note from Roland's mailbox and added it to his autograph collection. In place of Roland's writing, the fan left an identical note, save for the fact that it was in the fan's handwriting, not Roland's. There remained, however, the question of whether the signature on the original handwritten note was really that of Johnny Roland. Had Roland perhaps enlisted his wife or a neighbor to write the mailbox message? The question was answered a few months later when the fan received an envelope in the mail, postmarked Philadelphia. The envelope contained photographs signed by the former football star along with a handwritten note. Comparison of the signature on the photographs with the signature on the mailbox message confirmed that the

---

[5] Yogi Berra with Dave Kaplan, *When You Come to a Fork in the Road, Take It!* (New York: Hyperion, 2001), 156-157.

Eagles' coach really had written the note to the mailman. From two signatures, penned at different times and in different places, there emerged a principle: an autograph, known to be authentic, can be used to validate another autograph.

The law develops in a similar way. Underlying every principle of law are a series of experiences and events judged, from the standpoint of human behavior, to be right or wrong, authentic or false. Applying a principle reinforced by Frank Robinson, Jim Palmer judged Roberto Alomar to be wrong when Alomar failed to run hard after hitting a fly ball against the Braves. Similarly, baseball judged Frenchy Bordagaray and George Stovall to be wrong when they spit on umpires. Whether the year was 1913 or 1996, the principle remained the same. If it was wrong for George Stovall to spit on an umpire in 1913, it was equally wrong for Roberto Alomar to do it in 1996. The Stovall precedent was lost on Roberto Alomar. For students of the game, however, the Alomar precedent will serve as a guide to conduct on the baseball field well into the future.

Once a precedent has been established, whether in sports or in law, there remains the task of deriving the correct lesson from that precedent. During his twelve-year major league career with the New York Giants, Chicago Cubs, Brooklyn Dodgers and Philadelphia Phillies, outfielder Hack Wilson hit 244 home runs and compiled a .307 batting average. In the 1930 season, Wilson set a major league record that has never been equaled when, as a member of the Cubs, he drove in 190 runs. He stroked 56 homers that season while hitting .356. Like many ballplayers of his era, Wilson drank heavily when not on the field. Concerned for both Wilson's health and his performance on the field, one team used a novel approach to demonstrate the dangers of alcohol to Hack. A team official dropped a worm into a glass of whiskey. The worm perished within seconds. Confident that the lesson would not be lost on Wilson, the official asked, "What does that tell you, Hack?" Wilson replied, "It tells me that if I keep on drinking, I'll never get worms."

The precedent of the worm showed that alcohol can be fatal to living things. The lesson, as Wilson narrowly construed it, was that alcohol will kill worms. Either through innocence or creative wit, Wilson missed the point. He ultimately died at the age of 48, a chronic alcoholic who spent much of his time in the latter years of his life in the shadows of Baltimore's Memorial Stadium, living each day in defiance of the precedent of the worm.

On the field, the San Diego Padres baseball team of 1993 performed woefully—and for good reason. The Padres had sent away all of their established stars from the preceding years except for perennial .300 hitter Tony Gwynn. Catcher Benito Santiago, power-hitting first baseman Fred McGriff, third baseman Gary Sheffield, pitcher Bruce Hurst, and short-stop Tony Fernandez were all gone. With Gwynn surrounded by minor league-caliber players, the Padres won only 61 games. The preceding year, with a roster loaded with established stars, the Padres won 82 games. The precipitous decline did not sit well with Padres fans. Season ticket holders talked of filing a class action lawsuit.[6] The issue was simple. The fans had paid to see a major league product. The Padres were fielding a minor league team at major league ticket prices.[7]

Students of precedent could have predicted the results of a lawsuit against the Padres. Some twenty years earlier, a disgruntled basketball fan sued the New York Nets of the National Basketball Association after the Nets traded all-star forward Julius ("Dr. J") Erving to the Philadelphia 76ers. Led by Dr. J's exploits, the Nets had captured the American

---

[6] A class action suit is a lawsuit brought on behalf of many different people who have suffered similar injury or damages. For example, in the wake of the June 28, 1997 boxing match in which former heavyweight champion Mike Tyson was disqualified for biting both of the ears of opponent Evander Holyfield, a class action lawsuit was filed on behalf of closed circuit television spectators who had paid to see a boxing match—not a biting match.

[7] In the wake of the trade of Gary Sheffield to the Florida Marlins on June 24, 1993, three Padres' season ticket holders did file a lawsuit against the team. The ticket holders claimed they were deceived because the team had sent a letter in November 1992 promising that Sheffield and other Padres stars would not be traded. The lawsuit was dropped in August 1993 when the team agreed to change its ticket refund policy and promised to donate 1,000 tickets to charitable organizations.

Basketball Association championship during the 1975-1976 season. The next season, the Nets joined the NBA. To hype season ticket sales, the Nets structured an advertising campaign around Erving. The ads read, "See the fantastic Dr. 'J' in action." In spite of the advertisements touting Dr. J, the Nets sold the all-star to the 76ers at the start of the 1976-1977 season, depriving fans of the opportunity to "see the fantastic Dr. 'J' in action." The disgruntled season-ticket holder argued that he had entered into a contract with the New York Nets, paying money to the Nets in exchange for the right to see Dr. J play basketball. In the fan's view, by trading Erving to the 76ers, the Nets not only jeopardized their prospects for a winning season, they also made it impossible to fulfill their contract with the fan.

The judge was not sympathetic. He ruled that fans had no right to expect stability on team rosters, at least not in an era when athletes changed teams with regularity. To the contrary, the judge stated that fans assumed the risk that Dr. J might not play for the Nets.[8]

The sports were different. The Nets played basketball, the Padres baseball. The Nets traded one player—their only recognizable star. The Padres traded many players, leaving only one recognized star. In each case, however, the principle was the same: the law will not interfere with player trades.

The Julius Erving Principles of Trading "Franchise Players"

1. When sports fans buy season tickets, they are buying the right to watch a team and not individual players.
2. Teams are free to trade established stars, no matter how popular, for a good reason, a bad reason, or any reason at all.

---

[8] *Strauss v. Long Island Sports, Inc., doing business as the New York Nets*, 401 N.Y. Supp. 2d 233 (1978).

Chapter 2

Contracts in the Field of Play

At 3'7" in height and 65 pounds, Eddie Gaedel was far from the typical major league baseball player. Nonetheless, Gaedel could lay claim to having once appeared in a major league game. His appearance is documented in the *Baseball Encyclopedia*. Gaedel's single line of major league statistics stands tall between the records of Len Gabrielson and Gary Gaetti.

The St. Louis Browns, later to become the Baltimore Orioles, sent Gaedel to bat as a publicity stunt in the second game of a 1951 double-header against the Detroit Tigers. In the bottom of the first inning, the Browns' Frank Saucier, a rookie outfielder, was scheduled to lead off. Instead, Gaedel, carrying a toy bat, strode to the plate as a pinch hitter.[9] Home plate umpire Ed Hurley demanded proof that Gaedel really was on the Browns' roster. Anticipating this possibility, St. Louis owner Bill Veeck had signed Gaedel to a $100-per-day contract and mailed the papers to the American League headquarters the night before the game. Zack Taylor, the Browns' manager, showed Hurley a copy of the contract. Nothing in the rule book barred a midget, so the umpire was forced to

---

[9] Gaedel was wearing a tiny St. Louis uniform that belonged to nine-year-old Bill DeWitt, Jr., the son of the team's vice president. On the back of Gaedel's uniform was the number 1/8.

allow Gaedel to bat. Detroit pitcher Bob Cain walked Gaedel on four pitches, the last two of which were three feet over Gaedel's head. Two days later, the president of the American League, Will Harridge, voided Gaedel's contract. Harridge ruled that the contract was contrary to the best interests of baseball.[10]

A baseball player's contract is a legally enforceable agreement. The player agrees to play for a team. The owner of the team agrees to pay the player to perform for the duration of the contract. Contracts have three distinct elements: an offer, the acceptance, and consideration in the form of money or some other item of value or form of commitment. Eddie Gaedel's contract may not have been in the best interests of baseball, but there is no doubt that it was a valid agreement. The contract contained all of the essential elements. Gaedel was to play for the St. Louis Browns and, in return, would receive $100 each day. The three components of a valid contract, an offer by the Browns, acceptance of the offer by Gaedel, and consideration in the form of money, were present.

Eddie Gaedel was not the only undersized player signed to a contract with the Browns.[11] Never at a loss for promotional ideas, Bill Veeck also "signed" hundreds of babies born in St. Louis in the early 1950s to Browns contracts. The contracts were in the form of a document signed by Bill Veeck and bearing the name of a newborn baby. In the hope of enlisting the babies' families as fans, the Browns would send out the contracts to babies born in St. Louis hospitals. These baby contracts were often referred to as "Brownies."

---

[10] Richard Goldstein, *You Be The Umpire* (New York: Dell Publishing, 1993), 114-115.

[11] It can be argued that the Browns of the 1950s needed all the help they could get—from players of all sizes and ages. Under manager Marty Marion, the Browns won 54 games and lost 100 during the 1953 season. With both the team's performance and fan attendance lagging, the team moved to Baltimore and became the Orioles. The move did little to improve the team's performance. The 1954 Orioles finished the season with an identical record of 54 wins and 100 losses.

While Eddie Gaedel's contract satisfied the legal requirements for a binding agreement, the "Brownie" contracts did not. There was no consideration, in the form of money or other value, passing between the Browns and the babies. Moreover, the law does not consider contracts entered into by minor children to be legally binding. In both a legal and a practical sense, therefore, a clear distinction can be drawn between Eddie Gaedel's contract and the "Brownies." Gaedel possessed the legal capacity to enter into a binding contract; the St. Louis babies did not.

Legal capacity became an issue early in the career of another St. Louis ballplayer, future Hall-of-Fame pitcher Dizzy Dean. After signing with the Cardinals as a teenager, Dizzy was promoted to the parent club in 1932. Although he had not yet pitched a full season in the major leagues, Dean had already proclaimed himself as baseball's new "wonder boy."[12] Befitting that view, he was unhappy with his salary. In Dizzy's mind, his contract was not valid. Dizzy informed Sam Breadon, the Cardinals' owner, that he wanted his unconditional release. To justify his demand, Dizzy invoked a fundamental principle of contract law. "I'm not yet 21," he announced, "and my father didn't sign this year's contract like he did the others. So it's no good and I'd like to be turned loose."[13] Dizzy had correctly construed the law of contracts. At that time in Missouri, any person under 21 was a minor. In cases where minors do sign a contract, the

---

[12] As former Dallas Cowboy quarterback and Monday Night Football analyst Don Meredith was inclined to say, "if you can do it, it ain't bragging." Dizzy Dean could "do it." By the end of the 1932 season, he had served notice that he was a bona fide major league pitcher. That year Dean won 18 games and led the National League in innings pitched, strikeouts and shutouts. During his first five full seasons with the Cardinals, Dean won an average of 24 games per season. In his best year, 1934, he won 30 games and lost only 7.

[13] Robert Gregory, *Diz: The Story of Dizzy Dean and Baseball During the Great Depression* (New York: Viking Penguin, 1992), 86.

courts generally will allow them to break it. Dean, however, had difficulty separating fact from fiction.[14] He was correct in his understanding of contract law, but the facts were against him. The Cardinals' records showed Dean to be 22 years old.[15] The team confronted him. "Yah," he said, coming clean, "I'm 22 all right. I musta been thinkin' of my brother Paul's birthday. He'll be 22 one of these days. Or is it 20? Or 19? I reckon I'll have to ask him."[16]

At 22 years of age and poised to emerge as one of the top pitchers in baseball, Dizzy Dean could afford to take a decidedly whimsical approach to contractual matters. The Cardinals, in need of Dean's pitching talents to repeat as National League champions, could not. As Dean soon learned, signing a contract is a serious undertaking. Former professional high jumper Henry Hines and Hall-of-Fame outfielder Roberto Clemente learned the same lesson—Hines from words imparted by tennis player Arthur Ashe, Clemente from his mother. Upset with his pay on the professional track circuit, Hines complained to Ashe that all the money went to the "glamour boys" of track. Not holding the status of a "glamour boy," Hines felt unappreciated and underpaid. Ashe had little sympathy. He said to Hines, "Henry, did you sign? Did you sign? Once you have put your name on a contract, don't complain."[17]

---

[14] In a moment of introspection, Dean once offered some insight into a possible reason for his confusion. "The good Lord was kind to me," he said. "He gave me a strong body, a good right arm, and a weak mind. Armand Eisen, *Play Ball! Quotes on America's Favorite Pastime* (Kansas City: Andrews and McMeel, 1995), 278.

[15] Dean would have had an even more difficult case under the law today. Like most states, Missouri now allows anyone 18 years or older to enter into contracts.

[16] Gregory, *Diz: The Story of Dizzy Dean and Baseball During the Great Depression*, 86.

[17] Arthur Ashe and Frank Deford, *Arthur Ashe: Portrait in Motion* (New York: Carroll & Graf Publishers, Inc., 1993), 81.

Arthur Ashe's Principle of Contract Finality

Once you put your name on a contract, don't complain.

Roberto Clemente did things the right way, both on and off the field, sometimes with an assist from his mother. During his senior year of high school, 1953, nine major league baseball teams approached Clemente. After Clemente's graduation, the Brooklyn Dodgers offered him a bonus of $10,000 to sign a contract. It was one of the largest bonuses ever for a Latin ballplayer. Clemente told the Dodgers he would accept their offer. Less than a day later, the Milwaukee Braves offered Clemente a bonus of close to $40,000. Clemente turned to his mother for advice. His mother said sternly: "If you give the word, you keep the word."[18] Clemente signed with the Dodgers, passing up the $40,000 bonus from Milwaukee. He kept the word.

When Arthur Ashe asked Henry Hines, "Did you sign?", he knew well that Hines had signed. The lesson, of course, was that Hines should not have signed the contract unless he agreed with the terms and intended to fulfill them. Implicit in Ashe's question were two important points: *first,* the decision whether to affix one's signature to a document is one of the few aspects of life over which a person has near absolute control; and, *second,* once a person does sign a document, the consequences can be both severe and lasting.

Pat Boone, who enjoyed prominence as a singer and entertainer in the decades from 1950 to 1980, was both an active playground basketball player and an avid hoops fan. When the American Basketball Association announced its intent to start a team in Oakland, California, Boone signed

---

[18] Arnold Hano, "Man of Paradox," in *The Baseball Chronicles,* ed. David Gallen (New York: Carroll & Graf Publishers, Inc., 1991), 343.

on as a minority owner. For Boone, it seemed like an ideal situation. In exchange for lending his name and serving as president of the Oakland Oaks, he received a 10% stake in the team without having to invest any of his own money. He also had a written agreement indemnifying him from liability for any debts incurred by the team. When the team began to experience financial troubles, however, Boone was pressured to help out. One day, the majority owner asked Boone to sign a blank Bank of America check to pay off a team debt. Boone said, "There is no amount written on this check." The owner told him the check would be for either $245,000 or $251,000 but that he couldn't remember the exact amount and would have to fill it in later. Boone called his business manager for advice. The business manager told Boone it would be okay to sign because the other owners had agreed to indemnify him for any losses. Boone figured that, if worst came to worst, he could afford to pay the $250,000 anyway. He signed the check.

Worst did come to worst. It quickly became apparent that the Oaks were going bankrupt. Boone tried to break his ties with the team. It was only then that he learned the Bank of America check bearing his signature had been written in the amount of $1.3 million. Even worse, Boone found that he would not be indemnified for the loss. Boone considered suing the bank to recoup the money, but his lawyer cautioned against it. "How can you prove that the check was blank when you signed it?" the lawyer asked.[19] On the hook for $1.3 million, Boone was in desperate need of "some sort of miracle." Shortly thereafter, the miracle came in the form of an offer by a Washington, D.C. businessman to buy the team for $2.5 million. For Boone, it was a lasting lesson. If he had not signed the blank check, he never would have needed a miracle.

---

[19] Terry Pluto, *Loose Balls: The Short, Wild Life of the American Basketball Association As Told by the Players, Coaches, and Movers and Shakers Who Made It Happen,* (New York: Simon & Schuster, 1990), 95-96.

> **_Pat Boone's Principles of Signing Checks_**
>
> *1. There is no way to prove a check was blank when you signed it.*
> *2. Never, ever put your signature on a blank check.*

Years before Pat Boone's problems with the Oakland Oaks, it was not uncommon for members of the Brooklyn Dodgers to sign blank player contracts. In an era when contract negotiations were sometimes relatively informal, outfielder Duke Snider and shortstop Pee Wee Reese, among other players, trusted Dodgers general manager Buzzy Bavasi to fill in a figure on their contracts that was fair. One spring, Snider and Reese both reported unsigned to the Dodgers' Vero Beach, Florida spring training site. As the two prepared to take the field for their first workout of the spring, a team official told them they had to sign their contracts before they could take part in spring training. With that, Bavasi sent over blank contracts for Snider and Reese. They signed the contracts and then joined their teammates on the practice field. Not until later did they learn how much they would be paid for the season.

It is legally permissible for Pat Boone to sign a blank check, even if naive and ill-advised. However, when a player signs a blank contract, it may call into question the validity of the contract itself. As with contracts in other fields, a player's contract consists of offer, acceptance and consideration. The team makes an offer, the player accepts and there is consideration for the agreement, the player being entitled to a salary and the team being entitled to the player's best efforts on the field each game. When Duke Snider and Pee Wee Reese signed blank contracts, one of the essential elements to a contract—the offer—was lacking. In Duke Snider's words, "We actually didn't know what we were going to be paid until we received our first paycheck."[20] At common law, for a valid contract to

---

[20] Ron Luciano and David Fisher, *Remembrance of Swings Past* (New York: Bantam Books, 1988), 223

exist, there had to be a "meeting of the minds."[21] The law looked to see if both parties had agreed to the same deal. One can surmise that, when signing the blank contracts, Reese and Snider did not agree to "the same deal" as Buzzy Bavasi because only Bavasi knew how much Reese and Snider would be paid for the season. It is questionable, therefore, whether there was really a meeting of the minds. In the modern legal system, however, the common law standard of a meeting of the minds has given way to a more objective test. The law now focuses on whether the parties showed a mutual assent to be bound. The law asks whether a reasonable person would find that a contract had been formed. For purposes of the Reese and Snider contracts, therefore, the modern standard takes a more accommodating and practical stance. Surely, when signing the blank contracts, both Reese and Snider intended to be bound by the contracts and, in effect, to accept the salary levels dictated by the team. The players made a conscious decision to accept whatever salary Bavasi thought to be appropriate. Viewing the transactions from an objective standpoint, one would conclude that Reese and Snider both intended to enter into contracts with the Dodgers.

Nonetheless, there is a vast array of problems that can arise when the parties to a negotiation exchange blank contracts. False impressions may be created. Erroneous assumptions as to intent may be drawn. In the spring of 2001, Morgan State University was looking for a coach for its men's basketball team. Butch Beard, for many years a player in the

---

[21] The term "common law" is frequently used to refer to the judgments and decrees of the courts. The common law is distinguished from statutory law, which consists of the laws adopted by legislatures. The term "at common law" makes specific reference to the judgments that enforced the usages and customs prevalent in England in times before and contemporaneous with the colonization of America. When used in that sense, "common law" refers to the laws of England and the American colonies before the American Revolution.

National Basketball Association and a former coach at Howard University and with the New Jersey Nets, was the acknowledged front-runner for the Morgan State position. Inexplicably, however, the school's vice president of student affairs sent a blank contract for the coaching position to an assistant coach at South Carolina State, Francis Simmons. At the time, Simmons was also under consideration for the Morgan State position. Just as Morgan State officials were preparing to announce that they had selected Beard for the job, Simmons returned the blank contract to the school with changes that he had marked in the wording. Clearly, Simmons made his changes to the contract in anticipation of accepting the position. Morgan State Athletic Director David Thomas then had the undesirable task of informing Simmons that the school had sent the contract for informational purposes only. In explaining the school's predicament, Thomas asked rhetorically, "If you get a blank contract, does it mean that someone is making an offer?"[22]

Thomas' view was correct. Standing alone, a blank contract does not constitute an offer. For an offer to be valid, there must be a reasonable expectation created that no further action is necessary to form a contract other than accepting the offer. The test to be applied is whether a reasonable person standing in Coach Simmons' shoes would interpret the blank contract as giving Simmons an immediate power of acceptance. From all appearances, Morgan State University did not intend to give Simmons an immediate power of acceptance. The blank contract did not constitute an offer. Simmons' markup of the blank contract did not constitute an acceptance. There was no contract. Nonetheless, the situation clearly left Simmons disappointed and Morgan State University embarrassed.

In each contractual undertaking, the parties who negotiate the terms of the agreement must have the legal authority to negotiate. Similarly, the parties signing the contract must have actual authority to enter into a binding commitment. When Henry Hines signed his contract to participate in the professional track tour, there was no question that he was authorized to sign

---

the document in his own name. And when Pat Boone served as president of the Oakland Oaks, it was indisputable that he could sign contracts and other documents for the team. On occasion, however, an issue arises as to whether a person who signs a contract on behalf of an athlete or a team actually has the authority to make a binding commitment. In April 2002, Women's Sports Zone Inc. sued the tennis-playing sisters, Venus and Serena Williams, for allegedly reneging on a contract to play an exhibition match against John and Patrick McEnroe. Women's Sports Zone anticipated that it would earn $45 million from the match. The lawsuit contended that the agreement was signed by Richard Williams, the father of the two sisters, and that the father was functioning as an agent for his daughters. The lawsuit drew an immediate rebuttal from a lawyer for the Williams sisters. "The girls never gave authorization to do anything," the attorney stated.[23] Underlying the rebuttal was the simple principle that the sisters did not have to honor contracts signed by a person, even a parent, whom they had not empowered to serve as their agent.

As general manager of the ABA's Indiana Pacers, Mike Storen once wrote a letter to the Kentucky Colonels proposing that the two teams play a series of four exhibition games in the 1970 pre-season. Shortly after writing the letter, Storen quit the Pacers to become the general manager of the Colonels. Once situated in his office at the Colonels' headquarters, Storen came across the offer he had written on behalf of the Pacers. In his new capacity as the Colonels' general manager, Storen accepted the offer. He wrote back to the Pacers, "We would love to play those games." Storen assumed that he could both initiate an offer on behalf of the Pacers and accept the offer on behalf of the Colonels. His assumption was correct. A team's general manager typically possesses the legal authority to make decisions on playing pre-season games and to sign agreements regarding commitments to play exhibition games. Until the day he resigned his position as general manager of the Pacers, Storen had

---

[23] *Sports in Brief: Williamses Sued*, THE WASH. POST, April 23, 2002, D2.

the authority to sign agreements for the Pacers. Once he became the general manager of the Colonels, he possessed equivalent authority to make commitments for his new team. Even Storen recognized that the situation was a bit bizarre, however. "I made a deal for both teams myself," he said.[24]

Contracts form the foundation for assembling the playing rosters for professional sports teams. In addition to enabling teams to stabilize their rosters, contracts allow teams to set standards for player behavior and prohibit dangerous or unconventional behavior.[25] Contracts also ensure that teams are able to retain top-caliber coaching staffs. On January 8, 1999, former college basketball coach John Thompson shocked the sports world

---

[24] Pluto, *Loose Balls: The Short, Wild Life of the American Basketball Association As Told by the Players, Coaches, and Movers and Shakers Who Made It Happen*, 330.

[25] While playing for the San Francisco Giants, first baseman Will Clark was contractually prohibited from participating in a variety of outdoor activities, including woodchopping, ice-boating and spelunking (exploring caves). Martin J. Greenberg and James T. Gray, *Sports Law Practice* (Charlottesville, Virginia: Lexis Law Publishing, 1998), 483. Hall-of-Famer Rube Waddell, a major league pitcher from 1897 to 1910, had a penchant for eating crackers in bed. At the time, Waddell and his teammates slept two players to a bed while staying in hotels on road trips. Waddell's bedmate complained bitterly about the crumbs that Waddell would leave in the bed. In lieu of giving the pitcher a bed all to himself, Philadelphia A's owner and manager Connie Mack placed a clause in Waddell's contract prohibiting him from eating crackers in bed. George F. Will, *Bunts: Curt Flood, Camden Yards, Pete Rose and Other Reflections on Baseball* (New York: Scribner, 1998), 129. An injury suffered by pitcher Matt Anderson may cause the Detroit Tigers to draft a contractual provision prohibiting players from entering octopus-throwing contests. Anderson entered a May 20, 2002 octopus-throwing contest in the hope of taking home the prize, tickets to a Detroit Red Wings' playoff game. Not only did he not win the prize, he tore a muscle in his right shoulder, thereby proving that octopus-throwing is incompatible with pitching a baseball. The injury was expected to keep Anderson out of action for three months. The Tigers had to shoulder some of the responsibility for the injury. The contest was held at Detroit's home field, Comerica Park, and the team apparently acquiesced in Anderson's participation. *The Blotter: Sidelined*, SPORTS ILLUSTRATED, June 3, 2002, 22.

when he announced his sudden resignation as coach of the Georgetown University Hoyas. Few were ready to accept Thompson's decision. His players were stunned. Fellow college coaches tried to change his mind, as did Thompson's hand-picked successor, long-time assistant coach Craig Esherick. Only the University administrators, it seemed, were ready for Thompson's decision. While others pondered the impact of Thompson's departure, Georgetown officials were busy preparing for the future. By the afternoon of January 9th, one day after the momentous announcement, university officials were in the process of finalizing a long-term contract with Esherick, reportedly for four or five years. If Georgetown could not have Thompson back as coach, securing the services of Esherick, a former Georgetown player and Thompson's assistant for seventeen years, was the next best thing. To ensure Esherick's services, Georgetown needed to sign him to a contract. University officials proposed terms. Esherick agreed in principle.[26] Though it took longer than either Georgetown or the coach anticipated to complete Esherick's contract, the contract talks proceeded smoothly and without controversy. Less than two months after Thompson's surprise announcement, the university and its new coach were poised to sign the long-term deal.[27]

When the American Basketball Association opened its doors in the mid-1960s, one of its strategies was to attempt to quickly sign players from the rival National Basketball Association. The ABA franchise in the Bay Area, the Oakland Oaks, pursued Rick Barry, then with the NBA's San Francisco Warriors. The Oaks offered Barry $75,000 a year in salary and 15% ownership of the team. During the negotiations, Barry made it clear to the team's owners that he enjoyed living in the Bay Area and wanted to remain there. The owners promised Barry that if the team ever moved away from Oakland, he would not be obligated to continue playing for the team.

---

[26] Josh Barr, *Esherick Is Under Spotlight*, THE WASH. POST, January 9, 1999, D3.

[27] Ken Denlinger, *Esherick Weathers Georgetown's Storm*, THE WASH. POST, March 3, 1999, D4.

Unfortunately for Barry, the promise was never put in writing. "That was my fault," Barry said later. "I took their word and it came back to haunt me."[28]

Barry had high expectations for both the league and the Oakland Oaks. By the end of the team's second year in Oakland, however, the franchise was in financial disarray. Barry would later recall, "I had a verbal agreement with [owners] Pat Boone and Ken Davidson that I'd never have to leave the Bay Area if Oakland moved. I know I should have gotten it in writing, but I guess I just didn't expect the team to go broke and for someone else to buy it and move it to Washington."[29] To Barry's chagrin, that's what happened. After two years in Oakland, the owners sold the team to avert financial disaster. The new owner, Earl Foreman, moved the team to Washington. Relying on the verbal agreement, Barry thought he was relieved of his contractual obligation to the team. So, with two years remaining on his contract with the Oaks, he worked out a five-year contract to play for his old team, the Warriors. He even went to training camp with the Warriors before the start of the 1969-1970 season. Foreman took Barry to court. The court ruled that Barry could not play for the Warriors until he had fulfilled his contract with the Oaks-turned-Capitols. In the court's opinion, the skills that Barry would bring to Foreman's team would be "irreplaceable."[30]

The court had little difficulty reaching a conclusion in Barry's case. Whatever promises were made to Barry, the written word was far different. The court found that, when signing his contract with the Oaks, Barry had

---

[28] Pluto, *Loose Balls: The Short, Wild Life of the American Basketball Association As Told by the Players Players, Coaches, and Movers and Shakers Who Made It Happen*, 51.

[29] Pluto, *Loose Balls: The Short, Wild Life of the American Basketball Association As Told by the Players Players, Coaches, and Movers and Shakers Who Made It Happen*, 113.

[30] *Washington Capitols Basketball Club, Inc. v. Barry*, 304 F.Supp. 1193 (N.D. Cal. 1969).

clearly agreed to play for any team to which the Oaks assigned his contract. Paragraph 6 of the contract was unambiguous. It provided that:

> The Club shall have the right to sell, exchange, assign and transfer this contract to any other professional basketball club in the Association and the Player Agrees to accept such assignment and to faithfully perform and carry out this contract with the same force and effect as if it had been entered into by the Player with the assignee Club instead of with this Club.[31]

When Barry lost his court case, he got into his car, drove across the country and showed up ready to play for Foreman and his Washington Capitols.

The Rick Barry Principles of Contract Interpretation

1. Don't rely on oral assurances from Pat Boone or anyone else.
2. Don't forget to read Paragraph 6.
3. If your contract requires you to play in Washington, get in your car and drive to Washington.

During Rick Barry's year as a member of the Oakland Oaks, Alex Hannum, formerly both a player and coach in the NBA, coached the Oaks. Like Barry, Hannum took steps to ensure that he wouldn't have to move if the team left Oakland. Whereas Barry merely extracted a verbal promise from the team, Hannum had the provision written into his contract. When the Oaks relocated to Washington, Hannum had no obligation to go along. He remained in the Bay Area. The point was not lost on Rick Barry. He learned the law the hard way.

It was the same lesson that Bob "Hurricane" Hazle, a former outfielder for the Milwaukee Braves, had learned years earlier—again the hard way. Hazle was a one-season sensation. 1957 was his year. Thousands of major

---

[31] *Washington Capitols Basketball Club, Inc. v. Barry*, 304 F.Supp. at 1195.

league ballplayers have enjoyed longer careers than Bob Hazle. Relatively few, however, have garnered as many headlines as Hazle did. For a brief period in the summer and fall of 1957, Hazle attained near-mythical status. Thrust into the Braves' starting lineup by an injury to center fielder Billy Bruton, Hazle played in 41 games and went to bat 134 times. The results were extraordinary. He hit seven home runs, with a .403 batting average and 27 runs batted in.

No one, not Hazle and certainly not the Braves organization, expected such feats. Playing at the minimum major league salary of $6,000, Hazle was a real bargain. Once it became obvious that Hazle had earned a spot in the Braves' lineup, he asked general manager John Quinn for a raise in pay. "He kept telling me he'd take care of me," Hazle said long after his career had ended. "You're going great, you're going great," the general manager told Hazle, "and I'm going to take care of you." At season's end, after the Braves had defeated the New York Yankees to win the World Series, Quinn handed Hazle a "bonus" check for an additional $1,000. The check was far from adequate compensation for Hazle's contributions. Without a written agreement, with nothing to rely upon but the spoken word, Hazle gave the check right back to Quinn and went on home to Columbia, South Carolina.[32]

As Alex Hannum knew and Rick Barry would learn, there is a vast difference between an enforceable contract and a promise. Having promised Hazle "I'm going to take care of you," John Quinn may have had a moral obligation to reward Hazle for his contributions. The law makes it clear, however, that a moral obligation is not binding. Nor does a moral obligation transform a promise into a legal contract. In legal terms, a moral obligation cannot form the "consideration" for a contract. Without something more, John Quinn's promise to take care of Hazle fell short of adequate

---

[32] Skip Rosin, *One Step From Glory: On the Fringe of Professional Sports* (New York: Simon and Schuster, 1979), 210-211.

consideration and, therefore, one of the essential components of a contract was missing. Sadly for "Hurricane" Hazle, there was no enforceable agreement. As Hazle recognized, he had no choice but to pick up his bags and go home.[33]

There is often a very fine line between an enforceable contract and a promise. When Clemson University football coach Tommy Bowden was recruiting Roscoe Crosby, a wide receiver of great promise, Bowden resorted to a unique inducement. He promised Crosby that if the player enrolled at Clemson, Bowden would call a pass to him on the team's first offensive play of the 2001 season. For Bowden, it was not a commitment made lightly. "You've got to be careful what you promise," the Clemson coach commented, because "you can't make the same promise to everybody."[34] Crosby did enroll at Clemson—and Bowden made good on his word. Clemson's first play in the opening game of its 2001 season was a pass to Crosby, good for a 12-yard gain.

Two commitments, one by Tommy Bowden to Roscoe Crosby and one by John Quinn to Bob Hazle, produced two different results. One commitment was legally supportable, the other was not. Clemson had been one of many colleges competing for Roscoe Crosby's football talents. Crosby chose Clemson only after the coach promised to throw him the ball on the first play of the season. The pass play was an essential part of

---

[33] Though notoriously tight-fisted, Quinn did not always come out ahead in his dealings with players. In one contract negotiation with Braves' shortstop Johnny Logan, Quinn and Logan reached a stalemate after narrowing their differences to $500. Neither would budge. After weeks of continuing disagreement, Quinn called Logan at his home and suggested that they flip a coin to settle the issue. Logan said the coin flip would be okay but with one condition: his wife would have to flip the coin. Quinn agreed. Logan then put the phone down and returned after a few minutes. Upon picking up the phone, Logan advised Quinn that Mrs. Logan had already flipped the coin. Not surprisingly, Logan reported that he had won the coin toss. Luciano and Fisher, *Remembrance of Swings Past*, 220.

[34] Josh Barr, *Promises to Keep*, THE WASH. POST, September 3, 2001, D3.

the "deal." More than a promise, the pass play was a form of "consideration" in the contract between Crosby and Clemson. Crosby agreed to play
for Clemson and, in return, Tommy Bowden committed to sending the
season's opening play in Crosby's direction. In contract law, the commitment would be viewed as enforceable.

Bob Hazle's experience with the Milwaukee Braves was not unique.
When Donald Sterling, an eccentric millionaire and owner of the NBA's
Los Angeles Clippers, bought the Clippers in 1981, he invited prominent
lawyers and real estate agents to have lunch, meet the Clippers' players and
participate in a foul-shooting contest. The rules for the foul-shooting contest were simple. Each participant would attempt ten shots from the foul
line. The winner would receive a $1,000 prize. One of the participants
was Michael Spilger, a lawyer and the captain of San Diego State's 1969-
70 basketball team. Spilger made nine of his ten shots. When it came time
to give Spilger the $1,000 prize, Sterling tried to change the rules of the
contest. The team told Spilger that Sterling had rescinded the offer.
Instead of a $1,000 prize, the winner would receive a free vacation in
Puerto Rico, good for five days and four nights. However, Spilger
recounted, "There was one catch. The deal didn't include airfare, trans-
portation or food. I'd have to pay my own way." Spilger told Sterling that
he would prefer the $1,000. In much the manner of the Braves' John
Quinn, Sterling told Spilger that the Clippers' promotions department
would work things out. Two weeks later, the Clippers sent Spilger a letter
announcing that he had won a stay of three days and two nights in Las
Vegas. Spilger sued the Clippers for fraud. In an effort to compromise, the
team offered to donate $1,000 to a charity of Spilger's choice. Spilger
declined. "I'll see you in court," he told the Clippers. A couple of days
later—and more than a year after the foul-shooting contest—the Clippers
paid Spilger his $1,000 prize.[35]

---

[35] Franz Lidz, *Up and Down in Beverly Hills*, SPORTS ILLUSTRATED, April 17, 2000,
63.

By the time the foul shooting contest had been held, it was too late for Sterling to rescind his offer. If he had entertained any intention of rescinding the offer, he should have identified, in advance of the contest, the circumstances under which the offer might be rescinded. In the fall of 2000, newspapers around the country reported that Richard Violette, owner of the 18-hole Capital City Golf Course in Augusta, Maine, would give away his golf course to the person selected as the winner of an essay contest. The offer extended by Violette was simple: to enter the contest, entrants had to submit a $200 fee and write an essay of 200 words or less on why they would like to own and operate the Capital City Golf Course.[36] By November 2000, hundreds of entries had been received. Only one person could actually win the golf course and so, from a legal perspective, only one person could "accept" Violette's offer. The person accepting the offer would be that person who complied with all the entry requirements and whose essay was judged to be the winner.[37]

There was one catch. The offer could be rescinded if there were less than 20,000 entries. The contest rules specifically stated that Violette reserved the right to return all entry fees if he did not receive a minimum of 20,000 entries. At the March 21, 2001 contest deadline, there were less than 20,000 entries. Violette announced that he had rescinded his offer and would be returning all of the entry fees. Unlike Michael Spilger, participants in the Capital City Golf Course contest had no right to object. Violette had conditioned his offer on receipt of 20,000 entries. It was a condition that the contest participants willingly accepted when they entered the contest. In contrast, Donald Sterling had not specified

---

[36] *Golf Course Is Up for Grabs for $200, Essay*, THE WASH. POST, November 18, 2000, D2.

[37] Under the rules of the contest, the winning essay was to be selected "on the basis of originality and wit, inspiration, creativity, expression of thought, human interest, and the conveyance of a genuine desire to own the Capital City Golf Course."

any circumstances under which he might rescind his offer of $1,000 to the winner of his foul-shooting contest.[38]

The Vancouver Grizzlies basketball team would do well to learn from Donald Sterling's experience. On June 20, 2000, the Grizzlies worked out rookie guard prospects Speedy Claxton of Hofstra and Eddie Gill of Weber State. The Grizzlies had the good fortune of picking second in the year 2000 draft of collegiate and high school players. At the workout, Grizzlies player personnel director Tony Barone jokingly told Claxton and Gill, "I'm empowered to say that if you make a shot from center court, you'll be the Number 2 pick in the draft." As player personnel director, Barone really was empowered to make such a commitment, so his statement was cloaked with some credibility. "This for real?" Claxton asked. Barone nodded. Claxton then stepped up to center court and sank his shot. Gill followed, and he hit his shot as well. Even Barone could not commit to picking two players with a single draft pick. "I've done that 100 times, where you offer to buy the whole camp a soda if a guy sinks it," Barone said, "and in 20 years that has only happened one time."[39]

---

[38] In each case, the offers extended by Donald Sterling and Richard Violette were intended to be the prelude to a contract between the "offeror" and the person accepting the offer. There are other "offers" that do not form the basis for a binding contract. In a November 6, 2000 meeting with players on the Seattle Supersonics professional basketball team, Sonics coach Paul Westphal reportedly offered to resign. *Westphal Offered to Quit*, THE WASH. POST, November 18, 2000, D2. Westphal was frustrated by bickering and insubordination among the players. According to newspaper accounts, the Sonics' players would not let Westphal resign. Even if his players had favored Westphal's resignation, however, there would have been no obligation for Westphal to step down. Westphal's "offer" was not the prelude to a contract. He had not set the basis for a binding commitment in the same sense as had Sterling and Violette. Westphal had merely extended a promise that he might later have revoked without fear of legal consequences. There was no consideration for his promise. The promise was not enforceable.

[39] *Promising Prospects*, SPORTS ILLUSTRATED, July 3, 2000, 41.

Barone's "offer" was not for real, of course, and ultimately the Grizzlies did not make either Claxton or Gill the Number 2 pick in the draft. That distinction went to Stromile Swift, a 6'9" guard-forward from Louisiana State University. On one level, the incident reflects a classic case of offer and acceptance. Barone extended the offer, telling both players what they had to do to be selected as the Number 2 pick in the draft. Both players responded to Barone's offer and satisfied the condition that Barone had set. To that point, the situation is similar to offers extended by other businesses, such as when a department store advertises merchandise at promotional prices to the first person who shows up at the store on a specified day.[40]

A closer look at Barone's "offer," however, suggests that Barone really was joking. Clearly Barone and the Grizzlies could only take one player with the number two pick. By dangling the prospect of that single pick, on equal terms, to two different players, Barone was inviting a potentially impossible outcome. As Tommy Bowden knows well, "you can't make the same promise to everybody." Additionally, Claxton and Gill could not have been so naive as to think that a professional basketball team would base its all-important first round draft pick on a player's

---

[40] In one case, the Great Minneapolis Surplus Store ran a newspaper advertisement promising to sell, for one dollar, a Black Lapin Stole valued at $139.50 to the first person to come to the store "Saturday 9 a.m." When Morris Lefkowitz showed up at the store to buy the Black Lapin Stole, the store told him that, under "house rules," the promotion was open to women only. Lefkowitz sued. The court looked at the newspaper advertisement and judged that it was a clear, definite and explicit offer. As the first person to show up on Saturday at 9 a.m., Lefkowitz met the condition that the store had imposed. In the court's view, Lefkowitz accepted the offer, resulting in a valid contract. The store had to pay Lefkowitz $138.50—the value of the Black Lapin Stole minus one dollar. *Lefkowitz v. Great Minneapolis Surplus Store, Inc.*, 86 N.W.2d 689 (1957).

ability to hit a shot from half-court.[41] Most importantly, Barone's words themselves do not indicate a commitment. He told the players he was "empowered to say" that they would be taken with the Number 2 pick. He fell short of extending a firm offer. "Saying" that a player would be the Number 2 pick implies a commitment. Being "empowered to say" does not carry the same implication. As both Claxton and Gill would soon realize, Barone's offer was not "for real." Nonetheless, Barone would do well to heed the words written by a judge many years ago. The judge cautioned,

> Jokes are sometimes taken seriously by the young and inex-
> perienced in the deceptive ways of the business world and if
> such is the case, and thereby the person deceived is led to give
> valuable services in the full belief and expectation that the
> joker is earnest, the law will also take the joker at his word,
> and give him good reason to smile.[42]

Tony Barone's Principle of Bantering with Prospective Draft Picks

A Director of Player Personnel should not joke about things that players might think are "for real."

The Spirits of St. Louis, a professional basketball team in the short-lived American Basketball Association, can identify with Tony Barone's predicament. At every home game, the Spirits held a "Lucky Number Shootout." The team would draw a program number from a hat. The fan whose number was selected would come down to the court and attempt a

---

[41] This does not in any way detract from the feat that Claxton and Gill accomplished. In NBA arenas, mid-court is 47 feet from either basket. The shots by Claxton and Gill would have been extraordinary under any circumstances.

[42] *Plate v. Durst*, 24 S.E. 580 (1896).

shot from half-court. The prize was a trip around the world. Like Tony Barone, however, the Spirits gave little thought to having to make good on the offer. The Spirits had been staging the contest throughout the team's tenure in St. Louis. No contestant had ever come close to making a basket. During half-time of the Spirits' second-to-last game before the end of the 1975-76 season, the Spirits rigged the contest so that a friend of the Spirits' public address announcer was selected to attempt the "Lucky Number Shootout." With a smile on his face, the public address announcer introduced the friend, a man named David Elkin, as the lucky contestant. Elkin went to mid-court, bowed to the fans in the stands, dribbled the ball once and heaved it at the basket using one hand. Inexplicably, Elkin's shot swished through the basket. Unlike the tongue-in-cheek offer extended by Tony Barone, the Spirits fully intended their offer to stand as a binding commitment. They just never expected to have to pay off.[43]

Throughout the National Basketball Association's 2000-2001 season, there was rampant speculation as to where Sacramento Kings all-star forward Chris Webber would be playing when the NBA opened its doors the following season. After spending three seasons in small-town Sacramento, Webber became a free agent in the spring of 2001. There were reports that he wanted to join Michael Jordan and the Washington Wizards. Other reports had Webber, a frequent visitor to Los Angeles, ready to sign with the Lakers. Sacramento, a city that Webber found "lacking in a lot of diversity," seemed not to be high on his list of possible cities. The Kings' owners, Gavin and Joe Maloof, knew that it would take more than their millions of dollars to entice Webber to stay. They appealed to Webber with a billboard message positioned alongside Interstate 80, not far from the team's Arco Arena. The billboard pictured

---

[43] Pluto, *Loose Balls: The Short, Wild Life of the American Basketball Association As Told by the Players, Coaches, and Movers and Shakers Who Made It Happen*, 388.

Joe Maloof riding a lawn mower while Gavin extended a promise in extra large letters to Webber: "Chris, Joe will mow your lawn if you stay."[44]

There is little doubt that the Maloofs were joking, but the literal words on the billboard presented the appearance of a bona fide offer. In any event, few NBA insiders gave the Kings any reasonable chance of signing Webber. Joke or no joke, Joe Maloof probably gave little thought to ever having to mow Webber's lawn. On July 21, 2001, the "offer" became more than a moot point when Webber signed a seven-year, $122.7 million contract to stay with the Kings. "I looked at all my options," Webber told the press, "and after all the pluses and minuses, there was nothing better than being here."[45] Left unstated was whether Webber considered the prospect of having Joe Maloof mow his lawn to be one of the "pluses."

When it comes to being "for real," NBA Hall-of-Fame coach Lenny Wilkens, once an outstanding playmaking guard with Providence College and, later, the NBA's St. Louis Hawks, had a sterling reputation among the players he coached. When Wilkens was coaching the Seattle Supersonics, Sonics guard Gus Williams treasured his relationship with Wilkens. The bond between Williams and Wilkens was cemented in Williams' 1981 contract with the Supersonics. In a provision known as the "Wilkens Clause," the Supersonics agreed to attempt to trade Williams if Wilkens no longer held any decision-making authority with the Supersonics. Gus Williams, more savvy than Bob Hazle and less trusting of oral promises, required the Seattle Supersonics to put the "Wilkens

---

[44] Mark Heisler, *The Restless King: Webber Has Made Team Talk of Sacramento, But He's Fighting the Little-Town Blues*, LOS ANGELES TIMES, February 4, 2001, 1.

[45] *Webber Gets a Kings' Ransom: Seven-Year, $122.7 Million Deal*, THE WASH. POST, July 22, 2001, D7.

Clause" in writing.[46] As Williams knew and Hazle learned, it is difficult to force professional sports teams to adhere to promises that have not been set down in writing.

When *Sports Illustrated* reported the "offer" Tony Barone made to Speedy Claxton and Eddie Gill, it commented, "Lucky for the Grizzlies, this offer wasn't in writing." If the Grizzlies had put Barone's statement in writing, it might well have transformed the statement from an intentional joke to a binding commitment. The act of putting offers and agreements in writing brings a formality that is lacking in simple conversation. Putting contracts in writing helps to make the terms of an agreement clear. Without a written agreement, it may be difficult to determine whether a statement was made jokingly or "for real." Even when an agreement is for real and even when it is in writing, disputes may occur regarding the intention of the parties. Near the end of the 1964 season, the New York Yankees traded 28-year-old pitcher Ralph Terry to the Cleveland Indians. The contract that Terry signed with the Indians for 1965 included a provision guaranteeing him a bonus of $1,500 for every game he won in excess of ten. During the first half of the 1965 season, Terry won eleven games for the Indians. Once Terry won his eleventh game, the Indians decided it was time for a "youth movement." With the youth movement in place, the team used Terry only infrequently during the second half of the season. He ended up with 11 wins and 6 losses for the year. Terry felt the Indians purposely undermined the incentive clause in his contract. Upset with what he viewed as a dishonorable tactic, he told the team, "I ain't throwing

---

[46] Greenberg and Gray, *Sports Law Practice*, 256. The Commissioner of the National Basketball Association subsequently invalidated the "Wilkens Clause," ruling that it violated a provision in the Collective Bargaining Agreement that prohibited "no trade" clauses.

another pitch for you."[47] The Indians then traded Terry to Kansas City after the season.

Ralph Terry obviously thought that the Indians had acted in bad faith when they denied him the opportunity to pitch on a regular basis. Legendary Boston Celtics coach and general manager Arnold "Red" Auerbach would take a different view. Auerbach would argue that Terry negotiated the wrong terms—at least that is the way Auerbach viewed an incentive clause that was part of guard Paul Westphal's 1983-84 contract with the Phoenix Suns. The Suns had promised to pay Westphal an extra $250,000 if he played in 60 games during the season. As it turned out, Westphal played in only 59 games. Ralph Terry would have claimed bad faith. Westphal certainly did—because coach John MacLeod held Westphal out of two games in which he was available to play. Under similar circumstances, Terry resolved not to throw another pitch for his team. Westphal took a different approach. He sued the Suns for breach of contract. Westphal lost in court, a decision that Red Auerbach thought was the "correct ruling." Auerbach reasoned that the Suns had simply outsmarted Westphal and his agent during contract negotiations. In Auerbach's view, "if they had worded the perk correctly—specifying how many games Paul was *available* to play in, rather than how many games he actually played— they would have been able to pocket the dough."[48]

Auerbach's analysis suggests that Westphal should have made sure that the incentive clause was based on a factor that he could control, such as the number of games for which he was available. Instead, Westphal's incentive was based on the number of games in which he played, a factor he could not control. Auerbach's analysis applies to other contractual situations as

---

[47] Peter Golenbock, *Dynasty: The New York Yankees 1949-1964* (Englewood Cliffs, NJ: Prentice-Hall, Inc., 1975), 321.

[48] Red Auerbach with Joe Fitzgerald, *On & Off The Court* (New York: Bantam Books, 1986), 98.

well. In 1975, the American Basketball Association held its All-Star Game at the home arena of the San Antonio Spurs. The Spurs set out to make the game a showcase for the league and its players. The team enticed singer Willie Nelson, who had yet to become a widely known celebrity, to perform at the All-Star dinner the day before the game. Willie agreed to sing at the dinner, provided that he could also sing the National Anthem before the game. Nelson was well aware that the game would be carried on national television, and he craved the exposure that a nationwide broadcast would bring. Nelson sang at the All-Star dinner, fulfilling his part of the bargain. The next day, five minutes before the game was to begin, he showed up at the arena ready to sing the National Anthem. Willie walked out onto the court, jean jacket, bandanna, boots and all, and did a pleasing rendition of the Star-Spangled Banner. Unfortunately for Nelson's purposes, there was a mix-up on the timing and the TV broadcast began after he had finished singing. Both parties, the singer and the San Antonio Spurs, performed their duties under the contract. Only one party, the Spurs, got what they wanted—dinner entertainment by Willie Nelson. A more savvy Willie Nelson might have made exposure on national TV a specific requirement of the agreement.[49]

Under some circumstances, the law will infer an obligation by one of the parties to a contract to refrain from taking any actions that would undermine the benefit of the contract to the other party. Paul Westphal undoubtedly argued to the court that the Phoenix Suns had an obligation to play him in at least 60 games if he was physically capable of doing so. However, Red Auerbach did not believe the Suns were obligated to play him in 60 games and, more importantly, neither did the court that heard Westphal's lawsuit. A better example of a situation in which a court might infer an affirmative obligation to avoid undermining a contract occurred with the retirement of famed Boston Celtics center Bill Russell. At the time, Russell was

---

[49] Pluto, *Loose Balls: The Short, Wild Life of the American Basketball Association As Told by the Players, Coaches, and Movers and Shakers Who Made It Happen,* 307-08.

both a player and coach for the Celtics. Russell found the burden of his two jobs to be too demanding. At the end of the 1968-69 season, he told his boss, Red Auerbach, that he was going to retire. As a player, Russell was still in his prime. Auerbach thought Russell could easily play at an elite level for two or three more years. Auerbach asked Russell to think it over, but Russell said his mind was made up. Besides, Russell said, *Sports Illustrated* magazine had already paid him $25,000 to write an article announcing his retirement. The article was to be titled, "I'm Not Involved Anymore." "No problem," Auerbach said to Russell, "you can pick up another $25,000 by writing: 'Why I Changed My Mind!' "[50] If Russell had changed his mind, of course, there is no doubt that *Sports Illustrated* would have been harmed. The magazine certainly expected Russell's article to boost circulation. If Russell had continued to be "involved" with the Celtics, sports fans would likely have lost interest in reading "I'm Not Involved Anymore." In that situation, a court might well find that Russell had an obligation, by virtue of his contract with *Sports Illustrated*, to refrain from undermining the public appeal of his article.

When there is no written document, disagreements regarding contractual terms are apt to occur. In 1998, a Pontiac car dealer in the Washington, D.C. area provided several Washington Redskin football players with free cars and vans for their personal use. The Redskins were told that, in return, they might have to help in customer promotions, perhaps signing autographs at the dealership. Left guard Brad Badger, wide receiver Alvin Harper and others accepted the "free" vehicles. Badger drove a $23,000 conversion van for months. When he returned the van, the Pontiac dealer told Badger he would have to pay for the van—or trade it in for another vehicle and pay for that one. Other Redskins found repossession notations on their credit reports. After the players threatened

---

[50] Auerbach, *On And Off the Court*, 214.

legal action, the dealer relented and took the vehicles back without penalty.[51]

In the movie, *The Natural*, a contractual dispute set the stage for a magical season by aging baseball player Roy Hobbs. Hobbs showed up in the dugout of the mythical New York Knights with a contract signed by the Knights' chief scout. An incredulous "Pop" Fisher, the Knights' manager, demanded to see the contract. Perhaps no two characters in the history of sports were less equipped to debate the fine points of contract law than Pop Fisher, who "should have been a farmer," and Roy Hobbs, "a nobody from nowhere." Just as one need not be an athlete to talk sports, however, one need not be a lawyer to talk the law. So it was that Fisher and Hobbs felt perfectly comfortable arguing about the legality of Hobbs' contract in the Knights' dugout during the late innings of a loss to the Pittsburgh Pirates.

When Hobbs pulled the document out of his pocket, Fisher quickly pronounced that the contract was not legal. Hobbs countered that the contract had been signed by the Knights' chief scout, Scotty Carson, and that Carson said he had the authority to sign ballplayers. Hobbs, of course, had the law on his side. That was fortunate. Otherwise, moviegoers would have been denied the pleasure of witnessing his heroic feats—complete with scoreboard-shattering home runs and exploding floodlights—on the baseball diamond.

If the year had been 1961 instead of 1939, if it been the New York Football Giants instead of the New York Knights, and if it had been real life, the debate could have involved standout University of Mississippi running back Charlie Flowers instead of Roy Hobbs. In 1960 Flowers signed a

---

[51] Brooke A. Masters, *Sweet Car Deal For Redskins Takes Sour Turn*, THE WASH. POST, January 8, 1999, D3.

contract to play with the Los Angeles Chargers after he had already agreed to a two-year deal with the Giants. New York had signed Flowers to a contract before the 1960 Sugar Bowl, in which Mississippi was scheduled to play. By signing with the Giants, Flowers became a professional and, under collegiate rules, no longer eligible to play in the Sugar Bowl. However, the Giants agreed to keep Flowers' contract secret until after the Sugar Bowl, thereby enabling Flowers to play. In the days leading up to the Sugar Bowl, the Chargers offered Flowers a contract that would pay him more money than his agreement with the Giants. After the Sugar Bowl, Flowers returned his signing bonus to the Giants and signed with Los Angeles. In an effort to keep Flowers in New York's royal blue uniform, the Giants took the Chargers to court. The court found the Giants guilty of "unclean hands." The Giants had "soiled their hands," the court declared, by signing Flowers before the Sugar Bowl and then concealing the contract. The court ruled that Flowers was free to play for the Chargers.[52]

The Charlie Flowers Principle of "Soiled Hands"

If a player agrees to play for two different teams in the same season, the team with the "cleaner hands" will probably prevail.

Not everyone adheres to the principles espoused by Arthur Ashe. As Charlie Flowers' case illustrates, contracts in the sporting world do not guarantee loyalty or commitment. Nor does acceptance of a team's offer ensure performance. Charlie Flowers was not alone. At the same time that Flowers signed his name to conflicting contracts with the Giants and Chargers, All-American Billy Cannon, a halfback for Louisiana State University, signed contracts with both the Los Angeles Rams and

---

[52] *New York Football Giants, Inc. v. Los Angeles Chargers Football Club, Inc.*, 291 F.2d 471 (5th Circuit 1961).

the Houston Oilers. Cannon may have done so out of naivete. In the opinion of an appellate court judge, the 22-year-old Cannon was "a provincial lad... untutored and unwise."[53] The Rams' management, more savvy than Cannon but not necessarily any wiser, induced Cannon to sign his contract while he still had college eligibility remaining. The court found that the Rams, like the New York Giants, were guilty of "unclean hands."[54]

A person may communicate his acceptance of an offer in various ways. Sometimes acceptance of an offer can be implied from a person's actions. Before the 2001 major league baseball all-star game in Seattle, Florida Marlins outfielder Cliff Floyd spent nearly $16,000 to buy airplane tickets so that his family and friends could watch him play. Floyd was certain he would be selected to play for the National League team. Not only did he have a .341 batting average, sixth best in the league, and 70 runs batted in, he also had what he thought was a commitment from the National League manager, Bobby Valentine. Floyd had spoken with Valentine on the telephone before the manager announced his selection of the reserves for the NL team. Floyd received the distinct impression from the conversation that Valentine intended to pick Floyd as a reserve. Floyd thought

---

[53] *Los Angeles Rams Football Club v. Cannon*, 185 F.Supp. 717 (S.D. Cal. 1960).

[54] Flowers and Cannon suffered minor indignities during the court proceedings held to resolve their contractual obligations but both went on to enjoy productive careers in the American Football League. Other athletes have received more public condemnation for failing to "keep the word." In the 1998-99 school year, Ronald Curry played quarterback for the University of North Carolina football team and guard for the Tarheels' basketball team. During his senior year in high school, Curry, a native of Hampton, Virginia, verbally agreed to attend the University of Virginia. He then reneged on his verbal commitment and accepted a scholarship from North Carolina. Later, in a poll conducted by originators of the comic strip "Tank McNamara," Curry was voted "College Sports Jerk of the Year." University of Virginia fans voted early and often, accounting for most of the 2,424 ballots that Curry received. *U-Va. Fans Make Their Case*, THE WASH. POST, January 24, 1999, D8.

Valentine's assurance was ironclad. Valentine disagreed. Floyd "misunderstood the conversation," Valentine said. Floyd was adamant, however. "If he said I misunderstood, then he's lying," the player declared.[55] According to Floyd, Valentine had told him that he was on the team "if nothing crazy happens in the next 24 hours."[56]

Whatever Valentine said in the phone conversation with Floyd, it was, at most, a promise—and certainly fell far short of an enforceable contract. Nonetheless, the incident helps to demonstrate an important principle of contract law. If Valentine had extended a contractual offer to Floyd and the player agreed to accept, Floyd would not necessarily have had to inform Valentine, at least initially, of his acceptance. The fact that Floyd spent a significant sum of money in reliance on Valentine's offer, while the offer was still open, could have been construed as acceptance of the offer by Floyd. The player's expenditure of $16,000 for airline tickets in anticipation of fulfilling the terms of the purported contract could well provide a basis on which a judge might find that there had been an "implied contract."

When a contract is implied because either money or effort has been expended in expectation of performing duties under the contract, the courts will allow a reasonable period of time for the person receiving the offer to convey his formal acceptance to the party making the offer. During this period of time, the party making the offer will not be permitted to revoke the offer. In Roman law, it was said that "no one may change his plan of action to the injury of another." Implied contracts reflect this maxim. By analogy, in the typical sequence of events, if Bobby Valentine had extended an offer to Cliff Floyd, and Floyd—in reasonable reliance on the offer—spent $16,000 preparing to respond before

---

[55] *All-Star Spat*, THE WASH. POST, July 6, 2001, D7.

[56] *Floyd Named to NL Squad: Valentine's Late Pick Extends Mini-Drama*, The Wash. Post, July 9, 2001, D7.

Valentine revoked the offer, a contract would be implied. Based on the implied contract, Floyd would be given a reasonable period of time to inform Valentine that he accepted, even if Valentine had previously attempted to revoke the offer.

Professor Samuel Williston, a prominent legal scholar during the 1920s, wrote "it may fairly be argued that the fundamental basis of simple contracts historically was action in justifiable reliance on a promise."[57] In Cliff Floyd's case, the most important question to be answered was whether, in relying on Valentine's assurances, the reliance was "justifiable." Ultimately, Valentine did find a way to accommodate Floyd. Mets pitcher Rick Reed, whom Valentine had selected for the team, came up with a stiff neck in the days before the all-star game. Valentine named Floyd to take Reed's spot.[58]

Occasionally, in contract negotiations, the offer and acceptance take place in surprisingly quick fashion. Tom Heinsohn, a 6'7" forward for the Boston Celtics in the 1950s and 1960s, once negotiated a contract with the owner of the Celtics, Walter Brown, while the two stood side by side in the men's room of a Boston restaurant. "He asked what I wanted, and I told him," Heinsohn reported. "We made the deal before we zipped up."[59] Basketball player Don MacLean's experience while negotiating a contract with the Washington Bullets before the 1995-96 season was distinctly different. After receiving a written contract offer from the Bullets, MacLean signed the contract and then left the signed document on his kitchen table.

---

[57] Lon L. Fuller and Robert Braucher, *Basic Contract Law* (St. Paul, MN: West Publishing Company, 1964), 150.

[58] *Floyd Named to NL Squad: Valentine's Late Pick Extends Mini-Drama*, The Wash. Post, July 9, 2001, D7.

[59] Mark Bechtel, *Catching Up With Tom Heinsohn, Celtics Forward*, SPORTS ILLUSTRATED, February 8, 1999, 12.

After signing the contract, MacLean told reporters that he had agreed to terms with the Bullets and would be on the court the following morning. He told John Nash, the Bullets' general manager, the same thing. Nash reminded MacLean that the Bullets hadn't yet received the signed contract back, but MacLean said he would sign the necessary waivers to allow him to practice. Following MacLean's conversation with Nash, the Boston Celtics informed MacLean's agent that they wanted MacLean. The Celtics said they would make an offer to MacLean as soon as they were able to trade veteran point guard Sherman Douglas.[60] MacLean apparently concluded that he was free to accept an offer from the Celtics even though he had already signed the Bullets' contract. The act of signing a contract, MacLean seemed to believe, did not constitute acceptance. But MacLean did more than sign the contract. He also told the Bullets' general manager that he had signed it. Did MacLean, by signing the contract and then telling the Bullets that he had signed, accept the Bullets' offer? The Bullets apparently did not think so. In John Nash's view, for MacLean to accept the Bullets' offer, he had to return the signed contract to the Bullets' offices.

In the law of contracts, the offeror is the master of his offer. When accepting an offer, a person must follow the offeror's instructions. In Don MacLean's case, the Bullets insisted that MacLean, to show his acceptance of the offer, had to sign the contract and return it to the team. Don MacLean did not have the option of communicating acceptance through his conduct. If MacLean had simply played in the team's practices, it would not have signified acceptance. The Bullets had specified that MacLean could accept their offer only by returning the signed contract. In distinct contrast, the New Jersey Devils of the National Hockey League thought they had winger Claude Lemieux, the Most Valuable Player of the 1994-1995 NHL playoffs, signed and sealed for the 1995-1996 season. On June 30, 1995, Lemieux signed a copy of a contract that the Devils

---

[60] *MacLean Waits For an Offer From Celtics*, THE WASH. POST, October 7, 1995, D1-D3.

had sent to him over the fax machine. Under the contract, the Devils were to pay Lemieux $5.2 million for four years. Weeks later, Lemieux had second thoughts. Taking a page from Dizzy Dean, Lemieux informed the Devils that his contract wasn't valid because he had signed a fax copy, not the original document.[61] When Lemieux failed to report for the start of the new season, his team took the case to a hearing before an arbitrator. Not surprisingly, the arbitrator ruled in favor of the Devils. The only real surprise was that the hearing lasted two days and consumed seventeen hours. "We're not at all surprised by today's ruling," Lou Lamoriello, president and general manager of the club, said in a statement after the arbitrator's decision. "We've been saying all along that as far as we are concerned, Claude Lemieux was under contract to the New Jersey Devils...."[62] The arbitrator's ruling established that a facsimile copy of a contract is as good as the original. In signing the fax, it was as if Lemieux had signed the original.

> *The Lou Lamoriello Principle of Signed Contracts*
>
> *Whether a player signs a fax copy of a contract or the original document, the contract is valid and must be honored.*

It is not uncommon for professional athletes to lose interest in playing for their teams, just as Claude Lemieux lost interest in playing for the New Jersey Devils. Often but not always, the player's ambivalence can be traced to money issues. In 1970, the Carolina Cougars of the American Basketball Association signed Jim McDaniels, a 7'0"center from Western

---

[61] Joe LaPointe, *Pucks About to Drop Again*, THE N.Y. TIMES, September 10, 1995, Sec. 8, 5.

[62] Alex Yannis, *Devils Win Lemieux Case*, THE N.Y. TIMES, September 30, 1995, Sec. 1, 29.

Kentucky, to a contract. The contract called for McDaniels to receive a $50,000 signing bonus and $1,375,000, which was to be paid over twenty-five years. McDaniels played 58 games with the Cougars and spent many of his off-court hours trying to find a way to get out of his contract. Under the terms of his contract, the Cougars were supposed to provide McDaniels with a car. The Cougars provided the car, but it did not meet McDaniels' expectations. He claimed that his contract guaranteed his car would have a tilt steering wheel. The car provided by the Cougars came equipped with a standard, non-tiltable steering wheel. In McDaniels' view, the lack of a tilt steering wheel constituted breach of contract by the team. McDaniels, through his agent, sought additional compensation from the Cougars, including a payment of $50,000 as compensation for "the aggravation" of having to live in North Carolina.[63] Ultimately, McDaniels signed to play for the Seattle Supersonics in the NBA. The Cougars sued Seattle for inducing McDaniels to breach his contract. The two teams reached a settlement before the case went to trial.

Danny Ainge, a two-sport star at Brigham Young University, signed a contract to play baseball for the Toronto Blue Jays after completing his college career. Ainge, an infielder and outfielder, played for the Blue Jays from 1979 to 1981. In those three years, however, he never mastered major league pitching, hitting a collective .220. Ainge's third season, in which he appeared in only 86 games, was undoubtedly his most discouraging. In 246 plate appearances that year, Ainge hit a dismal .187 with six doubles, two triples and no home runs. The experience soured Ainge on major league baseball. He told the Blue Jays that he wanted to pursue a career in basketball. The Boston Celtics held the draft rights to Ainge and looked forward to adding him to their roster. Even though he was still under contract with the Blue Jays, Ainge signed to play for the Celtics.

---

[63] Pluto, *Loose Balls: The Short, Wild Life of the American Basketball Association As Told by the Players Players, Coaches, and Movers and Shakers Who Made It Happen*, 250-51.

The Blue Jays sued the Celtics to enforce their contractual rights to Ainge's performance. Toronto prevailed in court, with the judge ruling that Ainge's contract with the Blue Jays prevented him from becoming a professional basketball player.[64] In an aside, however, the judge noted that, under the law of contracts, Ainge would have been free to accept a job as a non-playing college basketball coach or other jobs that did not involve the playing of a professional sport.[65] After the decision was issued, the Blue Jays said the team's objective was simply to establish that Ainge was contractually obligated to Toronto. Like the New Jersey Devils in the Claude Lemieux case, the Blue Jays succeeded in proving the validity of their contract. After winning in court, the Blue Jays gave up their rights to Ainge and released him from his contract, reportedly in exchange for a $500,000 payment from the Celtics.[66]

Having purchased the rights to Ainge, only one other formality remained for the Celtics. To prevent the specter of Ainge's contract with the Blue Jays from ever again arising, the Celtics would likely have taken steps to show that the contract had been terminated. One way to do this would have been for Ainge and a Blue Jays' official to write void across the contract and affix their signatures. Another method would have been to simply rip up the contract and throw it away. In the days when teams from the National Basketball Association and the rival American Basketball Association were competing for the top players from the collegiate ranks, ABA teams used a variety of tactics to get college stars to sign. After 6'11" Bob McAdoo completed his college career at the University of North Carolina, the ABA's Virginia Squires signed him to a contract. Though McAdoo had completed his college eligibility, he was still in school. The Squires had reason to believe that the contract might not

---

[64] Greenberg and Gray, *Sports Law Practice*, 183.

[65] *Toronto Blue Jays Baseball Club v. Boston Celtics Corp.*, (S.D.N.Y. October 19, 1981).

[66] *Wherein Celtics Score Again by Signing Ainge*, Christian Science Monitor, Dec. 9, 1981, at 10.

stand up in court because McAdoo was under twenty-one when he signed. The Squires decided it was prudent to keep the contract secret. They placed it in a safe deposit box. The contract became of concern when the NBA's Buffalo Braves drafted McAdoo. Braves' owner Paul Snyder got wind of McAdoo's ABA contract and called the Squires. The Braves wanted McAdoo badly. Snyder offered the Squires $200,000 to forego their rights, if any, to McAdoo. Squires' owner Earl Foreman, thinking that his contract with McAdoo was illegal to begin with, was stunned. He quickly accepted Snyder's offer. Together, the two rival owners went to the safe deposit box and retrieved the contract. With the contract finally in his hands, Snyder wanted to ensure that the Squires would never try to assert any rights to McAdoo. Snyder lit the contract with a match and dropped it into a toilet bowl. He then flushed the contract down the toilet.[67] The contract, legally suspect in the first place, was now irretrievably revoked.

If contracts signed on fax paper are valid, then contracts written on other kinds of paper should be valid as well. There are no formal requirements governing the type of paper to be used in sports contracts. Adam Bernero, a rookie pitcher called up to the Detroit Tigers during the 2000 baseball season, signed his Tigers' contract on a napkin at a Denny's Restaurant.[68] Tigers scout Gary York wrote the words. Bernero and York both signed the napkin. The contract provided that "the hereby player, Adam Bernero, agrees to the terms of [Bernero's annual salary] with the Detroit Tigers professional baseball club."[69] Months after signing the contract, Bernero

---

[67] Pluto, *Loose Balls: The Short, Wild Life of the American Basketball Association As Told by the Players, Coaches, and Movers and Shakers Who Made It Happen*, 196.

[68] Dave Sheinin, *Youth Serves O's With Win*, THE WASH. POST, Aug. 8, 2000, at D6.

[69] There was no apparent difficulty in fitting the words of Bernero's contract on a napkin. Fitting one's entire life on a napkin would be considerably more difficult, though University of Utah basketball coach Rick Majerus claims to have done it. *See* Rick Majerus, *My Life on a Napkin: Pillow Mints, Playground Dreams, and Coaching the Runnin' Utes* (New York: Hyperion Press, 2000).

mused, "It makes me wonder sometimes if it was valid at all. But I am here now so I don't care."[70]

Bernero had good reason not to be concerned. Although a napkin is an unorthodox backdrop for a contract, there is nothing to prevent the use of napkins for this purpose.[71] Any paper or surface on which words can be written and preserved is sufficient. A napkin is not as good a medium as fax paper and fax paper may not be as sturdy as bond paper but, in the end, it is the intent of the parties that governs. So long as the courts are able to decipher the intent of the parties, as demonstrated by written words or other evidence, the material on which agreements are written is of little concern.

---

[70] Bernero reported to the Tigers on August 1, 2000 and remained with the team for the duration of the season. He appeared in 12 games, four as a starter and eight in relief, posting an 0-1 record. In 34⅓ innings, he recorded 20 strikeouts and yielded 16 earned runs, with an earned run average of 4.19.

[71] Adam Bernero's contract was not the first time that a napkin has been used to record a contract. In one case from the 1950s, a Virginia farmer signed an agreement to sell his farm on the back of a cocktail napkin while drinking at a bar. The farmer said he signed the contract in jest. Eyewitnesses had a different impression, however. A person who was at the bar testified that both buyer and seller appeared to have a sincere intention to enter into a valid contract. To the dismay of the farmer, the court ruled that the buyer had a legitimate agreement and required the farmer to turn over the farm to the buyer for the specified price. *Lucy v. Zehmer*, 84 S.E.2d 516 (1954).

Chapter 3

Assumption of the Risk

In 1929, the "Sultan of Swat," George Herman "Babe" Ruth made more money than then President Herbert Hoover. The Babe's explanation for the disparity in salary was simple. "I had a better year," he said.[72] Few could argue. Ruth had hit 54 home runs in 1928. Hoover never did that. As Babe Ruth knew well, statistics endow the world of sports with a measure of certainty found in few other areas of life.

> *The Babe Ruth Principle of Comparative Salary Levels*
>
> *If a person has a better year than the President, he or she deserves to get paid more than the President*

Statistics work both ways, however. When ballplayers are struggling, statistics provide a constant reminder of their difficulties. As a young outfielder with the Baltimore Orioles in the late 1980s, Brady Anderson was often overmatched at the plate. In 1988, he hit .198 in 53 games

---

[72] Martin J. Greenberg and James T. Gray, *Sports Law Practice* (Charlottesville, Virginia: Lexis Law Publishing, 1998), I, 947.

with the Orioles. Anderson did not fare much better in 1989, hitting .207 for the season. He was not alone. Anderson's teammate, Rene Gonzales, a utility infielder, was also struggling to adjust to major league pitching.

One night, the two teammates were driving on a darkened Maryland road during a heavy rain. Gonzales was behind the wheel. He was driving at a speed that, given the weather, was dangerously fast. Anderson grew progressively more concerned but refrained from cautioning Gonzales. Finally, Anderson turned to his teammate and said, "You know, Gonzo, if I weren't hitting .198, I'd ask you to slow down."

Eventually, the two ballplayers arrived safely at their destination. There never arose a need to determine whether Anderson, by continuing to ride with Gonzales, had assumed the risk of injury. Anderson could have asked "Gonzo" to slow down. He could have changed places with Gonzales and driven the car himself. He did neither. It could be argued that Anderson, by his inaction, assumed the risk of injury.

In sports, as in life, perils abound. Poor batting averages or not, reasonable people usually act to minimize the perils they face. Common sense dictates that people should avoid known dangers. The law expects no less. And the more maturity and experience a person possesses, the greater the expectation that a person will act prudently when there is a possibility of injury. In 1997, before a game at Pro Player Stadium between the Florida Marlins and the St. Louis Cardinals, the Marlins invited 100 children to participate in the team's "Bullpen Buddies" program. As the visiting Cardinals took pre-game batting practice, the Bullpen Buddies gathered in an area in the grandstands near the baseball field. Officials from the Marlins' front office fielded questions from the children while members of the Marlins team signed autographs for the kids.

Tragically, the team did not take any precautions to protect the Bullpen Buddies from stray baseballs. While taking his batting practice cuts, Cardinals outfielder Ray Lankford hit a line drive into the crowd of

Bullpen Buddies. Lankford's shot struck eight-year-old Andrew Klein on the left temple, causing permanent brain damage.[73] The Klein family sued the Marlins and Pro Player Stadium. A Florida jury determined that the defendants were negligent and awarded Andrew more than $1 million in damages. At the tender age of eight, Andrew could not have been expected to understand or take proper precautions against the risk of injury. Equally important, as a "Bullpen Buddy," Andrew was in the custody of the Florida Marlins. He relied on the Marlins to shield him from batting practice baseballs and other dangers. Andrew Klein required the law to step in when the Florida Marlins fail to provide the necessary protection. If Andrew had been older and better able to appreciate the risk involved, the jury would likely have been less sympathetic. Most certainly, the law would have been less protective.

In 1975, 27-year-old Elliott Maddox was a veteran of six years in the major leagues. For many of those six years, Maddox was tagged as a disappointment. He had made it to the big leagues with the Detroit Tigers in 1970, largely on the strength of his speed and glove. In his first three years in the American League, Maddox played for three different teams, never living up to the expectations of any of them. Between 1970 and 1973, his highest batting average was .252 and his lowest .217. In 1974, Maddox finally emerged as a productive hitter with the New York Yankees. In 137 games, he hit .303. The following year it was more of the same. After 55 games, Maddox was batting .307. During a night game at rain-soaked Shea Stadium on June 13, 1975, however, he injured his right knee. The injury required three separate surgical procedures to repair. Though Maddox continued to play major league ball until 1980, he never again hit above .300 and retired with a lifetime average of .261.

Maddox traced the decline of his career to the knee injury suffered at Shea Stadium. He claimed that, on the night of his injury, the outfield at

---

[73] *Injured Boy Awarded $1.05 Million*, THE WASH. POST, April 7, 2000, D9.

Shea was not suitable for play. There was standing water on the field. Earlier in the game, Maddox had complained to the grounds crew about the dangerous conditions. In the ninth inning, playing center field, he ran to his left in pursuit of a fly ball. As he tried to stop running, Maddox hit a wet spot. His left foot slid. His right foot stuck in a mud puddle, causing his knee to buckle. The injury ended Maddox's season. He sued for damages, alleging that the drainage system at Shea Stadium was ineffective to remove standing water.

The New York State Court of Appeals ruled against Maddox. The court found that Maddox was well aware of the dangerous conditions at Shea Stadium and had voluntarily assumed the risk of playing on the field. Having complained about the playing conditions, Maddox could not argue later that he was unaware of the potential risk.[74] No "Bullpen Buddy," Maddox certainly possessed the experience and maturity to take the actions necessary to protect himself, even if it meant removing himself from the game.

The Elliott Maddox Principles of Assumption of the Risk

1. Players have the right and obligation not to expose themselves to dangerous conditions.
2. If players willingly expose themselves to dangerous conditions, they assume the risk of injuries that may result.

A ballplayer named John Sipin, who played 60 games at second base for the 1969 San Diego Padres, chose to play baseball in Japan when his opportunities to play major league ball in the United States appeared limited. In violation of one of the unwritten rules of Japanese baseball, Sipin

---

[74] *Maddox v. City of New York*, 487 N.E.2d 553 (N.Y. 1985).

dared to show anger when opposing pitchers threw brushback pitches at him. On one occasion, Sipin attacked the pitcher. His conduct did not go over well in Japan. Sipin was suspended for three days and fined 100,000 yen ($500). The newspapers were highly critical of Sipin's predisposition for fighting, labeling his conduct "barbaric." One editorial in the Japanese sports pages likened Sipin to a gangster. Another newspaper wrote, "If Sipin doesn't want to get hit by the ball, he should jump out of the way."[75]

The message from the New York court to Elliott Maddox was essentially the same message that the Japanese newspaper delivered to John Sipin. From the court's perspective, Maddox had two options. He could have played and assumed the risk of injury, or he could have removed himself from the game. The preferred legal answer was that Maddox "jump out of the way," remove himself from the game, and avoid the danger. From the perspective of a ballplayer, however, and especially one playing for George Steinbrenner's Yankees, the court's solution was not particularly practical. For a ballplayer like Maddox, who was still trying to establish himself in the major leagues, the ramifications of removing himself from a game could have been severe. Teams have banished ballplayers from the major leagues for less. Rain-soaked field or not, Maddox would have risked a fine or suspension, at a minimum, if he had told Yankee manager Bill Virdon that he was not going to play in the game.

A few years after the decision in Elliott Maddox's case, an armed security guard who worked at Atlanta Braves games sued the Braves and the owners of Atlanta's Fulton County Stadium for injuries he suffered when he was shot by an armed robber. The security guard's job was to protect

---

[75] Robert Whiting, *You've Gotta Have "Wa"*, in The Armchair Book of Baseball II: An All-Star Lineup Celebrates America's National Pastime (New York: Charles Scribner's Sons, 1987), 414.

the cash receipts taken in at the Braves' concession stands. In his lawsuit, the guard claimed that the Braves and stadium authorities owed him a duty to keep the stadium safe. He also alleged that the defendants had negligently breached that duty. The security guard, like Elliott Maddox, lost in court. The judge reasoned that security guards, of all people, should understand that their jobs are inherently dangerous. The court concluded that the guard assumed the risk of injury from an armed robber when he accepted employment in the security business.[76]

Professional race car drivers participating in the Championship Auto Racing Teams (CART) circuit may not be familiar with either the Maddox case or the Fulton County Stadium case, but they seem to have an ingrained understanding of the assumption of the risk principle. On April 29, 2001, CART canceled the inaugural Firestone Firehawk 600 race at Texas Motor Speedway in Fort Worth. After practicing for the race in the days leading up to April 29, some drivers complained of feeling dizzy and disoriented. CART medical officials investigated and determined that the G-forces resulting from the gravitational pull on the 1.5-mile oval track were almost twice as high as at other race tracks. The Firestone Firehawk 600 was to consist of 250 laps around the track. CART officials found that the banking on the turns at the Speedway was 24 degrees—by far the most extreme banking at any CART race track. In contrast, the banking at Indianapolis Speedway is only 9 degrees. The steepest banking at any other track in the CART series is 18 degrees. CART's medical director expressed concern that drivers who were exposed to the steep turns during the race might lose consciousness. The G-forces were reported to be more than 5. According to conventional wisdom, race drivers cannot easily tolerate G-forces that are higher than 3. After taking his practice turns on the Texas Speedway, Michael Andretti, the biggest winner in CART history, said "You feel very compressed when you get down in the corners.

---

[76] *Atlanta Braves, Inc. v. Leslie*, 378 S.E.2d 133 (Ga. App. 1989).

Everything is just compressing your body. It's a feeling I've never had before."[77]

The CART drivers did what Elliott Maddox would probably have considered unthinkable. They refused to drive, necessitating cancellation of the Firestone Firehawk 600. When canceling the race, CART officials announced that they hoped to reschedule the event later in the year. For Speedway Motorsports Inc., the owner of the track, that was not good enough. The company sued CART over the cancellation. Court papers revealed that the cancellation caused the Speedway to issue refunds for more than 60,000 tickets. In its suit, Speedway Motorsports asked for the return of $2.1 million that it had previously paid CART and as much as $6 million in compensation for expenses, lost profits and damages. CART officials termed the lawsuit "meritless."[78] CART's pronouncements notwithstanding, later events suggested that the lawsuit may have had quite a bit of merit. On October 16, 2001, CART and Speedway Motorsports announced that they had settled the case. The track owner characterized the settlement as "favorable" but declined to reveal the actual terms. Knowledgeable sources, however, pegged the payment from CART to the Speedway at "millions of dollars."[79]

In the spring of 1999, country-western singer Garth Brooks took assumption of the risk to the extreme. Taking a page from Bill Veeck, the San Diego Padres signed Brooks to a professional baseball player contract and invited him to spring training with the big league club. However serious Brooks' interest may have been, fans recognized that his appearance in a Padres uniform was little more than a publicity stunt. Publicity stunt or not, however, Brooks played third base during the Padres' workouts. On the first day of practice, Padres farmhand Chris Jones drilled Brooks in the

[77] *Citing Safety, CART Won't Race: G-Forces Are a Problem in Texas*, THE WASH. POST, April 30, 2001, D4.

[78] *Sued*, SPORTS ILLUSTRATED, May 21, 2001, 24.

[79] *CART, Track Reach Settlement on Races*, THE WASH. POST, October 17, 2001, D2.

ribs with a line drive. Garth had forgotten a fundamental rule of baseball. He took his eye off the ball. According to one Padres player, the shot would have killed Brooks if it had him in the head.[80] If Brooks had been hit in the head, he would have had no one to blame but himself. He willingly undertook an activity that was inherently dangerous. Like Elliott Maddox, Brooks had ample opportunity to evaluate the risks. He could have declined to participate. Instead, he chose to play. It was a classic case of an individual assuming the risk of injury.

While assumption of the risk applies in many different contexts to professional and amateur sports, it is a principle with which those who earn their living from boxing are particularly familiar. When 26-year-old boxer Beethavean "Bee" Scottland died after being knocked unconscious in the 10th round of his June 26, 2001 fight against George Khalid Jones, it was the latest reminder of the severe nature of the risk assumed by boxers. In the aftermath of Scottland's death, there were indications that the fighter may have assumed more risks than most boxers. Scottland did not know that he would be fighting Jones until June 21, five days before the match. Scottland had been scheduled to fight another boxer, Dana Rucker, on June 21, but Rucker bowed out of the fight eight days before because of an injury. Coincidentally, Jones' scheduled opponent for June 26 suffered an injury as well, leaving Jones in need of an opponent. On June 21, promoters called Scottland to see if he wanted to fill in for Jones' injured opponent. Scottland jumped at the opportunity. As a result, however, he had little time to prepare for Jones beforehand.

Going into the fight, Scottland knew little about Jones other than that Jones had a career record of 15 wins and no losses. Jones was a bigger man than Scottland, having fought most of his career as a cruiserweight, which carries a weight limit of 190 pounds. Scottland fought either as a light

---

[80] *National League Notes*, USA TODAY BASEBALL WEEKLY, Feb 24-Mar 2, 1999, 12.

heavyweight, with a 175-pound limit, or a super middleweight, with a 168-pound limit. At the weigh-in, held the day before the fight, Scottland weighed 170 pounds. His opponent weighed 174. Observers suspected, however, that Jones may have gained as much as 11 pounds between the weigh-in and the time of the fight. Boxing experts pointed out that a fighter who is moving down in weight class, as was the case with Jones, often might gain up to 10 pounds, mostly in water, in the time between the weigh-in and the fight. A matchmaker who helped arrange the Scottland-Jones match commented that Jones looked like he weighed close to 185 pounds on the day of the fight.

In addition to his lack of knowledge about Jones, Scottland had other concerns. He had twisted his ankle while jogging two days before the bout. The day before the fight, while lounging in his New York hotel room, Scottland kept his ankle elevated in an effort to prevent additional swelling. Throughout the fight, whether due to the lingering effects of his ankle injury or Jones' superior punching, Scottland seemed overmatched. In round three alone, Jones landed 50 punches while Scottland landed only four. Finally, with 50 seconds left in the tenth round, Jones landed three punches in quick succession, a left hook, a short right, and a cross. Scottland fell to the canvas, still conscious but clearly hurt. Paramedics entered the ring and attended to Scottland, and then the fighter was taken by ambulance to a hospital. At the hospital, doctors determined that Scottland had suffered a swelling of the brain. He never recovered and, six days after the fight, passed away.

Scottland was well aware of the dangers of boxing. He readily accepted the risks. When other fighters suffered injuries or worse, Scottland was quick to say, "That's just a part of boxing." Scottland would tell his wife the same thing. When Denise Scottland worried about the effects of box-ing, her husband would simply tell her that risk was just a part of his job. In the end, it was that very risk that caused the fighter's death. Barry Jordan, the chief medical officer for the New York State Athletic Commission, was present at ringside when Scottland went down. Jordan came to Scottland's side and asked him where he was from. Scottland answered the question correctly. However, when Jordan asked Scottland the name of the city he was in at the time, Scottland had difficulty answering. Afterward, Jordan's comments sounded like words that Scottland himself might have spoken. "By the nature of this sport," Jordan said, "at times, things like this will happen."[81] Scottland's death raised some troubling questions for many, including U.S. Senator John McCain. A week after Scottland's death, McCain called for a thorough investigation of the Jones-Scottland fight. McCain expressed concern over the fact that Scottland took the fight on short notice and questioned whether Scottland was in proper condition to fight.[82]

The risks assumed by Elliott Maddox, Garth Brooks and Bee Scottland are similar to the risks undertaken by spectators when they attend sporting events. The most obvious risk is the possibility of injury from foul balls. When spectators attend a baseball game, they assume the risk of injury from batted balls. To ensure that spectators understand the risks and, equally important, to shield themselves from liability for injuries, major league baseball teams spell out the risks on the back side of their admission tickets. The warning that appears on tickets to games played by the Cleveland Indians at Jacobs Field is typical. The warning reads:

> The holder assumes all risk and danger incidental to the game of Baseball, whether occurring prior to, during, or subsequent to, the actual playing of the game including specifically (but not exclusively), the danger of being injured by thrown bats and thrown or batted balls ....

---

[81] Monte Reel and Micah Pollack, *A Boxer's Dream, Now a Nightmare: 'Bee' Scottland Died Doing What He Loved*, THE WASH. POST, July 8, 2001, D1, D11.

[82] William Gildea and Micah Pollack, *Sen. McCain Asks For Investigation Of Scottland Fight*, THE WASH. POST, July 11, 2001, D1.

The law books are full of cases in which fans have sued baseball teams for injuries suffered during games. Backed by the warning that appears on the admission tickets, the teams have prevailed in most of the cases. Usually the courts place baseball spectators in the same legal posture as Elliott Maddox. Once aware of the risk of injury, fans can choose whether to accept the risk and attend the game. If they decide to attend the game, they cannot later complain of injury. The courts have usually followed this view, but there have been exceptions. One exception occurred in 1957. The same year that Bob "Hurricane" Hazle and his torrid hitting led the Milwaukee Braves to the World Series, the Chicago Cubs tied the hapless Pittsburgh Pirates for last place in the National League.[83] For Cubs pitcher Bob Rush, 1957 was an unusually bad year. The *Baseball Encyclopedia* reveals just how bad it was. In each of the three years from 1954 to 1956, Rush won 13 games for the Cubs. His earned run average during those three years never exceeded 3.77. In 1957, Rush won only 6 games and lost 16. For every nine innings pitched, he allowed an average of 4.38 runs. It was the kind of year that causes baseball teams to trade players. In fact, before the next season started, the Cubs did trade Rush.[84]

Before Rush could get out of Chicago, however, he managed to hit a fan in the head with a wild pitch during a game at Wrigley Field. The fan, David Maytnier, was watching the game from the front row box seats, about ten to fifteen seats to the outfield side of the Cubs' dugout. Rush was warming up in foul territory along the left field line. During the sixth inning, Rush unleashed a pitch that went over the head of his bullpen catcher and into the stands. The pitch struck Maytnier in the head. The

---

[83] The Cubs and the Pirates both finished the season with identical records of 62 wins and 92 losses.

[84] On December 5, 1957, the Cubs sent Rush, outfielder Eddie Haas and pitcher Don Kaiser to the Milwaukee Braves in exchange for catcher Sammy Taylor and pitcher Taylor Phillips.

bullpen catcher that day was Gordon Massa, a Cub reserve. Massa stood six feet three inches. Even at that height, Massa could not reach Rush's pitch.[85] Maytnier sued Rush and the Cubs for his injuries. The judge ruled that Maytnier could not have been expected to keep his eye on two baseballs simultaneously, the ball that was in play during the game and the ball being thrown by Rush in the bullpen. In the judge's opinion, it was physically impossible for Maytnier to have seen or anticipated Rush's warmup pitch. Maytnier assumed the risk of injury from balls hit or thrown as a result of action on the field. He did not assume the risk of being hit by an unexpected pitch from the bullpen. The judge held Rush and the Cubs liable.[86]

The Bob Rush Principles of Assumption of the Risk

1. *Spectators at baseball games cannot be expected to keep their eyes on baseballs being thrown in the bullpen at the same time that a game is in progress.*
2. *Spectators do not necessarily assume the risk of injury if they get hit by a baseball thrown from the bullpen while a game is in progress.*

Johnny Lupoli, a teenager in Wallingford, Connecticut, can empathize with Bob Rush. As a nine-year-old Little League pitcher, Lupoli struck a spectator with an errant pitch at a game in May 1995. The spectator, Carol LaRosa, and her husband sued Lupoli for $15,000

---

[85] Massa's major league career was short-lived. He appeared in six games in 1957 and two more in 1958, all with the Cubs. In 21 plate appearances, he collected four walks and seven hits, good for a career batting average of .412.

[86] *Maytnier v. Rush and Chicago National League Ball Club, Inc.,* 225 N.E.2d 83 (1967).

in damages.[87] In the lawsuit, Carol LaRosa claimed to have suffered facial injuries that required 60 stitches and left her with headaches and a scar on her jaw.[88] LaRosa accused Lupoli, then in the third grade, of being careless. She claimed the pitcher failed to warn her that he was throwing the ball and that he threw the ball at a dangerous speed. Her husband claimed to have been injured by the resulting disruption in marital relations with his wife.[89] The LaRosas' lawsuit was dismissed on a technicality: the judge ruled that a minor child cannot be sued as a sole defendant.[90]

When investigating Johnny Lupoli's case, a reporter from *Sports Illustrated* magazine asked the LaRosas' lawyer whether Carol LaRosa had assumed the risk of injury. If the lawsuit had gone further, the court would have focused on the same question. As with Brady Anderson and Elliott Maddox, Carol LaRosa engaged in an activity where there was a clear risk of injury. Like Anderson and Maddox, she was capable of assessing the risk. By attending the game, especially one with a nine-year-old pitcher, she accepted that risk.

The risk that fans face at ice hockey games are similar to those with which baseball fans must contend. However, while the assumption-of-the-risk principle is well-settled in baseball cases, the results in hockey cases are not nearly so predictable. Under the right circumstances, courts have held that fans at hockey games assume the risk in the same way that their counterparts at baseball games do. However, it is not uncommon to

---

[87] Ironically, Lupoli's team in Connecticut's Yalesville Little League was sponsored by an insurance agency, Kovacs Insurance.

[88] Unlike Bob Rush, Lupoli was the sole defendant in the LaRosas' lawsuit. While David Maytnier sued the Chicago Cubs as well as Bob Rush, Carol LaRosa and her husband, for reasons that are not clear, sued only Johnny Lupoli.

[89] Jack McCallum and Kostya P. Kennedy, *The Windup, The Pitch, The Suit*, SPORTS ILLUSTRATED, January 15, 1996, 30.

[90] *Fanfare*, THE WASH. POST, February 22, 1996, D2.

have the courts rule in favor of hockey fans who were hit with a puck during games. In one case, a fan sitting in the first row of the hockey arena's balcony was knocked unconscious when a puck caromed off a player's stick and struck the fan in the head. The court ruled that the team owed the fan a duty to exercise ordinary care for the safety of spectators—and that it had breached that duty.[91] The outcome of ice hockey cases usually depends on whether the danger to a spectator of being hit by a puck is so open and obvious that he will be found to have assumed the risk.[92] During a game between the Los Angeles Kings and the San Jose Sharks, the Kings' Joe Murphy once hit a puck into the stands in frustration after the Sharks had scored a goal. The puck struck a fan in the head. The fan sued. The Kings ended up settling with the fan for $3 million. When commenting on the settlement, *Sports Illustrated* noted that when Murphy hit the puck, play was stopped. *Sports Illustrated* concluded that, though it was reasonably foreseeable that a puck might fly into the stands during game action, once play had stopped the fan could not anticipate that he might be hit with a puck.[93]

In a March 16, 2002 game between the Calgary Flames and the Columbus Blue Jackets, a 13-year-old cheerleader and soccer player, Brittanie Cecil, died after being hit by a puck. Brittanie was struck in the left temple on a shot by Blue Jackets center Espen Knutsen. Knutsen's shot was deflected by a Calgary defenseman and then ricocheted into the stands. Brittanie was sitting more than 100 feet from the rink. The stands were protected by an eight-foot-high sheet of plexiglass surrounding the rink, but the puck flew over the barrier. The impact inflicted a gash on Brittanie's head, but she was able to walk to a first-aid station for medical attention and later was taken to a hospital for observation. Unbeknownst to doctors,

---

[91] *Riley v. Chicago Cougars Hockey Club, Inc.*, 427 N.E.2d 290 (Ill. App. 1981).

[92] Greenberg and Gray, *Sports Law Practice*, 1255.

[93] L. Jon Wertheim, *No Penalty*, SPORTS ILLUSTRATED, April 1, 2002, 63.

the impact of the puck had torn Brittanie's right vertebral artery, which supplies blood to the back of the brain. The torn artery developed a clot. The clot, in turn, produced massive swelling, which impeded the flow of blood to the brain. Two days after being hit, Brittanie died, a victim of severely blocked arteries. David Milzman, a physician at Georgetown University Hospital and an expert on hockey injuries, termed the injury "incredibly rare."[94] Legal experts focused on whether Brittanie had assumed the risk of injury. There seemed little doubt that Brittanie had assumed the risk. Nonetheless, the Blue Jackets were inclined to compensate her family for her death, out of concern both for the tragic loss and to avoid unfavorable public reaction.[95]

Neal Lundell knows all about assumption of the risk. On June 20, 1978, Lundell gained temporary fame as the "victim" of a stray golf shot by former President Gerald R. Ford. Ford was playing in a professional-amateur golf tournament in Iowa City, Iowa. The ex-President had a well-deserved reputation for hitting spectators with golf shots. To underscore the point, before teeing off in Iowa City, Ford joked about his inability to keep the ball in bounds. "I'll try to keep the ball in the fairway," he said, "and I'll try not to do what Bob Hope accuses me of doing, and that's play four golf courses at once." On the first hole, Ford kept his word and hit a 220-yard drive down the middle of the fairway. A sigh of relief went up from the crowd. By the second hole, however, Ford was, in the words of the *New York Times*, "back in his familiar form." Ford sliced a shot and struck Lundell in the chest.[96]

Lundell was not hurt by the shot. Even if he had been injured, however, he would have been hard-pressed to complain. All of Gerald Ford's errant shots made the national news. His penchant for hitting shots into

<hr>

[94] L. Jon Wertheim, *Special Report: How She Died,* SPORTS ILLUSTRATED, April 1, 2002, 60.

[95] Wertheim, *No Penalty,* 63.

[96] Albin Krebs, *Notes on People,* THE N.Y. TIMES, June 21, 1978, C2.

the crowd was well-known. Neal Lundell and his fellow spectators had willingly joined the gallery for the pro-am tournament. Even if the former President had not been playing, there was a chance they might be hit. The presence of the former president and well-known slicer only increased the risk inherent in watching golfers play. Undeterred, the spectators willingly accepted the risk. In doing so, they forfeited the right to later complain of foreseeable injuries.

The Gerald R. Ford Principle of Assumption of the Risk

When a golfer's tendency to hit errant shots has been well documented in the newspapers, spectators should be ready to duck.

Long before Gerald Ford gained notoriety for hitting spectators, Brannon Morris, a Georgia golfer, plunked another golfer with one of his tee shots. When Gerald Ford hit Neal Lundell, it was with a slice. Morris hit F.W. Rose with a vicious hook on a tee shot that went off at a 17° angle. The ball struck Rose, who was standing 125 yards away on an adjacent fairway. Morris did not give warning when his shot went astray. Rose faulted Morris for not yelling "Fore." He sued Morris. The court ruled in favor of Morris, however.[97] In the court's view, being hit with a golf ball—from any source—was a risk that Rose assumed when he stepped on the golf course.[98]

---

[97] *Rose v. Morris*, 104 S.E.2d 485 (1958).

[98] Apparently, however, golfers do not assume the risk of being hit by their own shots that ricochet off "foreign" objects. That is the lesson to be learned from a 1995 decision by the Supreme Court for the State of Maine. The case arose when Jeannine Pelletier of Fort Kent, Maine hit a shot that bounced off nearby railroad tracks and struck her in the nose. Pelletier sued the golf course. The Maine Supreme Court allowed Pelletier to recover $40,000 in damages from the golf course. *Paying Through The Nose*, USA TODAY, July 20, 1995, 1C.

Assumption of the risk applies to a wide range of activities. Atlanta Braves pitcher John Smoltz once hurt himself ironing a shirt. In a bit of a hurry at the time, Smoltz decided to iron his shirt while he was wearing it. He applied a hot iron directly to his shirt and, in the process, burned his chest.[99] Smoltz had no one to blame but himself. He assumed the risk of injury from the iron. Even spectators at fishing holes are subject to the assumption-of-the-risk principle. In a 1941 case, Sam Rabiner suffered an eye injury at Kutshner's Country Club in Monticello, New York. Rabiner had been watching a fellow guest at the country club, Alex Rosenberg, fish for "Goldies" in a lake located at the resort. Using a flexible fishing pole five or six feet in length, Rosenberg hooked a fish. As he pulled the fish out of the water, it slipped off the hook. The sudden release of tension on his pole caused the fishing line to snap back and strike Rabiner in the eye.

At trial, the judge agreed that Rabiner had suffered a serious injury. However, the judge could not find anything that Rosenberg had done wrong. The judge applied baseball precedent. He concluded that the fact "plaintiff has suffered a painful and serious injury is not to be disputed. However, injury alone would not justify a judgment...."[100] The judge ruled that Rosenberg had acted prudently and that Rabiner had accepted the risk of sitting nearby. Rabiner should have known that a fishhook could cause injury, just as baseball fans know that foul balls might hurt them.

There are some risks that onlookers do not assume. For instance, fans at a baseball game do not assume the risk of being trampled by other fans. On May 15, 1955, the Milwaukee Braves played host to the Philadelphia Phillies in a game at Milwaukee County Stadium. A sixty-nine year-old fan, May Lee, was sitting in a box seat between home plate

---

[99] Ann Gerhart, *Dreams of the Well-Pressed Woman*, THE WASH. POST, June 16, 2001, C1, C2.

[100] *Rabiner v. Rosenberg*, 28 N.Y.S.2d 533 (1941).

and third base. A foul ball landed two rows in front of her chair. In pursuit of the ball, a dozen or so fans converged on Lee's seat. She was knocked off her chair and into the aisle. Some fans chasing after the ball stepped on Lee, fracturing her rib and causing severe bruises and abrasions. May Lee sued the Braves. She argued that the team owed her a duty of care while she was at the game. She faulted the ballclub for not having enough ushers in the area to protect her. The court agreed and awarded her $3,500 in damages. When fans attend a baseball game, the court said, they do not expect to be trampled. The risk was not apparent; it was not a risk that May Lee assumed.[101] The Braves surely did not intend for May Lee to be injured, so it was not an intentional tort. Nonetheless, the Braves breached their duty of care. It was a tort of negligence, an unintentional tort.

The May Lee Principle of Recovery in Negligence Cases

In order for a plaintiff to recover for injuries in a negligence case, four conditions must exist: (1) the defendant must have owed a duty of care to the plaintiff; (2) the defendant must have violated its duty of care; (3) the plaintiff must have suffered injury, damages or loss; and (4) the injury, damages or loss must have been caused by the defendant's actions or failure to act.

Just as May Lee did not assume the risk of being trampled, baseball fans do not assume the risk of having a stadium roof fall on top of them. In 1998, a 500-pound concrete and steel beam forming part of the upper deck of Yankee Stadium fell just as the New York Yankees and California Angels were about to begin batting practice, four hours before the scheduled start of their April 13, 1998 twilight game.[102] The beam landed atop

---

101 *Lee v. National League Baseball Club of Milwaukee*, 89 N.W.2d 811 (1958).

102 Randy Kennedy, *Yankee Stadium Closed As Beam Falls Onto Seats*, THE N.Y. TIMES, April 14, 1998, A1.

Seat 7 in the second row of Section 22 in "The House that Ruth Built." Baseball writers immediately dubbed Seat 7 "the Death Seat." No less an authority than New York Mayor Rudolph Giuliani commented, "You could see that if someone were sitting there at the time that the beam came down, that person would be dead."[103]

Babe Ruth may have "built" Yankee Stadium, but he wasn't responsible for maintaining it. The New York Yankees were. Had there been an injury or fatality from the falling beam, the Yankees would have had to shoulder the responsibility.[104] To maintain a lawsuit against the Yankees for negligence, four conditions would have had to exist. First, the Yankees must have had a duty to protect their patrons from harm. Second, the Yankees must have breached that duty or failed to conform to the customary standard of care. Third, there must have been actual injury, loss or damages; and, fourth, the injury suffered must have been caused by the Yankees' conduct. The law does not expect owners of sports facilities to protect fans from dangers that are beyond the owners' control. During World War II, German bombs struck the storied tennis stadium at Wimbledon in England several times during air raids. The bombs blew holes in the Centre Court roof. In the year 1940 alone, the Wimbledon courts were damaged four times during enemy air raids.[105] Unlike the falling beam at Yankee Stadium, the air raids were outside the

---

[103] Blaine Harden, *Letter from New York: One Steel Beam May Not Be Enough to Wreck the House That Ruth Built*, THE N.Y. TIMES, April 16, 1998, A2.

[104] The Yankees lease Yankee Stadium from the City of New York. The lease arrangement states that the Yankees are responsible for maintenance of the Stadium. The City of New York and the Yankees are jointly responsible for protecting spectators from injuries due to structural defects in the Stadium.

[105] Bud Collins and Zander Hollander, eds., *Bud Collins' Tennis Encyclopedia* (Detroit, MI: Visible Ink Press, 1997), 71.

control of the Wimbledon club. In the eyes of the law, the Wimbledon club would not have been liable for any injuries that may have been caused by the bombs.

May Lee's lawsuit against the Milwaukee Braves reinforced the principle that sports franchises must take precautions to ensure that fans are not trampled during games. However, when teams do take measures to prevent fans from being trampled, those measures must be reasonable. A case arising from a 1908 game at the Polo Grounds, home of the New York Baseball Giants, established an important legal standard regarding "imprisonment" of fans. The game pitted the Giants against the visiting Chicago Cubs. The baseball season was winding down, with the Cubs and the Giants tied for the National League lead. The winner of the contest would take a one-game lead in the standings. For both teams, it was the most critical game of the season.

When the gates outside the Polo Grounds opened before the game, fans surged into the ballpark. Wave after wave of fans passed through the gates. The ushers and security guards were quickly overwhelmed. Fearing that fans already inside the gates would be trampled, the Giants locked the outside gates. The fans who were inside the park found themselves trapped in an enclosed area between the stadium and the outside fence for about an hour. With the outside gates locked, they could not leave. One frustrated fan sued the Giants for false imprisonment. The court found the Giants liable. During the trial, it was revealed that there was another gate that the fans could have used to leave the stadium. However, stadium officials did not tell the fans about the alternate gate. The court found that the Giants' efforts to control the surging crowd, though well-intended, caused the fans to be imprisoned.[106] The simple remedy would have been

---

[106] *Talcott v. National Exhibition Co.*, 128 N.Y.S. 1059 (1911).

to let people know about the other exit. In the court's opinion, the failure to do so constituted a tort.[107]

The duty of care can extend to many different situations. In 1995 Ohio State running back Eddie George won the Heisman Trophy, college football's most coveted award. George received the trophy, a 35-pound sculptured bronze replica of a football player, at the prestigious Heisman dinner in New York City. After the dinner, George took a flight from New York's La Guardia Airport to his home in Columbus, Ohio. He carried the trophy with him. At the airport, the Heisman got stuck in an x-ray machine. The machine severed the tip of the trophy's right index finger and bent the middle finger.[108] When the damage to the Heisman occurred, the trophy was in the exclusive control of the x-ray machine operators. Eddie George expected that the airport personnel would take reasonable care to protect against damage. He entrusted the Heisman to their care. All they had to do was return the trophy in its original condition and with all the fingers intact. The airport failed its duty of care. Understandably, airport officials quickly offered to pay for repair of the trophy.

---

[107] The game itself was memorable because of "Merkle's bonehead." In the last of the ninth, the Giants had runners on first and third with the score tied and two outs. Fred Merkle was the runner at first. The batter drove the first pitch to center field, bringing home the runner at third. Seeing the winning run score, Merkle stopped halfway between first and second and, to avoid the surging crowd, headed for the Giants' clubhouse. The Cubs' Johnny Evers called for the ball and, as fans poured onto the field, Evers touched second base to force Merkle. It was the final out of the inning. The umpires were unable to clear the field. They declared the game a tie, with the game to be finished after the final regular season game. After completion of the season finale, the Giants and Cubs were tied for first place. When the two teams met to complete the suspended "Merkle's bonehead" game, the Cubs beat famed Giants pitcher Christy Mathewson, thereby winning the pennant.

[108] *George's Heisman Has a Chip on Its Block*, THE WASH. POST, December 15, 1995, B2.

> ## *The Eddie George Principle of the Duty of Care*
>
> *If a person who is under a duty to safeguard the Heisman Trophy or any other goods of value causes damage to the goods, the duty of care has been violated and a tort committed.*

The duty of care was not so clear in a tort case involving the manufacturer of basketball nets. A high school student, Christopher Conley of Nashua, New Hampshire, injured himself during a basketball game. The injury occurred as Conley was attempting to dunk the ball. He went up for the shot, apparently with his mouth open. As he descended, Conley caught his teeth on the basketball net, suffering severe dental damage. He maintained that Lifetime Products, the manufacturer of the basketball net, was responsible for his injury. Instead of going to a trial over Conley's injuries, Lifetime Products settled the case for $50,000.[109]

The injury that Conley suffered could readily be imagined. Catching a tooth, or several teeth, on the nylon strings of a basketball net could easily cause structural damage to a player's mouth as well as excruciating pain. To successfully sue Lifetime Products, however, Conley would have had to prove that the company, when manufacturing the net, had violated its duty of care to potential users. Conley would have also had to overcome another hurdle. He would have had to demonstrate that, when playing basketball with the Lifetime Products' net, he did not assume the risk of injury.

Just as Elliott Maddox assumed the risk of injury when playing baseball on the rain-soaked field at Shea Stadium, or as Sam Rabiner assumed the risk when watching Alex Rosenberg fish for Goldies, Conley was surely aware of the potential for injury if he caught his teeth on a nylon basketball net. The words that the New York court used in Sam Rabiner's "fish-

[109] Chuck Shepherd and Jim Sweeney, *News of the Weird*, WASHINGTON (D.C.) CITY PAPER, February 16, 1996, 16.

hook" case would seem to apply: "That plaintiff has suffered a painful and serious injury is not to be disputed. However, injury alone would not justify a judgment ...."

No players were injured when unseasonably warm weather caused a layer of condensation to form on the basketball court during the middle of a November 2001 collegiate contest between the University of Virginia and Michigan State University at the Richmond (Virginia) Coliseum. The game featured two powerhouse teams, with Virginia ranked ninth in the nation and Michigan State ranked twenty-second. It was being televised to a nationwide audience on the ESPN Sports Network. Just minutes after the start of the second half, however, officials were forced to cancel the game. The court had become dangerously slick, due to the condensation, and the officials worried that the players would be injured. The Coliseum had scheduled a professional hockey game for two days after the basketball game. According to Coliseum officials, there would not have been enough time to take up the ice before the basketball game and then install a new layer of ice for the hockey game. The Coliseum crew decided, instead, to lay the basketball floor on top of the ice, with a thin barrier separating the ice and the hardwood court. Under ideal conditions, the ice would not have affected the basketball game. Unfortunately, the weather in the days leading up to the basketball game was anything but ideal—at least for a hockey rink. At tip-off time between Virginia and Michigan State, the temperature outside the arena was 65 degrees and the ice was melting. Coliseum officials ran the arena's air conditioning units at full blast and turned on all of the available electric fans. Their efforts proved futile, however, leaving the basketball court wet and treacherous.[110]

---

[110] Jeremy Redmon, *Mayor Says City Should Refund Ticket Costs for Slippery Show*, RICHMOND TIMES-DISPATCH, November 30, 2001, A1, A8.

If players on either the Virginia or Michigan State squads had been injured, the situation would have presented a more compelling legal scenario than was the case with Christopher Conley's injury. The legal analysis would have focused on whether the injured players assumed the risk of injury. Experts would have looked for ways to distinguish conditions at the Coliseum from the circumstances in assumption-of-the-risk cases such as the Elliott Maddox decision. Several distinctions seem relevant. For one, officials at the Richmond Coliseum had complete discretion regarding preparations for the basketball game. It was their decision to lay the basketball court on top of the ice. In contrast, Shea Stadium had no control over the amount of rain that fell before the game in which Maddox was injured. Additionally, Maddox was well aware of the danger posed by the standing water in the outfield and, after assessing the danger, chose to play. The danger posed by the condensation at the Coliseum came from a source—the hockey rink—that was neither obvious nor within view of the players. With respect to assessing the danger, the basketball players were in a position that was dramatically inferior to the perspective enjoyed by Elliott Maddox at Shea Stadium.

When it comes to assumption of the risk, perspective is everything. If an individual is in a position to appreciate the danger, or has been forewarned about the danger, the courts are inclined to find that the individual assumed the risk of injury. Elliott Maddox was aware of the potential risk. May Lee was not. Maddox assumed the risk of injury. May Lee did not. As between Elliott Maddox and May Lee, the legal posture of the players in the Virginia-Michigan State basketball game was more akin to May Lee's situation. Like May Lee, the basketball players faced a risk that they could neither anticipate nor fully comprehend.

Chapter 4

Intentional Torts and the Perils of Pitching

Sunday, July 28, 1991, loomed as a big day in the life of New York Yankee rookie pitcher Scott Kamieniecki. He was scheduled to take the mound against the California Angels. Up to that point, the season had been quite a success for Kamieniecki. Relying on a fastball that traveled more than 90 miles an hour and a decent repertoire of breaking balls, Kamieniecki had posted a record of four wins against two losses. He had compiled a sparkling earned run average of 2.68. Kamieniecki had more incentive than usual to pitch well against the Angels. The Yankee Stadium crowd of 30,000 included his young wife and her parents, who had flown in from Michigan for the game. They were sitting in the box seats set aside for guests of the Yankee players.

Kamieniecki would soon have more to think about than simply impressing his wife and her parents. As he was getting set to pitch to California Angels second baseman Luis Sojo in the top of the second, a twenty-four-year-old exotic dancer named Laurie Stathopoulos, known professionally in Nyack, New York as Toppsy Curvey, strode onto the baseball field. Upon reaching the pitcher's mound, she planted a big kiss on Kamieniecki's cheek. Kamieniecki, obviously distracted and wearing a sheepish grin, let the baseball fall from his hands. Security guards then came to Kamieniecki's rescue and took Stathopoulos away.[111] When play resumed, Kamieniecki quickly gave up a two-run double to Sojo. The Angels went on to an 8-4 victory. After the game, Kamieniecki said his pitch to Sojo sailed too far out over home plate. He insisted, however, that Stathopoulos' kiss was not the reason. He said he simply did not have his good stuff.[112]

In 1995, a 27-year-old bond trader named John Murray ran onto the baseball diamond at Wrigley Field with more harmful intentions than a kiss in mind. Moments before, Chicago Cubs relief pitcher Randy Myers had given up a two-run home run to Houston Astros pinch hitter James Mouton. Mouton's homer gave the Astros a 9-7 lead and jeopardized the Cubs' bid for one of the four spots in the National League playoffs. No sooner had Mouton's blast cleared the fence than Murray leaped from the stands and ran toward the 6'1", 230-pound Myers. As Murray approached, it looked to the Cubs pitcher like Murray was reaching for a weapon. "I made sure his hands didn't go into his waistband and pull out a knife or a gun," Myers said later. Myers wrestled Murray to the ground. Wrigley Field security officers then escorted Murray out of the park and straight to the city's lockup facilities. Police charged him with assault and disorderly conduct.[113]

The law divides private legal actions into two broad categories, breach of contract and torts. A tort is any wrongful act, damage or injury done willfully, or unintentionally but negligently, that does not involve breach

---

[111] Richard Goldstein, *You Be The Umpire* (New York: Dell Publishing, 1993), 255-256.

[112] Filip Bondy, *Yankees Stripped of Victory*, THE N.Y. TIMES, July 29, 1991, C1, C3.

[113] *Cubs Pitcher Is Attacked By Spectator*, THE WASH. POST, September 29, 1995, D1, D8. Ultimately, Murray pleaded guilty to a charge of disorderly conduct. The court sentenced him to 18 months' probation and required him to perform 200 hours of community service. The court also banned Murray from attending Chicago Cubs home games during 1996.

of a contract. As the definition suggests, torts are classified as either intentional torts or unintentional torts.[114] The factual situations involving Laurie Stathopoulos and John Murray were different. From a legal perspective, however, there were clear parallels. Both Murray and Stathopoulos committed potentially tortious acts on the pitcher's mound.

An assault is an act that creates a reasonable apprehension of harmful or offensive contact. The act must be intentional. It must also result in a well-founded fear of peril. Clearly, John Murray assaulted Randy Myers. Murray intentionally entered the playing field. His actions created in Myers a well-founded fear of peril; Myers thought that Murray had a weapon. Whether Scott Kamieniecki was fearful of Laurie Stathopoulos is another question. The batter that Kamieniecki was facing, Luis Sojo, was a classic singles hitter. During the 1991 season, Sojo came to bat 378 times for the Angels. He collected 94 base hits, 76 of them singles. He had 14 doubles, a triple and 3 home runs. One of Sojo's 14 doubles came immediately after Stathopoulos kissed Kamieniecki. Sojo, a weak hitter, hit Kamieniecki's pitch with authority. The Yankee pitcher was no doubt surprised. But had Stathopoulos assaulted him? Like John Murray, Laurie Stathopoulos intentionally ran onto the baseball field. Did she create a reasonable apprehension of harmful or offensive conduct? Only Kamieniecki knows for sure. Newspaper accounts reported that the Yankee was left with a smudge of lipstick and a sheepish grin, suggesting amusement more than fright. Years later, when asked about the incident, Kamieniecki said that he was neither apprehensive nor afraid. He was surprised, however, because the stripper had first headed toward the Yankees' third baseman and then veered, unexpectedly, toward the pitching mound. He was also

---

[114] Intentional torts include assault and battery as well as other actions in which the wrongdoer intends to commit the act and does so in order to harm the victim. Invasion of privacy and infliction of emotional distress are examples of other actions that could be intentional torts.

embarrassed, he said, that the uninvited kiss took place in full view of his wife and in-laws.

> ## The Randy Myers Principles of Reasonable Apprehension
>
> 1. *If a spectator leaves his seat in the ballpark, walks onto the playing field and appears to be reaching for a weapon, the spectator has created a reasonable apprehension of harmful contact.*
> 2. *If the actions of the spectator are intentional and create a well-founded fear of peril, it is an assault.*
> 3. *For an assault to occur, there need not be actual contact between the assailant and the victim; a reasonable apprehension of harmful contact is sufficient.*

Battery is intentional contact that is harmful or offensive. Battery is a completed assault. Randy Myers was able to restrain his assailant before Murray could cause harmful contact. For this reason, Chicago police charged Murray with assault and not battery.[115] Stathopoulos, unlike

---

[115] The victims of assault and battery may sue for damages in a civil action under tort law and, at the same time, press criminal charges based on the same set of facts. For this reason, Myers could have filed a civil lawsuit seeking a monetary award against Murray for tortious assault. The components of criminal assault are generally the same as the elements that comprise assault under tort law. It sometimes happens that, in cases where a wrongdoer is the subject of both a civil lawsuit and criminal charges, the plaintiff may prevail in the civil action but the criminal case may be decided in favor of the defendant. That is what happened when former football star O. J. Simpson faced both criminal charges and a civil lawsuit in the death of his wife. One reason for the apparently contradictory results is that the specific elements of a crime are defined by law, and the courts are bound by the statutory definition. In contrast, a tort is usually not defined by law. Additionally, the standard of proof is different in a criminal case than in a civil lawsuit. To find Simpson guilty on the criminal charge, the jury would have had to conclude, beyond a reasonable doubt, that he had committed the act. In the civil suit, the jury was guided by a lesser standard. It had to find only that Simpson was responsible for the act based on a preponderance of the evidence.

Murray, completed the intended act. Kissing a stranger can be offensive conduct. If Kamieniecki considered the kiss offensive, the elements of a battery, intent plus conduct that is offensive or harmful, would exist. Most cases of battery, however, leave the victims angry. Stathopoulos left Kamieniecki with a sheepish grin and a smudge of lipstick, neither of which seemed to offend him.[116]

The Scott Kamieniecki Principles of Offensive Contact

1. *For a battery to occur, there must be intentional contact that is harmful or offensive.*
2. *If the intentional contact leaves a person with a "sheepish grin," it is probably not a battery.*

Philadelphia 76ers head coach Larry Brown got his start in coaching with the Carolina Cougars of the American Basketball Association. Wherever he played and coached, Brown was a fan favorite. He was also the kind of person that opposing fans loved to hate. Brown found the fans in San Antonio to be particularly abusive. To retaliate, Brown would take his case to the press. Once, in a moment of pique, he told newspaper reporters, "The only good thing about San Antonio is the guacamole salad." As Brown no doubt intended, the fans in San Antonio—at least those not in the business of making guacamole salad—took the insult personally. After one game, as Brown and his team headed to the locker room tunnel, some fans sitting in the stands above the tunnel entrance dumped a pile of gua-

---

[116] Kamieniecki's record speaks for itself, however. Stathopoulos' kiss seemed to mark a turning point in his season. Due in part to Sojo's two-run double, Kamieniecki lost to the Angels. He lost his next decision as well, finishing the year with four wins, four losses and an earned run average of 3.90.

camole and "all kinds of other stuff on him."[117] The fans may not have construed the dumping of guacamole as a battery, but Larry Brown certainly could have. Brown was not injured in the incident. However, the lack of injury does not preclude a finding of battery. As in the pitching mound encounter between Scott Kamieniecki and the stripper, the contact need only be offensive. Certainly, the fans intended to dump the guacamole on Brown. If Brown found the contact offensive, the incident would constitute a battery.

In distinct contrast to Scott Kamieniecki, the Houston Astros' Bill Spiers was not wearing a sheepish grin when he left the field in the middle of a game against the Milwaukee Brewers. Spiers, playing right field for the Astros on September 24, 1999, suffered a welt under his left eye and a bloody nose when a 23-year-old spectator, Berley Visgar, attacked him. As the Brewers came to bat in the bottom of the sixth inning, Visgar left the grandstands, entered the playing field, and jumped Spiers from behind. Other Astros players rushed to Spiers' defense and subdued the assailant. Milwaukee County sheriff's deputies then led Visgar away in handcuffs. The attack on Spiers combined all the elements of a battery. The assailant intentionally left his seat in the stands and jumped on Spiers. The attacker knocked Spiers to the ground, an offensive act under any circumstance. It was also harmful, as evidenced by Spiers' bloody nose and facial welt. The incident was potentially harmful to others as well. The Astros' starting pitcher against the Brewers, Mike Hampton, was one of the first players to come to Spiers' defense. Until teammates restrained him, Hampton pummeled the spectator. After being apprehended, Visgar explained to authorities that he had intended to jump on Spiers' back to attract the attention

---

[117] Terry Pluto, *Loose Balls: The Short, Wild Life of the American Basketball Association As Told by the Players, Coaches, and Movers and Shakers Who Made It Happen*, (New York: Simon & Schuster, 1990), 305-06.

of the 14,000 fans attending the game. Police charged him with two counts of disorderly conduct. Visgar was sentenced to 90 days in jail and fined $1,000.[118]

At the time of the attack, Hampton and the Astros were leading the Brewers 2-1. Newspapers reported that Hampton was "visibly upset" by the incident. Up to that point, Hampton had been enjoying a near perfect season. He entered the game against the Brewers with 20 wins for the year against only four losses. After the attack on his teammate, Hampton retired the side in the bottom of the sixth inning but gave way to Astro relief pitchers for the rest of the game. The relievers immediately yielded three runs. Hampton, one of the premier pitchers in the National League, may have contained the Brewers' hitters if he had stayed in the game. As it was, his premature departure cost him a chance for his twenty-first victory.

Team mascots, like baseball pitchers, seem to attract trouble. In 1995, a retired bus driver won $128,000 in compensatory damages for injuries suffered when the Philadelphia Phillies' mascot knocked him down. The mascot, the "Phillie Phanatic," hugged the bus driver, Carl Seidel, at a carnival. Seidel protested but to no avail. The mascot knocked Seidel down, injuring Seidel's back. Seidel sued both the Phanatic and the Philadelphia baseball club, which owned the rights to the Phanatic character. Seidel accused the Phanatic of assault. To prevail, Seidel would have had to prove that the Phanatic had caused a reasonable apprehension of harmful or offensive conduct, a well-founded fear of peril. The court concluded that the Phanatic had not assaulted Seidel. However, the court did find that the Phanatic's conduct had been negligent. The court ruled that the

---

[118] *Fan Sentenced*, THE WASH. POST, April 9, 2000, D11. Visgar had no prior criminal record. The judge handling the case, Circuit Court Judge Michael Brennan, noted that the 90-day jail term was particularly harsh for an individual with no prior record. However, Brennan hoped that Visgar's confinement would deter other fans from similar stunts.

Philadelphia Phillies were also negligent in failing to provide proper training for the Phanatic.[119]

"Burnie," the mascot for the Miami Heat professional basketball team, fared even worse than the Phanatic. During a 1994 exhibition game in San Juan, Puerto Rico, Wes Lockard, dressed in the Heat's fuzzy orange bird mascot costume, dragged Yvonne Gil-Rebollo out of her seat and onto the basketball court. Though the woman resisted participating in the gag, Lockard threw her down as if engaged in a mock wrestling match. Lockard was tried in criminal court and convicted. In the wake of the criminal conviction, Gil-Rebollo sued the Miami Heat, Lockard's employer, for $1 million in a civil lawsuit.[120] The jury found that Lockard had injured Gil-Rebollo and awarded her $50,000.[121]

There is often a fine line between a civil wrong, which may result in a private lawsuit seeking compensation for damages, and a criminal act for which a jail term or other criminal penalties may be assessed. In 1999, promising baseball pitching prospect Ben Christensen, who played for Wichita State University, shocked the collegiate baseball world when he deliberately threw a warm-up pitch at an opposing player. Just prior to the start of a game between Wichita State and the University of Evansville, Evansville infielder Anthony Molina knelt about 24 feet from home plate—near Wichita State's on-deck circle and some distance removed from Evansville's own on-deck circle. Christensen objected to Molina's location; he thought Molina should have stayed in his team's on-deck circle. After his fifth warm-up toss, Christensen threw a ball in Molina's direction. Molina was looking down at the time and never saw the ball until just before it struck him. The ball hit the Evansville batter near his left eye. Afterwards, Christensen maintained that he did not intend to hit Molina and that

---

[119] *Phils Must Pay*, THE WASH. POST, November 28, 1995, E3.

[120] *Animal Farm*, SPORTS ILLUSTRATED, November 20, 1995, 16.

[121] *Woman Wins Suit Against Heat*, THE N.Y. TIMES, February 15, 1997, 31.

he was merely throwing a "purpose" pitch. Christensen suspected that Molina was attempting to time his pitches and wanted to move him back. Whatever Christensen intended, the baseball fractured Molina's skull and left eye socket and caused severe lacerations to his face. An attending doctor said the blow was comparable to being hit by a sledge hammer.

The Wichita State pitching coach, Brent Kemnitz, came to Christensen's defense. "If the on-deck hitter is standing too close to home plate, you brush him back," Kemnitz said. "I teach that."[122] The reaction to Christensen's pitch and Kemnitz's teaching philosophy was swift. Commentators across the country condemned the Wichita State baseball program in general and Christensen in particular. Columnist Dave Kindred said Christensen's pitch was nothing short of "terrorism." Kindred found the act even more despicable because Christensen had been taught to react that way. "Once committed to a dishonorable act," Kindred wrote, "a man is liable for all consequences, even those unintended." Kindred noted, "There will be a lawsuit. There may be an arrest."[123]

Kindred was half right. There was a lawsuit—but no arrest. Anthony Molina underwent three operations to fix the damage done by

---

[122] Kemnitz' teaching was a throwback to more rough-and-tumble times. Pitcher Burleigh Grimes, a nineteen-year major league veteran, closed out his Hall-of-Fame career with ten appearances for the 1934 New York Yankees. Even after 269 career wins, most of which came with the Brooklyn Dodgers, the 40-year-old Grimes was desperate to squeeze out more victories and hang on to his playing days. While pitching against the Detroit Tigers, Grimes noticed that Detroit outfielder Goose Goslin, kneeling in the on-deck circle, was intently watching the pitcher's deliveries. Goslin was twenty feet off in foul territory. That didn't deter Grimes, however. He aimed a pitch directly at Goslin, decking the Tigers' star. Such tactics enabled Grimes to carve out one victory, against two losses, as a Yankee, leaving him with a career mark of 270 wins and 212 defeats. Richard Ben Cramer, *Joe DiMaggio: The Hero's Life* (New York: Simon & Schuster, 2000), 125.

[123] Dave Kindred, *Blind Ambition*, THE SPORTING NEWS, July 5, 1999

Christensen's pitch. The surgeries allowed Molina to resume playing baseball. He rejoined the University of Evansville team for his senior season and, in 20 games, hit .280. As Dave Kindred had predicted, Molina also filed a lawsuit. Fifteen months after he was hit, Molina sued Christensen for battery and negligence and asked the court to award $75,000 in damages. Molina also sued Christensen's school, Wichita State University, for negligence. The lawsuit lingered in the court system for more than two years, with lawyers arguing over whether Wichita State University should be a defendant in the case, or whether Christensen should stand as the sole defendant.[124] In February 2002, Christensen agreed to pay monetary damages to Molina, and the case was closed. Neither side revealed the dollar amount of the settlement. When the settlement was announced, Christensen's agent labeled the injury to Molina "an accident."

While Christensen steadfastly maintained that he did not intend to hit Molina, there is no question that he intended to throw close enough to intimidate the infielder. And although Molina may not have been kneeling in the Evansville on-deck circle, there was no indication that he purposely did anything to antagonize Christensen. A similar situation occurred in a major league game between the Red Sox and Orioles at Boston's Fenway Park on September 16, 1975. In Fenway, as in many parks, the bullpens are in clear view of the fans sitting in the outfield bleachers. Throughout the game, bleacher fans were heckling players in the Orioles' bullpen. Orioles pitcher Ross Grimsley was particularly upset at the heckling. In the latter stages of the game, Grimsley began to warm up in the bullpen. When Grimsley had finished his warmup throws, he intentionally threw a ball at the wire fence that separated the bullpen from

---

[124] Adam Knapp, *After 2 Years, Beaning Lawsuit Still Unresolved*, THE WICHITA EAGLE, May 4, 2001, 3C.

the bleacher seats. Grimsley's throw penetrated the fence and hit a fan, David Manning. Manning later sued Grimsley for battery and negligence.

The lawsuit against Grimsley was slated for a jury trial. On the battery count, however, the judge concluded that Grimsley had not intentionally thrown the ball at the hecklers and directed a verdict in favor of the pitcher. The allegation that Grimsley was negligent went to the jury, which ended up finding that Grimsley had not acted negligently. Both the judge and jury, it seemed, were swayed by the fact that the fans had been heckling Grimsley and other Orioles players sitting in the bullpen. Manning appealed the decision. On appeal, the court ruled that the trial judge had made a mistake in directing a verdict in Grimsley's favor on the battery count. The appeals court pointed out that Grimsley was an expert pitcher who, presumably, had good control over the accuracy of his pitches. The appeals court believed that a jury might well have concluded that Grimsley threw the ball with the intention of hitting Manning. The court sent the case back to the trial court for a jury to consider whether Grimsley had committed an intentional tort against Manning.[125]

The issue of intentional tort also arose in a case involving professional football player Dale Hackbart, a former defensive safety for the Denver Broncos, and running back Charles "Boobie" Clark of the Cincinnati Bengals. During one play in the first half of a game between the Broncos and Bengals, Clark ran an end zone pattern. Hackbart was covering him. The Bengals' pass was intercepted by the Broncos at the goal line. As the Broncos ran the ball back upfield, Hackbart tried to block Clark. In the process of blocking, Hackbart fell to the ground. With one knee on the ground, Hackbart turned to look upfield. Angry at the Bengals' turnover, Clark swung his right forearm and hit Hackbart in the back of his helmet. Hackbart played the second half of the game, but the next day he had to cancel a golf date because of persistent pain. The pain continued to affect Hackbart. Three weeks later, the Broncos released him.

---

[125] *Manning v. Grimsley*, 643 F.2d 20 (1st Cir. 1981).

After his release, Hackbart learned that he had suffered a serious neck injury. Hackbart sued Clark and the Bengals, alleging that Clark's forearm hit was so far outside the rules of football that it constituted reckless misconduct. If not reckless misconduct, Hackbart asserted, Clark was at least guilty of negligence. The court had to consider what actions a reasonably prudent football player would have taken if faced with the same circumstances that confronted Boobie Clark. The trial court considered Hackbart's allegations but ruled in favor of Clark. The court concluded that football is a violent game and Clark's hit was simply part of the "controlled rage" common at the professional level. The court also found that, in playing football, Hackbart assumed the risk of being hit unexpectedly.[126]

Hackbart appealed the court's decision. On appeal, Hackbart fared much better. The appeals court found that the lower court had erred by basing its decision on the fact that football is an inherently violent game. The appeals court criticized the lower court for using the rough play common to the National Football League as justification for insulating Clark from liability. The preferred approach, according to the appeals court, would have been for the trial court to consider whether Clark's hit was so far outside the rules of professional football that it amounted to reckless misconduct. In determining if Clark was guilty of reckless misconduct, the appeals court said, the trial court would have to consider whether the running back knew the potential danger to Hackbart or acted with knowledge of facts that would have alerted a reasonable person to the danger.[127] The appeals court sent the case back to the trial court for further consideration. Before the case could be retried, Clark and the Bengals settled with

---

[126] *Hackbart v. Cincinnati Bengals, Inc.*, 435 F. Supp. 352 (D. Colo. 1977).

[127] *Hackbart v. Cincinnati Bengals, Inc.*, 601 F.2d 516 (10th Cir. 1979).

Hackbart. Under terms of the settlement, Hackbart received $200,000 as compensation for his injury.[128]

Around the same time as Hackbart's injury, Rudy Tomjanovich, a star forward with the Houston Rockets and later the coach of the Rockets, was injured as the result of an even more violent hit by Los Angeles Lakers forward Kermit Washington. The sequence of events began when Rockets center Kevin Kunnert rebounded an errant Lakers' shot and, in the process, hit Washington in the face with his elbow. Washington took exception to being jabbed by Kunnert's elbow and began flailing away at his opponents. Players from both teams joined the scuffle. Tomjanovich sprinted toward Washington from the back. Washington spotted Tomjanovich's bright red Rockets jersey out of the corner of his eye and unleashed a right-handed punch squarely into Tomjanovich's face. The blow caused Tomjanovich to crumple to the floor with severe bleeding from his nose and mouth. Tomjanovich suffered multiple injuries, including fractures of his nose, jaw and skull, facial lacerations, a concussion and leakage of spinal fluid from the brain cavity.

Tomjanovich sued the Lakers for damages. He chose not to sue Washington personally but instead sought compensation from the Lakers on a two-part theory: *first*, that Washington, a well-publicized NBA "enforcer," was prone to dangerous tendencies; and, *second*, that the team, as Washington's employer, knew of his dangerous tendencies. Tomjanovich alleged that the Lakers were negligent in failing to control Washington. During the trial, one of the surgeons who had operated on Tomjanovich testified that the work required to reconstruct Tomjanovich's face was similar to putting a cracked egg back together with Scotch tape.[129] The jury awarded Tomjanovich $3.3 million. The Lakers appealed. While the appeal

---

[128] Robert C. Berry and Glenn M. Wong, *Law and Business of the Sports Industries: Common Issues in Amateur and Professional Sports* (Westport, CT: Praeger Publishers, 1993), 459.

[129] *Tomjanovich v. California Sports, Inc.*, No. H-78-243 (S.D. Tex. 1979).

was pending, the team settled out of court with Tomjanovich for an undisclosed amount.[130]

Harmful or offensive contact can occur on pitching mounds or basketball courts as easily as in other locations. The location is not significant. It is the contact itself that is of concern. If, after the contact, the "victim" is left wearing a smudge of lipstick and a sheepish grin, it is unlikely that either an assault or battery occurred. However, if the act creates a reasonable fear of harmful or offensive contact, it would likely constitute an assault or battery. As happened in the case of Randy Myers, an assault may occur when an assailant does not actually strike or touch the victim. If the assailant does strike or touch the victim, as happened to Bill Spiers, the act will likely be classified as a battery. If a player strikes an opponent in a way that is outside the normal rules of the game, as happened to Dale Hackbart, the act may be regarded as reckless misconduct. Regardless of how the acts are classified under the law, however, they all share the common element of being intentional torts—and not accidental in nature.

---

[130] Berry and Wong, *Law and Business of the Sports Industries: Common Issues in Amateur and Professional Sports*, 493.

Chapter 5

Criminal Law and Sports

On May 16, 1957, Dan Topping, the owner of the New York Yankees, woke up to bad news. Several Yankee players had been involved in a confrontation the previous evening at the Copacabana night club on West 51st Street in Manhattan. Outfielders Mickey Mantle and Hank Bauer, pitcher Whitey Ford, catcher Yogi Berra and the players' wives, along with Yankee second baseman Billy Martin and pitcher Johnny Kucks, had been out on the town to celebrate Martin's twenty-ninth birthday. After stopping at a club to hear singer Johnny Ray, the group went to the Copacabana, where Sammy Davis was the featured performer. One of the Copacabana's patrons, a Bronx delicatessen owner, began heckling Davis. Hank Bauer told the man to keep quiet. Before long, Bauer and the deli owner exchanged words. When the deli owner went into the men's room, Bauer followed. The deli owner ended up on the bathroom floor with a broken nose, hurt feelings, and an assortment of other injuries. Hoping to avoid further trouble, Bauer and the others in the Yankee party quickly left the Copacabana through the club's kitchen door.

The deli owner was treated at the hospital for his injuries. He then went to the police station to swear out a warrant for Bauer's arrest. Concerned that the incident would tarnish the Yankee image, Topping called on Yogi Berra, early the morning after, for an explanation. Topping knew that

Berra, of all the players involved, would tell the story straight. Berra did. "Nobody did nothin' to nobody," he told Topping. It was close to the truth. Bauer, sporting a .203 batting average at the time, denied hitting the deli owner or anyone else. With an air of innocence, Bauer said, "Hit him? Why, I haven't hit anybody all year." When telling his side of the story to the police, the deli owner was unable to remember specific details surrounding the incident and could not even say with certainty that it was Bauer who had hit him. Weeks later, the Yankee players were called to testify before a grand jury. The testimony confirmed that the Copacabana's bouncer, not Hank Bauer, had broken the deli owner's nose. The charges against Bauer were dropped.[131]

> ### *The Yogi Berra Principle of Criminal Law*
>
> *It's not a crime when nobody does nothin' to nobody.*

When "nobody does nothin' to nobody," the criminal justice system does not get involved. Even when somebody does somethin' to somebody, the criminal justice system may not get involved. On August 22, 1965, pitcher Juan Marichal of the San Francisco Giants came to bat in the third inning of a game against the Los Angeles Dodgers. The Dodgers led by a score of 2-1. Facing Marichal on the mound was the Dodgers' Sandy

---

[131] Yankee manager Casey Stengel made no attempt to hide his displeasure. He benched Ford and Berra for a game and relegated Bauer to the eighth spot in the batting order. Said Stengel, "We have twenty-five birthdays on this ball club, not to mention wedding anniversaries." What the skipper was really saying, the *New York Times* suggested, is that "no ball club could long survive rigorous observances of its members' personal milestones." McCandlish Phillips, *Yankee Is Linked to Fight In Café: But Bauer Denies That He Took a Swing at Fan in Copacabana 'Incident'*, THE N.Y. TIMES, May 17, 1957, 50. Even though the criminal charges were dropped, the Yankee players did end up paying $6,500 in settlement to the deli owner to ward off a civil lawsuit.

Koufax. Behind the plate, Dodgers catcher John Roseboro mishandled one of Koufax's pitches. The ball fell near home plate. Roseboro picked it up and, when returning the ball to Koufax, threw close to Marichal's head. Marichal took exception. He turned toward Roseboro and brought his bat down hard on the catcher's head. Blood streamed from Roseboro's face. Both benches cleared. Only the peace-keeping efforts of Giants center fielder Willie Mays and the umpires prevented a full-scale riot from erupting. National League president Warren Giles fined Marichal $1,750. At the time, it was the heaviest fine ever assessed by a league president. Giles also suspended Marichal for eight playing days. Giants fans thought the penalty was too severe. Dodger partisans thought Marichal should have been suspended for the rest of the season. Giles admitted that he tempered the punishment because a longer suspension would have hurt the entire Giants team, which was in the thick of the pennant race. *New York Times* sportswriter Arthur Daley commented, "It's a cinch... that Marichal would have landed in jail if he had perpetrated his outrageous attack at the corner of Market and Powell Streets in San Francisco instead of in Candlestick Park."[132]

Marichal didn't land in jail. Civil authorities, content to let baseball clean up its own mess, brought no charges. Marichal did issue an apology of sorts in which he said he thought Roseboro was going to hit him. Marichal claimed he was acting in self-defense. "First of all," Marichal told the press, "I want to apologize for using the bat. I am sorry I did that, but I was afraid of him." Marichal also contended that the throw from Roseboro that had precipitated the incident actually hit him. "It nicked my ear," Marichal explained. "I said to him, 'Why did you do that?' He didn't say anything, just came at me. I thought he would hit me with his mask so I hit him."[133] Roseboro didn't give Marichal's self-defense argument much credence.

---

[132] Arthur Daley, *Crime and Punishment*, THE N.Y. TIMES, August 25, 1965, 42.

[133] Leonard Koppett, *Marichal Says He Used the Bat To Hit Roseboro in Self-Defense*, THE N.Y. TIMES, August 24, 1965, 20.

Roseboro said Marichal was "scared to death" that Koufax would throw at him and was therefore on edge.

In the newspapers, Marichal's attack rekindled memories of a 1956 incident in which Giants pitcher Ruben Gomez had thrown a ball at Milwaukee first baseman Joe Adcock. Unlike Marichal's attack on Roseboro, when Gomez threw at Adcock, there was no question that it was in self-defense. Gomez and the Giants were playing against the Braves in Milwaukee. Gomez, who was in the midst of a disappointing 7-17 year, nicked Adcock with a pitch on the wrist. Adcock, who stood 6'4" and outweighed Gomez by 40 pounds, began walking to first, then abruptly veered toward Gomez. Gomez picked up the baseball and threw it at Adcock. Then Gomez fled the field in fright, with Adcock chasing after him. Before Adcock could catch him, the pitcher took refuge in the Giants' dugout and remained there until he was given a police escort back to his hotel room.[134]

Hank Bauer was not charged with a crime because "nobody did nothin' to nobody." Juan Marichal was not subject to criminal charges because his act took place at Candlestick Park and not "at the corner of Market and Powell Streets." Ruben Gomez was not subject to prosecution because his actions also took place in the confines of a ballpark—and he was clearly acting in self-defense. In each case, there was conduct that might have been subject to criminal prosecution. Before criminal charges could have been brought, however, the authorities would have had to find some basis to believe that a crime had been committed. The basis for all criminal charges lies in the laws that have been adopted. Laws vary from state to state. Each state has laws that prohibit violence against people and crimes against property.

The legal system recognizes self-defense as a proper justification for the use of force against another person. The self-defense argument must be

---

[134] Gerald Eskenazi, *Latest Giants-Dodgers Brawl Brings a Few Others to Mind*, THE N.Y. TIMES, August 23, 1965, 24.

plausible, however. With the towering Joe Adcock closing in on him, Ruben Gomez was attempting to defend himself when he threw the baseball at Adcock. Measured against the urgency facing Gomez, Marichal's claim of self-defense in his encounter with John Roseboro seems somewhat suspect. Gomez was ridiculed in major league dugouts for his unseemly exit from the playing field. One sportswriter maintained that the stigma caused by Gomez' cowering retreat from the muscular Adcock diminished Gomez' effectiveness on the mound for the rest of his major league career.[135] If there is virtue at all in Gomez' conduct, it lies in the fact that, when throwing the baseball at Adcock, his effort at self-defense was reasonably designed to protect himself from Adcock. It is a fundamental principle of law that a person, whether on a baseball field or at the corner of Market and Powell Streets, is not justified in using force against another unless it is proportional or reasonable to the harm threatened. Legal experts term this principle "the doctrine of proportionality."[136] Gomez' response was proportional to the threat facing him. Marichal, on the other hand, reacted to being "nicked" by clubbing Roseboro over the head. Marichal's response was not proportional to the threat. Arthur Daley no doubt had some variation of the proportionality doctrine in mind when he wrote of Marichal, "Only cowards use bats."[137]

---

[135] Daley, *Crime and Punishment*, THE N.Y. TIMES, August 25, 1965, 42. From 1953 to 1962, Gomez pitched for four teams, the Giants, Phillies, Indians and Twins. During this period, he compiled a record of 76 wins and 86 losses. After his abysmal 7-17 record in 1956, Gomez rebounded to go 15-13 in 1957 and 10-12 in 1958. However, he never recaptured the dominance he showed in 1954, when he won 17 games, lost only 9, and had an earned run average of 2.88. In 1967, after being out of the big leagues for four years, Gomez resurfaced briefly with the Philadelphia Phillies, when he appeared in 7 games without a decision. With that, his major league career was over.

[136] Joshua Dressler, *Understanding Criminal Law* (New York: Matthew Bender & Co., Inc., 1995), 37.

[137] Daley, *Crime and Punishment*, THE N.Y. TIMES, August 25, 1965, 42.

When Wichita State pitcher Ben Christensen injured Anthony Molina with a warm-up pitch, Molina filed a criminal complaint with the Wichita Police Department. It was left to the District Attorney for Sedgwick County in Kansas, the home of Wichita State University, to assess whether criminal charges should be brought against Christensen. The District Attorney deliberated long and hard. The question was whether Christensen should be charged with battery under the State of Kansas Aggravated Battery Statute. That law makes it a crime to intentionally or recklessly cause great bodily harm or disfigurement to another person. The District Attorney placed great weight on a statement by Christensen that he did not intend to hit Molina. After reviewing all of the relevant facts, the District Attorney concluded that Christensen should not be held liable for the unintended consequences of his brushback pitch. She found that Christensen's pitch was neither intentional nor reckless under Kansas criminal law. Therefore, the District Attorney ruled, there was no basis for criminal charges against Christensen. In reaching this conclusion, she considered several factors, including the nature of the offense, the characteristics of the offender, the possible deterrent value of prosecution, the probability of conviction under the applicable criminal law, and the fact that there were civil remedies available to compensate Anthony Molina for his injuries. The District Attorney concluded that, if criminal charges had been filed, it would have been difficult to prove criminal intent and, therefore, unlikely that Christensen would have been found guilty.[138]

The District Attorney considered other factors as well, including the fact that the participants in an athletic contest assume the risk of being subjected to "actions and behavior that may otherwise be criminal had it occurred in a non-athletic environment." As the District Attorney recognized, the law is more tolerant of aberrant behavior when it takes place

---

[138] Findings of Sedgwick County (Kansas) District Attorney Nola Foulston, filed November 23, 1999.

during a sporting event. Police and prosecutors are often content to let the game's referees administer punishment for excessively rough or violent play. Thus, Christensen escaped criminal prosecution for his "purpose pitch." Shortly thereafter, the Chicago Cubs selected Christensen in the first round of the major league draft.

Although civil authorities usually refrain from bringing criminal charges against participants in sports, there have been some notable exceptions. On January 15, 1999, Tony Limon, a 6'3" center for South San Antonio High School, elbowed an opponent, 5'11" guard Brent Holmes of East Central San Antonio High, in the face during a game. Limon threw his elbow with such force that it fractured Holmes' nose and cut his gum and lip. Holmes had to undergo plastic surgery to repair the damage. Limon's hit was called "one of the nastiest blows on a basketball court since Kermit Washington shattered Rudy Tomjanovich's face with a sucker punch in 1977."[139] Limon's hit on Holmes was captured on video, which showed Limon stepping into Holmes and hitting him squarely on the nose. Holmes' head jerked backward, and he crumpled to the floor. The prosecutor charged Limon with aggravated assault and intent to inflict bodily injury. After Limon pleaded no contest to the charges, the judge sentenced him to five years in prison. When issuing the sentence, the judge noted that Limon had previously pleaded no contest to two counts of attempted burglary. The judge left no doubt that the stiff sentence for the hit on Holmes was due, in large part, to the fact that the battery was Limon's second brush with the law.

In contrast to Tony Limon, former Boston Bruins hockey player Marty McSorley had no criminal record when he struck Donald Brashear of the Vancouver Canucks with his hockey stick in a National Hockey League game in Vancouver on February 21, 2000. Like Tony Limon's

[139] *Flagrant Foul*, SPORTS ILLUSTRATED, February 21, 2000, 22.

attack on Brent Holmes, however, McSorley's hit on Brashear was unprovoked. McSorley's hit was just as violent as Limon's, if not more so. With 2.7 seconds left in the game, McSorley skated up to Brashear from behind and struck him on the head with his stick. The blow hit Brashear in the right temple. The Canucks forward immediately collapsed and the back of his head struck the ice, causing his helmet to pop off. Brashear lost consciousness and had to be carried off the ice on a stretcher. Though the sports were different, McSorley's assault on Brashear was eerily similar to Juan Marichal's attack on John Roseboro—except for the fact that when Marichal hit Roseboro, the catcher saw the blow coming. Hoping to stave off criminal charges, the National Hockey League took quick, decisive action against McSorley. It held a disciplinary hearing two days after the attack and suspended McSorley for the remainder of the 2000 season and the playoffs, a duration of at least twenty-three games. It was the longest suspension ever imposed on an NHL player. As a result of the suspension, McSorley lost $72,000 of his $600,000 salary for the 1999-2000 season.

To the dismay of the hockey authorities, the Canadian criminal justice system moved almost as quickly as did the NHL. On March 7, 2000, British Columbia police arrested McSorley on the charge of assault with a weapon. He faced a maximum sentence of eighteen months in jail. It was the first time since Dino Ciccarelli of the Minnesota North Stars hit Toronto's Luke Richardson—twelve years before—that criminal charges were brought against an NHL player for a hit during a game.[140] NHL executive vice president Bill Daly, the league's chief legal officer, made no attempt to hide his disappointment. "The league dealt with the matter quickly, decisively and appropriately—and did not feel that any further action was warranted or necessary," Daly said. "We, therefore, would have preferred that the Crown not take

---

[140] Ciccarelli served one day in jail and was fined $1,000 for his attack on Richardson.

this action."[141] In September 2000, McSorley faced a non-jury trial before a judge. The trial lasted a week. McSorley testified that he was trying to hit Brashear in the shoulder and accidentally struck him on the head. Provincial Court Judge Bill Kitchen concluded that the attack was an "unpremeditated, impulsive act of violence" committed during the heat of competition. The judge found McSorley guilty but sentenced him to eighteen months of probation instead of jail. Under the decision, McSorley was obligated to avoid any criminal offenses for the duration of his probation. The judge also required him not to participate in athletic competition against Brashear for eighteen months. Slashing is part of the game of hockey, Judge Kitchen commented, but slashing an opponent in the head is not. Upon learning of the punishment assessed to McSorley, Washington Capitals defenseman Brendan Witt commented, "I think he shouldn't play in the league again. We don't need someone like that in our sport."[142]

In Judge Kitchen's view, there were several reasons for imposing probation instead of a jail sentence. For one, McSorley did not have a prior criminal record. The judge also recognized that slashing is part of the game. The fact that McSorley's attack came during the heat of competition was another mitigating factor. The level of competition also influenced the judge. At the professional level, hockey is a very physical and demanding sport in which players' emotions may reach a feverish pitch. In other sports, at lesser levels of competition, judges show less patience with violent acts. When Kevin Helland, a 37-year-old resident of Milwaukee, struck umpire Stuart Anderson and pushed him to the ground over a disputed call at the end of an amateur softball game, Waukesha County Circuit Judge Lee Dreyfus showed no tolerance at all

---

[141] Thomas Heath, *Bruins' McSorley Charged; Faces Up to 18 Months in Prison*, THE WASH. POST, March 8, 2000, D1, D8.

[142] Thomas Heath and DeNeen L. Brown, *McSorley Gets Probation For Slash: NHL Defenseman Avoids Jail Time*, THE WASH. POST, October 7, 2000, D1, D11.

for Helland's unprovoked violence. Helland pushed Anderson after the umpire had called a runner out at home plate. The player was charged with disorderly conduct. Though Helland did not have any prior brushes with the law, Judge Dreyfus sentenced him to serve ten days in jail. Helland referred to his attack on the umpire as "a five-second blur in judgment." Dreyfus warned Helland that he had lost perspective on where softball games fit in "the grand scheme of things."[143]

> *The Judge Lee Dreyfus Principle of Proper Perspective on Athletic Competitions*
>
> *It is important for athletes to retain a proper perspective on the role of recreational sports in the grand scheme of things.*

In one of the most tragic episodes in the history of the U.S. Naval Academy, three stellar graduates of the Academy died on December 1, 1993. Two of the individuals, Alton Grizzard and Kerryn O'Neill, died at the hands of Navy Lieutenant George P. Smith, who shot Grizzard and O'Neill in rapid succession and then turned the gun on himself. O'Neill, age 21, had been a track star during her four years at the Naval Academy. Grizzard, who was 24, had been a star quarterback for the Navy football team during his junior and senior years. Smith had completed the Navy's elite training program for nuclear submarine engineers. All three had known each other as midshipmen at the Academy, and O'Neill and Smith had been engaged to marry. Two days before the tragic incident, O'Neill had told Smith that she no longer wanted to marry him. On the day of the deaths, Smith, distraught over the end of his relationship with O'Neill, entered O'Neill's apartment at the Naval Amphibious Base in

[143] *Ump-Pushing Softballer Ordered to Cool Off in Jail*, THE WASH. POST, September 24, 1998, C2.

Coronado, California. He was carrying a gun. At the apartment, he encountered Grizzard, a long-time friend of O'Neill's. Smith shot the two star athletes and then turned the gun on himself. Friends and acquaintances had predicted great things for Grizzard. One Navy official expected that Grizzard would end up as a Navy admiral. A close friend used to tell people they would hear something great from Grizzard, "that he would die in some foreign land, defending his country. Instead, Grizzard died while trying to comfort a friend."[144]

Smith died in an ambulance while being taken to a hospital. If he had lived, the law would have had some difficult questions to answer. For starters, the law would have asked if Smith, in killing O'Neill and Grizzard, had committed murder or manslaughter. The law defines murder as a killing performed with malice. A person acts with malice when he or she kills another and there is no justification, excuse or mitigating circumstances that cause or motivate the killing. In contrast to murder, manslaughter is a killing without malice. There are three situations that may give rise to a charge of manslaughter: (1) when an individual kills another person in the sudden heat of passion as the result of some provocation; (2) when a person performs an act that is lawful in itself but does so without due caution and, as a result, kills another individual; and (3) when a person commits an unlawful act that is not a felony and, in the process, kills another individual.

When attempting to classify Smith's actions as either murder or manslaughter, it would have been necessary to determine whether Smith had some justification, such as self-defense, for the killings. If so, he likely would have been charged, at most, with manslaughter. Similarly, if Smith had some compelling excuse for his actions, such as diminished mental capacity, he may have been charged with manslaughter. Finally, if there was evidence that Smith was acting "in the sudden heat of passion"

---

[144] Fern Shen and Christine Spolar, *Three Lives Once Full of Great Hope: Young Officers' Deaths Shake Naval Academy*, THE WASH. POST, December 3, 1993, A1.

as the result of some provocation, the killings would probably have constituted manslaughter, not murder. However, in the absence of justification, compelling excuse or mitigating circumstances, Smith would likely have been charged with murder.

A crime differs from a civil wrong. A crime is an offense against society. The offense involves a violation of the criminal's obligation to promote a law-abiding society. Criminal cases require proof that the defendants possessed the intent to commit a crime. In a criminal matter, the standard of proof is higher than the traditional civil standard of preponderance of the evidence. The prosecutor must prove every element of a crime beyond a reasonable doubt. This is the highest burden in the law.[145] Injuries that are accidental or unintended are not the proper subject of a criminal proceeding.

When Arizona Diamondbacks pitcher Randy Johnson killed a dove with a fastball in a 2001 spring training game against the San Francisco Giants, there was no question as to Johnson's intent. Johnson was pitching to Giants batter Calvin Murray. The pitch left Johnson's hand and traveled about 45 feet before it collided with the dove. The dove was overmatched. At best, a dove can travel 70 miles an hour. Johnson's fastball routinely travels almost 100 miles an hour. As the ball hit the dove, a well-situated eyewitness, Arizona catcher Rod Barajas, said "all you see is an explosion." Clearly, Johnson's sole intent was to find a way to retire the Giants' batter. Killing the dove was both accidental and unintentional. Students of the law might be inclined to say that the dove, by flying so close to a Randy Johnson fastball, assumed the risk of injury. Certainly, National League batters knew better.

Nearly two decades before Johnson killed the dove, New York Yankee outfielder Dave Winfield killed a seagull with a throw in an August 4, 1983 game against the Toronto Blue Jays in Canada. In Winfield's case,

---

[145] Joshua Dressler, *Understanding Criminal Law* (New York: Matthew Bender & Co., Inc., 1999), 59-60.

there was some question as to the player's intent. Winfield, playing center field, was warming up between innings. He noticed a seagull napping in right-center field and threw the warm-up ball in front of the seagull with the intent, he said, of scaring it off. The ball took a bad hop, struck the seagull and killed it. Toronto fans were unforgiving. So were the police. For the rest of the game, the fans booed Winfield unmercifully. After the game, Ontario police escorted him to the police station and booked him for cruelty to an animal. Causing unnecessary suffering to any animal is illegal under the Canadian Criminal Code. Seagulls have special status in Canada because they are members of a protected species. Winfield posted a $500 bond and was released. Winfield viewed his arrest with more humor than did the Toronto police. "So here I am," he related, "it's after midnight and next to me is exhibit A, its feet sticking up in the air, stiff now and laying on a handkerchief." Winfield's manager, Billy Martin, also found some humor in the situation. "First time he hit the cutoff man all year," Martin said.[146]

When a person is charged with killing another human being, the law requires the prosecuting attorney to prove—beyond a reasonable doubt—the existence of four facts: (1) a person was killed; (2) the defendant was the killer; (3) the defendant intended to take a human life; and (4) the killing was unlawful. When Dave Winfield killed the seagull, the prosecutors would have faced a similar burden. They would have had to prove the same four elements of the "crime." If the prosecutors failed to prove each element of the crime, the court would have had to find Winfield not guilty. Proving that the seagull died would have been easy. After all, the police already had a stiff "exhibit A" with "its feet sticking up in the air." Proving that Winfield had killed the seagull would have been easy as well—there were more than 36,000

---

[146] Ray Sasser, *Dallas Morning News*, April 1, 2001.

potential witnesses.[147] The sticking point would have come in trying to prove that Winfield had criminal intent. Killing a seagull may be a violation of law, but attempting to scare one is not. Ultimately, after a lengthy telephone conversation with Winfield, Canadian prosecutors dropped the charges. The prosecutors were well aware of the difficulty they faced in trying to prove that Winfield intentionally killed the seagull. Later, Toronto city official Paul Godfrey, who was at the game as a spectator, apologized to Winfield for the way he was treated. "It's a day in the life of Toronto sports that we'd sooner forget," Godfrey said.[148]

In almost any controversy involving harmful deeds, the process of trying to determine an individual's intent is fraught with uncertainty. In the second game of the 2000 World Series, intent became an issue when New York Yankee right-hander Roger Clemens faced the catcher for the New York Mets, Mike Piazza, in the first inning. Clemens had his best fastball working that day. He had retired the first two Mets batters "in an angry spray of 98-mph fastballs."[149] Clemens threw another fastball to Piazza. Piazza swung and made contact, but the pitch shattered Piazza's bat into three pieces. The barrel of the bat bounced back to the pitcher's mound. Clemens instinctively picked the bat up with two hands and threw it in the direction of the Yankees' on-deck circle.

---

[147] There were 36,684 fans in attendance for the game, which the Yankees won by a score of 3-1. Winfield had two hits in four at-bats and two runs batted in. Afterwards, Yankee shortstop Roy Smalley offered to help reporters with their headlines for the next day's papers. "Winfield 2 for 4 With A Birdie," Smalley suggested. Following the game, the Yankee team was scheduled to leave Canada on a chartered flight departing from Hamilton Airport in Ontario. Winfield's booking delayed the flight. When Winfield finally boarded the plane, his teammates crowded the aisles to welcome him back. "Where's the convict's number on your back?" pitcher Rudy May inquired. Jane Gross, *Winfield Charges Will Be Dropped*, THE N.Y. TIMES, August 6, 1983, 29.

[148] *Winfield Gets An Apology*, THE N.Y. TIMES, August 9, 1983, B9.

[149] Tom Verducci, *Roger & Out*, SPORTS ILLUSTRATED, October 30, 2000, 40, 45.

Clemens underhand toss nearly hit Piazza, who had begun running to
first base. The bat "cartwheeled" in front of the Mets' catcher. Piazza,
thinking that Clemens had intended to hit him with the bat, yelled,
"What's your problem?" Clemens indicated that his only problem was in
mistaking the barrel of the bat for the baseball. In fact, onlookers reported that Clemens had "fielded" the bat as if it were a baseball. Clemens
said later that he was not even aware that Piazza was running to first.[150]
The two players, Clemens and Piazza, had distinctly different views of
what had happened. Piazza thought Clemens, in flinging the bat,
intended to hit him. Clemens' intent, apparently, was simply to field
and throw what looked to be a baseball. In attempting to prove criminal intent when Winfield killed the seagull, Toronto prosecutors would
have faced a similar problem. Intent is difficult to pin down, especially
when a person situated similarly to Roger Clemens or Dave Winfield
offers a plausible explanation for an action that could be interpreted as
being malicious.

The Roger Clemens Principles of Proving Intent

*1. In the heat of competition, a baseball bat may be mistaken for a
baseball.*
*2. When a person's actions are susceptible to two contradictory
interpretations, proving intent is difficult.*

No contradictory interpretations were possible when Daniel Stevens of
Baltimore approached John Lazzell, a 60-year-old club pro at Rocky Point
Golf Club in Essex, Maryland, at 5:00 a.m. one day in June 2001 as
Lazzell was getting ready for a tournament. Brandishing a gun, Stevens
forced Lazzell to open the safe in the pro shop. Lazzell feigned feeling sick.
The ploy distracted Stevens and allowed Lazzell to pick up a 9-iron and

---

[150] Verducci, *Roger & Out*, SPORTS ILLUSTRATED, October 30, 2000, 45.

swing it at Stevens. The force of the 9-iron knocked Stevens down. The two men then struggled for Stevens' gun. During the struggle, the gun discharged and struck Stevens in the leg. Stevens then fled the scene. Lazzell called the police, who quickly arrived and found Stevens out on the golf course.[151] From a legal perspective, faced with the threat of Stevens stealing money or property, Lazzell's response was reasonable. A person in Lazzell's situation is justified only in using force to the extent that it is proportional or reasonable in relation to the harm threatened. If the only potential harm was the loss of money or property, Lazzell would not have been justified in killing Stevens. The use of a 9-iron to deter Stevens was proportional to the threat; the use of a revolver to kill him would not have been.

Criminal law concerns itself with crimes against property as well as crimes against people. Shortly after the start of the 2001 baseball season, Chicago Cubs pitcher Jason Bere purchased a brand new silver Porsche 996 priced at $112,000. After buying the car, Bere drove it to Milwaukee, where the Cubs were to play the Brewers in a Saturday night game. Bere left his car with the valet parking service at a downtown Milwaukee hotel. After Bere had departed for the game, a stranger asked an unsuspecting hotel valet for the silver Porsche. The valet delivered the car to the stranger, who got behind the wheel and sped away. An hour later, the stranger drove the car back to the hotel and disappeared on foot.[152] To go joyriding in someone else's car, whether it's an old clunker or a brand new Porsche, is a crime. However, as happened in Jason Bere's case, if the criminal is not caught, the legal system is powerless to take any action. When the "wannabe" owner of a Porsche took Bere's new car for a joy ride, it was more than a violation of Bere's right to control the use of his car. The joy ride violated society's right to the protection of private property. It is not

[151] Kathy Orton, *Club Pro Quells Armed Man*, THE WASH. POST, June 21, 2001, D9.

[152] *Baby, You Can Drive My Car*, THE WASH. POST, June 7, 2001, D7.

likely, however, that the joy ride amounted to a larceny. Larceny is a "specific-intent" crime. It involves taking and carrying away the personal property of another person. Intent is an essential element of larceny. To commit a larceny, a thief must intend to deprive the owner of use of the property permanently. It is possible that the person who took Bere's Porsche intended, at the time he drove off, to keep the car permanently. In that case, his crime may have risen to the level of a larceny. However, his actions were more consistent with the lesser offense of joyriding, which is a temporary taking of an automobile but not with intent to deprive the owner of the car permanently. Joyriding is usually classified as a misdemeanor, whereas larceny involving an automobile is almost always a felony.[153]

In Tennessee, New York and many other states, it is illegal for individuals to "scalp" tickets to sporting events. Scalping involves selling tickets for a price above the price specified on the ticket. In each state, the determination as to what constitutes a crime depends on the legislature's view of the activities that are detrimental to the public welfare. In California, for example, scalping tickets is legal as long as it does not take place in the vicinity of the arena where the game is to be played. Each state has its own laws proscribing, in varying ways, a range of activities such as gambling and ticket scalping that are typically part of the sports world. On top of the state laws, there is a layer of federal laws proscribing activities such as sports bribery and other activities considered to be detrimental to society.

In November 1981, Rick Kuhn, a reserve forward on the 1978-79 Boston College basketball team, and four other men were found guilty of plotting to "fix" six Boston College basketball games. Kuhn and his co-conspirators were tried on charges of violating Federal laws prohibiting racketeering, conspiracy and interstate gambling. At the trial,

---

[153] The distinction between felony larceny and misdemeanor larceny commonly depends on the value of the property taken by the thief.

Federal prosecutors presented evidence that Kuhn and two other Boston College players had been paid to shave points during their games. Shaving points involves efforts by an "underdog" to lose a game by more points than reflected in the spread or betting line, or efforts by a favored team to win by fewer points than projected in the spread. Kuhn was sentenced to ten years in prison. The judge in Kuhn's case rejected pleas by Kuhn's lawyer for public-service work instead of prison. In the judge's opinion, Kuhn emerged "as a somewhat greedy individual." The judge expressed hope that the rather stiff sentence "will be recalled in the future by another college athlete who may be tempted to compromise his performance."[154]

If not for a bizarre discussion between Federal prosecutors and a Government informant named Henry Hill, the Boston College point shaving scandal may never have been uncovered. Hill had come under suspicion for a 1978 robbery of $5.8 million from the Lufthansa Airlines freight terminal at JFK International Airport in New York. Having turned informant, Hill casually referred to "fixing" basketball games when he was answering prosecutors' questions on the Lufthansa heist. A federal attorney asked Hill where he had been on a certain date. Hill replied that he was in Boston. The attorney then asked Hill what he had been doing during his stay in Boston. Hill answered, "fixing some Boston College basketball games."[155]

In baseball, the equivalent of shaving points is "throwing" games. In each case, players agree to compromise their performance for the sake of payoffs from gamblers or bookies. In Rick Kuhn's case, there was solid evidence that he had compromised his performance. In 1921, when eight

---

154 *Rick Kuhn Sentenced to 10 Years*, THE N.Y. TIMES, February 6, 1982, 17.

155 Robert C. Berry and Glenn M. Wong, LAW AND BUSINESS OF THE SPORTS INDUSTRIES: COMMON ISSUES IN AMATEUR AND PROFESSIONAL SPORTS VOL. II (Westport, CT: Praeger Publishers, 1993), 698.

members of the Chicago White Sox baseball team faced criminal charges for allegedly conspiring to lose the 1919 World Series in exchange for pay-offs from gamblers, the evidence was not nearly so persuasive—at least not to the jury hearing the case. Chicago prosecutors relied on confessions pur-portedly made to the grand jury by three players, "Shoeless Joe" Jackson, Eddie Cicotte and Claude "Lefty" Williams. Even with the confessions, however, the jury did not find guilt beyond a reasonable doubt. Questions were raised as to Jackson's alleged confession. Jackson was known to be illit-erate, casting doubt on whether he understood the full implications of the confession.[156] During the trial, the transcripts detailing the grand jury tes-timony of Jackson, Cicotte and Williams disappeared, reportedly taken by one of the bookies involved in the fix.[157] Due in part to the absence of the transcripts and the confessions they supposedly contained, all of the play-ers were acquitted.[158]

Shoeless Joe Jackson consistently maintained that he was innocent of any wrongdoing in the 1919 World Series. In an article that appeared under Jackson's byline in the October 1948 issue of *Sport Magazine*, Jackson recounted the events of 1919. "Sure, I'd heard talk that there was something going on," he said. "I even had a fellow come to me one day and proposi-tion me. It was on the 16th floor of a hotel and there were four other peo-ple there, two men and their wives. I told him: 'Why you cheap so-and-so!

---

[156] Illiterate or not, Jackson possessed a quick wit. Once, when the Chicago White Sox were playing a game in Cleveland, a fan took to heckling Shoeless Joe over his inabil-ity to read and write. The fan asked Jackson if he knew how to spell "illiterate." Jackson knew enough to take offense at the question. He responded by hitting a pitch to the out-field wall for a triple. Safely perched on third base, Jackson yelled at the fan, "Hey, big mouth, how do you spell 'triple'?" Roger I. Abrams, *Legal Bases: Baseball and the Law* (Philadelphia: Temple University Press, 1998), 156.

[157] Peter D. Vroom, *Cicotte And Jackson's Confessions Admitted*, THE CHICAGO EVENING POST, July 25, 1921, 1.

[158] *Chicago 'Black Sox' Acquitted*, SAN FRANCISCO CHRONICLE, August 3, 1921, 1.

Either me or you—one of us is going out that window.' "[159] Jackson chased the fixer out the door of the hotel room and never saw him again. Jackson also contended that on the night before the Series was to begin, he asked White Sox owner Charles Comiskey for permission not to play. Jackson knew there was talk that the White Sox had been paid to dump the Series. He reasoned that, if he didn't play, no one would be able to accuse him of participating in the fix. Comiskey, however, refused Jackson's request. "I went out and played my heart out against Cincinnati," Jackson said.[160] The record is supportive. Jackson hit .375 during the Series and led both teams in hitting. He also hit the only home run in the Series and handled 30 chances in the outfield without an error.

The Shoeless Joe Jackson Principle of False Accusations

When you play your heart out, it is not right for people to accuse you of a crime.

Ticket scalpers have been in operation in the United States for virtually as long as there have been competitive sporting events. At the 1919 World Series, scalpers were commanding $50 for a pair of tickets. Newspapers covering the Series carried frequent announcements that anyone who was speculating in the resale of tickets had to register with the Internal Revenue Service and pay a federal tax on half of the amount received over and above the face value of each ticket. The announcements did little to deter scalpers, however. There were few arrests, and scalpers ignored the law with abandon.[161]

---

[159] Shoeless Joe Jackson as told to Furman Bisher, *This Is the Truth!*, reprinted in THE BASEBALL CHRONICLES, ed. David Gallen (New York: Carroll & Graf Publishers, Inc., 1991), 61, 62.

[160] Jackson, *This Is the Truth!*, in THE BASEBALL CHRONICLES, 62.

[161] Eliot Asinof, *Eight Men Out* (New York: Henry Holt and Company, 1988), 81.

States that have adopted stringent "anti-scalping" laws view them as a way to ensure that all members of the public, regardless of stature or financial means, have an equal and fair opportunity to attend athletic events.[162] In 1992, a Connecticut ticket broker using the name "Concert Connection" sold tickets for the U.S. Tennis Open having a face value of $20 for prices ranging from $100 to $300. The company also sold $15 tickets to New York Yankee baseball games for $45. On at least three occasions, the Concert Connection resold overpriced tickets for events in New York to two different residents of New York and delivered the tickets to the buyers in New York. To the New York State attorney general's office,[163] the Concert Connection's practices amounted to illegal scalping of tickets. The attorney general's office charged the company with violating New York's anti-scalping law. The Concert Connection challenged the charges in court, arguing that New York's anti-scalping law imposed an unconstitutional burden on interstate commerce. The Concert Connection argued that the law should not be applied to out-of-state ticket brokers who sold tickets for events taking place within New York State. Nonetheless, a New York appeals court found the broker to be in violation of New York law and ordered it to compensate New York consumers for the amounts paid over and above the legal maximum.[164]

The New York courts have been equally tough on an individual who tried to sell the rights to season tickets for New York Knicks and New York

---

[162] *State v. Spann*, 623 S.W.2d 272 (Tenn. Sup. Ct. 1981).

[163] The New York law provides that the price of tickets offered by resellers may not exceed the price stated on the ticket plus the greater of $5 or 10 percent of the face value and applicable taxes.

[164] *Court's Ruling Just the Ticket For Keeping Scalpers in Check*, The National Law Journal, June 12, 1995, A27.

Rangers games at Madison Square Garden. In 1997, the owner of the season tickets decided to sell his tickets to a man named Mitchell Sahn. Sahn agreed to purchase the tickets and the right to subscribe to the same season tickets in the future for $90,000 above the face value of the tickets. The two parties, the season ticket holder and Sahn, entered into the agreement even though Madison Square Garden regulations specifically stated that the subscription rights to season tickets were not transferable. Roughly four months after the transaction, Sahn sold the season tickets and subscription rights to a James Haber. Under the agreement between Sahn and Haber, Haber paid $52,350 for the season tickets and $140,000 for the right to subscribe to the tickets in future years. The agreement also provided that if Madison Square Garden canceled the subscription rights or tickets, Haber "shall have no further rights against Sahn and Sahn shall have no further obligation pursuant to this agreement." Before Haber could use the season tickets, Madison Square Garden canceled the season ticket subscription and refunded the price of the tickets to the original season ticket holder. Following the cancellation, Sahn kept the $140,000 that Haber had paid for the subscription rights. Haber sued Sahn to get back the $140,000. Haber argued that the agreement with Sahn violated the New York State anti-scalping law. The court found that the contract between Haber and Sahn was in direct violation of the anti-scalping law. In its opinion, the court stated that it is the "strong public policy" in New York State to protect against the sale of sports tickets at exorbitant prices by individuals attempting to make enormous profits. The court faulted Sahn for reselling tickets at a price above the legal maximum and ordered him to repay Haber. In the court's view, the contract between Sahn and Haber violated New York law and was therefore illegal.[165]

---

[165] *Diversified Group Inc. v. Sahn*, 696 N.Y.S.2d 133 (A.D. 1 Dept. 1999).

Though race horse trainer Neil Terracciano denies doing anything illegal, the New York State Racing and Wagering Board collected evidence that Terracciano, or someone who worked for him, had doped his thoroughbred, Destination Home, before a race at Aqueduct Race Track in November 2000. The doctors who tested Destination Home after the race were dumbfounded at Terracciano's drug of choice. It appeared to be the sexual stimulant Viagra. The medical staff told Terracciano that Viagra could be harmful to horses. Terracciano, however, denied any wrongdoing. Nonetheless, in a curious rebuttal to the doctors, he disagreed that Viagra would harm horses. "My grandfather," Terracciano said, "he's 72, he takes Viagra. He's the fountain of youth."[166] Whatever benefits Viagra may provide for Terracciano's grandfather, the drug appeared to do little for Destination Home. The horse came in third at Aqueduct. The drug also did little for Terracciano—the Racing and Wagering Board suspended him for 60 days and fined him $2,000 for illegal doping.

A more common method of cheating in horse racing is to engage in a practice known as "milk-shaking." Trainers may "milk shake" a horse by feeding it a mixture of baking soda, sugar and water. The mixture causes the level of carbon dioxide in a horse's blood stream to rise. Higher levels of carbon dioxide block pain and muscle fatigue in a horse, allowing the horse to run faster. On August 17, 2000, a horse named Chicory Chap ran the fastest time ever at Hazel Park Harness Raceway in Michigan. After the race, Michigan Department of Agriculture authorities tested Chicory Chap for illegal substances. The horse's carbon dioxide reading was 37.02 millimoles per liter.[167] The legal limit in Michigan is 37 millimoles per liter.

---

[166] John Donovan, *Your Cheatin' Horse: Some People In Sports Just Can't Play By The Rules*, CNNSI, www.sportsillustrated.cnn.com/inside_game/john_donovan/news/2001/01/19/cheating.

[167] A millimole is a metric unit used to measure very small concentrations of substances in the bloodstream.

As a result of the violation, Chicory Chap's trainer lost her license for 60 days. The trainer denied any wrongdoing. "This doesn't look good on a resume," she said, and countered by suing the Department of Agriculture. In her lawsuit, the trainer maintained that a horse's level of carbon dioxide will increase naturally if the horse becomes dehydrated. On the day of the race, Chicory Chap had to travel two hours in stop-and-go traffic in hot weather, leading the trainer to conclude that the horse was dehydrated before the race. State authorities discounted the dehydration theory. The Michigan Attorney General's office insisted that the evidence clearly showed that Chicory Chap had ingested baking soda.[168]

In the State of Washington, professional gambling has historically been illegal. However, there is one exception: the Washington Horse Racing Act permits horse racing tracks in Washington to operate a parimutuel betting system. The Act applies only to certain breeds of horses. The state permits other types of racing, such as dog races, but without public gambling. In the 1960s, the Northwest Greyhound Kennel Association, Inc. launched an effort to establish parimutuel betting on greyhound races. The Association's motive was simple. As long as public gambling on dog races was outlawed in the State, it was economically impossible for dog racing to survive. The organization applied for a license to operate a parimutuel dog track, but the State denied its request on the grounds that the Horse Racing Act exempted only horse races from the state-wide ban on public gambling. The Northwest Greyhound Kennel Association then filed a lawsuit seeking to have the Horse Racing Act declared unconstitutional. The courts rebuffed the Association, finding that the only way that public betting on greyhounds could be authorized in the State would be for

---

[168] Kevin Lynch, *Horse Trainers Call New State Doping Law Unfair*, THE DETROIT NEWS, October 11, 2000, www.detnews.com/2000/oakland/0010/11/c04-133090.htm.

the legislature to pass a law permitting greyhound tracks to operate a parimutuel betting system.[169] Without such a law, any organization that established a parimutuel betting system for greyhound racing would risk criminal sanctions.

In the United States' system of criminal law, there are crimes against people and crimes against property. There are also crimes that result when an individual violates a law adopted to address a public concern, such as the laws against ticket scalping and betting on dog racing and other sporting events. In each criminal case, the authorities must find evidence that an individual acted in a manner contrary to the law. In the absence of such evidence, if in fact "nobody did nothin' to nobody," the law will not be able to obtain a conviction.

---

[169] *Northwest Greyhound Kennel Association v. State*, 506 P.2d 878 (1973).

Chapter 6

Women in Sports: From the Tunnel to the Clubhouse

During the 1974-75 basketball season, the Kentucky Colonels ranked among the elite teams in the American Basketball Association. The Colonels had one Brown, a woman named Ellie, as the owner and another Brown, the unrelated Hubie, as coach. Sparked by guard Louie Dampier, the best three-point shooter in the league, the Colonels won 22 of their last 25 games and beat the Indiana Pacers for the league championship. The Colonels played a stifling defense, anchored by 7'2" center Artis Gilmore, and featured consistent scoring from Dampier and Dan Issel. After the team beat the Pacers for the ABA title, Ellie Brown came to the Colonels' locker room to join in the celebration. Immediately, the players faced a quandary. By tradition, the team's owner was supposed to get thrown in the shower. The players were unsure, however, as to what tradition required when the owner was a woman. The players resolved the dilemma by resorting to the principle of equal opportunity: they threw Ellie Brown in the shower. Colonels guard Gene Littles explained, "After all, she was the owner, and owners get thrown in the shower."[170]

Not all of the issues involving women in sports are resolved so easily—or so evenhandedly. In the space the *Baseball Encyclopedia* reserves for a player's nickname, the moniker "Mr. October" appears next to Reggie Jackson's name. October is World Series time. It was Reggie Jackson's time. An imposing hitter in any month, Jackson played with special distinction during October. He appeared in 27 World Series games over the course of five different seasons and compiled a dazzling .357 batting average. More than any other World Series, it was Jackson's performance for the New York Yankees in the 1977 Series that earned him the distinction of being dubbed "Mr. October." In twenty plate appearances against the Los Angeles Dodgers, Jackson slammed five home runs, drove in eight runs and scored ten. He collected nine hits, good for a lofty .450 batting average. On the field, both teams played near-flawless baseball. In the six-game Series, the Dodgers committed only one error, the Yankees three. Since the inception of the World Series in 1903, no Series had witnessed fewer errors. Off the field, however, Major League Baseball Commissioner Bowie Kuhn, as well as the management of the Yankees and Dodgers, committed errors, and they were big ones. Prior to the Series, Kuhn issued an order barring women reporters from entering the teams' clubhouses to conduct post-game interviews. Both the Yankees and Dodgers complied with the edict.

Sports Illustrated magazine assigned reporter Melissa Ludtke to cover the Series. Ludtke had covered the Yankees' post-season games leading up to the Series. When New York played the Kansas City Royals during the American League playoff games, Ludtke enjoyed unrestricted access to Yankee manager Billy Martin's office after the games. Ludtke expected

---

[170] Terry Pluto, *Loose Balls: The Short, Wild Life of the American Basketball Association As Told by the Players, Coaches, and Movers and Shakers Who Made It Happen*, (New York: Simon & Schuster, 1990), 344.

that she would have similar access during the Series. And, before the Series began, the Dodgers told Ludtke that she would be permitted to enter their clubhouse after the games. Ludtke and *Sports Illustrated* were shocked, therefore, when the Commissioner's office informed Ludtke that she would be barred from both teams' clubhouses during the Series. In contrast, male reporters were able to freely enter the clubhouses and talk to the players and managers. Having exiled Ludtke, the Commissioner made special arrangements for her to talk to the ballplayers. Ludtke was told to stand in the tunnel leading to the clubhouses after the games. Kuhn gave a public relations director the responsibility of trying to bring players out of the clubhouse to speak with her.

Bowie Kuhn, a lawyer by training, should have known better than to discriminate on the basis of a reporter's sex. The New York Rangers hockey team, the National Basketball Association's Knicks and Nets, and the New York Cosmos soccer team certainly did. By 1977, the Rangers, Knicks, Nets and Cosmos, along with the vast majority of professional basketball and hockey teams, permitted women reporters to enter their locker rooms to talk to the players. The only basis for treating Ludtke differently was her gender. The distinction was inherently unfair. It was also unconstitutional.

Melissa Ludtke considered herself politically naive. She said she never thought much about discrimination until she saw how women were treated in the locker room controversy. "When I tried to get into the locker room," she said, "it was for obvious professional reasons. I went through all the proper steps, asked all the right people, explained my reasons. Then the door was slammed in my face. Literally, I mean."[171] Some of the ballplayers were appalled at the treatment that Ludtke received. Ludtke found Yankee outfielders Reggie Jackson and Roy White and infielder Fred Stanley to be particularly supportive during the controversy.

---

[171] Roger Angell, *Late Innings: A Baseball Companion* (New York: Ballantine Books, 1983), 146.

Bowie Kuhn was appalled that Ludtke would question his edict. He argued that he was merely protecting the privacy of players. Neither *Sports Illustrated* nor Ludtke was persuaded that the ballplayers' privacy required such extreme measures. In search of answers, they sued Kuhn and major league baseball. The judge presiding over the lawsuit, Constance Baker Motley, was not at all sympathetic to baseball's arguments. In the judge's view, the prohibition against women reporters only helped to maintain the locker room "as an all-male preserve." The judge considered Bowie Kuhn's logic flawed. If allowing Melissa Ludtke into the Yankee locker room infringed on Reggie Jackson's privacy, the judge reasoned, allowing women to watch a television interview with "Mr. October" from the locker room would have the same effect. If the players' privacy was the primary concern, Judge Motley ruled, Kuhn should have banned televised interviews from the locker room. He didn't. In the judge's eyes, the decision was easy. Baseball had violated Ludtke's rights to equal protection.[172]

The Judge Motley Principles of Equal Access to Clubhouses

1. *It is unconstitutional to expect women reporters to stand in a tunnel outside a clubhouse when men reporters are standing inside the clubhouse.*
2. *Professional sports cannot adopt policies that have the effect of creating "an all-male preserve."*

The Fourteenth Amendment to the Constitution guarantees women reporters equal protection under the law. Bowie Kuhn's edict took away that equal protection. It deprived Ludtke and other women of the right to pursue their chosen profession, a fundamental liberty protected by the Fourteenth Amendment. The Constitution aside, other factors argue for equal opportunity for women in sports reporting. Sportswriter Jane Gross

---

[172] *Ludtke v. Kuhn*, 461 F.Supp. 86 (S.D.N.Y. 1978).

has identified a few. "We women are interested in different things from the men writers, so we ask different questions." When Bob McAdoo was traded from the Knicks to the Boston Celtics,[173] Gross says, her first thought was, "How is his wife, Brenda, going to finish law school this year?" And, says Gross, his wife's law school career may have been the most important thing on Bob McAdoo's mind as well.[174] Gross felt that, as a woman, she had a special opportunity to get close to the players' wives and to report on aspects of professional sports that men reporters may never get to see.[175] The law guarantees women reporters the opportunity

---

[173] On February 12, 1979, the New York Knicks announced they had traded the 6'11" McAdoo to the Boston Celtics for three first-round draft picks. Two days earlier, the Knicks had played the Celtics at Madison Square Garden. Celtics owner John Y. Brown and his wife, sportscaster and former Miss America Phyllis George, attended the game, sitting in the company of Knicks owner Sonny Werblin. McAdoo's flair on the basketball court caught the eye of Phyllis George. She remarked to her husband that the Celtics could use a player like McAdoo. That same day, Brown and Werblin worked out the details of the trade. George Kalinsky and Phil Berger, *The New York Knicks: The Official 50th Anniversary Celebration* (New York: Macmillan Books, 1997), 141. The McAdoo trade was one of many incidents in which Brown usurped the responsibility of Celtics general manager Red Auerbach. After the trade was announced, Auerbach told Brown that he would resign his position with the Celtics unless Brown sold the team. Two weeks later, Brown sold his interest in the Celtics. Arnold "Red" Auerbach with Joe Fitzgerald, *On & Off The Court* (New York: Bantam Books, 1986), 86.

[174] Attendance at law school raises a whole other set of issues. When former NFL safety Brig Owens played with the Washington Redskins, he was enrolled in night classes at Georgetown University Law School. By attending classes at night, he was generally able to avoid conflicts with his day job. At times, however, such as when the Redskins played on Monday nights, the football schedule interfered with Owens' classes. On those occasions, Owens would ask his wife to attend class in his place. To her dismay, Owens' wife would find herself sitting in class taking notes on arcane points of law while the wives of other Redskin players were enjoying the spectacle of Monday Night Football at RFK Stadium.

[175] Angell, *Late Innings*, 152-53.

to ask "different questions." For a sports reporter, a team's clubhouse is the best setting in which to ask athletes those questions. Judge Motley found that most of the news written about baseball comes from clubhouse interviews. Requiring Melissa Ludtke, or any reporter, to stand in a tunnel while others are in the clubhouse is contrary to the law.

The Jane Gross Principles of Equal Access to the Sportswriting Profession

1. Professional sports need reporting by women sportswriters.
2. Women sportwriters ask different questions.

Lisa Olson, a reporter for the *Boston Herald*, had no problem getting into the New England Patriots' locker room. Once she got there, however, she found a most unpleasant environment. On September 17, 1990, Olson was trying to conduct a post-game interview with a Patriots player. During the course of the interview, Patriots tight end Zeke Mowatt allegedly exposed himself and made lewd remarks. Other players reportedly harassed Olson as well.[176] Patriots owner Victor Kiam immediately discounted Olson's version of the events and labeled Olson a "classic bitch." After the incident, Mowatt took a 5½-hour lie detector test that, according to his attorney, proved he had not harassed Olson. "This exonerates Zeke and shows just how poorly this entire episode was handled," Mowatt's attorney said at the time.[177] In the aftermath of the incident, NFL Commissioner Paul Tagliabue appointed Harvard Law Professor Philip Heymann to investigate Olson's allegations. Heymann's subsequent report was critical of Mowatt and teammates Michael Timpson and Robert Perryman. Based on Heymann's investigation, Tagliabue fined

---

[176] Christine Brennan, *Tagliabue To Probe Harassment: Woman Reporter Accuses Patriots*, THE WASH. POST, September 28, 1990, B5.

[177] *Polygraph Test Reportedly Clears Mowatt*, THE WASH. POST, October 7, 1990, C5.

Mowatt $12,500, and Timpson and Perryman $5,000 each. The NFL also fined the Patriots $25,000 for not adequately investigating and resolving the players' misconduct. Olson later sued the Patriots, alleging sexual harassment and violation of her civil rights. The suit was settled out of court in February 1992. Terms of the settlement were kept confidential, but the Patriots and Victor Kiam were reported to have paid Olson an amount ranging from $500,000 to $700,000.[178]

The incident involving Zeke Mowatt and the Patriots raised, once again, the issue of access by women reporters to men's locker rooms after practices and games. Former Washington Redskins defensive tackle Dave Butz used the occasion to suggest that players were entitled to privacy in the locker room. Butz came down in favor of equal opportunity and equal access for all reporters, male and female, but suggested that players should have a period of 20 minutes after games when they could shower and dress without being interrupted for interviews. As a player, Butz went well out of his way to accommodate reporters. He related that when Christine Brennan, a reporter who once covered the Redskins for *The Washington Post*, first appeared in the team's locker room after a game, he was both shocked and uncomfortable. When Brennan asked for an interview while Butz was in the process of dressing, Butz declined. However, as soon as Butz had a day off, he gave Brennan all the time she needed to get a story. Butz maintained that the value of obtaining comments from players immediately after a game is exaggerated. "Immediately after a game, in most locker rooms, there is much more perspiration than perspective," he observed.[179]

The case of *Ludtke v. Kuhn* may have solidified the law on equal access to clubhouses, but it did not erase the attitudes that led to Bowie Kuhn's

---

[178] Martin J. Greenberg and James T. Gray, *Sports Law Practice* (Charlottesville, VA: Lexis Law Publishing, 1998), I, 1278-79.

[179] Dave Butz, *Respect Should Keep Women Out of Men's Locker Rooms*, THE WASH. POST, October 7, 1990, C5.

edict in the first place. Pam Postema began working as a professional baseball umpire in 1977. In 1981, Postema was promoted to the Double A Texas League, becoming the first woman ever to umpire a professional baseball game above the Class A minor leagues. From 1983 to 1986, Postema umpired in the AAA Pacific Coast League. Other milestones followed swiftly. In 1987, she was hired by the Triple-A Alliance of Professional Baseball Clubs. She was behind the plate for the first Triple-A Minor League All-Star Game, held in 1989. She also umpired major league spring training games in 1988 and 1989. From 1987 to 1989, Postema received high praise from experienced baseball people, including Chuck Tanner, Tom Trebelhorn, Hal Lanier and Roger Craig, all of whom managed in the major leagues. Along the way, however, Postema also endured some of the same indignities that had been heaped upon Melissa Ludtke. Postema made national news when Houston Astros pitcher Bob Knepper said that, although she was a good umpire, women umpires were contrary to the teachings of the Bible. The manager of the minor league Nashville Hounds once kissed Postema on the lips when he handed her his team's lineup card before a game. During a 1988 spring training game, Pittsburgh Pirates manager Chuck Tanner asked Postema if she would like a kiss. Players and managers repeatedly asked her why she didn't pursue "women's work" instead of umpiring. Other players and managers were more abusive.[180]

Postema's career as an umpire began to unravel after the 1989 season. In October of that year, Postema's name was included on a list of candidates for major league umpiring positions submitted to the American League. The American League stated that it had no interest in hiring any of the umpires on the list because there were no vacancies on its umpiring staff. A month later, the Triple-A Alliance unconditionally released

---

[180] *Postema v. National League of Professional Baseball Clubs,* 799 F.Supp 1475 (1992).

Postema and others who had hoped to umpire in the big leagues. Postema charged that she was dismissed because of her sex. She sued both the major leagues and her employer, Triple-A, under Title VII of the Civil Rights Act.

Postema had no problem demonstrating the obstacles that she had encountered in her job. Even if Bob Knepper was wrong, even if female umpires are consistent with the teachings of the Bible, Postema faced a most difficult path to the big leagues. The former supervisor of umpires for the American League reflected the views of many in the baseball hierarchy when he said, "She's got to be better because of the fact that she's a girl." The assistant supervisor of umpires for the American League was more emphatic. "She's got to do the job twice as good as the guy," he said.[181] Unfortunately for Postema, it was easier to collect anecdotes demonstrating discriminatory attitudes than it was to prove actual discrimination. At a time when the major leagues were not hiring any new umpires, Postema was not the only umpire whose progress to the major leagues was stymied. The law required Postema to prove "a prima facie" case of discrimination.[182] She had to show that the major leagues prevented her from advancing because she was a woman. She could not meet the prima facie test because, when it came to handing out promotions to "the show," the major leagues treated Postema exactly the same as her Triple-A colleagues—they didn't hire any of them.

If Bob Knepper thought women umpires were contrary to the Bible, he most likely wouldn't have approved of women players—at least not on men's teams. Nonetheless, women have played—and starred—on men's

---

[181] *Postema v. National League of Professional Baseball Clubs*, 799 F.Supp at 1479.

[182] The "prima facie" standard applicable to discrimination in employment cases filed under the Civil Rights Act comes from a 1973 Supreme Court decision, *McDonnell Douglas Corp. v. Green*, 411 U.S. 792. In a lawsuit alleging discriminatory treatment based on gender, establishing a prima facie case requires the complaining party to demonstrate that, when compared to others who were similarly situated, he or she received unequal treatment.

teams. One of the earliest recorded instances of a woman playing with a men's professional team occurred in 1898 when Lizzie Arlington, a right-handed pitcher from Philadelphia, played with the Philadelphia Reserves in a game against a team from Richmond, Virginia. Her appearance with the Philadelphia Reserves was hailed as an opportunity for her to "show the professional players that the woman that can throw straight has at last been discovered."[183] That same season, Arlington also played with professional teams in the New York State and Western Leagues. In 1907, an 18-year-old woman named Alta Weiss played to even greater reviews. Trumpeted as "the girl wonder," Weiss led the Vermillions from Cleveland, Ohio to a 7-6 victory over Vacha's All-Stars on October 2, 1907. The *Cleveland Leader* reported Weiss' victory as front-page news. According to the *Leader*, Weiss was "graceful. And mighty pretty too." From all appearances, Weiss possessed a fastball capable of embarrassing her male opponents. "The arms are strong, the legs swift and the hands sure in catching the speedy balls," the newspaper gushed. Weiss' repertoire included a spitball. "For an evident reason," the *Leader* reported, "she chews gum. She's not a bit offensive about it. She makes a better delivery of the regular ball, although she keeps the men fooled by her variety." Weiss befuddled one of the All-Star batters by throwing a spitball for a strike on a 3-1 count. She followed up the spitball with a change-up for strike three. Weiss "laughed till her cheeks were red and the crowd laughed with her."[184]

From the sketchy news accounts available, it appears that Alta Weiss was having fun as she kept male batters "fooled by her variety." If Weiss encountered indignities when taking the field with a bunch of men, she apparently kept them to herself. Eighty-five years later, Julie Croteau, the

---

[183] *Miss Arlington's Tour: The Girl Pitcher to Twirl Against Professional Teams*, THE PHILADELPHIA PRESS, July 1, 1898, 10.

[184] Mariett M. Buggie, *Girl Tosser Wins Game, Also Fans: Chews Gum and Pitchers All-Star Team to Standstill*, THE CLEVELAND LEADER, October 3, 1907, 1.

first woman to play NCAA varsity baseball, felt compelled to quit her college team because "somewhere along the way, the game stopped being fun." The athletic director at Croteau's school, St. Mary's College in Maryland, confirmed that the first baseman had to fight a lot of battles during her three seasons with the St. Mary's varsity. Croteau quit the team in June 1991. The last straw, she said, was when she had to endure a bus trip with the team during which teammates read aloud from a degrading article about women that appeared in a men's magazine. Croteau left no doubt that there were other straws as well. Teammates told her she didn't belong on the team. She had to listen to members of the team describe players' inept performances as "feminine." Opposing pitchers would throw at her, apparently solely because she was female. "It wasn't easy," Jay Gardiner, the St. Mary's athletic director, said.[185]

Dot Richardson, the UCLA star who played a stellar shortstop for the 1996 and 2000 U.S. Women's Softball Teams, can certainly identify with Croteau. When Richardson was growing up, the coach of a boy's Little League team invited her to join his team. There was one catch, however. The coach told Richardson that she would have to pretend to be a boy. Richardson declined the invitation.[186] In 1990, Kelly Craig played on a boy's Little League team and, unlike Richardson, she didn't have to conceal her gender to do it. Craig, a pitcher and first baseman, gained fame as the first female ever selected to be the starting pitcher in a Little League World Series game. Craig played for the Trail team out of British Columbia. Facing a team from Matamoros, Mexico in a quarterfinal game, she faced three batters, yielding two singles and a walk. After the walk, Craig turned the mound duties over to a relief pitcher and moved to

---

[185] J.A. Adande, *'Boys Will Be Boys' Sad Excuse For Fouling Her Out, She Says: Female 1st Baseman Bids Insults Goodbye*, THE WASH. POST, June 25, 1991, E5.

[186] Marian Betancourt, *Playing Like a Girl* (New York: Contemporary Books, 2001), 71.

first base. In spite of the inauspicious start, Craig's team went on to post an 8-3 victory over Matamoros.[187]

When Duke University football coach Fred Goldsmith cut place-kicker Heather Sue Mercer from the Duke football squad in 1996, he added insult to injury by suggesting that the former all-state high school football player "try something like beauty pageants." Banished from the field, Mercer left her imprint on college football when she successfully sued Duke and was awarded $2 million in damages.[188] During the 2001 football season, Ashley Martin, a 20-year-old attending Jacksonville (Alabama) State University on a soccer scholarship, picked up where Mercer had left off. Playing in a more hospitable collegiate program than had Mercer, Martin made her debut as a varsity football player in Jacksonville State's August 30th game against Cumberland University. The team's second-string place-kicker, Martin entered the game in the first quarter after Jacksonville State scored its second touchdown. She booted the extra point through the uprights to give her team a 14-0 lead. The extra point attempt gave the 5'11", 160-pound Martin the distinction of being the first woman to play in a National Collegiate Athletic Association football game. In all, Martin kicked three extra points in Jacksonville State's 72-10 rout of Cumberland.

Like Mercer, Martin had been a successful high school football player. She was the first-string kicker for her East Coweta High School team in Sharpsburg, Georgia and had helped the team to records of 8-3 in her junior year and 10-1 in her senior season. The Jacksonville State football coach, Jack Crowe, decided to recruit Martin for his team when he looked out his office window one day and noticed her kicking footballs after soccer practice. Martin secured her place on the team by making 20 out of 22 extra point attempts during the team's preseason scrimmages. For Martin,

---

[187] *Little League Has Female Trail Blazer: Canadian Girl Starts In the World Series,* THE WASH. POST, August 22, 1990, D6.

[188] Mercer's lawsuit is discussed at greater length in Chapter 15.

the distinction of being the first woman player in an NCAA game was not cause for special celebration. "I'm not making a statement," she said, "I'm not trying to break a barrier—I just want to play a game and help the team win."[189] Others, however, refused to take Martin's feat in stride. The Jacksonville State bookstore quickly produced T-shirts with a caricature of Martin in her football uniform, wearing No. 89, and booting a Cumberland player through the uprights. Martin suffered few of the indignities that had been heaped upon Julie Croteau. The only time she felt uncomfortable around her new teammates, she said, was during the first team meeting in the preseason. According to one of her teammates, lineman Jerry Sullivan, Martin "just kind of blends in." "It was kind of funny to see a ponytail sticking out of a helmet at first," Sullivan said, "but after a while, it was like 'that's just another kicker.' "[190]

Julie Krone won more horse races than any other woman jockey in history. During her racing career, which stretched from 1981 to 1999, she won more than 3,500 races and earned in excess of $81 million. Krone didn't have it easy either. During a race in 1986, fellow jockey Miguel Rujano hit Krone in her ear with his whip. After the race, Krone turned the tables on Rujano. She found him in a vulnerable moment, punched him in the face and then whacked him with a lawn chair.[191]

In the early days of the American Basketball Association, one of Krone's predecessors, jockey Peggy Ann Early, played for the Kentucky Colonels. The Colonels signed Early to a professional basketball contract as a publicity gimmick, making her the first female pro basketball player. She sat on the team's bench for a couple of games and then got into one game for a brief moment during which she threw the basketball into play. The Colonels then promptly called a time-out and replaced Early with

[189] Ray Glier, *After Making the Team, She Is Making History*, THE WASH. POST, August 31, 2001, A3.

[190] Glier, *After Making the Team, She Is Making History*, THE WASH. POST, A3.

[191] Mark Beech, *Julie Krone, Star Jockey*, SPORTS ILLUSTRATED, May 21, 2001, 12.

another player.[192] Early, of course, was not serious about a basketball career. Nor were the Colonels serious about having her on the team. Another woman, Nancy Lieberman-Cline, took her basketball much more seriously. There was no denying Lieberman-Cline's talent and zest for the game. She grew up playing pickup games with boys on the asphalt courts in Harlem, New York. In 1976, when Lieberman-Cline was 18, she played on the U.S. woman's Olympic basketball team, becoming the youngest basketball player ever to win an Olympic medal. As a collegian, Lieberman-Cline led Old Dominion University to back-to-back AIAW National Championships in 1979 and 1980. Lieberman-Cline scored 2,430 points in her college career and passed for 961 assists. Twice she was selected as the woman's collegiate player of the year. In 1986, Lieberman-Cline became the first woman to play in a men's professional league when she was signed by the Springfield Fame of the United States Basketball League. The next year, Lieberman-Cline played with the Washington Generals. She spent the season with the Generals as they toured with the Harlem Globetrotters. It was not necessarily her competitive drive that led her to play with men. "I didn't want to play in a men's professional league," she said. "I wished that there was a women's professional league that I could play in. But I loved the game, so I decided to be a part of a men's team."[193]

Lieberman-Cline's counterpart in professional hockey was a woman named Manon Rheaume. On December 13, 1992, Rheaume, then 20 years old, became the first woman to play in a regular season professional hockey game when she tended goal for the Atlanta Knights against Salt Lake City in International Hockey League competition. The crowd of 9,027 gave Rheaume a standing ovation when she headed for the net. Rheaume saw

---

[192] Terry Pluto, *Loose Balls: The Short, Wild Life Of The American Basketball Association As Told By The Players, Coaches, And Movers And Shakers Who Made It Happen* (New York: Simon & Schuster Inc., 1991), 329-330.

[193] Betancourt. *Playing Like a Girl*, viii-ix.

five minutes and 49 seconds of action. In a game ultimately won by Salt Lake City, 4-1, she gave up one goal and stopped three shots.[194]

When Cammi Granato was named radio announcer for the Los Angeles Kings professional hockey team in 1998, her credentials for the job were impeccable. Hockey roots run deep in the Granato family. Granato's brother, Tony, is a veteran of the National Hockey League. Cammi Granato had been a stalwart on the Providence College women's hockey team during her college career. As a senior, she earned All-American honors. She was also the captain of the 1998 U.S. women's hockey team that captured the gold medal in Nagano, Japan. In October 1998, Granato began announcing the Kings' games. She soon found, however, that her hockey credentials were not enough. "I'm the only woman now doing this," she said, "and there were a lot of people objecting to it because I was a woman."[195]

If Cammi Granato takes to the radio waves like she took to the hockey rink, however, she should have it easy. Nonetheless, gender barriers are not easily broken. At the age of 19, Sarah Fisher, an automobile racer from Commercial Point, Ohio, began racing in the Indy Racing League. Her early performances were not particularly encouraging. In a race in Las Vegas in her rookie year, veteran driver Eliseo Salazar castigated Fisher for her role in a wreck that occurred on the track. "This is not powder-puff racing," Salazar fumed. Salazar suggested that Fisher "go race with girls." A year later, while racing at the Grand Prix of Miami, Fisher passed Salazar during the race. Salazar never caught up. Fisher finished in second place at the Grand Prix, the best finish in her brief racing career. When Fisher accelerated past Salazar, Salazar's boss, A.J. Foyt, screamed at him over the radio, "You just got passed by a girl!"[196]

---

[194] *Rheaume Plays First Game*, THE WASH. POST, December 14, 1992, C4.

[195] Rachel Alexander, *Cammi Granato Providing Color*, THE WASH. POST, February 3, 1999, D10.

[196] Mark Bechtel, *IRL's Leading Lady: Fisher Is Making Her Mark*, SPORTS ILLUSTRATED, June 4, 2001, 100.

When the Detroit Tigers named 28-year-old Heather Nabozny as their head groundskeeper in 1999, there were plenty of male groundskeepers who were passed by a "girl." Never before had a woman been in charge of a major league baseball field. Callers flooded the Tigers' switchboard. Overnight, Nabozny became a media sensation. Magazines and TV talk shows rushed to tell her story.[197] Heather Nabozny believes that the Tigers' decision to promote her to head groundskeeper was based strictly on her ability. Both the Tigers and Nabozny insisted the decision was not motivated by the publicity that was sure to follow.

The Heather Nabozny Principle of Promotions in the Field of Sports

Promotions should be based strictly on ability.

On those occasions when promotions in professional sports appear to be based on criteria other than ability, there are remedies available under the law. In the spring of 1998, a jury awarded an aspiring National Basketball Association referee, Sandra Ortiz-Del Valle, $7.85 million after the NBA repeatedly passed her over for a refereeing position. Ortiz-Del Valle had risen to second place on the list of referees in line to officiate in the NBA. Thereafter, her progress halted for no apparent reason. Ortiz-Del Valle sued the NBA for discrimination. The jury hearing her case found that the NBA had indeed discriminated.[198] The *Ortiz-Del Valle* decision affirmed a principle established twenty years earlier by Melissa Ludtke: the world of sports must permit equal opportunity for both men and women.

---

[197] Tom Verducci, *A Woman's Place Is on the Field*, SPORTS ILLUSTRATED, February 8, 1999, 117.

[198] A federal court later reduced the amount awarded to Ortiz-Del Valle in damages to $350,000. *Award Reduced*, THE WASH. POST, April 2, 1999, D6.

Chapter 7

Privacy in the Field of Play

Baseball player Ichiro Suzuki proved to be an immediate sensation when, after winning seven straight batting titles in Japan, he joined the Seattle Mariners for the 2001 major league baseball season. Early in his days with the Mariners, Suzuki's actions, both on and off the field, set him apart from other ballplayers. For starters, he informed the Mariners that he wanted to have his first name, not his last name, sewn on the back of his uniform jersey. In his very first month of major league ball, Ichiro performed well enough to earn Rookie of the Month honors. Entering the last week of May, he was third in the American League in batting with a .365 average. Ichiro kept up his torrid hitting all season, finishing the year at .350. He led the major leagues in batting average, hits and stolen bases. He was the first player since Jackie Robinson in 1949 to finish on top of the major leagues in both batting average and steals. At season's end, Ichiro was voted as both the Most Valuable Player in the American League and AL Rookie of the Year. Ichiro's heroics continued during his sophomore season. Entering the 2002 all-star break, he was batting .357 and was among the American League leaders in average, hits, runs, stolen bases and triples.

From every indication, Suzuki had adjusted well to life in the United States. He did concede, however, that he sorely missed his dog, which he had left behind in Japan. When reporters asked Suzuki the name of his dog, the ballplayer demurred. "I would not wish to say," he replied, "without first asking its permission."[199]

For former Supreme Court Justice Louis Brandeis, one of the primary functions of the Constitution of the United States was to protect a person's right to be left alone. Former basketball player Oscar Robertson, a perennial all-star with the Cincinnati Royals and Milwaukee Bucks, would no doubt agree. Robertson once ducked into the men's room at the Boston Garden just minutes before tip-off against the Celtics. As Robertson stood at the urinal taking care of business, a man approached and asked for an autograph. A stunned Robertson exclaimed, "Can't I even piss in peace?"

Oscar Robertson should have the right to "piss in peace." Ichiro Suzuki should have the right to protect the name of his dog. If Ichiro's concern for the privacy of his dog was a bit extreme, it was no more bizarre than some of the measures taken by other ballplayers to defend their right of privacy. While with the Cleveland Indians, former outfielder Albert Belle once threw baseballs at *Sports Illustrated* photographer Tony Tomsic to discourage him from taking pictures during pre-game warm-ups. As Belle was well aware, it is standard baseball practice for photographers to shoot pictures of baseball players when they are on the field. Nonetheless, Belle became enraged when Tomsic, positioned 100 feet away, took pictures of him playing catch in left field before a game. Belle retaliated by aiming baseballs at Tomsic's head.[200] Albert Belle seemed to believe he had a right to privacy even on the playing field before a game.

The Bill of Rights guarantees freedom of religion, freedom of speech and a host of other freedoms. There is, however, no express mention of the right to privacy anywhere in the Bill of Rights or elsewhere in the

---

[199] Jeff Pearlman, *Big Hit*, SPORTS ILLUSTRATED, May 28, 2001, 34, 39.

[200] Mark Maske, *AL President Orders Belle to Get Counseling*, THE WASH. POST, May 17, 1996, C1.

Constitution. Brandeis and other legal scholars have found the right of privacy to be an extension of the constitutional guarantees of life, liberty and the pursuit of happiness. For these scholars, the right to life includes the right to a quiet existence, out of the public gaze. Nonetheless, a person who places himself directly "in the public gaze," as Albert Belle did every time he stepped onto the playing field, necessarily must accept some loss of privacy.

Similarly, college football players who participate in public relations campaigns to bolster their All-American credentials may forfeit some of their privacy. Davey O'Brien, once a candidate for All-American honors at Texas Christian University, authorized the university to distribute his photograph for publicity purposes. T.C.U. sent O'Brien's photo to the Pabst Brewing Company, which used the picture on an advertising calendar. O'Brien sued for invasion of privacy, alleging that he was embarrassed and humiliated to be associated with an advertisement for beer. The court found, however, that O'Brien was a national football figure and had completely publicized his name and his pictures. According to the court, O'Brien had willingly forfeited his right to privacy by authorizing the distribution of his photograph.[201]

The O'Brien decision dates back to 1942.[202] In its ruling, the court did not focus on the issue of whether Pabst Brewing had unfairly exploited O'Brien's image for commercial purposes. The decision is at odds with more recent court cases recognizing that athletes have a proprietary interest

---

[201] *O'Brien v. Pabst Sales Co.*, 124 F.2d 167 (1942).

[202] TCU is undoubtedly more protective of its players' privacy in the modern era, if only because National Collegiate Athletic Association rules require it to be. Under Article 12.5.2.2 of the NCAA Bylaws, if an athlete's name or picture is used to promote a commercial product without the knowledge or consent of the athlete, the athlete or his or her school must take steps to stop the promotion. If the athlete or the school fails to take appropriate action to stop the promotion, the NCAA could bar the athlete from participating in intercollegiate sports.

in protecting their public personality. In 1970, for example, major league baseball players successfully brought a lawsuit against a manufacturer of baseball table games that had used the names of players without entering into royalty or license agreements. In its games, the manufacturer used the names and statistical information of more than 500 major leaguers, listing each player's uniform number, playing position and other identifying information. The lawsuit was filed in the name of Ted Uhlaender, then an outfielder with the Minnesota Twins.

In *Uhlaender v. Henricksen,* the court determined that an athlete had the right to prevent companies from using the athlete's name and accomplishments for commercial purposes. In contrast to the ruling in the *O'Brien* case, the court was not bothered by the fact that the players had placed themselves in the public gaze. On this point, the court stated, "to hold that such publicity destroys a right to sue for appropriation of a name or likeness would negate any and all causes of action, for only by disclosure and public acceptance does the name of a celebrity have any value...."[203] In any analysis of the privacy rights of athletes, there are two questions that must be answered. *First,* has the athlete placed himself or herself in the public gaze, as did Albert Belle? *Second,* has the athlete signed away his or her right to privacy, as Davey O'Brien apparently did? The context of the athlete's activity becomes critical. There is a vast difference between Oscar Robertson using a public restroom and Albert Belle playing catch on a baseball diamond before a paying audience. Similarly, there is a vast difference between an All-American candidate complaining about the distribution of publicity photos and college athletes seeking to keep their academic records private.

When pro basketball player Marcus Camby was a student at the University of Massachusetts, school officials distributed a copy of Camby's academic record to *The Boston Globe.* To Camby's dismay, the

---

[203] *Uhlaender v. Henricksen,* 316 F.Supp. 1277 (1970).

Globe published his grades in the newspaper. In distinct contrast to Davey O'Brien's case, Camby never authorized the university to release his academic record. Shortly afterwards, Camby notified the school that he intended to sue.[204]

When athletes do not invite the public gaze, it stands to reason that they should have a right to privacy. Marcus Camby should be able to keep his academic record private. Legal scholar William Prosser has identified four protections that are inherent in the right of privacy. According to Prosser, the right of privacy entitles an individual to protection from: (1) intrusion upon his solitude or into his private affairs; (2) public disclosure of embarrassing private facts; (3) publicity which places a person in a false light in the public eye; and (4) appropriation of the individual's name or picture for the advantage of another person.[205] Other legal experts are quick to point out, however, that there is an inherent conflict between an individual's interest in preventing intrusions into his or her private affairs and the public's "right to know." The *Boston Globe* determined that its subscribers would have an interest in reading about Marcus Camby's grades because he was a prominent athlete. The *Globe* apparently concluded that the intrusion was warranted. Camby disagreed. If he had taken counsel from Albert Belle, Camby might well have resorted to hurling basketballs at the *Globe*'s editors—and with some justification.

Former University of Maryland basketball guard Duane Simpkins surely can identify with Camby. During his career at Maryland, Simpkins ran up a series of campus parking fines. The National Collegiate Athletic Association suspended Simpkins for three games for having improperly borrowed money to pay the parking fines. Simpkins, his father and university officials all declined to reveal the amount of the parking fines. The public became aware of the amount of the fines—totaling more than

---

[204] *Five U-Mass. Players File Suit*, THE WASH. POST, December 15, 1995, B4.

[205] Dean William Prosser, *Privacy*, 48 Cal.L.Rev. 383, 289.

$8,000—only because Carrie Doyle, the director of eligibility appeals for the NCAA, released it to the press. Doyle said she revealed the figure because of "misinformation" in news accounts.[206]

Does Duane Simpkins have a right to keep his record of parking violations private? Under Prosser's definition of the right of privacy, he probably would. In the absence of other circumstances, the fact that Simpkins had accumulated $8,000 in fines would seem to be a private fact. Certainly, disclosure of the amount embarrassed Simpkins. The right of privacy protects athletes from emotional injury stemming from unwanted publicity. In 1992, former Denver Broncos wide receiver Vance Johnson sued Home Box Office for violation of his right of privacy. HBO had broadcast a show titled "Inside the NFL" that contained video scenes from the Broncos' locker room after a 1992 playoff victory. One of the scenes showed the wide receiver after he had removed all of his football gear and before he had dressed. The cameraman who had taken the pictures warned HBO that there were scenes of a naked player. HBO disregarded the warning and included the scenes in its show. Johnson sued for invasion of privacy. HBO and Johnson settled the lawsuit out of court. HBO was reported to have paid $50,000 to Johnson under the terms of the settlement.[207]

The right to privacy may also protect one's right to be "remembered" in a preferred way. Corey Hirsch, a goaltender for the Canadian Olympic hockey team in 1994, had the misfortune to give up the goal that won the gold medal for Sweden at the Lillehammer Olympic Games. In recognition of the dramatic goal, scored by Peter Forsberg, Sweden announced that it would issue a commemorative postage stamp showing Forsberg slipping the puck past Hirsch. Hirsch was not pleased. "It's not the way I

---

[206] Mark Asher and David Nakamura, *Simpkins's Tab $8,000, Says NCAA*, THE WASH. POST, February 21, 1996, F1.

[207] Martin J. Greenberg and James T. Gray, *Sports Law Practice*, 2nd ed. (Charlottesville, VA: Lexis Law Publishing, 1998), I, 686.

want to be remembered," he said. He turned to the law and threatened to file an image-appropriation lawsuit against the Swedish government.[208]

The late Arthur Ashe, a former U.S. Open tennis champion and captain of the U.S. Davis Cup team, was forced to grapple with a more tragic invasion of his right to privacy. Ashe contracted AIDS as a result of a blood transfusion. The disease ultimately led to his death. Ashe wished to keep the nature of his illness private. Many of his close colleagues in the professional tennis ranks and in the journalistic community were aware of his illness but, out of respect for Ashe's wishes, kept it secret. When *USA Today* learned of the illness, the newspaper engaged in a lengthy debate over whether it should announce Ashe's condition. A friend of Ashe's informed the former tennis player that the newspaper was considering publication. With that news, Ashe felt he had no option but to break his silence on his illness. At a hastily scheduled news conference, Ashe and his wife disclosed that he was suffering from AIDS. Ashe remarked that *USA Today* "had put me in the unenviable position of having to lie if I wanted to protect our privacy." "No one," he said, "should have to make that choice."[209]

The Arthur Ashe Principle of Protecting One's Privacy

No person should be placed in the position of having to lie to protect his or her privacy.

Measured against the gravity of Arthur Ashe's situation, the invasions of privacy suffered by Marcus Camby and Duane Simpkins—or even Vance Johnson—seem almost trivial. Nonetheless, the same principles apply. Every invasion of privacy, whether trivial or tragic, must be analyzed from

---

[208] *Stamp of Disapproval*, SPORTS ILLUSTRATED, April 17, 1995, 12.

[209] Arthur Ashe and Arnold Rampersad, *Days of Glory: A Memoir* (New York: Ballantine Books, 1993), 17.

the perspective of whether the athlete subjected himself to the public gaze and whether the athlete, because of his own conduct, has forfeited the right to privacy. As Arthur Ashe's situation highlights, however, the balance between the right of privacy and the constitutional guarantee of freedom of the press is often uneasy.

When university officials revealed Marcus Camby's grades, the unauthorized disclosure at least had the virtue of being true. In the case of Hall-of-Fame pitcher Warren Spahn, an author fabricated substantial segments of a book that he passed off as a biography of Spahn. The writer portrayed Spahn as the recipient of a Bronze Star for valor during his military service in World War II. In fact, Spahn, though injured during the war, was not awarded the Bronze Star. The biographer reported that Spahn "raced out into the teeth of the enemy barrage." By his own admission, Spahn did no such thing. The book reported that Spahn's father taught him to pitch and that his father provided advice to Spahn before he signed his first professional contract. Neither statement was true. Among other errors, the book inaccurately depicted Spahn's relationship with baseball figures Casey Stengel, Jackie Robinson and Lew Burdette.

Spahn sued both the publisher and author for humiliation and mental anguish. He did not want friends and acquaintances to think that he had embellished his war record.[210] Spahn also wanted to correct the notion that a close father-son relationship was a necessary ingredient for a successful

---

[210] From all indications, Spahn was deeply disturbed by the distortion of facts in the biography. Years after the lawsuit, when Spahn was well into retirement, sports law professor Ray Yasser encountered the noted pitcher at a baseball card show. Yasser, accompanied by his son, stood in line to obtain Spahn's autograph. While Spahn was signing for Yasser's son, Yasser said, "Mr. Spahn, if you have a minute, would you be interested in talking to me about your lawsuit?" Spahn immediately stopped the line, stood up and told the crowd, "I'm going to take a break." He put his arm around Yasser and explained, "I've been dying to talk about this case for years." The two then spent the next fifteen minutes talking about the lawsuit. Spahn made it clear that he was embarrassed by the overly laudatory statements in the book. He was especially bothered by the thought that friends and relatives who were familiar with the details of his Army career might think that he had made up fictitious stories about his "heroics" while serving in Europe.

career in baseball. As he did so often on the mound, Spahn prevailed in court. The judicial decision made it clear that if the biography had been accurate, there would have been no infringement of law. The court stated that if the affairs of an individual fall within the category of current news or information in which the community has a legitimate interest, the right of privacy must yield. Therefore, an individual's right to privacy does not apply to articles which, though not strictly news, are informative and educational and which make use of the names or pictures of living persons.[211] When the information being reported falls outside the bounds of legitimate news or information, however, the privilege of reporting on a public figure ceases.[212] The *Spahn* court found numerous "factual errors, distortions and fanciful passages" in the purported biography. The court concluded that both the writer and the publisher had shown a careless disregard for the responsibility of the press and ordered them to pay Spahn $10,000 in damages.

The Warren Spahn Principle of Biographical Distortion

The right of privacy protects athletes and other celebrities against "distortions and fanciful passages" in print, no matter how flattering the writing may be.

Warren Spahn's court case makes it clear that the privacy rights of a Marcus Camby, a Duane Simpkins or even an Arthur Ashe must be balanced against the public's legitimate interest in the dissemination of current events or informative and educational news. The public interest in the dissemination of newsworthy information does not extend, however, to situations where there has been a careless disregard for the truth. The annals of sport are filled with examples of careless disregard for the truth.

---

[211] Indeed, the abundant references in this book to the names of living persons are possible because the book is in the nature of an informative and educational publication.

[212] *Spahn v. Julian Messner, Inc.*, 250 N.Y.S.2d 529 (1964).

In the 1958 World Series, Warren Spahn's Milwaukee Braves faced the New York Yankees. The Yankee pitching staff included Art Ditmar, who pitched 3⅔ scoreless innings in the sixth game, helping the Yankees notch a 4-3 win over Spahn. Ditmar pitched again for the Yankees in the 1960 World Series, facing the Pittsburgh Pirates. This time, he did not fare well. Ditmar started the first and fifth games of the Series, both of which the Pirates won. In the two games, Ditmar yielded six hits and four runs in 1⅔ innings. In baseball, as in other areas of life, however, statistics can be misleading. "There was nothing wrong with starting Ditmar or with his pitching," Yankee manager Casey Stengel said after game five. "The Pirates didn't overpower or overwhelm him. They were bouncing balls through holes and over heads, and our fielders didn't field too good behind him, either." Yankee pitching coach Eddie Lopat took a similar view. "There is no substitute for experience and stuff," Lopat said, "and Ditmar had both. But he didn't have any luck...."[213]

Game 5 ended Art Ditmar's appearances in the 1960 World Series. It did not, however, end his bad luck. In the seventh game, future Hall-of-Famer Bill Mazeroski unloaded a ninth-inning, game-winning home run off Yankee pitcher Ralph Terry. On radio, play-by-play announcer Chuck Thompson told a different story. As Mazeroski's hit cleared the left field fence, Thompson reported the score as 10-0 instead of 10-9. He also told the listening audience that the homer had been hit off Art Ditmar, not Ralph Terry. Years later, Thompson explained, "I think I had just seen Ditmar warming up in the bullpen." For Thompson, "it was easily the most embarrassing moment of my career behind the microphone." After the Series, the Pirates offered Thompson an opportunity to correct his play-by-play for use in a souvenir record they were producing. He

---

[213] Louis Effrat, *Stengel Defends His Selection of Ditmar Over Stafford as Starting Pitcher: Ditmar, 15-Game Winner, Had No Luck and Little Help, Says Stengel*, THE N.Y. TIMES, October 11, 1960, 59.

declined. According to Thompson, "I figured it had gone on the air that way, so it wouldn't be honest to change it."[214]

Thompson's decision to live with his mistake meant that Art Ditmar would have to live with it as well. Thompson's error might have eased gracefully into the shadows of World Series history if Budweiser Beer had not selected Thompson's play-by-play as the backdrop for a television commercial during the 1985 World Series. The commercial showed young boys outside a barbershop listening to the radio as Thompson described Mazeroski's dramatic home run. The Budweiser commercial ran for the first two games of the 1985 Series. After publication of a newspaper article pointing out Thompson's erroneous reference to Ditmar, Budweiser took the commercial off the air for the third, fourth and fifth games. Inexplicably, however, Budweiser aired the commercial again during games six and seven.

Budweiser Beer had nothing to do with Chuck Thompson's error. However, it compounded the error by using the replay on nationwide TV. Budweiser's commercial came twenty-five years after the original broadcast and more than twenty years after Ditmar had retired from the game, when he was well out of the public gaze. Did the Budweiser commercial invade the former pitcher's privacy? Using William Prosser's legal standard, the commercial would seem to have placed Ditmar in a false light in the public eye. A good case could also be made that Budweiser appropriated Ditmar's name for its own commercial advantage. F"displayed a careless—indeed, an obvious—disregard for the truth.

---

[214] Chuck Thompson, *Ain't the Beer Cold!* (South Bend, IN: Diamond Communications, Inc., 1996), 101.

Ditmar ultimately sued Budweiser for damages in an Ohio court. The judge assigned to the case demonstrated little understanding of the significance that Mazeroski's home run holds in baseball lore. Ditmar lost his lawsuit. However, if the case had been brought in New York, where the Mazeroski home run remains a source of irritation to many, the outcome might have been different. Well after the lawsuit was over, Ditmar commented, "I still feel that no company has a right to misuse your name in a situation they knew was incorrect."[215] The results of the Ditmar lawsuit notwithstanding, when it comes to privacy issues, television and the print media are not permitted to take liberties with the truth. Assuming the press avoids a careless disregard for the truth, however, it is permitted to disseminate current events and informative news. Always, however, the public's right to know must be balanced against the risk of intruding upon a person's right to be left alone.

Closely aligned with the right of privacy is the right of publicity. The right of privacy protects individuals from emotional injury stemming from unwanted publicity; it protects feelings. The right of publicity preserves a person's interest in using his own name or picture for commercial gain. In the wake of baseball slugger Mark McGwire's record-breaking home run season in 1998, Christopher Morris of Hardy, Arkansas began producing and distributing fake $70 bills containing a picture of McGwire in the center of the bill. The bills bore the signature of "Mac A. Tack" and otherwise could clearly be identified as bogus. McGwire objected to the bills; Morris agreed to stop the unauthorized printing. Later, however, when Morris didn't stop selling the bogus bills, McGwire sued.[216] In suing Morris, McGwire was asserting his right of publicity. He was affirming the principle that an athlete's image cannot be exploited for commercial benefit without proper consent.

---

[215] Seth Swirsky, *Every Pitcher Tells A Story: Letters Gathered by a Devoted Baseball Fan* (New York: Times Books, 1999), 118.

[216] *Sued*, SPORTS ILLUSTRATED, January 15, 2001, 26.

If it is not permissible to reprint and sell pictures of Mark McGwire's face, it stands to reason that other identifiable parts of an athlete's body cannot be exploited for commercial gain either. In 1997, Frank Sheftel, owner of the Candy Factory of North Hollywood, California, attempted to capitalize on the notoriety generated when heavyweight boxer Mike Tyson took a bite out of Evander Holyfield's ear during their June 28, 1997 title bout. Sheftel created ear-shaped chocolates with fake teeth marks and sold them as "Earvander-Tyson Bites." Not surprisingly, customers ate them up. The Candy Factory sold 300 boxed pairs of "Earvander-Tyson Bites," earning $600 in profit.[217] Just as Christopher Morris did not obtain McGwire's approval for the "Mac A. Tack" bills, the Candy Factory failed to get Holyfield's permission for the "Earvander-Tyson Bites." Holyfield directed the Candy Factory to stop selling the fake ears and to turn over the proceeds of the sales. Sheftel claimed his product was legal and vowed to continue selling the candies.

Both the "Mac A. Tack" bills and the "Earvander-Tyson Bites" suggest classic cases of unlawful appropriation of image. Appropriation of name or image is a form of invasion of privacy. The law applies a two-part test for appropriation of image. First, there must be no doubt as to the identity of the person being depicted. Second, the person's name or likeness must be used without permission, for financial gain or some other benefit. When there has been appropriation of a person's name or image, the right of publicity entitles the person to obtain a court injunction prohibiting further use of his name or likeness. Courts have ruled that it is permissible to make "incidental" use of a person's name or image. Neither the "Mac A. Tack" bills nor the "Earvander-Tyson Bites" were incidental, however. If Christopher Morris had used a picture of McGwire's hands holding a baseball bat, and the hands were not identifiable as McGwire's, there would have been little risk of liability. In the same way, if the Candy Factory had simply sold chocolates in the shape of an ear, Evander Holyfield would have had no

---

[217] *A Chocolate Ear Flap*, THE WASH. POST, September 14, 1997, D2.

complaint. Even if the Candy Factory had added bite marks to the ear but did not link the chocolates to Holyfield's name, the fighter might not have had much of a case. But the combination of a chocolate ear, distinguishable bite marks, and the label "Earvander-Tyson Bites" left no doubt that the company was attempting to profit from Evander Holyfield's image.

The law recognizes that a person has an exclusive right to "trade" on his own name. Hockey player Tony Twist, a former winger with the St. Louis Blues, accused the creator of the "Spawn" comic book series of trading on Twist's name. The comic books used the name "Antonio Twistelli" for a mobster character. Twist sued. He alleged that the creator of "Spawn" had stolen his name without consent. A St. Louis Circuit Court jury agreed and awarded Twist $24.5 million in damages.[218] As the Tony Twist case suggests, the right of privacy and the right of publicity are held in great esteem in the American legal system. The degree of control that an athlete is entitled to exert over his likeness is illustrated by reference to sports trading cards. When an athlete or an organization negotiating on behalf of an athlete, such as the Major League Baseball Players Association, gives a producer of sports cards the right to reproduce the player's face and image, that right is usually not transferable to others. In 1973, for instance, authors Brendan Boyd and Fred Harris published *The Great American Baseball Card Flipping, Trading, and Bubble Gum Book*. The book was an offbeat look at major league baseball that highlighted some of the more entertaining aspects of the careers of different players. The authors displayed a special penchant for obscure facts, such as the revelation that the person pictured on the 1969 Topps baseball card of California Angels third baseman Aurelio Rodriguez was not Rodriguez at all, but rather a bat boy for the Pittsburgh Pirates. The authors explained, "This is in the nature of a little joke by Aurelio who could very easily be mistaken for a bat boy, except that most bat boys could easily outhit him."[219] When

---

[218] *Sports in Brief*, THE WASH POST, July 7, 2000, D2.

[219] Brendan C. Boyd and Fred C. Harris, *The Great American Baseball Card Flipping, Trading, and Bubble Gum Book* (Boston: Little, Brown and Company, 1973), 39.

Boyd and Harris published their work, they included reproductions of 243 baseball cards and one football card—that of Baltimore Colts quarterback Johnny Unitas—that had been distributed by Topps Chewing Gum.[220] Prior to publishing, Boyd and Harris obtained permission from Topps to reproduce the cards. However, from a legal perspective, Topps was only authorized to assign to others those rights for which it had bargained. In the current era, the baseball card contracts signed between card companies and professional athletes do not give card companies the right to authorize others to reproduce a player's image.

When Topps or another card company plans a set of baseball cards, it signs a contract with Major League Baseball that allows the company to reproduce team logos. Similarly, Topps also signs a contract with the Major League Baseball Players Association, on behalf of the individual players, that gives Topps the right to reproduce pictures taken of the players. However, the contracts do not give Topps permission to assign those rights to other parties. A card company can only grant to others the permission to reproduce items over which they hold the original creative rights. If other authors were to attempt, in the future, to recreate a book similar to *The Great American Baseball Card Flipping, Trading, and Bubble Gum Book*, they would have to obtain permission on three levels: *first*, from the athletes or the players' association representing the athletes, the right to reproduce the images and facial portraits of the players whose cards would be reproduced; *second*, from Major League Baseball, the right to reproduce the teams' insignias and logos appearing on the baseball caps and uniforms; and, *third*, from the card company, the right to reproduce the artistic work that goes into making a card, such as the borders, creative designs and background colors, as well as the card company's logo.

During the 1994 strike by baseball players, baseball fan and songwriter Seth Swirsky found that a vital part of his summer was missing. Baseball,

---

[220] According to the authors, the Unitas card was inserted because they "just wanted to see if you were still paying attention."

Swirsky says, "is the background music for my summer." He found a unique way to fill the void. He sent out letters to former major league players, in care of their old ballclubs, asking questions relating to their careers. For instance, Swirsky wrote to former Red Sox infielder Dave Stapleton, who had served as the team's defensive replacement for Bill Buckner throughout the 1986 season. Referring to Bill Buckner's critical error on Mookie Wilson's ground ball during the 10th inning of Game Six of the 1986 World Series, Swirsky asked Stapleton whether he was surprised that Red Sox manager John McNamara had not put him in for Buckner in the late innings of the game. Stapleton replied that he was surprised because he had already loosened up and was ready to play. Stapleton also remarked that, when the Red Sox released him after the 1986 season, it was because McNamara did not want him around as a reminder of his managerial miscue.[221] As the letters flooded in from ex-major leaguers, Swirsky pondered the idea of publishing the letters in book form. In deference to both the players' privacy and the law, Swirsky wrote back to all the players who had answered his inquiries, told them of his desire to publish the letters, and asked the players to sign release forms authorizing public dissemination.[222] As Swirsky recognized, under the right of publicity, the publication of personal correspondence from athletes without consent could have been construed as trading on the names and personalities of the players.

There are bounds on how far the right of publicity extends. After golfer Tiger Woods' stunning victory in the 1997 Masters Tournament in Augusta, Georgia, artist Rick Rush captured a scene from the tournament in a painting entitled "The Masters of Augusta." The painting depicted

---

[221] Seth Swirsky, *Baseball Letters: A Fan's Correspondence with His Heroes* (New York: Kodansha America, Inc., 1996), 19. Swirsky would later publish a second book of a similar nature, titled *Every Pitcher Tells A Story: Letters Gathered by a Devoted Baseball Fan.*

[222] Tim Wendel, *Pass Time With This Litany Of Baseball Love Letters*, USA TODAY BASEBALL WEEKLY, November 6-12, 1996, 26.

Woods in play during the tournament. To the displeasure of Woods and his marketing company, a publishing company sold reproductions of the painting. In an effort to protect his right of publicity, Woods sued the publisher. However, a federal judge upheld the publisher's right to distribute the prints. The judge ruled that the prints were "an artistic creation seeking to express a message." As an artistic creation, the judge held, the artist's work was entitled to constitutional protection under the First Amendment.[223]

The Corey Hirsch Principle of the Right of Publicity

I have the right to determine whether I want to be pictured as the losing goalie on a postage stamp.

The right of privacy protects an athlete from unwanted publicity. The right of publicity protects an athlete from unauthorized use of his or her name or likeness. There is no easy test for determining when the protections inherent in the right of privacy and the right of publicity come into play. Canadian goalie Corey Hirsch may have hit upon a useful starting point, however, when he stated, "It's not the way I want to be remembered."

Hirsch didn't want to be remembered as the hapless goaltender on Peter Forsberg's historic score. Warren Spahn didn't want to be remembered as a soldier who had puffed up his war record. Tony Twist didn't want to be remembered as the inspiration for a comic book gangster. The right of privacy and its counterpart, the right of publicity, afford an athlete control over the way his or her name and image are used. These rights offer athletes control over the way they are remembered.

---

[223] *Tossed Out*, Mark Mravic, ed., SPORTS ILLUSTRATED, April 24, 2000, 28.

Chapter 8

Misrepresentation: Tall Tales On and Off the Playing Field

Catcher Charles "Gabby" Street's major league career was lackluster at best. From 1904 to 1912, Street played for four teams, with his batting average never once topping .238.[224] For his career, Street hit .208. His most memorable moment in baseball came, not on a ball field, but at the Washington Monument. Street successfully caught a baseball dropped from the top of the Monument, gaining him instant fame.

Gabby's heroics prompted rivals to try to go him one better. Wilbert "Uncle Robbie" Robinson, seventeen years a major league catcher, was coaxed into trying to catch a baseball thrown from an airplane. Uncle Robbie's stunt took place in Florida while the Brooklyn Dodgers, whom Robinson managed, were in spring training. A Dodgers' clubhouse man went up in the airplane, equipped with two baseballs. The first time the plane flew over the ball park, the clubhouse man miscalculated the speed of the plane. He dropped the baseball a half mile outside the park. The

---

[224] Street retired from the game after the 1912 season when he was 30 years old. Nineteen years after his retirement, however, at the age of 48, Street appeared in one game for the 1931 St. Louis Cardinals. He handled two chances in the field for the Cardinals, without error, and went to bat once but failed to hit safely.

clubhouse man's timing was no better on the plane's second pass. Again, the ball fell outside the park. With his supply of baseballs exhausted, the clubhouse man was in a quandary. Reluctant to ask the pilot to land the plane to get more baseballs, the clubhouse man spied a sack of Florida grapefruit in the plane. He instructed the pilot to make another pass over the field. This time, throwing a grapefruit instead of a baseball, the clubhouse man's timing was impeccable. From ground level, Uncle Robbie lined up under the falling grapefruit, fully expecting a baseball. "I got it, I got it!" Robbie yelled. The grapefruit landed in Robbie's glove and, on impact, exploded. The force of the grapefruit knocked Robbie to the ground. Juice and pulp splashed all over his face.[225] In a panic, Robbie yelled, "I'm bleeding to death. Help me!" His plea for help produced massive laughter among the onlookers. The episode earned Robinson the enduring nickname, "Grapefruit."[226]

Uncle Robbie's Principle of Straight Shooting

If I am expecting a baseball, don't throw me a grapefruit.

A "misrepresentation" is an assertion that is not consistent with the facts. Misrepresentations typically bear the same relationship to truth as

---

[225] Robinson was lucky. At least he wasn't knocked out. Hall-of-Fame pitcher Nolan Ryan once knocked out a cameraman with a grapefruit. The incident occurred while Ryan was filming a television commercial for the Texas Department of Agriculture after he had retired from baseball. Ryan was supposed to throw a grapefruit toward a sheet of Plexiglas. The cameraman was stationed behind the Plexiglas. His job was to film Ryan's delivery and record the impact of the grapefruit. A bit more wild in retirement than during his playing days, Ryan missed the Plexiglas but hit the cameraman. Even in retirement, however, Ryan still possessed a blazing fastball—and proved it by knocking out the cameraman. Ray Sasser, DALLAS MORNING NEWS, April 1, 2001.

[226] Lawrence S. Ritter, *The Glory of Their Times: The Story of the Early Days of Baseball Told by the Men Who Played It* (New York: William Morrow and Company, Inc., 1992), 214-15.

Uncle Robbie's grapefruit bore to a baseball. Misrepresentations come in many forms. In the sports world, some misrepresentations are best described as ruses; others are little more than "white lies."

When his professional baseball career came to an end in the United States, former Los Angeles Dodger infielder Jim Lefebvre played five seasons in Japan's major leagues. A fiery competitor, Lefebvre became enraged one day when his manager on the Lotte Orions took him out of a particularly important game. At the time he was removed, Lefebvre was in the middle of infield warm-ups. He had to endure the indignity of coming off the field and yielding his position to another player. Lefebvre walked off the field and flung his glove at the dugout wall. The manager, thinking that the glove was aimed for him, challenged Lefebvre to a fight. Lefebvre was eager to oblige, but coaches quickly separated the two men and restored peace. The manager got the last word, however—or at least appeared to get it. He fined the "troublemaker" $10,000. With fines in Japan usually amounting to no more than $250, Lefebvre's fine was way out of line. He refused to pay the money. The manager was equally adamant. Having announced the fine, he would lose face if he backed down. The team's front office and coaches tried to find a way out of the impasse. They hit upon a novel idea—resorting to misrepresentation. The coaches proposed that the team secretly rescind the fine but announce publicly that Lefebvre had paid the $10,000. The plan appealed to everyone, except Lefebvre. He would not consent to the ruse. When it became clear that Lefebvre would not play along, the team quietly dropped the fine and reinstated him.[227]

For St. Louis Cardinals manager Tony La Russa, a ruse is a useful device for protecting his players from unwanted media attention. The day before the Cardinals were to play the Atlanta Braves in the opening game of the

---

[227] Robert Whiting, *You've Gotta Have "Wa"*, in The Armchair Book of Baseball II: An All-Star Lineup Celebrates America's National Pastime (New York: Charles Scribner's Sons, 1987), 413.

National League's 2000 first-round playoff series, La Russa sent veteran pitcher Darryl Kile to the interview room set up for reporters.[228] The other pitcher in attendance was four-time Cy Young award winner Greg Maddux, the obvious choice as the Braves' opening day pitcher. From all appearances, La Russa intended to tap Kile to face Maddux in the opening game. For a time at least, both the Braves and the media were primed to see Kile pitch in the first game. When the game started, however, 21-year-old rookie Rick Ankiel, not Kile, was on the mound for the Cardinals.

La Russa defended the ruse as necessary. "We wanted to avoid making it tough for [Ankiel]," he said. "This is a big enough challenge as it is." La Russa was quick to add that Kile hadn't been untruthful when talking to reporters; he never told the press he would be pitching the first game. "We didn't lie," La Russa said.[229]

> *The Tony La Russa Principle of Acceptable Ruses*
>
> *There is nothing wrong with ruses that don't involve telling a lie.*

Tony La Russa might be troubled by ruses that involve telling lies. Former New York Yankee center fielder Mickey Mantle was most certainly not—especially if the ruse was for the purpose of playing golf. One day during spring training in Florida, Mantle's golfing buddy, teammate

---

[228] Kile, widely regarded as one of the warmest and most generous players in the game, died an untimely death on June 22, 2002 as a result of coronary arteriosclerosis. He was 33 years old and at the height of his career. In a tribute at Busch Stadium, teammate and fellow pitcher Dave Veres saluted Kile as "an angel."

[229] *La Russa's Deception*, THE WASH. POST, October 4, 2000, D5. Even La Russa could not have anticipated how big a challenge the game would pose for the rookie pitcher. After pitching splendidly in the final two months of the season, Ankiel succumbed to playoff jitters against the Braves. The left-hander lasted only 2⅔ innings during which he gave up four walks and threw five wild pitches. "I was trying to do too much instead of relaxing,"Ankiel explained.

Whitey Ford, had been excused from workouts. It looked like a promising day for golf. Mantle phoned Yankee skipper Casey Stengel and told him he had a stomachache. "I don't feel well," Mickey told the manager. For sure, it was an assertion that was not consistent with the facts. Mantle felt fine, but not as well as he would feel on the golf course. "Can I have the day off?" Mantle asked the manager. Stengel told him to take the day off from practice to recuperate. Mickey went directly to the links to "recuperate" with his buddy, Ford.[230] The ruse worked perfectly until the twosome encountered Yankee general manager George Weiss on the eighteenth green. "How's your stomachache, Mickey?" Weiss asked. Mantle replied, "Eighteen holes are the best thing in the world for a stomachache."

No stranger to white lies, Mantle also made up stories to explain some of his more unusual off-the-field injuries. In 1957, Mantle suffered a serious leg injury during a golf outing with Yankee second baseman Billy Martin. The teammates had rented golf carts and were using the carts to race each other from hole to hole. The races evolved into a game of bumper cars. The Yankee stars began ramming each other's cart at full speed, each trying to tip his teammate's cart over. As they made their way to the seventh green, Martin faked a turn to the right and then abruptly zigzagged left. He hit Mantle's cart broadside, causing the cart to roll over. The cart fell on Mantle's leg, disabling the center fielder. The Yankees told reporters covering the team that Mantle had hurt himself stepping in a hole during fielding practice.[231] Though more than a white lie, the story of Mantle's leg injury was nothing that was "actionable" in a legal sense.

Whether on the golf course or in the clubhouse, Mantle displayed a sincerity that was convincing. Stengel seemed not to doubt his stomachache, just as reporters readily accepted Mantle's account of stepping into a hole in

---

[230] Peter Golenbock, *Dynasty: The New York Yankees, 1949-1964* (Englewood Cliffs, NJ: Prentice-Hall, Inc., 1975), 195.

[231] Golenbock, *Dynasty: The New York Yankees, 1949-1964*, 194.

the outfield. Others have not been so lucky. The producers of CBS Sports have been called to task for their practice of using audio recordings of bird sounds to create a more "natural" background for televised Professional Golf Association tournaments. The ploy came to light after CBS inserted the song of a canyon wren, a bird not found east of Texas, into its broadcast of the Buick Open golf tournament in Michigan during the summer of 2000. CBS followed up the Buick Open by dubbing the chirp of a white-throated sparrow into its August 2000 telecast of the PGA Championship from Kentucky. As bird watchers know—and CBS would learn—white-throated sparrows do not frequent the South during the summer. With tongue in cheek, the *Washington Post* noted that at the NEC Invitational, played during the last week of August, the white-throated sparrow "called again in a place it does not belong —Ohio."[232] The bird sounds were as authentic as Mickey Mantle's golf-induced stomachache, and produced the same result—a little embarrassment but no harm.

Just as a baseball player should avoid being seen on a golf course when he's supposed to be nursing a stomachache, tennis players should not be caught on a dance floor when they are supposed to be nursing leg injuries. When tennis player Andy Roddick withdrew from the 2001 French Open with a strained hamstring, observers had no reason to doubt the severity of his injury. On television sets around the world, Roddick was seen writhing in pain on the clay courts at Roland Garros stadium in Paris.[233] Hours after abruptly retiring from play during his third-round match against Lleyton Hewitt, however, there were reports that Roddick was seen dancing at a local bar in Paris. The news of Roddick cavorting on the dance floor led to speculation that his injury may have been more imagined than real.[234] As things turned out, the accounts of Roddick dancing were not

---

[232] D'Vera Cohn, *TV Golf, Botching the Birdies: Sharp-Eared Viewers Hear False Notes in 'Ambient Sound'*, THE WASH. POST, September 2, 2000, C1.

[233] The famed stadium and tennis complex is named after Frenchman Roland Garros, a heroic aviator who was killed in World War I.

[234] Rachel Alexander Nichols, *Roddick Recovers*, THE WASH. POST, June 7, 2001, D3.

true. He did go out to dinner after withdrawing from his match with Hewitt, but he denied doing any dancing. Tongue in cheek, Roddick invited those who had seen him dancing to critique his style on the dance floor. Unlike Mickey Mantle's stomachache, Roddick's injury was real. Shortly after his match, Roddick had undergone an ultrasound that confirmed he was suffering from a strained hamstring.[235] Unlike Mantle's encounter with George Weiss at the eighteenth green, there was no one who could confirm that Roddick was actually dancing. Nor was there any misrepresentation by Roddick.

Former New York Yankee play-by-play announcer Phil Rizzuto, one of Mickey Mantle's teammates in the early 1950s, would resort to misrepresentation to avoid discussion of the more earthy aspects of life. During one broadcast of a Yankee game from Chicago's Comiskey Park, Rizzuto took a break to go to the men's room. His broadcast partner, Fran Healy, informed listeners that Rizzuto had gone to the bathroom. Rizzuto found Healy's candor unsettling. He asked Healy simply to tell listeners that Rizzuto was visiting White Sox general manager Bill Veeck. In subsequent innings, Rizzuto made repeated trips to the men's room. Each time, Healy would dutifully announce that Rizzuto had gone to see Bill Veeck. Finally, when the pattern of misrepresentation became obvious, Rizzuto was forced to explain. "When you drink a lot of coffee on a cold night, you have to visit Bill Veeck often," he told his audience.[236]

Misrepresentations in sports are commonly passed off as "gamesmanship." If you're running a collegiate basketball team, you might list your 6' 10" center as 7' 0" in the team's program. Bob Kurland, a seven-foot basketball player during the 1940s, was once considered too tall by college

---

[235] Roddick also had an MRI performed the next day, but he refused to disclose the results. S.L. Price, *Andy Roddick's Breakthrough: New American in Paris*, SPORTS ILLUSTRATED, June 11, 2001, 93.

[236] Ron Luciano and David Fisher, *Remembrance of Swings Past* (New York: Bantam Books, 1988), 265.

coaches. "Coaches didn't want to take the time to develop boys like me," Kurland said. "The six-footers were faster and more poised." Oklahoma A&M coach Henry Iba was an exception. He gave Kurland a scholarship and set out to refine his game. Iba changed Kurland in other ways as well. On the university's game-day programs, he listed Kurland's height as seven feet. Years later, Kurland conceded that he was not that tall. "I'm 6' 10 ½" —about as close to seven feet as 98 cents is to a dollar," he said. "The school stretched me because they figured the idea of a seven-foot basketball player would capture the imagination of the fans."[237]

If it is acceptable to engage in a bit of hyperbole with a tall man, it should be equally permissible to exaggerate the height of a shorter player. Michigan State University listed its former star shooting guard, Shawn Respert, as 6' 3" on its programs. When Respert was preparing for the National Basketball Association draft, however, pro scouts measured him at just under six-feet, one-inch. The only person hurt by the misrepresentation was Respert. "If he's 6-feet-3, he's Joe Dumars," said former American University coach Ed Tapscott. The revelation of Respert's true height, however, gave many NBA teams second thoughts.[238]

In 1950, the New York Yankees had a similar problem. Their pitching staff was in need of help and the best available prospect in the farm system was Edward "Whitey" Ford. At 5'8" in height, however, Ford was just a "runt." Not many self-respecting major league pitchers stood less than 5'10". The Yankees cured the problem by raising Ford's height to 5'10" in the game programs.[239] And so the 5'8" Ford officially gained two inches. To this day, *The Baseball Encyclopedia* lists Ford's height as 5'10". Runt or not, Ford helped to lead the Yankees to the American League pennant in

---

[237] *The Tall Tale of Bob Kurland*, SPORTS ILLUSTRATED, November 6, 1995, 18.

[238] J.A. Adande, *Respert Shooting for the Big Time: Michigan State's Top Scorer Impresses Scouts with Range, But Height Is a Shortcoming*, THE WASH. POST, June 24, 1995, C3.

[239] Richard Ben Cramer, *Joe DiMaggio: The Hero's Life* (New York: Simon & Schuster, 2000), 292.

1950, winning nine games against only one loss after he was called up from the minor leagues in mid-season. It was the first of fourteen excellent seasons that Ford would enjoy in the major leagues.

There are several reasons why colleges find it advantageous to list a Bob Kurland as 7' 0" or a Shawn Respert as 6' 3". Height does capture the imagination of the fans. It also may help to intimidate opponents or confuse their pre-game strategy sessions. In Respert's case, it may have garnered a bit more attention from the NBA scouts. When a team stretches the truth in this way, the misrepresentation may have passed the point of being a white lie, but it falls short of being a material misrepresentation. When Kurland was playing for Oklahoma A&M, fans purchased tickets to see a seven-footer. They ended up watching a player who was only 6' 10". What the fans really paid to see, however, was a player who, by virtue of his height, could dominate the opposition. That's exactly what they received. Whether listed at 6' 10" or 7' 0", Kurland stood tall. The deception was not material. Indeed, a degree of "puffing" is to be expected when colleges promote their sports teams.

Similarly, when Michigan State fans bought tickets to see Respert play, it mattered little whether he stood 6' 1" or 6' 3". The fans paid to see a collegiate guard whose forte was sinking three-point shots. That's what they got. As a college senior, Respert was eighth in the country in scoring, averaging over 25 points per game. He took 251 shots from beyond the three-point arc and hit nearly 50 percent of them. In the professional ranks, an inch or two of height makes a more dramatic difference than at the collegiate level. For this reason, NBA teams interested in drafting Respert possibly might have been harmed by the deception. However, professional teams have a readily available protection—the pre-draft measuring stick. Misrepresentations become of legal significance when others rely on them to their detriment. The Portland Trailblazers drafted Respert in the first round of the 1995 NBA draft. The Trailblazers then traded him to the Milwaukee Bucks. Both the Trailblazers and the Bucks knew Respert's exact height—and a lot more about him in addition—well before the draft. If Respert had told the Bucks that he was six-foot-three and if height was a material factor in the decision to sign him to a contract, the team may have had cause to cancel his contract. Under the law, however, it would have been a difficult case to prove. Among other things, the law would require the Bucks to show that the team had relied on the misrepresentation when entering into the contract with Respert.

By the time professional teams are ready to announce their first round draft picks, they have compiled an extensive physical and personality profile of the prospects. The scope of the pre-draft research ensures that teams are intimately familiar with the physical strengths and shortcomings of a player. With an abundance of scouting reports in front of them, it would strain credibility for either the Trailblazers or the Bucks to allege that they had relied on the misrepresentation of Respert's height. In other situations, misrepresentations do influence hiring decisions and other legal commitments. It is one thing for a basketball player to exaggerate his height. It is quite another for a team to misrepresent the ages of its players—especially when those players are dealt to opposing teams. When the Baltimore Orioles traded shortstop Mike Bordick to the New York Mets just before the July 2000 trading deadline, they acquired Mets pitcher Leslie Brea in return. Baseball publications listed Brea as 21 years old. The Mets knew better. Brea was actually 26 years old. From the Orioles' perspective, Brea was a key part of the trade. As a 21-year-old, he would have had several years to develop his talent. As a 26-year-old, there was concern that time might be running out.[240]

The Baltimore Orioles' Principle of Detrimental Reliance

Misrepresentations become legally significant when others rely on them to their detriment.

---

[240] Jason La Canfora, *Spurgeon Up, Brea Down*, THE WASH. POST, Aug. 15, 2000, D4.

Brea was not the first ballplayer to have taken a few years off his age. The practice has a lengthy history. John Tortes "Chief" Meyers, a member of the Cahuilla tribe from the San Jacinto Mountains, was a catcher for the New York Giants, Brooklyn Dodgers and Boston Braves in a career that lasted from 1909 to 1917. Meyers played for John McGraw, caught for Christy Mathewson, and was a teammate of famed 1912 Olympian Jim Thorpe. Born in 1880, Meyers was twenty-eight years old when he made it to the big leagues and thirty when he first got the opportunity to play regularly for the Giants. Facing a career that was late in blooming, Meyers "cheated a little on my age, you know, so they always thought I was a few years younger." Meyers may have been able to fool the record books, but he couldn't fool Father Time. "When the years started to creep up on me," he once said, "I knew how old I was, even if nobody else did."[241]

When a ballplayer misrepresents his age, the purpose is not to fool Father Time, merely to fool the major league teams. While working as a scout for the Pittsburgh Pirates, Syd Thrift concealed the real age of pitching prospect Woody Fryman. Fryman was 26 years old at the time. Thrift and Fryman agreed to shave four years off Fryman's age. "We knew we wouldn't be able to sign him as a 26-year-old," Thrift recounted. "But he was good, so we all agreed to say he was 22." The ploy worked. Fryman did sign with the Pirates and spent 18 seasons in the big leagues, winning 141 games. Only after retiring did he reveal his true age.[242]

Former major league pitcher Rollie Sheldon was easier to figure out. When Sheldon made the jump from Class A baseball to the New York Yankees in 1961, the newspapers reported that there had been "mystery" about Sheldon's age. Most of the mystery was created entirely by Sheldon.

---

[241] Ritter, *The Glory of Their Times: The Story of the Early Days of Baseball Told by the Men Who Played It*, 179.

[242] Peter Slevin and Dave Sheinin, *An Age-Old Numbers Game: Amid Visa Crackdown, Many Dominican Players Aren't as Young as Thought*, THE WASH. POST, March 2, 2002, D1, D3.

He passed himself off as 21 years old. He may have been able to fool the Yankees, but he couldn't sneak the misrepresentation past the press. After some digging, the *New York Times* reported that Sheldon spent four years in the Air Force and, after his stint in the military, played varsity basketball for the University of Connecticut in 1960. Near the end of the Yankees' spring training camp in 1961, after Sheldon had already won the Dawson Memorial Award as the outstanding rookie in camp, he admitted he was actually 24 years old.[243]

In February 2001, Cuban refugee Andy Morales, a third baseman who clubbed a three-run homer in the Cuban national team's 12-6 exhibition victory over the Baltimore Orioles in 1999, agreed to terms with the New York Yankees. Morales' contract reportedly was for four years and $4.5 million. Immediately after the signing, however, questions were raised about Morales' actual age. At the time of his defection from Cuba, Morales reported his age as 25. He was listed as 26 years old in baseball's record books, though most baseball scouts believed he was closer to 29.[244] Morales started the 2001 season with the Yankees' Class AA farm team, the Norwich Navigators. At mid-season, he was hitting a mediocre .237 with one home run, a triple and three doubles. When Yankee executives confirmed that Morales was actually three years older than his reported age, they voided his contract and released him. Morales was certainly not alone in his deception. "From the beginning of time," a knowledgeable source says, "Latin American ballplayers have been shaving years from their ages."[245]

---

[243] *Sheldon, Pitcher, Wins Award As Bombers' Leading Rookie*, THE N.Y. TIMES, April 6, 1961, 41.

[244] Charles Nobles, *Yanks Agree to Terms With Defector*, THE N.Y. TIMES, February 14, 2001, D2.

[245] Steve Fainaru and Ray Sánchez, *The Duke of Havana: Baseball, Cuba and the Search for the American Dream* (New York: Villard Books, 2001), 209.

Fourteen-year-old pitcher Danny Almonte didn't do anything that Chief Meyers, Rollie Sheldon and Andy Morales hadn't done before him. With the help of his parents and his Little League coach, Almonte shaved two years off his age. Almonte, the undisputed star of the 2001 Rolando Paulino "Baby Bombers" Little League All-Star team from the Bronx, New York, paid for the deception in a way that Meyers, Sheldon and Morales never did. A native of the Dominican Republic, Almonte used a 70-mph fastball and an assortment of breaking balls to overwhelm opposing batters and lead his team to the U.S. Little League championship game. Along the way, Almonte pitched a no-hitter in the Eastern Regional final on August 14, 2001 and a perfect game in round-robin play on August 18, 2001. With each successive outing, Almonte's stellar efforts caused the parents and coaches of opposing teams to question his age. Under Little League regulations, players had to be twelve years old or younger to be eligible. Any player born before August 1, 1988 was not eligible to participate in Little League play in 2001. Opponents were convinced Almonte was overage; some went to extraordinary lengths to prove it. A group of adults in Staten Island even hired a private investigator, at a cost of $10,000, to research the ages of Almonte and other players on his team.

Throughout the controversy, officials of the Rolando Paulino Little League maintained that Almonte was twelve years of age. On more than one occasion, Rolando Paulino, the league's founder and a popular sportswriter for a Spanish-language newspaper in New York, produced a birth certificate for Almonte that appeared to be legitimate. The birth certificate showed Danny Almonte's birth date as April 7, 1989, placing his age at twelve. When the questions persisted, *Sports Illustrated* magazine sent a reporter to review the official birth records in Moca in the Dominican Republic, Almonte's birthplace. The official records showed that a Danny de Jesús Almonte had been born on April 7, 1987, making the pitcher two years too old for Little League play.[246] When the deception was con-

---

[246] Ian Thomsen and Luis Fernando Llosa, *One for the Ages*, SPORTS ILLUSTRATED, September 3, 2001, 63.

firmed, Little League officials acted quickly to strike Almonte's name from the record books, wiping out his no-hitter and perfect game. The officials also ruled that the Baby Bombers would have to forfeit all of their victories in their march to the U.S. championship game.[247] Authorities in the Dominican Republic brought criminal charges against Almonte's father, Felipe de Jesús Almonte, for falsifying his son's birth certificate and announced that he would be arrested as soon as he returned to his native country. The senior Almonte, who was living with his son in New York City when the charges were announced, faced a jail term of three to five years if convicted.[248]

The consequences of Danny Almonte's case extended far beyond Little League. Within months, the U.S. consulate in Santo Domingo began clamping down on professional ballplayers applying for visas to travel to the United States. Before the Almonte controversy, ballplayers from the Dominican could routinely obtain a visa without undergoing a personal interview or submitting a birth certificate. Under newly implemented procedures, however, when a professional athlete from the Dominican requested a visa to play ball in the United States, the U.S. consulate required the athlete to appear in person for an interview. The athlete also had to submit his birth certificate. If there was reason to suspect that a player's birth certificate had been altered, the consulate required the player either to obtain a certification from the Dominican Electoral Committee or present a new passport reflecting his proper birth date. If, in the process, a player was found to have lied about his age, U.S. officials required the player to notify his team in the United States and obtain written assurance that the team still desired to employ him.[249]

---

[247] Sally Jenkins, *Let the Little Kids Play—Without The League*, THE WASH. POST, September 1, 2001, D1, D5.

[248] *Almonte's Father Could Face Charges*, THE WASH. POST, September 5, 2001, D2.

[249] Slevin and Sheinin, *An Age-Old Numbers Game: Amid Visa Crackdown, Many Dominican Players Aren't as Young as Thought*, D3.

One player from the Dominican Republic, Los Angeles Dodgers pitcher Odalis Perez, was found to be younger—by five days—than his original birth certificate indicated. Perez was the exception. Several players emerged from the process older, if not wiser. Shortstop Ed Rogers, the fifth-ranked prospect in the Baltimore Orioles' farm system, was found to be 23 years old, not 20 as previously reported. The addition of three years to Rogers' age threatened to stymie his progress in the Orioles' chain. When promoted from the Orioles' Class A team to Class AA during the 2001 season, he had struggled offensively. When Rogers was thought to be 20 years old, the Orioles could afford to be patient with his development. A weak-hitting 23-year-old, however, was not nearly as attractive to the organization. Suddenly, it appeared that time was running out for Rogers. His stature as a major league prospect was expected to drop precipitously.[250] Other players who were found to have lied about their ages included Rogers' brother, Omar, also an Orioles' farmhand, starting pitcher Bartolo Colon of the Cleveland Indians and shortstop Rafael Furcal of the Atlanta Braves. Both Colon and Furcal were two years older than their listed ages. Second baseman Marcus Agramonte of the Texas Rangers went from being a 19-year-old to a 25-year-old. The deception cost Agramonte his job. After learning his true age, the Rangers released him.

There is no doubt that, when ballplayers misrepresent their ages or when teams do it for them, there is the potential for harm to others. When the New York Mets traded Leslie Brea to the Orioles as a "21-year-old," the Orioles were cheated out of five formative years in the pitcher's development. When Danny Almonte competed against overmatched twelve-year-olds, teams that complied with the rules suffered. When 22-year-old Benjamin "Benjie" Davis of Pinehaven, New Mexico, fought a 16-year-old, Louis Wade, in the novice class of a Golden Gloves boxing tournament in Albuquerque, New Mexico in February 1982, Davis was two

---

[250] Dave Sheinin, *Rogers Is Caught in Age Game*, THE WASH. POST, March 2, 2002, D3.

years over the age limit for the novice class. With a six-year difference in age, Davis would seem to have enjoyed a distinct advantage over his opponent. Instead, it was Wade who held the upper hand. By the second round of their bout, Davis was offering little resistance to Wade's persistent jabs. In the middle of the round, Wade noticed that Davis' eyes had turned "glassy." The tournament quickly took a tragic turn. Before the round was over, Davis had crumpled to the canvas. In a remote corner of the ring, Wade fell to his knees in prayer for his stricken opponent. Twenty-four hours after the fight, Davis was dead, a victim of his own misrepresentation and the seemingly cavalier attitude of tournament officials toward enforcing the rules.[251]

When athletes lie about their ages, it is clearly a misrepresentation. Some misrepresentations are innocuous. The more serious ones, however, may constitute material misrepresentations. Similarly, when a coach incorrectly states that he played in 147 games for a national team, it is more than a white lie, more than mere puffing. In 1996, after Jon Clark took over as the acting coach of the U.S. Olympic men's field hockey team, *The Daily Telegraph* of London reported that Clark had misrepresented his background on the resume he submitted to the U.S. Field Hockey Association (USFHA). During his playing days, Clark had been an excellent goalkeeper in England's top professional league. Not convinced that his credentials were sufficient, however, Clark stated on his resume that he was also a member of Britain's bronze-medal-winning team at the 1984 Olympics. In fact, he was never on the Olympic team. Even more, while he claimed to have played 147 games for the English and British national teams, he only played 15 games for those teams. "It was deemed necessary to talk up my playing record to impress the [U.S.] players," Clark explained.[252]

---

[251] Frank Deford, *The World's Tallest Midget: The Best of Frank Deford* (Boston: Little, Brown and Company, 1987), 91, 100.

[252] Jack McCallum and Kostya Kennedy, *Pre-Games Stretch*, SPORTS ILLUSTRATED, April 15, 1996, 20.

It is not uncommon for people to inflate their resumes to enhance job prospects. In resumes, as with the game-day programs for sporting events, a certain degree of puffing can be expected. To Jon Clark, the exaggerated resume was simply a matter of "talking up his playing record." To the U.S. Olympic Committee, it may have been more significant. If the Olympic Committee were so inclined, it could have sought to cancel the contract with Clark. To void the contract, the Olympic Committee would only have had to show that: (1) Clark had falsely stated his credentials; (2) the misrepresentations were material; and (3) the Olympic Committee had relied on the misrepresentations when making the decision to hire Clark.

The Jon Clark Principle of Voiding Contracts

When a person is induced to enter into a contract because of misrepresentation by the other party, the contract can be voided if the misrepresentation is material.

On December 8, 2001, Notre Dame University introduced Georgia Tech football coach George O'Leary as its new head coach. Five days later, O'Leary was gone, a victim of his own misrepresentations. O'Leary's resume represented that he had received a master's degree from New York University. It also stated that he had played varsity football for three years at the University of New Hampshire. Neither statement was true. O'Leary had taken courses at New York University but never earned a degree from the school. He had graduated from the University of New Hampshire but, due to a bout with mononucleosis and a knee injury, he never played football at the school. Both misrepresentations were long-standing. O'Leary had claimed to be a former member of the New Hampshire football varsity when he applied for an assistant coaching position at Syracuse University in 1980. And, in 1987, prior to O'Leary's first season as an assistant at Georgia Tech, the Georgia Tech media guide reported that O'Leary had earned a master's degree in 1972. As misrepresentations go, the inaccuracies reflected on O'Leary's resume were not of earthshaking proportions. Whereas Jon Clark's misrepresentations undoubtedly influenced the U.S. Olympic Committee's decision to hire him as coach of the field hockey team, Notre Dame hired O'Leary because of his coaching record at Georgia Tech. O'Leary's misstatements were largely irrelevant to the hiring decision. In football circles, earning a varsity letter from the University of New Hampshire is not the kind of credential that will open a lot of doors under any circumstance. Even a master's degree, by itself, is hardly a surefire entree to a prestigious college football coaching position. Nonetheless, when the lies were uncovered, the outcome was inevitable. Even though Notre Dame had not relied heavily on the misrepresentations, O'Leary had to go. For Notre Dame, the lies constituted "a breach of trust that makes it impossible for us to go forward with our relationship."[253]

Former Chicago White Sox pitcher Bob Locker would have had little difficulty proving that he relied on the White Sox' misrepresentations during his 1968 salary negotiations. For much of his 10-year career, Locker was one of the most successful relief pitchers in the American League. He also had one remarkable season, 1967, in which he saved 20 games, won 7 more, limited opposing teams to 2.09 earned runs per nine innings, and struck out nearly four times as many batters as he walked. After that season, Locker asked the White Sox for a raise to $18,000. The White Sox countered with an offer of $16,000. The Sox prevailed in the negotiations but only by resorting to tactics that were clearly underhanded. Locker's exceptional season came one year after fellow pitcher Phil Regan had enjoyed a truly stellar year for the Los Angeles Dodgers. Regan had won 14 games in relief for the Dodgers in 1966 and lost only one. He led the National League with 21 saves and recorded a miserly 1.62 earned run average. Regan's performance that year set the contemporary standard for relief pitchers.

---

[253] Josh Barr and Robert E. Pierre, *O'Leary Resigns as Coach at Notre Dame: Falsified Credentials Lead to Downfall*, THE WASH. POST, December 15, 2001, D1.

When Bob Locker asked for $18,000, White Sox general manager Ed Short countered by pointing to Regan's contract. Short argued that Locker's price was out of line because Regan had just signed with the Dodgers for $23,000. Short's ploy was persuasive. Locker, perhaps a bit too honest and certainly too gullible, said to Short, "If Regan is making only $23,000 then I'm asking too much. You check that. If he signed for $23,000, I'll sign for $16,000." The next day Short called Locker and said, "I called Buzzie Bavasi (the Dodgers GM) and he told me Regan was making $23,000 this year." "All right," Locker said, "I'll take the $16,000." After Locker signed his contract, he wrote Regan a letter "just for the hell of it." Locker asked Regan if he would mind telling him how much he was making. Regan wrote back saying that he had signed for $36,500. "You know, you don't mind a guy deceiving you a little during contract negotiations," Locker concluded. "You get used to it. They all do it. But when a guy just outright lies right to your face, that's too much."[254]

Bob Locker's Principle of Acceptable Deception in Contract Negotiations

It's okay when people engage in a little deception during contract negotiations, but when they tell outright lies, they have crossed the line.

Legal analysts would view the negotiations between Ed Short and Bob Locker as a classic case of deception and reliance. They would pose two questions: *first*, did Locker have a right to rely on the White Sox' representations regarding Phil Regan's salary?; and, *second*, did Locker actually rely, to his detriment, on Short's word? Locker was entitled to rely on Short's word. Equally important, he did rely on the misrepresentation.

---

[254] Jim Bouton, *Ball Four: My Life and Hard Times Throwing the Knuckleball in the Big Leagues* (Cleveland, Ohio: The World Publishing Company, 1970), 212.

The damages were evident. Locker's misplaced reliance on Short's honesty had cost him $2,000.[255]

The Busch Gardens theme park in Williamsburg, Virginia once fell victim to a costly deception by one of its security supervisors. The year was 1995. The employee, a 40-year-old with dreams of glory, was named Greg Light. He portrayed himself as an Olympic-caliber athlete. His specialty was purportedly the shot put. He told Busch Gardens that he had qualified for the 1996 U.S. Olympic track and field trials in the shot put with a throw of 65-feet, 10-inches. According to Light, his best effort measured 69 feet, a distance that would have been good for the silver medal in the 1992 Olympics. As an added touch, Light said that he had played two years with the New England Patriots in the National Football League. Busch Gardens found Light's story to be credible and trumpeted his Olympic aspirations. The theme park issued a press release highlighting Light's story and gave him travel funds. The press release exclaimed, "This is far more than a pursuit, it is fast becoming a reality." Busch Gardens also released color photographs of Light posing with Izzy, the official mascot of the 1996 Olympics.

---

[255] The introduction of salary arbitration in major league baseball has allowed an unprecedented glimpse into negotiations between baseball players and their teams. If salary arbitration had been in use when Locker was negotiating with the White Sox, he would have had a much better feel for his market value. In most arbitration cases, the players believe their talents are worth more to the team than does the team. Typically, a ballplayer's asking price is higher than the amount the team thinks it should have to pay. However, there have been some curious exceptions. In 1982, pitcher Mike Flanagan, then with the Baltimore Orioles, filed for $485,000 in arbitration hearings. Lacking a firm idea as to how much Flanagan would be seeking, the Orioles offered $500,000. It was only the second time in the arbitration process that a player had asked for less than his club offered. In that situation, of course, resolving the arbitration was easy. Flanagan "settled" for $500,000. Ron Luciano and David Fisher, *Remembrance of Swings Past* (New York: Bantam Books, 1988), 230.

Light's representations did not ring true to the Richmond, Virginia *Times-Dispatch*. The newspaper learned, for example, that a shot put of more than 65 feet would have placed Light among the top 10 shot putters in the United States. The *Times-Dispatch's* suspicions were confirmed when a spokesman for USA Track and Field said that Light was not on a list of shot putters credited with throws of more than 57 feet in competition. When the newspaper attempted to confirm Light's NFL experience, the Patriots reported that they had no record of him. Four days after the *Times-Dispatch* reported the inaccuracies, Light left his job at Busch Gardens.[256]

Greg Light passed himself off as an Olympic shot putter, gaining photographs with Izzy, travel funds and public acclaim in the process. Leroy Fulton, a 74-year-old homeless man, engaged in misrepresentation for more compelling reasons. Fulton suffers from emphysema. In constant need of medical treatment, Fulton relied on one of the few assets he had gained over the years—a thorough knowledge of the baseball career of former Detroit Tiger ace and New York Yankee nemesis, Frank Lary. Until police caught up with him in May 2000, Fulton crisscrossed the country for the better part of ten years, pretending to be the noted "Yankee Killer." Lary had last pitched in the major leagues in 1965.[257] Fulton traded on Lary's identity to gain admission to hospitals. Fulton also freely penned "Frank Lary" autographs for unsuspecting hospital staff members. After he

---

[256] *Olympian Effort for Naught*, RICHMOND TIMES-DISPATCH, November 23, 1995, D1, D3.

[257] In his heyday with the Tigers, from 1955 to 1961, Frank Lary won 117 games and lost 93. He enjoyed a hugely successful season in 1961, when he won 23 games and lost only 9. Thereafter, his star dimmed. He pitched two more full seasons for the Tigers, 1962-1963, but won only six games in that span against 15 losses. Lary retired in 1965 after brief stints with the New York Mets, Milwaukee Braves and Chicago White Sox. For his career, he won 128 games and lost 116.

was caught, Fulton pleaded guilty to fraud and received a jail sentence equivalent to the time he had already spent in jail after his arrest.[258]

Fulton, homeless and suffering from emphysema, engaged in misrepresentation out of need. There was a certain charm in Fulton's impersonation of Frank Lary. At age 74, Fulton undoubtedly retained some boyish enthusiasm for the sport of baseball—or at least a reverence for the exploits of a former star. Scott Simon, the host of National Public Radio's *Weekend Edition*, introduced his book *Home and Away*, with the words, "There was a time when I was Billy Pierce, the high-kicking left-handed pitcher of the Chicago White Sox (211 career wins, 169 losses). But being only about two and a half feet tall, my impact on the game was small."[259] When Simon's mother would address him as "Scotty," Simon would respond, "What did you say my name was?" As Simon recounts it, his mother would be profusely apologetic. "Ohmigosh, *Billy*," his mother would say, "*Billy*, I almost forgot." Later, well-established in his career with National Public Radio, Simon encountered Billy Pierce when the two served as pallbearers at the funeral of Jack Brickhouse, the former play-by-play announcer for both the Cubs and the White Sox. Simon told Pierce how, as a boy, he would imitate Pierce. "I used to think I was you, Billy Pierce," Simon explained. At the end of the funeral, Pierce said to Simon, "Tell you what, pal. For the next twenty years or so, I'll pretend to be you."[260]

If Simon's impersonation of Billy Pierce was innocuous, Leroy Fulton's impersonation of Frank Lary was only slightly more troubling. If accumulating riches was Fulton's objective, he could have chosen a more prominent athlete to impersonate. And if there was fraud in Fulton's act of passing off his signature as that of Frank Lary, his fake autographs at least

---

[258] *Frankly, This Imposter Wasn't Very Truthful*, USA TODAY BASEBALL WEEKLY, Sept. 20-26, 2000, 3.

[259] Scott Simon, *Home and Away: Memoir of a Fan* (New York: Hyperion, 2000), 1.

[260] Simon, *Home and Away: Memoir of a Fan*, 357.

brought some pleasure to inveterate baseball fans. Other impersonators are not so endearing. For the better part of two years, a man named Anthony Lemar Taylor used the identity of golf superstar Tiger Woods to steal $17,000 worth of goods. Taylor obtained a driver's license using Tiger's given name, Eldrick T. Woods. Though he bears little resemblance to the golfer, Taylor was also able to obtain credit cards in Woods' name. Taylor then used the credit cards to purchase a 70-inch television, stereos and a used luxury car. When authorities caught up with Taylor, they learned he had been convicted of twenty crimes over a seventeen-year period. In April 2001, a Sacramento, California judge sentenced Taylor to a prison term of 200 years to life.[261]

A man named Canh Oxelson took a different approach to impersonating Tiger Woods. Like Anthony Lemar Taylor, Oxelson impersonated Woods for financial gain. Unlike Taylor, Oxelson never attempted to do it fraudulently. Oxelson bears a striking resemblance to Woods, both facially and in terms of build, particularly when dressed in golfing togs. Oxelson has made as much as $3,000 a day impersonating Tiger Woods at weddings, golf outings and corporate functions. When Oxelson impersonates his famous look-alike, he does so without misrepresenting his own identity. Those who pay for Oxelson to attend social functions know they are getting a person who looks like Woods but is not nearly as accomplished on the golf course. Oxelson has even been paid to stand in for the real Tiger Woods during commercial shoots for American Express. "Up close you can tell us apart," says Oxelson, "but people want to believe they're meeting a celebrity."[262] In June 2001, Oxelson received his master's degree in education from Harvard University. While Anthony Lemar Taylor used Woods' name to purchase luxury items, Canh Oxelson used the money he earned from impersonating Woods to help pay for graduate school. Taylor broke the law; Oxelson did not.

---

[261] *Woods Imposter Gets 200 to Life*, THE WASH. POST, April 29, 2001, D2.

[262] *Picture This*, SPORTS ILLUSTRATED, May 28, 2001, 28.

When material misrepresentations occur, the truth often emerges eventually. On occasion, the truth explodes—as severely as did the grapefruit when it hit Uncle Robbie's glove. The truth exploded on University of Texas football player Ron Weaver at a most inopportune time. Using the alias Joel Ron McKelvey, Weaver was set to play for the University of Texas in the Sugar Bowl on Sunday, December 31, 1995. Listed in the Sugar Bowl program as a 23-year-old, Weaver played defensive cornerback for the Longhorns. The day before the Sugar Bowl game, *The Californian* newspaper, based in Salinas, California, reported that Weaver was playing for Texas under a false identity. After the story broke, and just hours before his big game, Weaver left New Orleans, the site of the Sugar Bowl, without telling his team. Within days, the Austin (Texas) *American-Statesman* reported that Weaver was actually 30 years old and had previously used up all four years of his college eligibility. Unbeknownst to the University of Texas, Weaver had once played college football at Cal State-Sacramento. His college eligibility expired in 1989.

After his eligibility expired, Weaver enrolled at Los Angeles' Pierce Community College. To conceal his prior college experience, Weaver took both the name and the social security number of an acquaintance, Joel McKelvey. He played two years at the community college under the name "McKelvey." His hard-nosed play at Los Angeles Pierce Community College drew raves from college recruiters, and the University of Texas, among other schools, awarded Weaver a full athletic scholarship. Still using the name McKelvey, Weaver enrolled at Texas in August 1995.[263] After the 1995 Sugar Bowl, federal prosecutors launched an inquiry.[264] Weaver was under investigation for possible wire fraud, mail fraud and violation of the social security laws. In the end, he pleaded guilty to a federal charge of misusing social security numbers. The judge ordered Weaver

[263] *Texas Considers Suing Imposter*, THE WASH. POST, January 3, 1996, F4.

[264] In the Sugar Bowl, Texas fell victim to a stellar Virginia Tech team. Virginia Tech won handily, 28-10.

to repay the University of Texas for his scholarship, which amounted to $5,000.[265]

The Ron Weaver Principle of the Emergence of the Truth

Sometimes the truth emerges at the most inopportune moments.

When it comes to material misrepresentations, there is no such thing as a "white lie." When others rely on those misrepresentations, there are often financial consequences and legal exposure. If Bob Kurland was as close to 7-feet tall as 98 cents is to a dollar, Greg Light was a full dollar shy of being an Olympic-class athlete. Similarly, Jon Clark was not the person that the U.S. Olympic Committee bargained for when it hired him to coach the men's field hockey team. The Chicago White Sox' misrepresentations cost Bob Locker $2,000 and possibly even more money in salary during subsequent years. Ron Weaver's misrepresentation cost the University of Texas $5,000 and caused the federal government to expend substantial time and effort on his prosecution. In each case, there was a loss of money, credibility and trust.

---

[265] *Imposter Pleads Guilty*, THE WASH. POST, March 16, 1996, B7.

Chapter 9

Sports Agents

Catcher Charles Johnson was caught by surprise when the Baltimore Orioles traded him to the Chicago White Sox midway through the 2000 baseball season. The trade did not shock Johnson so much as the way the Orioles explained it. The word from the Orioles' front office was that the team did not expect to have an easy time re-signing Johnson when his contract expired because they found his agent, Scott Boras, to be a difficult individual with whom to nail down a deal. The relationship between Boras and Orioles owner Peter Angelos, was, at best, "uneasy." Johnson was disappointed. "But he works for me," Johnson protested.[266] For Johnson, the relationship was simple: he called the shots, not Boras. Boras was the agent, not the boss.

In the current era, dealing with agents is a way of life for teams in all professional sports. And as Charles Johnson made clear, agents work for the players. It is the players who call the shots in negotiating their contracts—or at least should be calling the shots. The role of agents in sports is a relatively recent development. As late as the 1960s, player agents were virtually nonexistent. Athletes had to negotiate their contracts by themselves because agents were not welcome in the front offices of professional sports teams.

---

[266] Dave Shenin, *O's Send Three On Their Way*, THE WASH. POST, July 30, 2000, D1.

In February 1957, the New York Yankees acquired pitcher Art Ditmar in a twelve-player trade with the Kansas City Athletics.[267] Ditmar was fresh off a modest 12-22 campaign for the last-place Athletics. He had joined the team as a twenty-five-year-old rookie in 1954 and had amassed 25 wins in the majors before his twenty-eighth birthday. With several outstanding games to his credit, including a two-hitter against the Chicago White Sox in 1955 and a one-hitter, also against the White Sox, in 1956, Ditmar's stock was on the rise.[268] He looked to have a promising career ahead. In the days before being traded to the Yankees, Ditmar had held contract talks with the Athletics for the 1957 season. He had tentatively agreed with the Athletics on a salary of $14,500 for the upcoming season but had yet to sign a contract. The $14,500 salary was good pay for Kansas City but less appealing in the more costly environs of New York City.

Ditmar greeted the trade to New York with mixed emotions. He was content playing in Kansas City.[269] Not having signed his 1957 contract

---

[267] In addition to Ditmar, New York also acquired pitcher Bobby Shantz and infield prospect Cletis Boyer, as well as three players, Wayne (Footsie) Belardi, Curt Roberts and Jack McMahan, who would never suit up for the Yankees. In return, the Yankees sent pitchers Tom Morgan, Rip Coleman and Mickey McDermott, outfielder Irv Noren, and infielders Billy Hunter and Milt Graff to the Athletics.

[268] Joe McGuff, *Athletics in 13-Run Inning, Ditmar Spins 1-Hitter*, THE KANSAS CITY STAR, April 22, 1956, C1.

[269] The Athletics had known little success since moving to Kansas City before the 1955 season. With Lou Boudreau as manager, the team finished sixth among the eight American League teams in 1955 and were dead last in 1956, with a woeful 52-102 record. Nonetheless, members of the team seemed to enjoy playing in Kansas City, and Ditmar's ambivalence about being traded to the Yankees was not unique. A's outfielder Roger Maris had a similar reaction when he joined the Yankees in 1960 after two productive seasons in Kansas City. "I'm not all that happy about coming to New York," Maris told New York writers after being traded. "I liked Kansas City," he said. "I expected to play out my career there." David Halberstam, *October 1964* (New York: Villard Books, 1994), 158-59.

with the Athletics, Ditmar assumed he was not bound to play for $14,500 in New York. Yankee general manager George Weiss assumed otherwise. Weiss was well aware that Ditmar had agreed to play for the Athletics for $14,500. Weiss informed Ditmar that he would have to play for the same salary in New York. Ditmar thought that the Yankees, as perennial American League champs, could do better. Weiss refused to budge. Ditmar called home to consult with his father. The senior Ditmar advised, "Don't rock the boat." It was sound fatherly advice. Relatively inexperienced in contract negotiations, and without the benefit of either a lawyer or an agent, Ditmar stood little chance of getting the best of George Weiss. The pitcher ended up signing his contract for $14,500.[270]

The Art Ditmar Principle of Contract Negotiations

If I agree to play for $14,500 in Kansas City, that doesn't mean that I agree to play for the same salary in New York.

Contract negotiations have changed dramatically since Art Ditmar's experiences in the 1950s. At the end of the 2000 baseball season, outfielder Manny Ramirez, a four-time all-star, opted for free agency. Ramirez was represented by prominent sports lawyer and agent Jeffrey Moorad.

[270] Ditmar enjoyed several excellent seasons with the Yankees, including a 13-9 season in 1959 and a 15-9 campaign the following year. He got off to a slow start with the Yankees in 1961 and was traded back to the Athletics in mid-season. He finished the 1961 season with Kansas City and saw limited action with the Athletics the next year before retiring from baseball. A man of many talents, Ditmar designed the uniforms that the Athletics wore during the 1962 season. At the time, in Ditmar's view, most of the American League teams attempted to pattern their uniforms after the staid pinstripes worn by the Yankees. Ditmar advised Athletics owner Charles O. Finley to break the trend and adopt a pattern that Kansas City could claim as its own. Ultimately, Finley took Ditmar's advice to the extreme and outfitted his team in a distinctive gold and green combination.

The Boston Red Sox proved to be Ramirez's most ardent suitor. At a pivotal point in the negotiations with the Red Sox, Boston general manager Dan Duquette flew to California to meet with Moorad and his staff. The discussions began when Brian Murphy, a member of Moorad's team of lawyers and an avid Red Sox fan, brought in a framed picture of Boston's Fenway Park. Murphy wanted Ramirez's hefty bat in the Red Sox lineup. He told Duquette, "I'll do whatever I can to get this done." Shortly thereafter, the deal did "get done." Ramirez and his agent agreed to a $160 million, eight-year contract to play for Duquette and the Red Sox.

Separated in time by more than forty years, the experiences of Art Ditmar and Manny Ramirez vividly illustrate the evolution of contract negotiations in professional sports. Ditmar had to conduct his negotiations entirely by himself and in the somber confines of the Yankee offices, with a phone call to his father being his only resource. Ramirez, relying on an experienced team of sports lawyers whose sole focus was to get the deal done, was thousands of miles away when his contract negotiations were taking place. Symbolic of the leverage held by Ramirez and many of his contemporaries, the Red Sox general manager flew clear across the country to meet at Moorad's offices.

Legendary Green Bay Packers coach Vince Lombardi, for one, would not have easily embraced the changes in player-owner negotiations. In 1967, when the Packers' dynasty was at its height, Lombardi traded center Jim Ringo, a seven-time All-Pro, to the Philadelphia Eagles. It was a trade that suited both the Packers and Ringo. Lombardi suspected that Ringo was nearing the end of his stellar career. Lombardi sorely wanted the draft choices that a trade for Ringo would bring. Ringo was from Philadelphia and wanted to play in his hometown. The trade satisfied the objectives of both the Packers and Jim Ringo. A very different story emerged in the press. "I talked to Vince Lombardi on the phone first," Ringo was reported to have said. "I told him I had an agent. I told him my agent was going to Green Bay to represent me." Lombardi was supposed to have replied, "Agent? What the hell are you talking about?" As legend has it,

Lombardi met briefly with Ringo's agent in Green Bay and then excused himself to call Philadelphia. It is said that, after the phone call, Lombardi sat down with the agent and told him, "I am afraid you have come to the wrong city to discuss Mr. James Ringo's contract. Mr. James Ringo is now the property of the Philadelphia Eagles."[271]

More than thirty years later, the truth finally came out. It was true that Jim Ringo hired an agent to negotiate his 1967 contract. It was also known that Lombardi did not care for agents. However, according to Pat Peppler, the Packers' personnel director at the time, other details of the events surrounding the trade were not factual. The trade was not an impulsive act. Lombardi had been working on it for a long time. Moreover, Ringo's agent talked contractual matters with Peppler, not Lombardi. Peppler has also reported that Lombardi himself spread the fictitious report of his alleged meeting with Ringo's agent. Lombardi found the story useful because it discouraged his other players from hiring agents or making difficult contract demands.[272]

Lombardi would have been comfortable with the approach taken by the Milwaukee Bucks' shooting guard Ray Allen. Allen, out of the University of Connecticut, averaged 19.5 points per game for the Bucks in the 1997-1998 season, only his second year as a pro. Allen's plans for the future were modest. He wanted to stay in Milwaukee and play for the Bucks, even though it meant staying on a small-market team. Before the 1999 NBA season, Allen negotiated a six-year, $71 million contract directly with the Bucks' owner, U.S. Senator Herb Kohl, without benefit

---

[271] This anecdotal version of the Ringo trade is widely reported in various sports law texts to illustrate Vince Lombardi's antipathy toward sports agents. *See,* for example, Martin J. Greenberg and James T. Gray, *Sports Law Practice,* 2nd Ed. (Charlottesville, VA: Lexis Law Publishing, 1998), 948-49.

[272] David Maraniss, *When Pride Still Mattered: A Life of Vince Lombardi* (New York: Simon and Schuster, 1999), 354-55.

of an agent.[273] Allen felt comfortable calling his own shots in the negotiations and, equally important, was confident that the Bucks would deal with him fairly.

One of the first sports agents was Charles C. "Cash and Carry" Pyle. University of Illinois football legend Red "The Galloping Ghost" Grange hired Pyle to negotiate Grange's first professional football contract. In 1925, "Cash and Carry" Pyle opened negotiations with the Chicago Bears on Grange's behalf. Pyle's efforts resulted in a contract that paid Grange $3,000 per game and an additional $300,000 for endorsements and movie rights.[274] Today, most professional athletes hire agents to negotiate their contracts.[275] Up until 1968, however, teams in the National Football League refused to allow advisors to accompany players to contract negotiations. The management in professional baseball was no more enlightened. In the winter of 1966, Bob Woolf, a Boston lawyer, helped former Red Sox hurler Earl Wilson negotiate his contract for the 1967 baseball season with the Detroit Tigers.[276] Woolf, however, was not present for the negotiations. Wilson met with the Tigers' general manager at the team's offices. Woolf stayed in a hotel room located a few blocks from the Tigers' offices.

---

[273] Allen did, however, retain the services of a lawyer to assist in the legal technicalities. Allen paid the lawyer an hourly fee of $500, substantially less than the 4% to 10% fee that agents typically charge for their services. *Secret Agent*, SPORTS ILLUSTRATED, February 15, 1999, 28.

[274] Greenberg and Gray, *Sports Law Practice*, 2ND ed., 946.

[275] There are notable exceptions, however. In addition to the Bucks' Ray Allen, all-pro basketball players Grant Hill and Tim Duncan have negotiated their professional basketball contracts without using an agent.

[276] Woolf went on to gain widespread recognition as the dean of professional sports agents. Among his most notable clients were basketball players Larry Bird, John Havlicek, Julius Erving and Marvin Barnes as well as baseball players Carl Yastrzemski, Thurman Munson, Mark Fidrych and Ken Harrelson. Woolf also drew attention for his adamant adherence to ethical standards. He believed that athletes had an obligation to fulfill the terms of their contracts and refused to assist clients in renegotiating with their teams during the life of an existing contract. *Bob Woolf, Athletes' Agent, Dies*, THE WASH. POST, December 1, 1993, B2.

When the pitcher reached the stage where he needed his agent's advice, he excused himself from the meeting, went to a phone outside the office and called Woolf's hotel room. "In those days," Woolf explained, "third parties of the financial persuasion were not welcomed in the same room when teams were telling their athletes how much they would be paid."[277] Wilson ended up signing a contract for 1967 that paid him $65,000.[278]

Welcome or not, by the late 1960s, "third parties of the financial persuasion" were starting to make their presence felt in sports negotiations. One year before Earl Wilson retained Bob Woolf, all-star Los Angeles Dodgers pitchers Sandy Koufax and Don Drysdale used an agent to help them become the first major league pitchers to earn more than $100,000 in a season. Koufax and Drysdale had led Los Angeles to the 1965 World Series, in which the Dodgers defeated the American League champion Minnesota Twins, four games to three. Koufax won twenty-six games during the regular season and two more in the World Series. Drysdale was nearly as dominant, winning twenty-three regular season games and one more in the Series. At the suggestion of Drysdale's wife, the two pitchers jointly negotiated their 1966 contracts with the Dodgers. They hired J. William Hayes, a Hollywood movie producer, to negotiate for

---

The Sandy Koufax and Don Drysdale Principle of Contract Negotiations

Two front-line players can most effectively create clout in contract talks by negotiating their contracts jointly.

---

[277] Greenberg and Gray, *Sports Law Practice*, 2nd ed., 949.

[278] Even at $65,000, a handsome salary for a baseball player in the 1960s, Wilson proved to be a bargain. He recorded his best season in the major leagues in 1967, winning 22 games and losing only 11. Wilson's 22 wins tied Boston Red Sox pitcher Jim Lonborg and San Francisco Giants pitcher Mike McCormick for the most wins in the major leagues.

them. With the help of Hayes and an extremely favorable negotiating position,[279] Koufax signed for $125,000, Drysdale for $115,000.[280]

Chicago White Sox pitcher Bob Locker, negotiating without an agent and relying on his general manager's word, earned $16,000 for the 1968 season—two years after Koufax and Drysdale, with the help of an agent, each signed for more than $100,000. The experiences of Koufax and Drysdale help to explain Vince Lombardi's disdain for agents. The emergence of agents has severely weakened the overwhelming leverage that teams like the White Sox once enjoyed over players like Bob Locker. A savvy agent will use a variety of techniques to gain leverage for his clients. Agent Tony Attanasio often brought a player's wife to her husband's salary arbitration hearings. For one hearing, a player's wife showed up eight months pregnant. Attanasio explained, "I want the arbitrator to know it's more than a statistical argument. Statistics are important. But we're talking about human beings."[281]

For the players, however, the emergence of sports agents has been a mixed blessing. Cases of unethical conduct by players' agents have been repeatedly documented. Pete Newell, the general manager for the Los Angeles Lakers in the 1970s, frequently found himself competing with rival American Basketball Association teams for the contractual rights to college stars. Newell maintained that, in some situations, agents convinced the players they represented to sign with ABA teams even though the players stood to make more money from the Lakers. "I'm convinced," Newell once said, "that the ABA was paying agents under the table to send kids to their league." Wayne Embrey, the long-time general manager for

---

[279] With a combined total of 49 victories during the 1965 season, Koufax and Drysdale brought considerable clout to the bargaining table. The other pitchers on the Dodgers' 1965 staff accounted for only 48 wins between them. Behind Koufax and Drysdale, the Dodgers' top pitcher was Claude Osteen, who won 15 games. No other pitcher had more than seven wins.

[280] Greenberg and Gray, *Sports Law Practice*, 2nd ed., 947-48.

[281] Greenberg and Gray, *Sports Law Practice*, 2nd ed., 154.

the NBA's Cleveland Cavaliers, concurred. "I know the ABA was paying off agents," Embrey said. Embrey pointed to the fact that players who went to the ABA often ended up with contracts "that were good for no one but the ABA and the agent."[282]

---

[282] Pluto, *Loose Balls: The Short, Wild Life Of The American Basketball Association As Told By The Players, Coaches, And Movers And Shakers Who Made It Happen*, 179.

Chapter 10

The Trading of Professional Athletes

Willie Kamm was the regular third baseman for the Chicago White Sox from 1923 to 1930 and, for several years, the best glove man to play the hot corner in the majors. In 1924, Kamm's second season in the majors, he led all American League third basemen in putouts, assists, double plays, and fielding percentage. In each of the next five seasons, Kamm recorded the best fielding percentage of all American League third basemen. In four of those seasons, his fielding percentage was the highest of any third basemen in either the American or National League. In 1930, however, Kamm suffered through a subpar season, finishing next-to-last in fielding percentage among regular American League third basemen and committing a career-high 23 errors.

Predictably, the White Sox traded Kamm early in the 1931 season. Kamm learned that a trade was in the works from an operator for the telephone company. A week before the trade, the telephone operator called Kamm. "You're going to be traded to Cleveland," the operator said. Kamm dismissed the operator as "some nut." In fact, the operator, having eavesdropped on telephone conversations between the two teams, was not just some nut. A couple of days after her first phone call to Kamm, the operator called again. "It's getting closer and closer," she said. The operator called again the following Saturday. "The deal went through," she told Kamm, "you're traded to Cleveland." The next morning, Kamm read of the trade in the Chicago sports pages. He went to the ballpark, emptied out his locker and paid a visit to the White Sox' front office. "Yeah, you've been traded," he was told.[283] Kamm's official notice of the trade came in the form of a terse sheet of paper titled "Notice To Player Of Release Or Transfer" signed by White Sox owner

```
COPY FOR PLAYER                          No. A 1258

       NOTICE TO PLAYER OF RELEASE OR TRANSFER
                    AMERICAN LEAGUE

                                   MAY 17, 1931

  To Mr.    Wm Kamm

  You are hereby notified as follows:
  1. That you are unconditionally released.
  2. That your contract has been assigned to the Cleveland
  Club of American League.    (a) Without right of recall.
                              (b) With right of recall.

          in exchange for Lew Fonseca
  ............................................................
  ............................................................
     (Cross out parts not applicable. In case of optional agreement, specify all conditions affecting player.)

             AMERICAN LEAGUE BASEBALL CLUB OF CHICAGO

                 Chas a Comiskey  President

  Copy must be delivered to player; also forwarded to President of League of which Club is a member and to the
  Commissioner..
```

[283] Lawrence S. Ritter, *The Glory of Their Times: The Story of the Early Days of Baseball Told by the Men Who Played It* (New York: William Morrow and Company, Inc., 1992), 290-91.

and president Charles Comiskey. The notice informed Kamm that his contract had been assigned to Cleveland. With that, Kamm's career in Chicago was over and, for the next four years, he played third base for Cleveland. His flair for fielding returned. In both 1933 and 1934, Kamm led all major league third basemen in fielding percentage, committing only 14 errors over the two-year period.

Bob Cerv, a substitute outfielder for the New York Yankees in the early 1950s, recalled how he learned he had been traded to the Kansas City Athletics in 1956. Cerv was standing near Yankee manager Casey Stengel one day. Without warning, Stengel blurted, "Nobody knows this yet, but one of us has been sold to Kansas City." Cerv looked around. He and Stengel were the only people present. Since managers are not commonly traded, Cerv concluded that he would soon be on his way to Kansas City.[284] Decades later, the trading process has become considerably more intricate. Before the start of the 2000 season, the Baltimore Orioles entered into trade discussions with the New York Mets involving incumbent Orioles left fielder B.J. Surhoff. Surhoff's contract allowed him to name six teams to which he could refuse a trade. However, he never had reason to anticipate a trade and so had never identified the six teams. When Surhoff learned of the trade talks with the Mets, his agent quickly dashed off a list of the six "no-trade" teams and sent it to the Orioles' front office. The Mets were at the top of Surhoff's list.

The trade talks between the Orioles and Mets ultimately broke down and Surhoff, one of the most popular players in the Orioles' clubhouse,

---

[284] Trades involving managers are rare but not unheard of. On August 10, 1960, the Cleveland Indians traded the team's manager, former Yankee second baseman Joe Gordon, to the Detroit Tigers. In return, the Indians received Tiger manager Jimmy Dykes, himself an infielder for 22 years with the Philadelphia Athletics and Chicago White Sox. The trade did little to improve the fortunes of either team. Gordon piloted the Tigers to a finish of 26 wins and 31 losses. Dykes fared no better in Cleveland. His Indians won 26 and lost 32 during the same period.

remained with Baltimore for the better part of the 2000 season. On July 31, 2000, however, the Orioles shipped Surhoff and pitcher Gabe Molina to the Atlanta Braves for pitching prospect Luis Rivera, outfielder Trenidad Hubbard and catcher Fernando Lunar. Atlanta was not among the six no-trade teams that Surhoff had designated.[285]

In July 2002, the Montreal Expos pulled off a stunning eight-player trade with the Florida Marlins that landed the Expos power-hitting outfielder Cliff Floyd. No one was more stunned by the trade than left-handed relief pitcher Graeme Lloyd, who went from the Expos to the Marlins.[286] Lloyd's contract with Montreal allowed him to name twelve teams to which he could not be traded. Florida was one of the twelve "no-trade" teams that Lloyd had identified. For this reason, when newspaper reporters leaked rumors of the trade to Lloyd on July 11th, he informed the reporters that the Expos were prohibited from trading him to the Marlins. Minutes later, the deal was officially announced, leaving Lloyd to wonder about his no-trade provision. To his dismay, Lloyd later learned that, under the terms of his contract, he was required to submit his list of no-trade teams to the Expos by November 1, 2001. Lloyd and his agent

---

[285] Even so, the trade was a deep disappointment to Surhoff and a shock to his team-mates. He had played in Baltimore for four years and four months. Those years, he said, were his best years in baseball. The trade was even more shocking because of its timing. Major league teams had until 4:00 p.m. on July 31st to complete player trades for the season. After the 4:00 p.m. deadline, deals could only be made using waivers, a process in which the Orioles would have had to give all other major league teams the chance to claim Surhoff. Though the Surhoff trade had been completed at 3:40 p.m., the news did not reach Surhoff until after 4:00 p.m. Surhoff was getting ready to take pre-game batting practice with the Orioles when he was told of the trade. Quite naturally, he had assumed he was safe. William Gildea, *Difficult Goodbye For Surhoff, And the Orioles,* THE WASH. POST, August 1, 2000, D1, D6.

[286] The trade sent Floyd, infielder Wilton Guerrero and pitcher Claudio Vargas, the Marlin's minor league pitcher of the year for 2000, to the Expos in exchange for Lloyd, infielder Mike Mordecai, and pitchers Carl Pavano, Justin Wayne and Don Levinski.

did not submit the list until after that date, in effect negating the benefit of the no-trade provision.[287]

Surhoff and Lloyd had limited no-trade clauses in their contracts. The contracts for other players, such as former Tampa Bay Devil Rays first baseman Fred McGriff have contained absolute no-trade clauses. McGriff's contract with the Devil Rays ran through the 2002 season. Under the terms of the contract, the Devil Rays were precluded from trading McGriff for the duration of his contract. The only exception would be if McGriff agreed to waive his no-trade clause, thereby allowing Tampa Bay to deal him to another team. On July 8, 2001, the Devil Rays worked out a tentative deal that would have sent McGriff to the Chicago Cubs. The Cubs, positioning themselves for the pennant race, were in need of a consistent power hitter to bat behind Sammy Sosa. McGriff seemed to fill the bill perfectly. To the Cubs' dismay, however, McGriff was not anxious to change teams. After consulting with his family, McGriff exercised his rights under the no-trade clause and nixed the deal to Chicago. As baseball commentator Joe Morgan would say later, though, it was a "soft no." Less than a month after McGriff declined the trade to Chicago, the Devil Rays again approached him about waiving the no-trade provision in his contract. This time, McGriff was more receptive. After further discussions with his family and after reviewing all the alternatives, McGriff agreed to accept a trade to the Cubs. The trade was completed on July 27, 2001.

Two days later, McGriff was in a Cub uniform and playing first base for his new team in a nationally televised Sunday Night Baseball game against the St. Louis Cardinals. McGriff paid immediate dividends for the Cubs, getting one hit in three at-bats, with a run batted in. In an interview played during the telecast, McGriff explained his reasons for waiving his no-trade clause and agreeing to join the Cubs. His family was supportive, he said, and he felt he would be better able to control his career options in Chicago. It was also important, McGriff commented, that the Cubs were

---

[287] Dave Sheinin, *Covering the Bases*, THE WASH. POST, July 14, 2002, D7.

playing well and, to top it off, Chicago was home to "Ron of Japan," his favorite Japanese restaurant.

In the current era, no-trade clauses are often granted to players whose stature gives them sufficient leverage in contract negotiations. In years past, even established stars could be traded at the whim of a team owner, without notice or warning. In 1954, the St. Louis Cardinals traded outfielder Enos Slaughter, a hero of the Cardinals' 1946 World Series championship team and an eventual Hall-of-Famer, to the New York Yankees.[288] Slaughter was devastated. Newspaper photographs captured him weeping in front of his locker. Slaughter's trade gained international attention. The magazine *Soviet Sport* criticized the trade as "flesh peddling." The magazine cited the trade to illustrate that "beizbol bosses care nothing about sport or their athletes, but only about profits."[289]

Tim Fortugno, a career minor leaguer, pitched for 15 different teams. During his baseball career, Fortugno was the "property" of six different major league organizations. Being traded was a way of life for him. Even Fortugno, however, was probably shocked to learn, in 1989, that the Reno (Nevada) Silver Sox had traded him to the Milwaukee Brewers organization in exchange for twelve dozen baseballs and $2,500.[290] Former pitcher Jim Bouton recalls that, whenever he was traded, one of his first questions was, "Who I was traded for?" Bouton explained, "You like to hear a big name on the other end. It's good for your morale."[291] Bouton's morale

---

[288] Slaughter hit .320 in the 1946 Series and, in the seventh game, dashed home from first base with the decisive run to capture the championship for the Cardinals. In contrast, Stan Musial, who led the National League in hitting during the 1946 season with a .365 average, hit only .222 in the seven Series games.

[289] David Pietrusza, Matthew Silverman and Michael Gershman, eds., *Baseball: The Biographical Encyclopedia*, (Kingston, NY: Total Sports Publishing, 2000), 1047.

[290] Tim Kurkjian, *Swing Shift*, SPORTS ILLUSTRATED, January 23, 1995, 70, 74.

[291] Jim Bouton, *Ball Four* (Cleveland, Ohio: The World Publishing Company, 1970), 324.

plummeted in 1969 when the Seattle Pilots traded him to the Houston Astros for pitcher Dooley Womack. "Maybe it's me for a hundred thousand, and Dooley Womack is just a throw-in," Bouton wrote. "I'd hate to think that at this stage of my career I was being traded even-up for Dooley Womack."[292] It has been said that all pitchers think alike. If Tim Fortugno thinks like Jim Bouton, he no doubt was looking to see if the twelve dozen baseballs were just a "throw-in" in his trade to the Brewers.

There is no question that the Milwaukee Brewers had the right to trade or give away twelve dozen baseballs—provided, of course, that they owned the baseballs. The trading of a player, however, invokes different principles. Baseballs constitute property; people do not. What gives teams the right to trade players? Why did the Reno Silver Sox have the right to trade Tim Fortugno for cash and 144 baseballs?

The views of *Soviet Sport* notwithstanding, player trades are an integral part of major league sports. Player trades are also consistent with the contractual nature of professional athletics. When the St. Louis Cardinals traded Enos Slaughter to the Yankees and the Baltimore Orioles traded B.J. Surhoff to Atlanta, the process involved an "assignment" of player contracts. The Cardinals assigned Slaughter's contract to the Yankees; the Orioles assigned Surhoff's contract to the Braves. Whether the sport is baseball, basketball, football or hockey, any player trade starts with the player's contract. Teams can trade a player only if they have bargained for that right, as reflected in the terms of the contract. Bob Cerv's contract

---

[292] In fact, Bouton was not traded even-up for Womack. The Astros also sent minor league pitcher Roric Harrison to the Pilots. The inclusion of Harrison probably did little to improve Bouton's morale. At the time of the trade, Harrison was still three years away from making his major league debut and had yet to show that he was a major league prospect. Dooley Womack pitched for five years in the big leagues, winning 19 games, losing 18, and recording an impressive earned run average of 2.95. Roric Harrison also spent five years at the major league level, with a record of 30 wins and 35 losses. His career ERA was 4.24. During his ten-year career, Bouton recorded 62 wins and 63 losses and allowed 3.57 earned runs per nine innings.

with the New York Yankees in 1956 included a clause allowing the Yankees to assign the contract to another team. The words of the assignment clause provided, in essence, that "the Player agrees that his contract may be assigned by the Club to any other Club."

B.J. Surhoff signed a three-year deal with the Orioles in December 1998. Under terms of the contract, Surhoff was to receive $3 million for playing baseball during the 2000 season. In return, Surhoff agreed to play to the best of his ability and to allow the Orioles to trade him to any other major league team—aside from the six no-trade teams he was to designate—during the life of his contract. When a team enters into a player trade, it transfers both its rights and obligations to the player's new team. The trade of B.J. Surhoff to the Braves would have been meaningless if his new team did not have an obligation to pay him the money owed under his contract. From a legal perspective, a trade involves two parallel actions: (1) an assignment to the new team of the right to the player's performance; and (2) a delegation to the new team of the duty to pay the player's salary.[293]

In the current era, a standard major league player contract includes the usual words by which the player agrees to allow his team to assign his contract to any other team. The standard player's contract also includes words recognizing that the team and a player may agree to limit or eliminate the team's right to assign the contract. The Orioles and B.J. Surhoff agreed to a partial limit on the team's trading rights. Taking B.J. Surhoff's contract one step further, the Tampa Bay Devil Rays and Fred McGriff agreed to

---

[293] In an era when multi-million dollar salaries for players are routine, teams are increasingly reluctant to accept a high-salaried player in trade unless the player's former team agrees to pay a portion of the player's future pay. When the Baltimore Orioles traded first baseman Will Clark to the St. Louis Cardinals on July 31, 2000, Clark's contract called for a salary of $5.5 million for the 2000 season. As part of the deal with the Cardinals, the Orioles agreed to absorb part of Clark's remaining salary, thereby making the trade possible. Dave Sheinin, *O's Ship Clark to Cards and Surhoff to Braves In Deals for Reserves and Minor Leaguers*, THE WASH. POST, August 31, 2000, D1.

eliminate the team's trading rights altogether. As an established major league hitter, McGriff was in a position to demand a no-trade clause. Tim Fortugno, like most ballplayers, never attained that stature.

Player contracts in the National Football League are similar. A standard NFL contract states, "It is mutually agreed that the Club shall have the right to sell, exchange, assign or transfer this contract and the Player's services hereunder to any other Club in the League." In the late 1960s, Los Angeles Rams quarterback Roman Gabriel was one of the marquee players in the NFL. A collegiate standout at North Carolina State, Gabriel was the National Football League's Most Valuable Player in 1969. Gabriel asked for, and received, a no-trade provision in his contract with the Rams. In 1973, Gabriel's stature suffered when the Rams acquired fellow quarterback John Hadl from the San Diego Chargers. Gabriel did not welcome the prospect of sharing playing time with Hadl; he wanted out of Los Angeles. Coincidentally, the ownership of the Rams had changed hands the previous year. The new owner, Carroll Rosenbloom, acquired the team after Gabriel had signed his contract with the Rams. Seeking to force a trade, Gabriel claimed that the previous owners of the Rams had violated the no-trade clause in his contract when they sold the team to Rosenbloom. Gabriel's lawyer explained, "Gabriel has an agreement in writing with a company no longer in existence, and without his approval, his contract could not be assigned." Gabriel sued the Rams and asked for $5,000 in damages for violation of his contract. The lawsuit alleged that, with the change in ownership of the Rams, Gabriel's contract with the team was no longer valid. Gabriel's lawyer was also quick to acknowledge that the tactic might not work. "This hasn't been tried before, but he's got nothing to lose," the lawyer said. "If he loses, he'll be right back where he is now."[294] Ultimately, the Rams agreed to trade Gabriel to the

---

[294] *Gabriel Files Suit Disputing Ram Contract*, THE WASH. POST, May 10, 1973, D4.

Philadelphia Eagles. Shortly before the teams finalized the trade, Gabriel withdrew his lawsuit.[295]

Though trades are an accepted part of professional sports, being traded is not easy on players. Former major league pitcher John Curtis once commented, "I've been traded twice myself, so I know the short-term nature of baseball friendships, but that doesn't make it any easier."[296] While playing for the San Francisco Giants, Curtis developed close friendships with teammates Gary Thomasson and Gary Alexander, both of whom were later traded. A thoughtful man, Curtis noted that ballplayers, like most other people, look for stability in their surroundings and their friendships. Curtis used to enjoy spending evenings at Thomasson's house, until the Giants traded Thomasson to the Oakland Athletics in 1978. "You need your friends in this business," Curtis said.[297]

The John Curtis Principle of Friendships In Professional Baseball

You need your friends in this business.

Curt Flood would have understood John Curtis' feelings. When the St. Louis Cardinals traded Flood to the Philadelphia Phillies in 1969, Flood refused to report to the Phillies.[298] He disliked the way black players were treated in Philadelphia and had concerns about the Phillies' organization. Moreover, Flood had business interests in St. Louis and was unwilling to

---

[295] *Gabriel Suit Dismissed*, THE WASH. POST, May 31, 1973, D5.

[296] Before his baseball career ended in 1984, Curtis would be traded a third time, from the San Diego Padres to the California Angels.

[297] Roger Angell, *Late Innings: A Baseball Companion* (New York: Ballantine Books, 1983), 71.

[298] Flood was traded along with Cardinal teammates Tim McCarver, Joe Hoerner and Byron Browne for the Phillies' Dick Allen, Cookie Rojas and Jerry Johnson. When it became apparent that Flood would not report to Philadelphia, the Cardinals sent Willie Montanez and Bob Browning to the Phillies to complete the trade.

accept the upheaval that would result. A decade earlier, Jackie Robinson, the first African-American to play in the major leagues, had balked when the Brooklyn Dodgers attempted to trade him. On December 13, 1956, the Dodgers completed a deal that would have sent Robinson to the New York Giants for pitcher Dick Littlefield and $30,000 in cash. The trade rankled Robinson. He found it inconceivable that he would have to wear the uniform of the Dodgers' archrival. He retired instead, and the trade was subsequently canceled.

In recent years, the increasing tendency of players to refuse to accept trades has been a source of particular concern to the National Basketball Association. Under the terms of the standard player's contract, an NBA player can be suspended and his salary withheld if the player does not report to his new team within 48 hours of a trade. To some players, however, the threat of a suspension carries little import. Pat Riley, president and coach of the Miami Heat, likened a player's refusal to accept a trade to blackmail. In Riley's view, "an owner is going to sue a player and his agent for damages for killing a trade or not wanting to go somewhere else." John Nash, general manager with the Washington Bullets and later the New Jersey Nets, was of the same opinion. "When they sign," said Nash, "they know their contract can be reassigned, and if they don't report, it's a breach of that contract."[299]

The Pat Riley Principle of Trades

Players who refuse to report to a new team after a trade should be sued for violation of contract.

Even when all the players involved in a trade report to their new teams, the teams sometimes do not receive everything for which they bargained. In 1972, during George Allen's heyday as head coach of the Washington

---

[299] Phil Taylor, *Hell, No, They Won't Go*, SPORTS ILLUSTRATED, March 2, 1998, 80.

Redskins, the Redskins agreed to a trade with the San Diego Chargers in which the Chargers would send veteran players to the Redskins in exchange for multiple draft choices. The trade backfired when the Chargers learned that the Redskins had previously traded away, to another team, the same draft choices that Allen had promised to the Chargers. The National Football League fined Washington $5,000 for the transgression.[300]

During the short-lived history of the American Basketball Association, team executives sometimes felt little compulsion to abide by league rules when trading players. During the 1972-73 season, the ABA's Virginia Squires featured both Julius Erving, later to be known as "Doctor J"[301] and George Gervin, who was destined for superstar status in both the ABA and the NBA.[302] The 1972-73 season was Erving's second year with the Squires and Gervin's first. Neither had yet established a nationwide reputation. In need of money, the Squires sold Erving to the New York Nets in the summer of 1973.[303] The following winter, the Squires sold

---

[300] Dave Brady, *Rams Escape Fine In Draft Deal Oversight*, THE WASH. POST, March 9, 1973, D2.

[301] The Squires had signed Erving to a professional contract after his junior year at the University of Massachusetts. Erving acquired the nickname "Doctor" during his first pre-season training camp with the Squires. After watching Erving make one impressive dunk after another, Squires teammate Willie Sojourner would say, "There's the doctor digging into his bag again." Eventually, as other players picked up the expression, "Doctor" became "Dr. J."

[302] Terry Pluto, *Loose Balls: The Short, Wild Life of the American Basketball Association As Told by the Players Players, Coaches, and Movers and Shakers Who Made It Happen* (New York: Simon & Schuster, 1990), 300.

[303] With the Squires, as with several ABA teams, financial difficulties were a way of life. One night Virginia was scheduled to play the Indiana Pacers. Before the game, the Squires' owner called the Pacers and asked that the game be canceled. The owner explained that he had been unable to pay $2,000 to the manufacturer of the team's uniforms and a sheriff was coming to repossess the uniforms. The owner of the Pacers intercepted the sheriff at the arena and pointed out that the uniforms had been used and so held little resale value. After considering the matter, the sheriff allowed the Squires to keep their uniforms and the game went on as scheduled.

Gervin to the San Antonio Spurs for $225,000. The Squires' owner, Earl Foreman, traded Gervin under duress and not without severe misgivings. Of particular concern, the ABA's All-Star game was to be played in Virginia that season. Gervin was slated to represent the Squires in the All-Star game, and the hometown fans were sure to heap abuse upon the Squires if Gervin did not play in the game—or worse, if he played in the game wearing an opponent's uniform. To solve the predicament, the two teams agreed to keep the Gervin trade quiet until after the All-Star game, still several months away. In working out the details of the trade, the owner of the San Antonio Spurs, Angelo Drossos, proposed to Earl Foreman, "I'll pay you the $225,000 now. We'll wait until right after the All-Star Game and then you deliver George to me. Until then, you can keep him."[304]

Only three people in the world knew that George Gervin had been traded—and Gervin wasn't one of them. He continued to play for the Squires right up to the All-Star Game, even though his contractual rights belonged to the San Antonio Spurs. When the details of the trade were revealed, the commissioner of the league, Mike Storen, was irate. The trade was clearly in violation of the league's rules. Storen sued the Spurs to force them to cancel the trade and return Gervin to the Squires. Storen's reasoning was flawless. *First*, the trade was illegal under league rules. *Second*, at the time of the trade, the owner of the Squires was trying to sell the team. Storen feared that Gervin's trade, following so closely upon the trade of Julius Erving, would deplete the team of all its marketable players and discourage prospective buyers. Storen insisted that he was acting in the "best interest" of the league. As it turned out, however, his arguments fell on deaf ears. He filed his lawsuit against the Spurs in the Federal District Court in San Antonio, hardly a neutral location. He also had the

---

[304] Pluto, *Loose Balls: The Short, Wild Life of the American Basketball Association As Told by the Players Players, Coaches, and Movers and Shakers Who Made It Happen*, 298-99.

misfortune of having his case heard by a judge who was a Spurs' season-ticket holder. Not surprisingly, the judge ruled in favor of San Antonio.

In his days as commissioner of Major League Baseball, Bowie Kuhn received greater deference from the courts than did Mike Storen. During a tumultuous two-day stretch in June 1976, the owner of the Oakland Athletics, Charles O. Finley, traded three of his most prominent players for cash. Finley sent outfielder Joe Rudi and relief pitcher Rollie Fingers to the Boston Red Sox for $2 million and then dealt fire-balling left-hander Vida Blue to the New York Yankees for $1.5 million. Invoking his authority as commissioner, Kuhn scheduled a hearing on the trades. One day after the hearing, Kuhn announced that he would not approve the deals. Echoing some of the same concerns that Mike Storen had cited in the George Gervin trade, Kuhn ruled that the trading of Rudi, Fingers and Blue would be contrary to the best interests of baseball. Kuhn felt the trades would debilitate the Athletics and lessen the competitive balance in the American League. Finley wasted no time in reacting. Ten days after completing the trades, he sued Bowie Kuhn in Federal District Court.[305] Finley lost in court. The judge found that the major league owners had given the commissioner broad authority to prevent "any act, transaction or practice that was not in the best interests of baseball." Finley later appealed the decision, but it was to no avail.[306] Though Rudi, Fingers and Blue all remained with Oakland for the duration of the 1976 season, the turmoil caused by the aborted trades effectively ended the tenure of Rudi and Fingers with the Athletics. Rudi became a free agent at the end of the

---

[305] Finley filed his lawsuit in Illinois—and not in a court near the Athletics' fan base in California. Thus, Finley did not receive the benefit of the same sympathetic judicial environs as had the San Antonio Spurs in the dispute over the Gervin trade. As best as can be determined, however, Finley was not a particularly popular figure in California anyway, and his attempt to sell players of the stature of Rudi, Fingers and Blue may have produced an openly hostile courtroom setting in California.

[306] *Finley v. Kuhn*, 569 F.2d 527 (7th Cir. 1978).

1976 season and signed to play for the California Angels. Fingers also became a free agent and signed with the San Diego Padres. Under the newly established rules of free agency, neither the California Angels nor the San Diego Padres were required to pay any compensation to Finley for signing his former stars. Vida Blue remained with the Athletics until March 1978, when he was dealt to the San Francisco Giants in a trade that brought Gary Thomasson, Gary Alexander and five other players to the Athletics.[307]

Regardless of the sport, player trades rarely become entangled in court proceedings. The trades involving Gervin, Rudi, Fingers and Blue were exceptions to the rule. And, the Enos Slaughter trade aside, player trades invariably proceed without generating controversy outside of the sports world. Whether one views the trading of players as "flesh peddling" or simply as part of the game, however, there are certain undeniable characteristics of the trading process:

> 1. Regardless of a player's popularity with fans or team-mates, teams will trade a player whenever it is in the team's best interest to do so.
> 2. Trades will sometimes reduce a ballplayer to tears.
> 3. When circumstances permit, players will often seek to limit a team's ability to trade them, either through full or partial no-trade clauses or simply by threatening not to report to their new team if they are traded.

---

[307] If, as Jim Bouton suggests, it is good for a ballplayer's morale to see a "big name" among the players for whom they have been traded, Vida Blue's morale must have gone off the charts after his trade to the Giants. The Athletics gave up only Blue in the trade. In exchange, the Athletics received Thomasson, Alexander, Mario Guerrero and Dave Heaverlo, who were all established major leaguers, plus prospects Alan Wirth, John Henry Johnson and Phil Huffman, each of whom would later spend considerable time in the majors. The Giants also paid $390,000 in cash to the Athletics.

4. As long as a player's contract gives his team the right to assign his contract to another team, trading the player is permissible from the perspective of the law, whether the trade is for another player or for twelve dozen baseballs.

5. League commissioners, acting in the "best interests" of the sport, generally have the authority to overrule trades, with the possible exception of trades that have the potential to bring a player of George Gervin's caliber to a team whose fan base includes members of the judicial community.

Chapter 11

Baseball's Antitrust Exemption and the Road to Free Agency

Tony Lupien, known as "Lupe" to his friends, was in trouble. It had been another late night. In his haste to get home, Lupien had taken his prized new Ford sedan around a bend at an alarmingly fast speed. The car, as well as Lupe and his passenger, Lexington, Massachusetts neighbor Bill Pollock, survived the hazardous turn. The two hubcaps on the passenger side of the sedan did not. In making the turn, Lupien had popped the hubcaps. They rolled noisily off into the night. That night, for fear his wife would notice the missing hubcaps, Lupien backed his car into the driveway, exposing only the driver-side hubcaps to plain view. Early the next morning, Lupien drove to his Ford dealer to replace the hubcaps. With the Ford restored to its pristine condition, Lupien returned home without fear of incurring his wife's anger.

Away from home, Lupien was not nearly so timid. He proved capable of handling both fastballs and baseball management with equal aplomb. In March 1945, as a twenty-seven-year-old ballplayer and a veteran of three full major league seasons, Lupien was inducted into the U.S. Navy. He spent the duration of World War II at the Sampson Naval Base in upstate New York. When the war ended, the Navy discharged Lupien in time for him to play in fifteen games for the Philadelphia Phillies at the tail end of the 1945 season. For the year, Lupien collected 17 hits in 54 at-bats, for an impressive .315 average. During those 15 games, however, Lupien would hit no home runs. Home runs had never been his forte and, even in his best years, Lupien's home run totals never reached double digits. He was a doubles hitter who had the misfortune to play first base, traditionally a power-hitting position. Nonetheless, Lupien was caught off guard when the Phillies announced, early in 1946, that they intended to sell his contract to a minor league team, the Hollywood Stars of the Pacific Coast League. To replace Lupien, the Phillies had traded for first baseman Frank McCormick.

Though six years older than Lupien, McCormick hit with more power. In his eight full major league seasons with Cincinnati, he had hit 18 or more home runs four times.[308] McCormick also possessed the "look" of a first baseman, standing 6'4"—a good five inches taller than Lupien. Unlike Lupien, McCormick had not lost any time to World War II. Lupien did not take his demotion quietly. As a returning veteran, he felt he was entitled to a position on a major league roster. Even worse, it was a former ballplayer, one-time New York Yankee pitcher Herb Pennock, who was responsible for demoting Lupien. Pennock had completed his Hall-of-Fame career in 1934. He then turned to baseball management and, in 1946, was serving as Philadelphia's general manager. Lupien visited Pennock and reminded him of the Veterans Act. "Don't you know that a returned serviceman is allowed at least a year's grace at getting his old job back?" Lupien railed. Unfazed, Pennock told Lupien, "That doesn't apply to baseball." Sensing he was getting nowhere, Lupien yelled at Pennock, "Who the hell are you to think that you're above the

---

[308] McCormick turned 35 years old midway through the 1946 season, his first with the Phillies. In 135 games that season, he hit .284 but managed only 11 home runs and 66 runs batted in.

federal government?"[309] On that note, both the meeting with Pennock and Lupien's career with the Phillies ended.[310]

Baseball's rules and the law both seemed to be on Lupien's side. According to major league rules, a returning serviceman was required to have at least 30 days in spring training before his team made a decision on the player's future. Lupien had spent less than a month with the Phillies in 1945 and was not invited to spring training in 1946. Furthermore, the U.S. Selective Service Board had advised Lupien that he had a valid case to claim his old job under the Veterans Act.[311] Even with the law on his side, Lupien had neither the money nor the appetite for engaging the major leagues in lengthy litigation. He decided to report to the minor leagues for the 1946 season and leave the lawsuits to others. He also resolved to share his experiences with other returning veterans who encountered similar difficulties.

In 1946, it wasn't hard to find other ballplayers who were being denied their rights under the Veterans Act. In April of that year, Lupien learned that one-time Red Sox infielder and former Navy lieutenant Al Niemiec had been released by the minor league Seattle Rainiers. The Rainiers had waived Niemiec even though the team's manager admitted that "Al has quite a bit of good baseball left in him." Niemiec was better poised than Lupien to pursue his legal rights. After his release, Niemiec visited the

---

[309] Lee Lowenfish, *The Imperfect Diamond: A History of Baseball's Labor Wars* (New York: Da Capo Press, Inc., 1991), 130.

[310] Tony Lupien did report to the Hollywood Stars for the 1946 season and eventually worked his way back to the major leagues for one last season. In 1948, at age 31, Lupien became the regular first baseman for the Chicago White Sox. Playing in all 154 games for the last place Sox, he hit .248, with six homers and 54 runs batted in. Lupien led the major leagues in putouts that season with 1,436, and his 617 at-bats were the most of any White Sox player. With those modest accomplishments, Lupien closed out his career in baseball.

[311] Lowenfish, *The Imperfect Diamond: A History of Baseball's Labor Wars*, 131.

draft board in Seattle. To the draft board, it was an easy case: the Rainiers had violated the Veterans Act. The draft board offered Niemiec the services of a lawyer. The case came before Federal Judge Lloyd Black who, in June 1946, ruled that baseball had no discretion "to repeal an act of Congress."

Al Niemiec was a month shy of 35 years of age when he was released by the Rainiers. During the trial, the Rainiers' management depicted Niemiec as an older player who had passed his peak and no longer deserved a spot on the team's roster. Judge Black found otherwise. Niemiec had played in five games for the Rainiers before being released, and the Rainiers had won three of those contests. In the five games, aside from one error, Niemiec had fielded flawlessly. Judge Black took his analysis one step further. The judge heard testimony that Niemiec's manager with the Rainiers, Bill Skiff, had played until he was 39 years old. The judge found ample evidence that Niemiec, at the age of 35, could still perform capably on the field. After Niemiec's release and before Niemiec filed his lawsuit, Skiff had written a letter of recommendation for Niemiec. The letter touted Niemiec's play. Skiff had written, "Al still has a lot of fine baseball left, we are sure...."[312]

Judge Black ordered the Rainiers to pay Niemiec his salary for 1946, less any amounts that Niemiec might earn playing baseball for any other team that season. In his decision, the judge expressed little sympathy for professional baseball. He noted that, under then prevailing case law, professional baseball did not involve interstate trade or commerce and was not subject to antitrust law. Though the antitrust exemption was not central to the Niemiec case, the judge speculated that perhaps the time had come for the U.S. Supreme Court to re-examine the validity of the exemption. Judge Black left no doubt that, in his opinion, baseball should be subject to the antitrust laws.[313]

---

[312] *Niemiec v. Seattle Rainier Baseball Club, Inc.*, 67 F. Supp. 705 (W.D. Wash. 1946).

[313] *Niemiec v. Seattle Rainier Baseball Club* at 712.

The issue of whether Niemiec was still capable of playing baseball was pivotal to the lawsuit. There was ample evidence that Niemiec could still hold his own on the baseball field. If the testimony had shown that Niemiec's skills on the diamond had deteriorated significantly, his case would have been severely weakened. For the flip side of Niemiec's case, one need look no further than former pitcher Steve Sundra. A 6'1" right-hander, Sundra began his major league career with the New York Yankees in 1936. From 1936 to 1944, Sundra won 56 games in the major leagues, splitting time with the Yankees, Washington Senators and St. Louis Browns. His best season came in 1943, when he pitched 208 innings and led the Browns' staff with 15 wins. Inducted into the Army in May 1944, Sundra remained on active duty until February 1946. Upon his return from the Army, Sundra signed a contract with the Browns for the 1946 season. The Browns agreed to pay Sundra $8,000 for the year. After two months with the team, though, Sundra had appeared in only two games, pitching four innings and giving up nine hits and three walks. He was not effective. A couple of months into the 1946 season, the Browns released Sundra. In turn, the pitcher sued under the Veterans Act.

The logic underlying the *Niemiec* decision worked against Steve Sundra. The essential factor in Judge Black's ruling in *Niemiec* was that "the veteran must be qualified to perform the duties of his position." Niemiec was qualified. Sundra was not. It was that simple. St. Louis Browns catcher Joe Schultz told the *Sundra* court that Sundra no longer threw very hard. Zach Taylor, the Browns' manager, testified that Sundra was no longer capable of helping the team. The court found that Sundra, a fastball pitcher, was a victim of the passage of time. "The pitching life of fastball pitchers," the judge noted, "is less in most instances than that of other pitchers."[314]

---

[314] *Sundra v. St. Louis American League Baseball Club*, 87 F. Supp. 471 (E.D. Miss. 1949).

In the *Niemiec* decision, Judge Black suggested that the Supreme Court might someday overturn baseball's antitrust exemption. More than fifty years have passed since the *Niemiec* decision. Baseball continues to be exempt. Alone among professional sports, baseball enjoys court-sanctioned freedom from the antitrust laws. The antitrust exemption arises from an opinion written by Supreme Court Justice Oliver Wendell Holmes in 1922. The case was the result of an appeal by Ned Hanlon, the owner of the Federal Baseball Club of Baltimore, a team in the upstart Federal League. Hanlon alleged that the owners of the American League and National League professional baseball teams had conspired to "wreck and destroy" the rival Federal League in violation of the antitrust laws. Hanlon offered evidence that the American and National Leagues had engaged in bribery to induce some of his fellow Federal League owners to disband the Federal League.

Under the applicable antitrust laws,[315] Congress had outlawed attempts to impose artificial restraints on trade, or exercise monopolistic control of the production of goods, or otherwise stifle commercial competition in the marketing of goods and services in interstate commerce. A federal jury found that the American and National Leagues had engaged in activities designed to illegally undermine the existence of the Federal League. The jury awarded Hanlon damages in the amount of $80,000. The American and National Leagues appealed the decision. The Court of Appeals reversed the jury's decision, ruling that baseball was a sport, not a trade, and did not constitute "commerce" as that term was used in the antitrust laws. Hanlon took the adverse Court of Appeals decision to the Supreme Court.

In a decision written by Justice Holmes, the Supreme Court concluded that baseball games were purely "state affairs"—and not interstate in

---

[315] There were two antitrust laws that arguably governed the operations of professional baseball, the Sherman Antitrust Act of 1890 and the Clayton Antitrust Act of 1914.

nature. Holmes wrote that the games involved the personal effort of ballplayers and "personal effort, not related to production, is not a subject of commerce."[316] Taking the analysis one step further, the opinion held that whatever actions the American and National League team owners may have taken, they did not, by definition, interfere with commerce among the states. There was, the Court found, no violation of the antitrust laws. The Supreme Court's decision in the *Federal Baseball Club of Baltimore* case has consistently been interpreted as granting major league baseball an exemption from the antitrust laws. From the days of Justice Holmes to the early 1970s, the decision was much criticized but never overturned. In 1972, major league outfielder Curt Flood gave the Supreme Court an opportunity to review the legal underpinnings of the antitrust exemption.

Flood had come up through the Cincinnati Reds' farm system. A 5'9", 165-pound outfielder, he excelled at every minor league stop on his way to the majors. Flood first made it to the major leagues with Cincinnati in 1956, appearing in five games, most of which were as a pinch runner. In 1957, Flood again had a "cup of coffee" with the Redlegs, playing two games at third base and one game at second. During that season, he hit the first of his 85 home runs in the major leagues. On December 5, 1957, after Flood had played only eight games in a Redleg uniform, Cincinnati traded him to St. Louis. Accompanying Flood to St. Louis was journeyman outfielder Joe Taylor. In exchange, the Redlegs received three pitchers, Willard Schmidt, Marty Kutyna and Franklin Delano Roosevelt ("Ted") Wieand. Of the three pitchers, only Schmidt had experience in the major leagues at the time of the trade. Kutyna and Wieand would later see limited action in the majors. The trade would ultimately be judged as extremely one-sided in favor of St. Louis. Schmidt, a winner of 10 games

---

[316] *Federal Baseball Club of Baltimore, Inc. v. National League of Professional Baseball Clubs, et al.*, 259 U.S. 200 (1922).

for the Cardinals in 1957, would win only six games in two years with Cincinnati before retiring. Wieand appeared in only one game for the Redlegs during the span of two years and never recorded a victory in the majors. Kutyna never made it to the majors with Cincinnati.

By all accounts, being traded to the Cardinals had a substantial impact on Flood, then an impressionable 19-year-old. It mattered little to him that St. Louis would be judged to have received the better end of the deal. Of greater concern was simply the nature of the trading process, whereby teams could trade ballplayers at whim or, as Flood would later depict it, "like a bottle cap." With his speed, bat control and flair in the outfield, Flood quickly became a key man in the St. Louis lineup. He went on to have several excellent seasons with the Cardinals. After the 1968 season, in which Flood hit for a .301 average, he asked the Cardinals for a $30,000 raise. The request did not sit well with Cardinal owner August "Gussie" Busch. Busch determined it was time to get rid of Flood.[317] On October 7, 1969, Busch traded his center fielder to Philadelphia in a deal that brought slugger Dick Allen and infielder Cookie Rojas to St. Louis.

At the time of the trade, Flood was thirty-one years old and a twelve-year major league veteran. His family was comfortable in St. Louis, and Flood had business interests in the city. He was at the top of his game, having been anointed "baseball's best center fielder" by *Sports Illustrated* in 1968. Flood was particularly displeased with the prospect of moving to Philadelphia. Having decided that he would not play for the Phillies, Flood implored Commissioner Bowie Kuhn to allow him to negotiate with other teams. Kuhn offered Flood two options: play in Philadelphia or find another career. Flood chose a third option. He filed a lawsuit against major league baseball.

---

[317] Roger I. Abrams, *Legal Bases: Baseball and the Law* (Philadelphia, PA: Temple University Press, 1998), 65.

> ## *The Curt Flood Principle of Leaving the Game on One's Own Terms*
>
> *A ballplayer has a right to go out like a man and not like a bottle cap.*

At the trial of Flood's lawsuit, the baseball owners prevailed. The judge ruled that the precedent established by Justice Holmes in his 1922 *Federal Baseball Club of Baltimore* decision governed and that baseball was immune from federal antitrust laws. In a rebuke to Flood and his legal team, District Court Judge Irving Ben Cooper warned against undue concentration by anyone or any group on commercial considerations. "The game is on higher ground," said the judge, and "it behooves every one to keep it there."[318] Flood appealed the decision, but the result was the same. Again, the "higher ground" prevailed, and Flood lost. Undeterred, Flood took his case to the U.S. Supreme Court. He argued that the reserve system forced him into "peonage" and was an unreasonable restraint of trade in violation of federal antitrust laws. This line of attack clearly implicated the 1922 Supreme Court decision.

In an opinion that legal experts have termed an "embarrassment,"[319] Justice Harry Blackmun held that baseball—alone among professional sports—was not subject to antitrust regulation.[320] Blackmun recognized that professional baseball's unique status under the law was an "anomaly," but considered it an anomaly that only Congress could correct. Justices Marshall, Douglas and Brennan were not so easily persuaded, but a majority of the justices agreed with Blackmun's analysis.[321] The dissenting justices, William

---

318 Abrams, *Legal Bases: Baseball and the Law*, 65.

319 Roger Abrams notes that, though Justice Blackmun would later earn a much deserved reputation as a distinguished jurist, his opinion in the *Flood* case was based on an "awkward judicial formalism." Blackmun opened the decision with an entirely too sentimental anthem of praise for baseball mythology that included a reference to the poem "Casey at the Bat." The late Justice Byron White, winner of the Heisman Trophy as a collegiate football player and no stranger to professional sports, found Blackmun's introduction so offensive that, although he agreed with the outcome of the case, he refused to join in with the first part of the opinion. Abrams, *Legal Bases: Baseball and the Law*, 66.

320 Abrams, *Legal Bases: Baseball and the Law*, 67.

321 *Flood v. Kuhn*, 407 U.S. 258 (1972).

Douglas, Thurgood Marshall, and William Brennan, found the decision hard to swallow. Douglas considered Holmes' 1922 decision "a derelict in the stream of the law" and characterized Flood and other ballplayers as "victims" of the reserve system.[322] Marshall went even further. In Marshall's view, the reserve system "virtually enslaved" the ballplayers. Marshall believed that Holmes' decision made the ballplayers "impotent" and urged his fellow justices to correct the error. Notwithstanding the eloquent pleas of Justices Douglas and Marshall, the Court left Holmes' decision in *Federal Baseball Club of Baltimore* standing.[323] Flood had reached the end of the line, both in terms of the court system and his baseball career.[324]

The *Flood* decision confirmed what Boston Red Sox slugger Ted Williams had known all along. In 1958, Williams testified before the United States Senate's Subcommittee on Antitrust and Monopoly. Williams told the senators, "when you sign in baseball, as I understand it, you are their property then until they sell you, trade you, or release you, and I think once you sign, why, that's the way it goes for a ballplayer."[325]

---

[322] *Flood v. Kuhn* at 286-87.

[323] By the time of the Supreme Court=s decision in Curt Flood=s case, major league baseball had clearly become heavily involved in, and dependent upon, interstate commerce. Even Justice Holmes might have agreed that, in the 50 years since his opinion in Federal Baseball, the decision had become Aa derelict in the stream of the law.@ As a jurist, Holmes had little use for blind adherence to legal precedents. In a critical assessment of the role of precedent in the law, he once said, AIt is revolting to have no better reason for a rule of law than that so it was laid down in the time of Henry IV. It is still more revolting if the grounds upon which it was laid down have vanished long since, and the rule simply persists from blind imitation of the past.@ Address on AThe Path of the Law,@ reprinted in Richard A. Posner, ed., The Essential Holmes: Selections from the Letters, Speeches, Judicial Opinions, and Other Writings of Oliver Wendell Holmes, Jr. (Chicago: University of Chicago Press, 1996), 160.

[324] Flood appeared in 13 games with the American League's Washington Senators in 1971, but his major league career effectively ended on the day the Cardinals dealt him to Philadelphia. He missed all of the 1970 season and when he returned to baseball in 1971, both his skills and his zest for the game had deserted him.

[325] David Gallen, ed., *The Baseball Chronicles* (New York: Carroll & Graf Publishers, Inc, 1991), 384.

The singular focus of Curt Flood's lawsuit and Ted Williams' testimony was baseball's reserve system. Baseball's rules stipulated that "there shall be no negotiations or dealings respecting employment, either present or prospective, between any player, coach or manager and any club other than the club with which he is under contract... or by which he is reserved." Each player's contract contained an option clause. As interpreted by baseball's owners, the option clause allowed a team to extend an existing player's contract from one year to the next for an indefinite period. The option clause, coupled with a team's right to "reserve" its players, effectively allowed teams to exercise a property right over the players.

The early days of Topps baseball cards provides a useful analogy for explaining how baseball's reserve system turned ballplayers into "property." When Al Ferrara, an outfielder for the 1963-1968 Los Angeles Dodgers, was asked why he wanted to be a baseball player, he explained his choice of careers in a way that most people could readily understand. Ferrara would tell people that he always wanted to see his picture on a bubble gum card. In all, Ferrara's picture appeared on eight different cards issued by Topps Chewing Gum. For the duration of Ferrara's major league career, Topps was the only game in town. There was no competition from Fleer or Upper Deck or other card companies that would later enter the market. Topps had started in the baseball card business in the early 1950s. At that time, the Bowman Gum Company held exclusive licensing agreements with most of the major league players to use their pictures on baseball cards. Topps purchased the licensing rights from Bowman. In the 1950s and 1960s, Topps signed contracts with nearly every major league baseball player. The contracts gave Topps the exclusive right to use the players' pictures on cards sold alone or with gum, candy or confectionary products. After a player had been in the major leagues for two years, Topps would sign the player to a renewal contract. The renewal contract lasted for several years. Under Topps' interpretation of the law, a player could not sign a contract with any other card company while the player's contract with Topps was still in effect. To sign with a competing card company, a player first had to allow his contract with Topps to expire.[326] In almost all cases, Topps renewed the players' contracts before they could expire. In effect, the players were perpetually under contract to Topps.[327] Baseball's reserve system worked in much the same way: the owners were forever able to keep the players under contract. So long as the reserve system remained in effect, players could only negotiate with the one team that held their contractual rights.

Baseball was not the only professional sport to use a reserve system to its advantage. Player contracts in the National Basketball Association contained a reserve clause which enabled teams to contractually retain the services of their players for a one-year period after expiration of the contract. Basketball player Rick Barry sat out the 1967-68 basketball season as a result of the reserve clause contained in his contract with the San Francisco Warriors. The 1966-67 season was Rick Barry's second year with the Warriors. That year, he led the NBA in scoring, averaging 35 points a game. Barry, however, did not enjoy the regimented ways of Warriors coach Bill Sharman. George Mikan, the first commissioner of the rival American Basketball Association, thought that Barry might be inclined to sign with the ABA's Oakland Oaks if the Oaks hired Barry's college coach and father-in-law, Bruce Hale, to be the coach. Barry's initial contract with the Warriors was for two years, so the only provision binding him to the Warriors after 1966-67 was the reserve clause in his initial contract. The Oaks did hire Bruce Hale as coach and, as Mikan had predicted,

---

[326] Rival card companies could sell trading cards with products that were not gum, candy or confectionary. To avoid the label "confectionary," it was necessary to reduce the level of sugar in a product. Fleer tried selling cards with a cookie that contained so little sugar that it was not a confectionary product. The results were disappointing. It quickly became apparent that children had a strong preference for cookies containing sugar.

[327] Marvin Miller, *A Whole Different Ball Game: The Sport and Business of Baseball* (New York: Simon and Schuster, 1991), 144-146.

Barry was receptive to signing with the Oaks. Barry knew that his contract with the Warriors contained a reserve clause. He consulted with lawyers to determine if he was free to sign with the Oaks. The lawyers advised Barry that the reserve clause would probably not hold up in court. Emboldened by the legal advice, Barry agreed to a three-year contract with the Oaks for $75,000 per year and 15 percent ownership of the team. The Warriors took the Oaks to court. The judge examined the reserve clause in Barry's contract and ruled that it was valid. Therefore, the Warriors held the rights to Barry for one more year; he was not a free agent and not available to play for the Oaks until he had sat out a year. To enforce his ruling, the judge issued an injunction preventing Barry from playing for the Oaks until his option year with the Warriors expired. Under the ruling, Barry could either play for the Warriors for the 1967-68 season or sit out the season. He decided against playing for the Warriors. Instead, Barry served as a commentator on TV broadcasts of the Oaks' games and spent the year playing against high school faculties as a member of radio station KYA's basketball team.[328]

Zelmo Beaty, a 6'9" center for the Atlanta Hawks, became the second player to jump from the NBA to the ABA. Beaty's experience paralleled that of Rick Barry. When Beaty signed a contract with the ABA's Los Angeles Stars in 1969, the Hawks sued to enforce the reserve clause in his contract. Beaty, too, had to sit out a year. The Hawks obtained a ruling that precluded Beaty from playing or practicing with the Stars. For the year covered by the reserve clause in his contract with the Hawks, Beaty worked at a bank in Los Angeles. At night, when the Stars were playing at home, Beaty would attend the games and sit with the fans. After the reserve clause expired, Beaty joined the Stars for the 1970 season. By then,

---

[328] Terry Pluto, *Loose Balls: The Short, Wild Life Of The American Basketball Association As Told By The Players, Coaches, And Movers And Shakers Who Made It Happen* (New York: Simon & Schuster, 1991), 50.

the team had relocated to Utah. Beaty played for the Stars from 1970 to 1974, leading the team to the ABA title in 1971.[329]

In 1975, major league baseball owners lost their grip on the reserve system. Though Curt Flood had lost his case at every level of the judicial system, his legal challenge of the reserve clause inspired similar thinking among other players.[330] Three years after the Supreme Court's ruling, pitcher John Alexander "Andy" Messersmith was unable to reach agreement with the Los Angeles Dodgers on what he considered to be a fair salary for the 1975 season. In 1974, Messersmith started 39 games for the Dodgers and won 20 of them, with 13 complete games. Along the way, he pitched three shutouts, lost only six games and gave up only 2.59 runs every nine innings. His performance propelled the Dodgers to the World Series. Messersmith sought a substantial raise for 1975. The Dodgers balked. Messersmith refused to sign a contract with the Dodgers for 1975, and so the team invoked its option clause and unilaterally renewed his contract at a modest increase in salary.

After the 1975 season, Messersmith filed a grievance under the collective bargaining agreement between players and owners. In his grievance, Messersmith challenged the validity of the reserve system. Since he had not signed a contract for 1975, he believed he had escaped the clutches of the reserve system. The last contract he had signed was for the 1974 season. That contract gave the Dodgers the right "to renew this contract for the period of one year on the same terms." Under Messersmith's interpretation, the Dodgers' right of automatic renewal extended for only one

---

[329] Pluto, *Loose Balls: The Short, Wild Life Of The American Basketball Association As Told By The Players, Coaches, And Movers And Shakers Who Made It Happen*, 207-08.

[330] Flood died on January 20, 1997. At his death, he was hailed as a true champion. Donald Fehr, head of the Major League Baseball Players Association, said of Flood, "when it came time to take a stand at great personal risk and sacrifice, he stood firm for what he believed was right." Thomas Boswell, *Quite Simply, a Hero*, THE WASH. POST, January 22, 1997, D3.

year. Messersmith gave the Dodgers the one year to which they were entitled. After that one year, Messersmith believed that he was a free agent and
able to sign with any team. The Dodgers insisted otherwise. In their view,
every time they renewed Messersmith's contract, they also bought themselves another year of automatic renewal.

As required by baseball's collective bargaining agreement, Messersmith's
dispute was referred to an arbitrator. The arbitrator, Peter Seitz, examined
major league baseball rules, the collective bargaining agreement and the
standard player contract. In particular, Seitz reviewed the one-year option
clause in Messersmith's contract. Seitz believed the option clause extended
for one year only and not perpetually, as the owners argued. In a decision
issued in December 1975, Seitz ruled that teams could not legally reserve
the services of players, such as Messersmith, who were no longer under
contract. Seitz made it clear that the players could have entered into an
endless contract, if that was their intention, but found no evidence of such
an intent. The law, Seitz noted, frowned upon contracts that were
designed to be renewable by one party forever. Seitz declared Messersmith
to be a free agent.[331]

The Peter Seitz Principles of Free Agency

*1. The parties to an agreement are free to create an "endless contract"
but must do so by clear and explicit words.*
*2. The contract that Andy Messersmith signed in 1974 gave the Los
Angeles Dodgers the option of renewing his contract for one year.*
*3. A one-year option clause means exactly that—an option for one year
and not a perpetual right of renewal.*

---

[331] Seitz knew that the team owners would fire him as baseball's contract arbitrator
as soon as he issued his decision. The owners wasted no time. They fired Seitz within five
minutes after receiving word that he had declared Messersmith a free agent. Abrams,
Legal Bases: Baseball and the Law, 127.

Free of the reserve system, Messersmith exercised his free agent rights and, on April 10, 1976, agreed to play for the Atlanta Braves.[332] It was the sort of freedom for which Curt Flood had fought long and hard. Finding themselves on the short end of the Messersmith decision, the owners tried to implement a form of the reserve system through negotiations with the Players Association. The players would have none of it, however. Eventually, both players and owners agreed on a system that allowed the teams to reserve each player for six years before the players gained free agent status.[333]

---

[332] The Braves assigned Messersmith uniform number 17. When attempting to affix Messersmith's last name to the back of his uniform jersey, the Braves discovered that his name contained too many characters to fit neatly. Braves owner Ted Turner asked Messersmith if he had a nickname. Upon learning that Messersmith had no nickname, Turner assigned Messersmith the nickname "Channel." With "Channel" sewn to the back of his jersey, Messersmith became a walking advertisement for Turner's UHF television station, Channel 17, whenever he took the field. Messersmith's new "nickname" lasted for only a couple of games before Commissioner Bowie Kuhn ordered the Braves to remove "Channel" from the jersey.

[333] At nearly the same time that Seitz' ruling gave rise to free agency in professional baseball, players in the National Basketball Association gained free agency with a settlement in the case of *Robertson v. National Basketball Ass'n*, 389 F. Supp. 867 (S.D.N.Y. 1975). The case was initiated by Oscar Robertson, then president of the NBA Players Association and the only player in NBA history to average in double digits in points, rebounds and assists for an entire season. Robertson's historic season came in 1961-62 when he averaged 30.5 points, 12.5 rebounds and 11.4 assists per game. In 1970, under Robertson's leadership, the NBA players filed lawsuits against the league challenging the reserve clause contained in player contracts, the NBA's draft of college players and the league's merger with the American Basketball Association. In 1976, the players and the NBA agreed to a settlement that eliminated the reserve clause and allowed players to become free agents when their contracts ended. Under the free agency put into place, a player's former team was allowed the opportunity to match any offers the player received from other clubs.

In 1946, Judge Lloyd Black predicted that the Supreme Court would someday reverse its course and rule that professional baseball is subject to the antitrust laws. That day has yet to come. Nonetheless, the conditions that caused Ted Williams to look at ballplayers as "property" and Thurgood Marshall to see them as "enslaved" have changed dramatically. The decision in the Messersmith arbitration case opened the doors to a limited—but lasting—form of free agency. Due to the foundation established by Curt Flood and to Peter Seitz's ruling, major league ballplayers no longer have to worry about being forced into "peonage." And, in a belated tribute to Curt Flood, Congress made an historic incursion into baseball's antitrust exemption in 1998 when it passed legislation titled the "Curt Flood Act." The Curt Flood Act, signed into law by President Bill Clinton on October 27, 1998, revoked baseball's antitrust exemption with respect to labor relations matters. The Act did not change the effect of Holmes' *Federal Baseball* decision in other areas, such as franchise relocation, league expansion or the minor leagues. Nonetheless, with passage of the Curt Flood Act, it now seems clear that major league baseball players will have the option to pursue a lawsuit for antitrust violations in any future labor relations dispute.[334]

Baseball did not have to wait long for the next labor relations dispute to arise. Immediately after the end of the 2001 World Series between the New York Yankees and the Arizona Diamondbacks, baseball's owners boldly invited a confrontation with the players. In the waning hours of November 4, 2001, Diamondbacks slugger Luis Gonzalez had singled off the Yankees' Mariano Rivera in the seventh game of the Series to drive in the decisive run for Arizona in a dramatic come-from-behind, 3-2 victory. Two days later, baseball's owners voted to eliminate two major league teams. In announcing the decision, the owners declined to identify the two teams that would be eliminated, but speculation focused on the two

---

[334] *Antitrust Exemption Is Partly Revoked,* THE N.Y. TIMES, October 28, 1998, D7.

most unprofitable teams, the Montreal Expos and the Minnesota Twins. The Expos had ranked last among major league teams in revenue generated during the 2001 season, the Twins next to last. The decision was widely viewed as an affront to both players and fans, especially fans in Montreal and Minnesota.[335]

The owners' decision was unprecedented in the modern history of baseball. Dating back to 1961, when two expansion teams, the Los Angeles Angels and the Washington Senators, joined the American League, baseball's owners had moved steadily in the direction of franchise expansion. At the end of the 1960 season, there were sixteen major league teams in existence, eight in the American League and eight in the National League. Forty years later, there were 30 major league teams. If players and fans were comfortable with 30 teams, the owners were not. In the owners' view, the steady pace of expansion had placed teams in cities that were not capable of adequately supporting a baseball franchise. For this reason, the owners voted to reverse the trend toward expansion and, in the process, introduced a new term to baseball: "contraction." The stated objective of the contraction effort was to cut back to 28 teams.

In Washington, D.C., the contraction vote generated little sympathy among politicians, with the possible exception of President George W.

---

[335] There was speculation that, in the wake of the contraction announcement, the Expos and Twins would have little incentive to put out their best efforts on the playing field during the 2002 season. Ironically, the contraction announcement seemed to spur the two teams to unexpected heights. As of April 25, 2002, both teams had identical records of 13 wins and 8 losses, a won-lost percentage of .619. The Expos were the undisputed leaders of the National League's East Division, two games ahead of the New York Mets. The Twins were sitting comfortably in second place in the American League's Central Division, one game behind the Division-leading Chicago White Sox. Both the Expos and the Twins were playing particularly well in front of their hometown fans. The Expos had won 8 of their 12 home games. The Twins were even more impressive at home, winning 8 of 9 games at the Metrodome.

Bush. A week after the owners' vote, Senator Paul Wellstone, a Democrat from Minnesota, introduced a bill in the Senate titled the "Fairness in Antitrust in National Sports Act of 2001." In the House of Representatives, Rep. John Conyers, a Democrat from Michigan, introduced identical legislation. The proposed legislation would have made all aspects of baseball subject to the antitrust laws. In February 2002, in response to judicial rulings compelling the Twins to play the 2002 season in the Minnesota Metrodome, major league owners abandoned their plans for contraction, at least temporarily. In turn, Congress set aside the proposals to eliminate baseball's antitrust exemption. Nonetheless, Congressional reaction to the contraction vote served as a very visible reminder that Congress possesses the authority to rescind the antitrust exemption, even if the Supreme Court continues to avoid the issue.

Chapter 12

Baseball and the National Labor Relations Board

From 1940 to 1946, Ernie "Tiny" Bonham was a front-line pitcher for the New York Yankees. To his teammates, Bonham was as "grand a guy as any of us will meet in this game."[336] For one season, 1942, he also was one of the best pitchers any of his teammates would meet in the game. That season, Bonham was a bona fide superstar, leading the American League in complete games (22) and winning percentage (.808) and placing second in total wins (21) and earned run average (2.27). On a staff that included two future Hall-of-Famers, Lefty Gomez and Red Ruffing, Bonham was the best the Yankees had to offer. For one year, he was the ace.

By 1946, Tiny Bonham's star had dimmed. The newly acquired Allie Reynolds and Vic Raschi, the "Springfield Rifle," were set to emerge as pitching stars for the Yankees. The Yankees dealt Bonham, then 33 years old, to the Pittsburgh Pirates.[337] Bonham enjoyed three creditable years

---

[336] John Drebinger, *Defeat by Indians Reduces Yankee Lead Over Idle Red Sox to 2½ Games: Old Mates Mourn Bonham*, THE N.Y. TIMES, September 16, 1949, 39.

[337] In exchange for Bonham, the Pirates sent 28-year-old lefty Cookie Cuccurullo to the Yankees. In three years with the Pirates, 1943-1945, Cuccurullo had won three games and lost five. Those three years would be the extent of his career in the major leagues; he never appeared in a game for the Yankees.

with the Pirates. Though a chronic bad back and other injuries reduced him to the role of a spot starter, he won 24 games in his three seasons with the Pirates. On August 28, 1949, Bonham pitched the Pirates to an 8-2 victory over the Philadelphia Phillies. A week later, he was admitted to the hospital for an appendectomy. Complications set in after the surgery. Bonham never recovered. Less than three weeks after his triumph over the Phillies, Bonham passed away. He was 36 years old.[338]

Unwittingly, Bonham was the inspiration for the formation of the Major League Baseball Players Association, the labor association that represents major league ballplayers. With Bonham's death, his widow was entitled to receive the pension money that Bonham had earned as a ten-year veteran of the major leagues. However, there was not enough money in the ballplayers' pension account to pay his widow the money owed. To make up the shortfall, the commissioner of baseball, Happy Chandler, hurriedly sold the television and radio rights for the World Series and the all-star game to the Gillette Safety Razor Company for $1 million a year over the next six years.

Bonham's death prompted serious questions about the management of the pension fund. With the Gillette deal, Chandler deftly avoided a financial crisis. To the players' dismay, however, Chandler had vastly underestimated the value of the television and radio rights. Less than a year after acquiring the broadcast rights, Gillette transferred its rights to the Mutual Broadcasting System, which proceeded to sell the World Series and all-star game package to the National Broadcasting Company for $4 million per year.[339]

---

[338] Baseball records listed Bonham's playing weight as 215 pounds, but that did not take into account considerable extra poundage. Bonham's obituary in *The New York Times* noted that "the nickname 'Tiny' was the paradoxical reflection of his physical proportions." *'Tiny' Bonham Dies; Baseball Star, 36,* THE N.Y. TIMES, September 16, 1949, 27.

[339] Lee Lowenfish, *The Imperfect Diamond: A History of Baseball's Labor Wars* (New York: Da Capo Press, Inc., 1991), 183.

In the years immediately following Bonham's death, the players repeatedly demanded that baseball's owners provide an accounting of the pension funds. Their pleas fell on deaf ears; neither the owners nor Happy Chandler's successor, Ford Frick, felt compelled to honor the demands. Frick responded to the players' questions by flippantly assuring them that he was taking care of the fund.[340] When the owners continued to ignore the requests for an accounting, the players became increasingly militant. Finally, in December 1953, the players voted to form a union.[341] The players elected one-time teenage pitching phenom and future Hall-of-Famer Bob Feller to be the first president of the Major League Baseball Players Association.[342] Feller's perspective on the game made him an ideal, if somewhat cynical, union leader. A reflective man, he once commented that "baseball was made for kids, and grown-ups only screw it up."[343]

Bob Feller's Principle of the Purpose of Baseball

Baseball was made for kids.

Long before the formation of the Major League Baseball Players Association, major league players had frequently voiced concerns about labor issues. Baseball owners were notoriously heavy-handed in their dealings with players. In 1911,

---

[340] Lowenfish, *The Imperfect Diamond: A History of Baseball's Labor Wars*, 183.

[341] Lowenfish, *The Imperfect Diamond: A History of Baseball's Labor Wars*, 188.

[342] In addition to being one of the dominant stars in the major leagues during the post-World War II era, Feller was well-respected by players, owners and fans alike. He had attained the status of a national hero even while in high school. In the 1930s, Feller's schoolboy pitching heroics had gained such attention that his high school graduation was broadcast live on national radio. Feller was inducted into the U.S. Navy shortly after the Japanese attack on Pearl Harbor in December 1941. His induction ceremony was also carried on national radio.

[343] John Helyar, *Lords of the Realm: The Real History of Baseball* (New York: Ballantine Books, 1994), preface.

Washington Senator pitching ace Walter Johnson, widely regarded as both a consummate gentleman and a voice of reason, had written an article entitled, "Baseball Slavery: The Great American Principle of Dog Eat Dog."[344] Johnson wrote that baseball represented "the direct application of the great intelligent American business principle of dog eat dog…. The employer tries to starve out the laborer, and the laborer tries to ruin the employer's business. They quarrel over a bone and rend each other like coyotes."[345]

> *Walter Johnson's Principle of "Dog Eat Dog"*
>
> *The employer tries to starve out the laborer, and the laborer tries to ruin the employer's business.*

A year after the appearance of Johnson's article, players staged the first labor strike in baseball history. In a game in New York, fans had taken to heckling the visiting Detroit Tigers. The fans directed their most abusive language at Tigers star Ty Cobb. In the fourth inning, the cantankerous Cobb jumped into the stands and attacked the loudest fan. After the incident, Ban Johnson, who as a member of the three-person "National Commission" exercised near absolute power over the game, suspended Cobb for ten days. The Tiger players announced they would go on strike unless Johnson reinstated Cobb. Johnson refused to back down and the Tigers, led by infielder Jim Delahanty, walked out of a scheduled game against the Philadelphia Athletics. The Tigers hastily recruited replacement players, hiring, it was said, "any ballplayer who could stop a grapefruit from rolling uphill."[346] The replacement players lost to the Athletics by a score of 24 to 2. Just as quickly, the strike ended. When Ban Johnson

---

[344] Lowenfish, *The Imperfect Diamond: A History of Baseball's Labor Wars*, 75.

[345] *Baseball* magazine, July 1911.

[346] Lowenfish, *The Imperfect Diamond: A History of Baseball's Labor Wars*, 77.

threatened to expel the striking players from baseball, Cobb urged his teammates to go back to work. Cobb sat out his suspension and was reinstated. The incident, however, left its mark on the players. Jim Delahanty believed the episode demonstrated that there was a compelling need for a ballplayers' association. "It is about time we got together and formed a union," Delahanty told reporters.[347]

The Jim Delahanty Principle of the Unionization of Labor

When our job security is threatened by the unilateral actions of baseball management, it's time to get together and form a union.

There would be no significant union of the players during Delahanty's lifetime.[348] However, throughout the fifty-year period that followed the Tigers' one-game strike of 1912, the "dog-eat-dog" attitude described by Walter Johnson produced periodic owner-player skirmishes. In 1946, Robert Murphy, a Harvard-trained labor organizer, toured the major league baseball spring training camps in Florida. He hoped to organize the players. A graduate of Northeastern University Law School in Boston, Murphy knew ballplayers who lived in the Boston area. He was aware that run-of-the-mill big leaguers earned less than $3,500. Other injustices caught his attention. He discovered that major league owners did not pay ballplayers for the time they spent in spring training. Murphy was particularly sympathetic to ballplayers such as slugger Jimmie Foxx, who spent twenty years in the major leagues and, at his retirement, had little in savings to show for it.[349]

---

[347] Lowenfish, *The Imperfect Diamond: A History of Baseball's Labor Wars*, 78.

[348] Ironically, Delahanty died in October 1953, just two months before the players voted to form the Major League Baseball Players Association.

[349] Lowenfish, *The Imperfect Diamond: A History of Baseball's Labor Wars*, 140.

In April 1946, Murphy formally established the "American Baseball Guild" as a labor organization. He had an aggressive agenda, vowing to bring "a square deal to the players, the men who make possible big dividends and high salaries for stockholders and club executives."[350] Murphy called for a minimum player salary of $6,500, impartial arbitration of salary disputes and, when a player was sold, payment of 50 percent of the sale price to the player. He sent a letter to every major leaguer asking the players to support the Baseball Guild. Murphy focused his initial efforts on organizing the Pittsburgh Pirates. Pittsburgh's steel mills were hotbeds of union activity, and Murphy thought he would find a cordial audience in the city. He sent a letter to the Pirates' owners requesting an election to see if the ballplayers wanted the Baseball Guild to serve as their representative for collective bargaining. The owners refused, instead suggesting a meeting with Murphy after the 1946 season had ended. From the owners' perspective, the purpose of the proposed meeting would be to discuss whether a labor union was even appropriate for baseball. The owners were being both arrogant and cagey; conducting effective labor discussions with the players after the season had ended would be impossible once the players left the city for their off-season homes and jobs. Murphy set a deadline of June 5, 1946 for the Pirates to act on his request for a player vote. Not surprisingly, with the deadline only hours away, the Pittsburgh owners announced that they needed more time to look at the details of Murphy's request.

> *The Robert Murphy Principle of the Economic Contribution of the Players*
>
> *It is the ballplayers who make possible big dividends and high salaries for stockholders and club executives.*

---

[350] Lowenfish, *The Imperfect Diamond: A History of Baseball's Labor Wars,* 141.

The National League schedule for June 5, 1946 pitted the Pirates against the Brooklyn Dodgers in a night game at Pittsburgh's Forbes Field. When the players learned that the owners had no intention of complying with Murphy's deadline, most wanted to strike—beginning with that night's game. Murphy urged restraint. He persuaded the players to play the game, in large part because the fans had already filed into Forbes Field. The game went on as scheduled but only after a dramatic eleventh-hour confrontation in the Pittsburgh dressing room. The Pirates took pre-game batting practice at 6:30 p.m. and then retreated to their clubhouse. Murphy informed team officials that the players would not play unless the Pirates' president and chief owner, William Benswanger, met with the players. At 7:45 p.m., Benswanger appeared. It was his first visit to the clubhouse in twelve years.[351] He spoke with the players, and the game went on at its scheduled 8:30 p.m. starting time.[352]

To keep the pressure on the owners, Murphy set a new strike deadline for June 7, two days later. The Pirates were scheduled to play the New York Giants. The possibility of a strike was real. Pirates manager Frankie Frisch made plans to field a lineup of replacement players. His "contingency" lineup featured Frisch himself, then forty-eight years old, at second base and seventy-two-year-old coach Honus Wagner at shortstop. Two hours before game time, Benswanger again met with the players in the clubhouse. This time Murphy was outmatched; security guards made it impossible for him to enter the clubhouse. By prior agreement, the players

---

[351] *Guild Threatens Strike by Pirates: No Giants Game Tomorrow Night Unless Club Agrees to Bargaining Election*, THE N.Y. TIMES, June 6, 1946, 26.

[352] The Pirates lost to the Dodgers 5-3, as Dodger pitchers Kirby Higbe and Rube Melton held the Pirates to six hits. It was Melton's first appearance for the Dodgers after returning from service with the Army in Korea. The crowd of 26,206 "spent a great part of the evening booing the Bucs when they weren't cheering a couple of good Brooklyn plays." Roscoe McGowen, *Dodgers Vanquish Pirates by 5-3 As Higbe and Melton Excel in Box*, THE N.Y. TIMES, June 6, 1946, 26.

planned to skip the game only if two-thirds of the team supported a strike. Counting the team's coaches and trainers, there were 36 individuals eligible to vote; 24 votes were needed for a strike. When the final tally was taken, 20 voted in favor of striking, sixteen against. There would be no strike. Clearly, some of the players feared losing their jobs if they went out on strike. Others were persuaded by the strenuous anti-union comments of the team leaders, pitcher Truett "Rip" Sewell and infielder Jimmy Brown. Not coincidentally, Sewell and Brown were the only members of the team who earned more than $10,000 a year. Sewell was quoted as saying, "I'd hate to see baseball unionized, as a player has no limit on what he can earn in this game."[353]

The Rip Sewell Principle of the Unlimited Earning Power of Ballplayers

A player has no limit on what he can earn in this game.

Murphy met with no more success in other major league cities. Quickly, the team owners realized that the best way to stave off unionization was to improve the lot of the players. In July 1946, the owners convened a special reform committee. They invited player representatives to express their concerns to the committee. Among other things, the players asked for the establishment of a minimum salary level, elimination of daytime doubleheaders after night games and payments for participation in spring training. The owners found these concessions preferable to the possibility of a union. Before the 1946 season ended, the owners announced that they were instituting a minimum player salary of $5,500. And, for the first time, team owners agreed to pay spring training expenses. Each player would receive $25 per week during spring training. With a tip of their caps to Robert Murphy, the players referred to the spring training expense

---

[353] Lowenfish, *The Imperfect Diamond: A History of Baseball's Labor Wars,* 147.

allotments as "Murphy Money." Additionally, the owners announced their intention to create a pension fund—the same fund that, three years later, was supposed to provide support for Tiny Bonham's widow. The pension plan was to be funded by the owners with contributions from the players. Under the plan, all players who had spent more than five full years in the major leagues would be eligible for pension payments at the age of 50. With the announcement of these changes, the owners thwarted Robert Murphy's attempt at unionization.

Murphy himself was able to derive small consolation from the knowledge that team owners never considered any meaningful improvements in player conditions "until the American Baseball Guild threatened the very foundation—sometimes rotten—of their baseball empire."[354] Some of the changes did not last long. Even before the 1946 season had ended, the owners announced they were scaling back the minimum salary to $5,000. Within a year, however, Murphy was no longer a presence in major league baseball. He left with an understated assessment of the players' gains. "The players have been offered an apple," he said, "but they could have had an orchard."[355]

> ## *The Robert Murphy Principle of the Effects of Unionization*
>
> *By forming a united labor organization, players can turn apples into an orchard.*

The concept of labor unions did not come easily in the United States. It took a tragic circumstance—the Great Depression of the 1930s—before labor unions would gain acceptance. Until the Depression, policies at both the state and federal levels were antagonistic to unions. Workers who

---

[354] Lowenfish, *The Imperfect Diamond: A History of Baseball's Labor Wars,* 150.

[355] Lowenfish, *The Imperfect Diamond: A History of Baseball's Labor Wars,* 151.

tried to strike faced the threat of an injunction issued by federal courts. Employers clearly held the upper hand, wielding near dictatorial control over employees. In 1930, Congress responded to the effects of the Depression by passing the Norris-LaGuardia Act. This law removed the threat of federal injunctions against workers who engaged in peaceful strikes. Five years later, Congress passed the National Labor Relations Act of 1935, also known as the Wagner Act. The Wagner Act recognized the right of workers to organize into unions. It also imposed an obligation upon employers to negotiate with the unions in good faith. Congress hoped that the Act would be a cure for the lingering effects of the Depression. Unions offered the prospect of greater bargaining power for workers and, in turn, increased wages. The Wagner Act also created a new administrative agency, the National Labor Relations Board, otherwise known as the NLRB. The NLRB was empowered to hear complaints from workers about any instances of unfair labor practices by management. The NLRB also had the authority to issue orders or impose sanctions to correct unfair practices. The Wagner Act, together with changes introduced later by the 1947 Taft-Hartley Amendments and the Landrum-Griffin Act, form the essence of the National Labor Relations Act.

Under the National Labor Relations Act, workers have the right to engage in peaceful strikes. The National Labor Relations Board has the responsibility of ruling on labor disputes that allege violations of federal labor law, but only for companies that are engaged in interstate commerce.[356] The National Labor Relations Act requires management and

---

[356] There are obvious similarities between federal antitrust laws and the National Labor Relations Act. In each case, Congress' authority to adopt laws is based on the "commerce clause" in Article I, Section 8, of the U.S. Constitution. The commerce clause provides that Congress shall have the power to regulate commerce among the states. The framers of the Constitution intended that commerce which was conducted entirely within the boundaries of a single state would be regulated by the state. When Justice Holmes found, in the *Federal Baseball* decision, that professional baseball was engaged in intrastate, not interstate, commerce, it set in motion baseball's storied exemption from federal antitrust law.

6666666666

666666

666

labor to negotiate in good faith on issues involving the terms and conditions of employment. The "terms and conditions" of employment include all subjects relating to employee hours, wages and related matters. Management and labor may also negotiate other issues not involving the terms and conditions of employment. However, the law does not compel the parties to negotiate on these other issues.

After baseball players established the Major League Baseball Players Association in 1953, the question arose as to whether the National Labor Relations Board could certify the association as the representative of the players. When Congress passed the Wagner Act in 1935, it did so under the authority of its constitutional power to regulate commerce between the states. Clearly, Congress had intended—and the Constitution required—that the NLRB, as an agency of the federal government, would assert authority only over companies that were engaged in interstate commerce. One plausible view was that the NLRB lacked jurisdiction over major league baseball because, at least for purposes of Justice Holmes' *Federal Baseball* decision, baseball was not engaged in interstate commerce.

> *The National Labor Relations Act's Principles of Workers' Rights*
>
> *1. Workers have the right to organize into unions.*
> *2. Employers must negotiate with labor unions, in good faith, regarding hours, wages and other terms and conditions of employment.*
> *3. Workers have the right to engage in peaceful strikes.*

The National Labor Relations Board had recognized the National Basketball Players Association as the collective bargaining unit for NBA players in 1962. Five years later, the NLRB recognized the National Football League Players Association as the competitive bargaining unit for players in the National Football League and the National Hockey League Players Association as the competitive bargaining unit for professional hockey players.[357] Even with the recognition of the players' unions in basketball, football and hockey, it was not clear, in view of the *Federal Baseball* decision, whether the NLRB could recognize the Major League Baseball Players Association. If the NLRB could not recognize a union of professional baseball players, it would also be powerless to rule on any allegations of unfair labor practices raised by the players.[358] The issue that would later prove to be a thorn in Curt Flood's side also posed a formidable hurdle to NLRB recognition of the Major League Baseball Players Association.

In 1969, the National Labor Relations Board had occasion to tackle, head-on, the issue of baseball and interstate commerce. The opportunity arose when the umpires working in the American League sought to organize for the purpose of bargaining collectively with the League over the terms and conditions of their employment.[359] The umpires petitioned the NLRB for recognition. The American League opposed the umpires' petition, arguing that the NLRB had no authority over major league baseball. The American League based its argument squarely on the principle established in the *Federal Baseball* decision. There was much at stake. Clearly, if baseball games did not involve interstate commerce, then all of the participants—owners, players and umpires—would be affected in the same way. If the NLRB found that it was powerless to rule on disputes involving owners and umpires, it would also be powerless to act on owner-player disputes. Conversely, if the NLRB decided that it did have jurisdiction over labor issues involving owners and umpires, it would also have authority over owner-player issues.

Presented with a situation in which it had clear authority over professional basketball, football and hockey, the NLRB found that it would defy

---

[357] George W. Schubert, Rodney K. Smith and Jesse C. Trentadue, *Sports Law* (St. Paul, MN: West Publishing Co., 1986), 154.

[358] Roger I. Abrams, *Legal Bases: Baseball and the Law* (Philadelphia, PA: Temple University Press, 1998), 76.

[359] Abrams, *Legal Bases: Baseball and the Law,* 77.

logic if it somehow lacked authority over professional baseball. Viewed another way, the NLRB reasoned that if basketball, football and hockey games involved interstate commerce, then baseball games must involve interstate commerce as well. The NLRB also took note of the reality of the situation: baseball was an industry in which millions of dollars in goods and services crossed state lines.[360] In a decision that represented a major victory for the umpires and established a firm foundation for later recognition of the players' union, the NLRB ruled that it had jurisdiction over baseball. Shortly thereafter, in an election supervised by NLRB employees, the umpires voted to be unionized. The NLRB then certified the union as the exclusive bargaining representative for all American League umpires.

From that point on, there was no question that the NLRB had jurisdiction over owner-player disputes. Over the years since the NLRB first recognized the umpires' union, it has steadily asserted its jurisdiction over employer-worker disputes in the baseball industry. While the National Labor Relations Act recognizes the right of workers to strike in an effort to obtain more equitable pay and working conditions, it also recognizes the right of employers to carry on their businesses. In an important 1938 case interpreting the Wagner Act, *National Labor Relations Board v. Mackay Radio & Telegraph*, the Supreme Court ruled that employers have the right to replace striking employees with other workers. The Court stated, "It is not an unfair labor practice to replace the striking employees with others in an effort to carry on the business."[361]

For baseball players, the impact of the *Mackay Radio & Telegraph* decision hit home when the Major League Baseball Players Association went on strike in August 1994. At issue was the owners' desire to control their rapidly rising salary costs. The owners insisted on a "salary cap," which would impose a ceiling on how much money a team could spend on its player payroll. The Players Association responded with a proposal for a "luxury

---

[360] Abrams, *Legal Bases: Baseball and the Law*, 78.

[361] *NLRB v. Mackay Radio & Telegraph*, 304 U.S. 333 (1938).

tax," under which owners who dramatically exceeded the average payroll for all major league teams would have to pay a tax that would be distributed to less affluent teams. The intent of the luxury tax was to achieve some degree of balance in the revenue taken in by the various teams.

> *The National Labor Relations Board's Principle of Interstate Commerce*
>
> *When an industry such as baseball results in millions of dollars in goods and services crossing the boundaries between the states, that industry is engaged in interstate commerce.*

The dispute proved contentious. When no agreement seemed imminent, the owners canceled the 1994 World Series. When the time for spring training rolled around in 1995, the two sides were still far apart. The owners made plans to open the season with replacement players, as they were permitted to do under *Mackay Radio & Telegraph*. The strike was resolved just prior to the scheduled opening day when U.S. District Judge Sonia Maria Sotomayor, acting at the request of the National Labor Relations Board, ruled that the owners had committed unfair labor practices. Judge Sotomayor ordered the owners and players back to the bargaining table to negotiate in good faith. Days later, the impasse was resolved. The 1995 season began on April 26, with only three weeks of the new season having been lost.

> *The Mackay Radio & Telegraph Principle of Replacement Workers*
>
> *Under the National Labor Relations Act, when a company's workers have gone out on strike, the employer has the right to hire replacement workers to carry on the company's business.*

Today, the baseball players' union, which took its first tentative steps shortly after Tiny Bonham died, has become a force in baseball. The union generates millions of dollars in revenues for players from lucrative licensing agreements. More importantly, with timely assists from both the NLRB and Judge Sotomayor, the union has steadily gained important rights for the players through the collective bargaining process.

In November 2001, when baseball's owners voted in favor of "contracting" two major league teams, it set the stage for yet another confrontation between players and owners. Contraction threatened to reduce the number of baseball player jobs at the major league level by 50 and the number of minor league jobs by approximately 100. In the players' view, the collective bargaining agreement between players and owners required the owners to negotiate the contraction issue—and specifically the elimination of jobs—with the union. Speaking for the players, pitcher Rick Helling, the union's American League representative, said, "from our position, contraction affects the players, and anything that affects the players has to be negotiated."[362] Not surprisingly, the owners maintained they had a right to contract teams without consulting with the union. Further complicating the proceedings was the fact that baseball's collective bargaining agreement had expired at midnight on November 7th, one day after the owners voted to contract.

The owners viewed contraction simply as an effort to control rising costs, particularly player salaries. Imbedded in the contraction issue, however, were several significant legal questions, not the least of which involved the fate of the players on the teams to be eliminated. Under the owners' plan, the teams that remained in existence after contraction would conduct a dispersal draft to assign players from the contracted teams to other ballclubs. From the players' perspective, the owners had moved much too quickly. Donald Fehr, chief of the players' union, criticized the owners for reaching the decision "unilaterally, without any attempt to negotiate with the players, apparently without any serious consideration

---

[362] Dave Sheinin, *Union Challenges Contraction Bid*, THE WASH. POST, December 5, 2001, D3.

of other options, including relocation, and seemingly with little concern for the interests of the fans." Fehr contended that the decision was "inconsistent with the law, our contract and perhaps, most important, the long-term welfare of the sport."[363] On November 8, the union filed a grievance claiming that the decision to implement contraction violated baseball's labor contract. The grievance was to be decided by baseball's permanent arbitrator.[364]

The owners planned on implementing contraction before the start of the 2002 season. The players were skeptical. Hearings on the players' grievance began on December 5. If the union's arguments proved successful, contraction would be all but impossible before the start of play in 2002. If the owners prevailed in the arbitration hearings, the players planned to appeal the arbitrator's decision to the NLRB. However, the outcome of such an appeal was uncertain. In cases submitted to the National Labor Relations Board, the Board's general counsel has the authority to select those cases in which the Board will actually consider the appeals. Historically, the players have fared well at the NLRB when the general counsel was appointed by Democratic administrations. However, if the players appealed the contraction issue, the appeal would be reviewed by an appointee of Republican President George W. Bush—a fact which did not bode well for the players.[365]

Like so many labor issues that have arisen in baseball over the years, the contraction issue was sure to spark plenty of controversy. With all its implications for players, fans and particularly the cities of Montreal and

---

[363] Bill Shaikin, *Strike 2? Major Leagues Plan to Cut Pair of Teams*, L.A. TIMES, November 7, 2001, 1.

[364] Bill Shaikin, *Players' Union Files Grievance*, L.A. TIMES, November 9, 2001, 1.

[365] Sheinin, *Union Challenges Contraction Bid*, THE WASH. POST, December 5, 2001, D3.

Minneapolis-St. Paul, contraction was the latest in a lengthy history of player-owner confrontations that date back to the suspension of Ty Cobb in 1912. Ultimately, NLRB involvement in the contraction issue was rendered unnecessary, at least for the time being, when baseball Commissioner Bud Selig announced in February 2002 that Major League Baseball would not contract any teams for the 2002 season.

Chapter 13

Relocation and Contraction of Professional Sports Franchises

Twenty-four-year-old righthander Art Ditmar started and won the Philadelphia Athletics' last game of the 1954 season. The win came against the New York Yankees at Yankee Stadium. Ditmar faced a Yankee lineup that manager Casey Stengel had purposely juggled to send as many big bats to the plate as possible. Stengel put his power-hitting center fielder Mickey Mantle at shortstop, cleanup hitter Yogi Berra at third base, and first baseman Bill "Moose" Skowron at second. Ditmar's

Athletics Hammer 'Power-Laden' Yankees, 8-6; In Season Finale, Ditmar Gains First Victory

NEW YORK, N.Y.   SEPTEMBER 26, 1954

PHILADELPHIA (AL)	AB	R	H	O	E
Suder, 2b, 3b	4	1	2	1	0
DeMaestri, 3b	2	0	1	0	0
Power, 1b ...	5	1	1	10	0
dLimmer, 1b .	1	0	1	1	0
Finigan, 3b .	1	0	1	0	0
Joost, 2b	4	1	3	1	0
Zernial, lf	5	1	1	0	0
Renna, rf ...	4	0	1	5	0
Wilson, cf	5	0	1	1	0
Littrell, ss	3	2	1	3	0
Astroth, c	5	2	2	4	0
Ditmar, p	2	0	1	0	1
Fricano, p	1	0	0	1	0
Totals	42	8	16	27	1

NEW YORK (AL)	AB	R	H	O	E
Bauer, rf...	0	0	0	1	0
Slaughter, rf .	1	0	1	0	0
Robinson, 1b	3	0	1	6	0
aCollins, 1b	1	0	0	3	0
Mantle, ss .	2	1	1	4	0
Berra, 3b	5	0	0	1	0
Noren, cf	5	1	1	0	0
Skowron, 2b	5	2	3	2	1
Cerv, lf	5	1	2	1	0
Berberet, c ...	3	1	1	8	0
Byrne. p	2	0	1	0	1
Konstanty, p ..	0	0	0	0	0
bLeja	1	0	0	0	0
Morgan	0	0	0	0	0
cMcDougald	1	0	0	0	0
Grim	0	0	0	0	0
Totals ..	34	6	11	27	2

a—Ran for Robinson in fourth.   c—Grounded out for Morgan in seventh.
b—Popped up for Konstanty in sixth.   d—Singled for Power in ninth.

PHILADELPHIA ....020 031 200—8
NEW YORK ....021 002 100—6

Pitchers	IP	H	R	ER	BB	SO
Ditmar (Winner, 1-4)	5⅓	7	5	4	8	3
Fricano	3⅔	4	1	1	1	1
Byrne (Loser, 3-2)	5	9	5	5	3	4
Konstanty	1	1	1	1	2	0
Morgan	1	3	2	2	0	1
Grim	2	3	0	0	1	1

U—Soar, Flaherty, Grieve and Honochick. T—2:41. Atttendance—11,670.

effort was not pretty, but it was effective. He yielded four earned runs and seven hits in $5^1/_3$ innings and then turned the game over to reliever Marion Fricano, who preserved the victory. It was the first win of Ditmar's career. It was also the last game in the history of the Philadelphia Athletics. The next season, Ditmar and his teammates found themselves playing in Kansas City.

The Athletics' move to Kansas City came despite assurances from owner Roy Mack, the son of Connie Mack, that the team would not leave Philadelphia. "We'd never leave Philadelphia," Mack had told his fellow owners. Mack's pious words were too much for Bill Veeck, maverick owner of the St. Louis Browns. Veeck retorted that the Athletics would most assuredly be the next franchise "to take wing." "Oh, no," Mack replied. "No. Never."[366] Technically, Mack didn't leave Philadelphia. He and his brother simply sold the team to Chicago real estate mogul Arnold Johnson, who relocated the A's to Kansas City in time for the start of the 1955 season. And, technically, Veeck was wrong: the Athletics were not the next team "to take wing." That distinction fell to Veeck's beloved Browns. Financially distressed and having burned too many bridges with his fellow owners, Veeck sold the team to a Baltimore syndicate after the 1953 season. The new owners promptly relocated the team to Baltimore.

Veeck himself had hoped to relocate the St. Louis Browns to Baltimore in time for the start of the 1953 season. In December 1952, he notified his fellow owners of his interest in relocating the team. To gain approval for the move, Veeck needed favorable votes from a three-fourths majority of the American League owners. A vote was scheduled for March 1953. With eight teams in the American League at the time, Veeck required the votes from five owners in addition to his own vote. When the vote was taken, the owners rebuffed Veeck's bid to move, with six votes opposed and two in favor. The outcome of the vote left Veeck in shock. Citing the antitrust

[366] Bill Veeck with Ed Linn, *Veeck As In Wreck* (Chicago: The University of Chicago Press, 2001), 285.

laws, his lawyers advised him that it was illegal for a group of individuals to get together to cause injury or loss to another person.

Veeck's lawyers forgot one thing. They failed to take into account the effect of the Supreme Court's decision in the *Federal Baseball Club of Baltimore* case, written 30 years earlier by Justice Oliver Wendell Holmes.[367] With that case as support, the American League owners could seemingly band together anytime they wanted to cause financial harm to a fellow owner.

Irrespective of the sport, the owners of professional teams have a natural incentive to control the timing and location of franchise changes. In the 1950s, baseball owners didn't want Bill Veeck to relocate his Browns to Baltimore, apparently out of distaste for Veeck's maverick inclinations. In the 1990s, baseball owners refused to allow the Pittsburgh Pirates to relocate to Washington, D.C., this time out of deference to Orioles' owner Peter Angelos.[368] In *Los Angeles Memorial Coliseum v. National Football League*, a federal court of appeals ruled that the National Football League violated antitrust laws when it refused to allow Al Davis and his Oakland Raiders to play in Los Angeles.[369] At the time, NFL rules required the approval of three-fourths of the member teams before a team could move to a new city. It was abundantly clear that the NFL owners did not want Davis in Los Angeles. They turned down his relocation bid by a vote of 22-0, with five owners abstaining. Davis was not the only disappointed party. The Los Angeles Coliseum had hoped to host the Raiders and, in fact, had signed an agreement with Davis for the 1980 season. The Coliseum sued the League and its member teams. In 1982, a federal district court ruled

[367] *Federal Baseball Club of Baltimore, Inc. v. National League of Professional Baseball Clubs, et al.*, 259 U.S. 200 (1922).

[368] Jeffrey Gordon, *Baseball's Antitrust Exemption and Franchise Relocation: Can A Team Move?*, FORDHAM URBAN LAW JOURNAL, XXVI (1999), 1201, 1248.

[369] *Los Angeles Memorial Coliseum v. National Football League*, 726 F.2d 1381 (1984).

that the League could not interfere with the Raiders' proposed relocation. The Raiders were awarded $11.55 million in damages. The Los Angeles Coliseum was awarded another $4.86 million. On appeal, the U.S. Court of Appeals for the Ninth Circuit, based in San Francisco, affirmed the lower court ruling. In its decision, the court advised the NFL's owners that if they had problems with the dictates of the antitrust laws, they should look to Congress, not the courts, for a solution.

The owners of major league baseball teams are in an enviable position. They already have a "solution" under the law. They can restrict franchise relocations and get away with it. As the *Los Angeles Memorial Coliseum* decision makes clear, professional football owners are obligated to avoid actions that violate the federal antitrust laws, and interference with the movement of franchises does violate those laws. The same holds true for other professional sports—every sport but baseball. In various decisions, the courts have applied the antitrust laws to hockey, tennis, golf, horse racing and bowling. The cumulative effect of these decisions leaves no doubt that the antitrust exemption granted to baseball by Justice Holmes is an anomaly that reaches to no other major professional sport.

In 1992, two Pennsylvania residents, Vincent Piazza and Vincent Tirendi, signed a letter of intent to buy the San Francisco Giants for $115 million. Piazza and Tirendi hoped to move the Giants to St. Petersburg, Florida. Baseball's owners considered the proposed relocation and voted against it. A lawsuit soon followed. In *Piazza v. Major League Baseball*, a federal district court held that baseball's antitrust exemption applies only to baseball's player reserve system and not to franchise relocations.[370] The *Piazza* decision is in conflict with a host of other decisions that take a much broader reading of the antitrust exemption. As an example, when the Milwaukee Braves left Wisconsin after the 1965 season and relocated to Atlanta, the State of Wisconsin sued the team. The lawsuit alleged that

---

[370] *Piazza v. Major League Baseball*, 831 F.Supp. 420 (E.D. Penn. 1993).

the Braves and baseball's owners had unfairly restrained trade and commerce. The allegations were not far wrong. In fact, the Braves and the American League had agreed to refrain from playing any future exhibition games in Milwaukee. The court took note of the agreement and construed it as a restraint of trade. Nonetheless, the court said it was powerless to provide a remedy because baseball is exempt from the antitrust laws.[371]

On March 28, 1984, Robert Irsay, owner of the NFL's Baltimore Colts, quickly and quietly moved his team to Indianapolis. In the dark of night, the Mayflower Moving Company backed its vans up to the Colts' headquarters in Baltimore and loaded all of the team's possessions, football equipment as well as office furnishings, onto the trucks. By morning, the Colts were gone. The City of Baltimore immediately filed an action in court to exercise its powers of eminent domain over the football franchise. If successful, the lawsuit would have enabled the city to "condemn" the Colts franchise and thereby keep the team in Baltimore. As in any condemnation proceeding, the city would have had to pay Irsay for the value of the "property" being condemned. The theory underlying the lawsuit may have been valid, but it was a day late. "It is axiomatic," the reviewing court stated, "that the [city's] power to condemn property extends only as far as its borders and that the property to be taken must be within the … jurisdictional boundaries." Unfortunately for the City of Baltimore, the Colts were long gone. As Bill Veeck would have put it, they had "taken wing." "The inescapable conclusion," the court said, "is that the franchise is beyond the jurisdictional reach of Baltimore City."[372]

Under the prevailing law, professional sports teams are free to "take wing" whenever they choose—except in baseball. In baseball, the *Piazza* decision notwithstanding, an owner who seeks to relocate his or her team

---

[371] *Wisconsin v. Milwaukee Braves Inc.*, 144 N.W.2d 1, cert. denied, 385 U.S. 900 (1966).

[372] *Mayor and City of Baltimore v. Baltimore Football Club Inc.*, 624 F.Supp. 278 (D.Md. 1985).

to a different city must still obtain approval from fellow owners. "Taking wing" is always possible, but the process of relocation involves significantly more planning, deliberation and cajoling than in other sports. For baseball owners, fleeing a city abruptly in the middle of night is not an option.

The November 6, 2001 decision by major league baseball owners to eliminate two major league teams through "contraction" stimulated legal action on several fronts. Though the owners did not identify the teams to be eliminated, speculation focused on the Montreal Expos and the Minnesota Twins as the likely targets. The Expos and Twins were among the franchises hit hardest by small-market economics. For teams in any market, the primary sources of local revenue are the rights from TV and radio broadcasts and income from ticket sales, luxury suite rentals, concessions and parking. Lacking lucrative fees for broadcast rights, both the Expos and Twins were particularly hamstrung by playing in older ballparks that did not have a large number of luxury suites.

Shortly after the owners announced their plans for contraction, the Major League Baseball Players Association filed a grievance. The union contended that the owners were required by law to consult with the players before voting on contraction. The U.S. Congress got involved as well. Proposals were introduced in both the House and Senate to strip baseball of its antitrust exemption. Congressman John Conyers, the ranking Democrat on the House Judiciary Committee, was particularly critical of baseball's owners. "Any time 30 of the wealthiest and most influential individuals get together behind closed doors and agree to reduce output, that cannot be a good thing for anyone but the monopolists," said Conyers.[373]

The contraction controversy presented professional sports with a range of legal issues never before encountered. It soon became clear that the issues would not be resolved quickly. In Minnesota, the Metropolitan

---

[373] Bill Shaikin, *Players' Union Files Grievance*, L.A. TIMES, November 9, 2001, 1.

Sports Facilities Commission filed a lawsuit to compel the Twins to honor their lease to play in Minnesota's Metrodome in 2002.[374] On November 16, 2001, the Hennepin County District Court issued an injunction in favor of the Metropolitan Sports Facilities Commission. Under the terms of the injunction, the Twins were required to play the 2002 season in the Metrodome.[375] Baseball's owners immediately appealed the decision. On December 6, 2001, the House of Representatives Judiciary Committee held hearings on the proposal to eliminate baseball's antitrust exemption. Bud Selig, the Commissioner of Major League Baseball, and former professional wrestler Jesse Ventura, the Governor of Minnesota, were called to testify before the Committee. Selig staunchly defended the antitrust exemption. To support his arguments, he raised the specter of the Colts' hasty middle-of-the-night departure from Baltimore. If baseball is subjected to the antitrust laws, Selig testified, there would be no way to prevent teams from leaving in the night. Ventura, seated next to Selig, quickly responded, "what is the difference between leaving in the night and being contracted?"

From a legal perspective, there is a big difference. With the antitrust exemption in place, a major league baseball team cannot abandon its home city in the middle of the night. Assuming that the labor and stadium issues could be resolved, however, major league owners would be free to "contract" one or more teams at will. From a practical perspective, the answer to Jesse Ventura's question is more simple. When a team leaves in the middle of the night, it closes its doors in one city but at least it reopens the doors in another locale. But if the major league owners were to contract a team, the team would close its doors—and those doors

---

[374] Bill Shaikin, *Strike 2? Major Leagues Plan to Cut Pair of Teams*, L.A. TIMES, November 7, 2001, 1.

[375] Mark Asher, *Setback for Contraction: Courts' Rulings Strain Timetable for '02 Season*, THE WASH. POST, December 1, 2001, D5.

would stay shut permanently. Or, as sportswriter Tom Boswell suggested, with contraction, there are "no telltale tire tracks."[376]

On January 22, 2002, Minnesota's Court of Appeals upheld the Hennepin County District Court decision requiring the Minnesota Twins to play baseball in the Metrodome during the 2002 season.[377] Two weeks later, the Minnesota State Supreme Court voted not to review the appellate court decision, thereby ensuring that there would be major league baseball in Minnesota in 2002. Buffeted by the adverse court decisions, Bud Selig announced on February 5, 2002 that contraction would not take place until the 2003 season at the earliest.[378] With that announcement, contraction discussions were shelved for another year, and major league baseball swung into the 2002 season with the full complement of 30 teams in place.

[376] Thomas Boswell, *Ventura Works High and Tight to Selig*, THE WASH. POST, December 7, 2001, D1, D5.

[377] Dave Sheinin and Mark Asher, *Twins Are Ordered to Stay Put*, THE WASH. POST, January 23, 2002, D2.

[378] *MLB Contraction Reset for 2003*, MLB Press Release, February 5, 2002.

Chapter 14

Sports-Related Injuries

In the fall of 1905, Theodore Roosevelt, Jr., then a student at Harvard University, tried out for a spot on the Harvard football team. Shortly thereafter, in his role as both concerned father and President of the United States, Theodore Roosevelt, Sr. held a lengthy afternoon conference with the head football coaches at the universities of Harvard, Yale and Princeton. The Presidential conference focused on the "many brutal features" of football. Specifically, President Roosevelt was anxious to eliminate excessively rough play on the gridiron. The President was of the opinion that the only way to reduce the level of injuries in football was to make radical changes in the rules. Roosevelt was sufficiently concerned to schedule another conference for the end of the football season.[379]

Most athletes do not have the benefit of direct Presidential interest in their health and welfare. Whatever the level of competition, concern for the health of athletes usually extends no further than the doctors and trainers employed by a school or team. Often, conflicts arise between the obligations of trainers and physicians to their employer, whether a professional

---

[379] *Roosevelt Would Oust Football's Brutal Features*, THE PHILADELPHIA INQUIRER, October 10, 1905, 1. The meetings initiated by President Roosevelt led to formation of the Intercollegiate Athletic Association of the United States, which later became the National Collegiate Athletic Association (NCAA). Due to his groundbreaking efforts, President Roosevelt is looked upon as the founder of the NCAA.

team or an educational institution, and their obligations to the athletes they are treating. "There are team doctors and there are company doctors," former Washington Redskin offensive tackle Jim Lachey once said. The difference, according to Lachey, is that a team doctor looks out for the best interests of the athletes, while a company doctor will do whatever it takes to get athletes back on the field.[380]

Jim Lachey's Principle of the Distinction Between "Team Doctors" and "Company Doctors"

1. A team doctor looks out for the best interests of the athletes in his or her care.
2. A company doctor does whatever it takes to get athletes back on the field.

By Lachey's definitions, former Philadelphia Flyers team doctor, orthopedic surgeon John Gregg, would qualify as a company doctor. Gregg operated on Glen Seabrooke, a 21-year-old left wing with the Flyers' minor league team, the Hershey Bears, during the 1988-89 season. Seabrooke had injured his left shoulder when he crashed into a goalpost, suffering a massive tear in his rotator cuff. Gregg later prescribed an aggressive—and painful—therapy for Seabrooke. According to Seabrooke's agent, the program ruined Seabrooke's arm. Seabrooke later sued the doctor. At trial, Seabrooke introduced internal memos in which the physical therapists who supervised his rehabilitation had assured the Flyers that they would be "beating on Seabrooke all summer" to get him back for the next season. During his therapy, Seabrooke had passed out several times from the extreme pain. The rehabilitation program placed Seabrooke's career

---

[380] Ken Denlinger, *A Prescription For Pain? Trust Is Tenuous Between Athletes, Team Doctors*, THE WASH. POST, October 31, 1995, E1.

in jeopardy. In 1995, he received a $5.5 million judgment against Dr. Gregg.[381]

In the Seabrooke case, as happens with medical malpractice cases in sports generally, the court looked to see whether the doctor and his staff exercised a level of care that was consistent with the skill and knowledge common to other physicians, in and out of sports. Even in the sporting world, medical staffs do not typically "beat on" players all summer. Medical staffs certainly are not in the practice of administering treatments that cause players to pass out. Thus the court in the Seabrooke case had little difficulty finding that Dr. Gregg had been negligent.

When a team physician perceives the team's owner as his client, the physician can easily lose sight of his obligation to his patients. When the team physician is the team owner, the physician's commitment to his patients may be nonexistent. Long-time Boston Red Sox team physician Arthur Pappas was more than a company doctor. In addition to his medical practice, Dr. Pappas was also part owner of the team. With his ownership interest, Pappas had more reason than most team doctors to protect the franchise.

In June 1989, in a game between Boston and the Toronto Blue Jays, former Red Sox second baseman Marty Barrett was injured while running out a routine grounder to the Toronto third baseman. The third baseman's throw went wide of the bag, causing Blue Jays first baseman Fred McGriff to shift to the home plate side of the base. Fearing a collision with McGriff, Barrett attempted to run around the first baseman and touch the inside part of the base. As he maneuvered to avoid McGriff, Barrett heard a pop in his right knee and immediately fell in pain.

Two days after Barrett's injury, Dr. Pappas performed surgery. After the operation, Pappas held a press conference. The doctor announced that the

---

[381] J. Nocera, *Special Report: Bitter Medicine*, SPORTS ILLUSTRATED, November 6, 1995, 81.

Red Sox second baseman had suffered torn cartilage in the knee and had stretched a ligament. Contrary to the doctor's pronouncement, however, Barrett had actually ruptured his anterior cruciate ligament, a potentially career-threatening injury. The report that Pappas filed at the hospital after the surgery indicated that he had removed much of what was left of Barrett's ruptured anterior cruciate ligament. According to Barrett, Dr. Pappas never told him the true extent of the injury, just as the doctor had hid Barrett's ruptured ACL from the press. Bolstered by Pappas' diagnosis of torn cartilage, Barrett underwent rehabilitation and returned to the lineup six weeks later without surgical reconstruction. The next season, Barrett played in 62 games for the Red Sox but was not effective at the plate. In 159 at-bats, he hit only .226. The Red Sox handed the second base job to Jody Reed and waived Barrett.[382]

Barrett sued Dr. Pappas. In his complaint, Barrett alleged that Pappas knew the Red Sox needed Barrett back in the lineup quickly if the team was to contend for the 1989 American League pennant. Barrett pointed out that if the Red Sox could compete for the pennant, the franchise and all of the team's owners stood to profit. Barrett also charged that Pappas was well aware that proper repair of the anterior cruciate ligament required a year of rehabilitation. In his suit, Barrett demanded compensation from the doctor for having cut short his playing career.[383] In 1995, a Massachusetts court agreed with Barrett's allegations and ordered Dr. Pappas to pay the former ballplayer $1.7 million.[384]

Dr. Pappas owed multiple obligations to Barrett. The doctor owed, *first*, the obligation to render a proper diagnosis. *Second*, the doctor was obligated to provide proper treatment. *Third*, the doctor had an obligation to

---

[382] Barrett signed with the San Diego Padres for the 1991 season but appeared in only twelve games with the team. A career .278 hitter, Barrett could muster only a .188 average for San Diego. He retired after his brief stint with the Padres.

[383] Nocera, *Special Report: Bitter Medicine*, 74, 76.

[384] *Around the Majors*, THE WASH. POST, October 26, 1995, D7.

adequately inform his patient about the nature of the injury and alternatives for treatment. "There is huge pressure to keep players on the field," Dr. Rob Huizenga, an internist with the Oakland Raiders from 1983 to 1990, once said.[385] From all appearances, when treating Marty Barrett, Dr. Pappas succumbed to that pressure. He failed in his obligations to his patient, neither providing Barrett with an accurate diagnosis nor providing proper treatment.

The Marty Barrett Principle of the Duty of Care Owed by Physicians

A team doctor has multiple obligations to athletes in his or her care:
1. The obligation to render a proper diagnosis.
2. The obligation to provide proper treatment and/or surgery.
3. The obligation to adequately inform the patient about the nature of the injury and the alternatives for treatment.

The difficulties encountered by former San Francisco 49ers lineman Charles Kreuger are eerily similar to Barrett's case. Kreuger was hit on his knee in a game in 1970. Immediately after being hit, Kreuger felt a "piece" break off in his left knee. The 49ers' staff gave Kreuger codeine and authorized him to return to the game. Kreuger played out the season. Unbeknownst to Kreuger, he risked permanent injury by playing without having the knee surgically repaired. The 49ers never informed him of the risk.

Kreuger retired from football in 1973. His injured knee went untreated until 1978. In that year, for the first time, Kreuger was shown x-rays that had been taken after his knee was hit in 1970. It was also the first time that Kreuger learned that he would have permanent disability in the knee. Kreuger sued the 49ers for fraudulent concealment of essential medical information. At trial, the court ruled against Kreuger on the grounds that

---

[385] Denlinger, *A Prescription For Pain? Trust Is Tenuous Between Athletes, Team Doctors*, E1.

he would likely have continued to play anyway even if he had been told the extent of his injuries. Kreuger appealed the decision. The appellate court ruled in favor of Kreuger. This time, the court focused principally on whether the team had fully disclosed the nature of the injury to Kreuger. The court concluded that: (1) the 49ers had not made full disclosure of the nature and extent of the injury to Kreuger; (2) the 49ers had a vested interest in inducing Kreuger to continue playing in spite of his injury; and (3) Kreuger was entitled to rely on the team's physicians for full disclosure of his injury. These three elements, the court found, were sufficient to prove fraudulent concealment by the 49ers.[386]

Even in cases where a doctor is intent on providing proper diagnosis and treatment, the unique bond between physician and team may disrupt the normal doctor-patient relationship. In June 1965, New York Yankee home run champion Roger Maris injured two of the fingers in his right hand when he tried to score from second base on a single. As he slid into home, Maris caught his fingers on the spikes of home plate umpire Bill Haller. Days later, while batting in a game against the Washington Senators, Maris heard a pop in the palm of his hand as he swung the bat. Maris had broken his hand, though he did not realize it. Doctors took three different sets of x-rays on the injured hand. Throughout the season, the Yankees issued bulletins saying that Maris was almost ready to play. In fact, the hand was broken so badly that Maris couldn't even turn a doorknob, much less hit a baseball. At the insistence of the team, Maris took batting practice every four or five days but was unable to swing without pain. His hand worsened to the point that he could not hold a baseball. Not until a week before the end of the season did the Yankees tell Maris that he had broken his hand.

There was no suggestion that the doctors had failed to read the x-rays accurately or recommend proper treatment. Maris, himself, believed that

---

[386] *Kreuger v. San Francisco Forty Niners*, 234 Cal. Rptr. 579 (Cal. App. 1987).

Yankee officials, and not the doctors, were responsible for hiding the truth about his injury. "It was a broken hand," Maris said. "Someone was told not to tell me; I can't say it was the doctor."[387] With the Yankees serving as the intermediary between physician and patient, the channel of communications between the doctor and Maris broke down. As one of the team's stars, Maris helped to draw fans to the ballpark by appearing in a Yankee uniform, even if he couldn't play. By listing Maris as "almost ready," the Yankees perpetuated the myth that fans might see the home run champ in action. The Yankees were loath to announce, in June, that Maris' season was finished. Maris was convinced the untreated injury hastened the end of his career. "Once I broke the hand," he said, "really, it was all over for me.... I would swing the bat and have that hand slip right out there."[388] Roger Maris did not seek relief in the courts. "You end up sitting back and saying, 'Let it quiet down,' " he explained.[389]

When first baseman David Segui injured his wrist early in the 2002 season during a collision at home plate, the Baltimore Orioles' team doctor told him that his tendon was torn. Taking a page from the 1965 Yankees, however, team officials told the press that Segui had merely bruised his tendon. Like the Yankees, the Orioles appeared to have a hidden agenda. Segui favored having surgery, so that the tendon could be permanently repaired. His team, already short on power hitters, preferred to see if the tendon would heal by itself, with the help of periodic rest and cortisone shots. With a yearly salary of approximately $7 million, Segui was the highest paid player on the Orioles' roster. The Orioles feared that if Segui underwent surgery, he would miss the rest of the season. Segui was livid when he learned of the diagnosis released by team officials. He ripped up and threw away a statement the team had prepared for him to read.

---

[387] Peter Golenbock, *Dynasty: The New York Yankees 1949-1964* (Englewood Cliffs, NJ: Prentice-Hall, Inc., 1975), 302.

[388] Golenbock, *Dynasty: The New York Yankees 1949-1964*, 302.

[389] Golenbock, *Dynasty: The New York Yankees 1949-1964*, 302.

Even Orioles manager Mike Hargrove seemed to take issue with the team's handling of Segui's injury. "Saying it's a bruise is downplaying it," Hargrove said. "To say it is just a bruise paints it as a player who just doesn't want to play. And that's not the case. David Segui is as tough a player as I've ever been around."[390]

One day after the Orioles labeled the injury a bruise, Segui was back in the lineup as a designated hitter. He was as strident as ever, however, in his criticism of the team. "I'm upset about the lying," he told reporters. "One day I'm told it's torn, then the next day I'm told it's not.... I saw it, the MRI film. I saw the tear, the doctor pointed it out...." Even as his name was being written into the starting lineup, Segui mocked the team's diagnosis. "It feels good right now," he said, "it feels like a bruise, you know, bruise-ish."[391] Ten days after the dispute erupted, Segui exercised his contractual right to receive a second opinion and was examined by a surgeon not affiliated with the team. The examination confirmed that Segui's tendon was torn, and surgery was quickly scheduled.[392]

During their playing careers, Portland Trailblazer center Bill Walton and legendary Chicago Bear linebacker Dick Butkus experienced more medical troubles than most athletes. Walton was hampered by problems with his left foot, Butkus with irreparable damage to his right knee. Both placed the responsibility for their ailments on inadequate medical care by team doctors. As a result of lawsuits brought by Walton and Butkus, professional sports teams began to give players the right to a second medical opinion—paid for by the team—in cases where the players were not comfortable with the diagnosis given by the team's doctor. The right to a second opinion is

390 Dave Sheinin, *O's, Segui Have Dispute About His Wrist Injury*, THE WASH. POST, May 8, 2002, D5.

391 Tarik El-Bashir and Dave Sheinin, *Injured Segui Returns to O's Lineup*, THE WASH. POST, May 9, 2002, D8.

392 Preston Williams, *Surgery for Segui, Out 10-12 Weeks*, THE WASH. POST, May 18, 2002, D5.

now guaranteed in the standard player contracts in professional baseball, basketball, football and hockey.[393] When requesting a second opinion on his "bruise," therefore, David Segui was merely exercising a right extended to him by virtue of his contract.

If "company doctors" tend to be too aggressive in trying to get ballplayers back on the playing field, the doctors at Northwestern University might have been too conservative—at least too conservative for basketball star Nick Knapp's liking. During his high school career at Peoria Woodruff High in Illinois, Knapp was one of the top guards in the state. In 1994, during his junior year at Peoria Woodruff, Knapp committed to play collegiate ball at Northwestern. The following September, Knapp went into cardiac arrest during a pickup game and collapsed. Knapp sat out his senior year of high school basketball, but in the summer after his graduation, he played in more than 50 all-star and pickup games without incident. Nonetheless, after the Northwestern team physician reviewed Knapp's medical records, the university refused to let him play varsity basketball. Northwestern did, however, guarantee that it would honor Knapp's scholarship. That was not enough for Knapp. He wanted to play. After Knapp suffered the cardiac arrest in high school, he had a defibrillator installed in his stomach. A defibrillator is a device that restarts one's heart after the heart stops functioning. Following installation of the defibrillator, four doctors examined Knapp and declared him fit to play basketball. In an effort to persuade Northwestern officials to let Knapp play, Knapp and his father agreed to absolve the school of any liability if playing basketball caused additional medical trouble. Still, the university remained adamant; school officials asked Knapp to try out for a less strenuous sport.[394]

Knapp sued Northwestern University. He asked the court to order the university to let him play basketball. At trial, the four cardiologists who

---

[393] Nocera, *Special Report: Bitter Medicine*, 84.

[394] *The Heart of the Matter*, SPORTS ILLUSTRATED, November 27, 1995, 26.

had examined Knapp testified that playing basketball posed little risk to Knapp. United States District Court Judge James Zagel heard the case. Based on the cardiologists' testimony, the judge ruled that the risk of injury or death was not serious enough to bar Knapp from playing.[395] Northwestern appealed the decision. A federal appeals court then ruled against Knapp, holding that any decision regarding whether there was a substantial risk of future harm to Knapp should be made by the university and not by a court of law.[396] Knapp then took his case to the U.S. Supreme Court, but the Court allowed the appeals decision to stand. Knapp never realized his dream of suiting up for Northwestern University.

One player who certainly could have identified with Nick Knapp's desire to get back on the court is hockey player Esa Tikkanen. In 1995, Tikkanen, then with the Vancouver Canucks, had to miss several weeks of play with bone chips in his right knee. Tikkanen was in such a hurry to resume playing that he declined surgery even though there was a risk of permanent injury. Tikkanen's solution was to buy private insurance that would protect him in the event that he suffered further injury. If the Canucks and the team's coach, Rick Ley, were concerned about Tikkanen incurring permanent injury, Tikkanen did not share the same concern. "If Ricky doesn't play me, I'll kill him," Tikkanen said. "I won't listen to him. I've been waiting for this day too long. I want to play." The coach replied, tongue in cheek, "Well, I can't take a chance on getting killed."[397]

Nick Knapp undoubtedly felt that both Northwestern University and the court system let him down. If the university's medical philosophy had been more closely aligned with the attitudes of "company doctors," Knapp would have stood a better chance of playing varsity basketball. Yet the

---

[395] *Judge Rules Recruit Can Play Despite Heart Attack*, THE. WASH. POST, September 11, 1996, B3; *Knapp v. Northwestern University*, 942 F.Supp 1191 (1996).

[396] *Knapp v. Northwestern University*, 101 F.3d 473 (7th Cir. 1996), *cert. denied*, 520 U.S. 1274 (1997).

[397] *Tikkanen Rarin' to Go*, THE WASH. POST, December 17, 1995, D10.

examples of Marty Barrett and Charles Kreuger serve as sobering reminders of the harm that can be done by "company doctors." If left to their own devices and deprived of competent medical advice, professional-caliber athletes will invariably want to play. In doing so, they may jeopardize both the longevity of their athletic careers and their long-term health.

Outfielder John Paciorek made his major league debut in 1963 as an 18-year-old, appearing in the Houston Colt .45s' final game of the season. Paciorek collected three hits in three at-bats, walked twice, scored four runs and drove in three. Shortly after his auspicious beginning, Paciorek experienced problems with his back and never again appeared in a major league game. He retired with a major league batting average of 1.000.[398]

The landscape of professional sports is littered with the names of players who, like John Paciorek, were forced into premature retirement by debilitating injuries. Paciorek at least had the opportunity to appear in one big league game. During a career shortened by injury, left-hander John Sielicki pitched for both the San Francisco Giant and New York Yankee organizations. Unlike John Paciorek, Sielicki never once appeared in a regular season game in the majors. In 1974, while with the Giants, Sielicki required surgery on his left elbow. The next year, he re-injured the elbow. He pitched in the minor leagues throughout the 1976 and 1977 seasons without experiencing any recurrence of elbow trouble. In March 1978, Sielicki went to spring training with the New York Yankees. From the beginning of training camp through April 7, he pitched a total of nine innings. On April 7, he threw three more innings in an exhibition game against the Baltimore Orioles. That game would be Sielicki's last appearance in a major league

---

[398] Paciorek's better known brother, Tom, spent 18 years in the major leagues with six different teams. The Pacioreks had a younger brother, Jim, who played in 42 games for the Milwaukee Brewers in 1987.

uniform. The next day, he felt a tightness in his left elbow and muscle spasms in his left arm. Shortly afterwards, the Yankees released him. Sielicki consulted with doctors, who found evidence of ulnar neuritis. Sielicki's career was over. The doctors told Sielicki the condition was caused by the strain of pitching. Lacking the financial security of an established major leaguer, Sielicki filed a claim for workmen's compensation benefits from the Yankees.

Like other employers, professional sports teams participate in workmen's compensation insurance programs to cover athletes who suffer disabling injuries. Workmen's compensation is regulated on a state-by-state basis. All states have workers' compensation laws, but not all states require employers to take out private insurance policies to cover their workers. Workmen's compensation is based on the notion that an employee is automatically entitled to benefits when he or she suffers a personal injury in the course of employment. The right of a professional athlete to collect workmen's compensation benefits for a career-ending injury rests on a simple test: was the player's injury work-related? Typically, workmen's compensation policies provide protection for injuries caused by accident as well as injuries resulting from repeated trauma.

The Yankees denied Sielicki's claim for workmen's compensation benefits. The team argued that his disability was due to continuing trauma over the course of his career and not to any accident that occurred in his last appearance in a Yankee game. Sielicki sued. The lawsuit focused on whether the team's workmen's compensation policy covered only discrete accidents or extended to injuries caused by repeated trauma. At the trial, a sports medicine specialist testified that Sielicki's injury was the result of the pitcher attempting to throw too hard too early in the season. Based on the medical testimony that Sielicki presented, the court concluded that the pitcher's injury involved repeated trauma, up to and including the date of his last spring training game with the Yankees. The court decided that it wasn't necessary for Sielicki to prove that he had suffered a specific accident, because workmen's compensation covers injuries caused by repeated trauma.[399]

Former Baltimore Oriole outfielder Albert Belle never made it past the end of the Orioles' 2001 spring training. Before training camp had finished, Belle announced that his degenerative hip, which had begun causing problems at least a year earlier, prevented him from playing baseball any more. Months earlier, *Washington Post* sportswriter Tom Boswell had an inkling that Belle's hip was troubling him more than he let on. Boswell was walking through the Orioles' clubhouse one day during the 2000 baseball season when he heard a deep voice call out "Hi, Boz." The voice was that of Albert Belle, who was normally not inclined to engage sportswriters in casual conversation. Shortly thereafter, Boswell saw Orioles skipper Mike Hargrove. He told Hargrove that Belle's hip must be bothering him badly. Hargrove asked Boswell how he knew. Boswell said the real tip-off came when Belle had said, "Hi, Boz." There is a maxim in baseball, Boswell explained, "They learn to say hello when it's time to say goodbye."[400]

For most professional athletes, the time to say goodbye comes all too quickly. John Paciorek had to say goodbye after only one game. The careers of Marty Barrett, Charles Kreuger and Roger Maris were significantly longer. Nonetheless, neither Barrett, Kreuger nor Maris had the privilege of leaving the playing field on their own terms. In each case, improper medical treatment hastened their passage into retirement.

---

[399] *Sielicki v. New York Yankees*, 388 So.2d 25 (1980).

[400] Thomas Boswell, *On His Way Out, Belle Takes A Swing At Introspection*, THE WASH. POST, March 7, 2001, D1.

Chapter 15

Equal Opportunity in Sports

The Civil Rights Act of 1964 prohibited discrimination on the basis of race, color or national origin.[401] Buddy Gilbert, a professional baseball player years before Congress got around to adopting the Civil Rights Act, didn't need Congress to teach him the difference between right and wrong. Gilbert was color-blind. It was instinctive.

On September 26, 1959, Gilbert, a rookie, played right field for a Cincinnati Redlegs team that included future Hall-of-Famer Frank Robinson and all-stars Vada Pinson, Gus Bell, and Johnny Temple. Gilbert drove a pitch from Pittsburgh Pirates hurler Jim Umbricht into the outfield stands for his first home run in the big leagues. When Gilbert returned to the Reds' dugout, manager Fred Hutchinson approached him. "Gilbert," Hutchinson yelled, "you ran those bases so fast that the cameras

---

[401] Due in large part to the efforts of President Lyndon B. Johnson, the Civil Rights Act became law on July 2, 1964, 78 Stat. 253, 42 U.S.C. § 2000e et seq. (1964). Title II of the Civil Rights Act prohibits discrimination or segregation on the basis of race, color, religion or national origin in the operation of a place of public accommodation. As originally adopted, Title VII of the Civil Rights Act prohibited discrimination on the grounds of race, color, religion or national origin in employment. In 1972, Congress amended the Act to also prohibit discrimination in employment on the basis of sex.

couldn't keep up with you!" The next day, playing in the Redlegs' final game of the season, Gilbert again hit a home run.

Just as quickly, the promise faded. Gilbert played two more years of baseball, with Triple-A Seattle in 1960 and Double-A Nashville in 1961, but the major leagues never again beckoned.

Buddy Gilbert made his contributions to baseball in other ways. In the mid-1950s, he was the center fielder for the Cincinnati farm team in Savannah, Georgia. Gilbert was an above-average ballplayer. He hit with power. He consistently compiled a batting average of .280 or better. He was a prospect. He was not, however, the team's best prospect. That distinction belonged to Curt Flood, an African-American, who played third base. In the mid-1950s, the South was less than hospitable to Flood. On trips to games in other cities, the team bus would stop at restaurants along the way. The white ballplayers would empty out of the bus to eat; Flood would remain behind. By law and custom, he could not eat with his teammates. Eating alone was perhaps the easiest part of Curt Flood's daily routine. At ballpark after ballpark, wherever the Savannah team played, fans would shout racial epithets at Flood. Gilbert recoiled at the insults directed toward his teammate. Gilbert heard many of the words the fans yelled at Flood because when the Savannah team would take the field for a game, Gilbert would jog side by side with Flood. Gilbert would bring Flood food from the restaurants. He invited Flood to his home. He helped Flood endure the racial taunts and the cruel language. Gilbert himself drew the animosity of a few of his teammates simply because of his efforts to befriend a lonely teammate. Some players criticized Gilbert for getting "too close" to Flood. In his defense, Buddy would simply explain, "I just like people."[402] By 1964, Buddy Gilbert was out of baseball and carving

---

[402] David Halberstam, *October 1964* (New York: Villard Books, 1994), 114.

out a career in business.[403] At the same time, Curt Flood was quietly establishing himself as a major league star. In 1964, Flood registered one of the best seasons of his major league career. Patrolling center field for the St. Louis Cardinals, Flood played in all of his team's 162 games. He led the National League in plate appearances, with 679, and hits, with 211. He hit .311 for the year and played a key role in the Cardinals' drive to the 1964 National League pennant and the team's World Series victory over the New York Yankees. Outside of baseball, 1964 witnessed the dramatic result of years of effort by the National Association for the Advancement of Colored People (NAACP) and its chief lawyer, Thurgood Marshall, who served as head of the NAACP Legal Defense Fund. Throughout the 1940s and succeeding decades, Marshall and his associates mounted an all-out attack on racial discrimination in the United States. Marshall likely did not know of Curt Flood's experiences in Savannah, but he wouldn't have tolerated them any better than did Buddy Gilbert. With Marshall serving as its point person, the NAACP was instrumental in gaining passage of the Civil Rights Act of 1964. The Act represented Congress' attempt to remedy racial violence and respond to the awakening of the African-American protest movement.

When Buddy Gilbert befriended Curt Flood in baseball stadiums throughout the South, he was following in impressive footsteps. A decade before, Brooklyn Dodger shortstop Pew Wee Reese had taken Jackie Robinson, the first African-American in the modern era of the major leagues, under his wing. In the minutes before Robinson's first

---

[403] Gilbert's major league career consisted of 20 at-bats in seven games. He collected only three hits in his 20 trips to the plate. His career did produce one notable claim to fame, however: his ratio of one home run for every 10 plate appearances represents a better mark than for every noted slugger in the history of baseball, including Babe Ruth (one home run for each 12 times at bat), Roger Maris (one homer for every 19 plate appearances), Hank Aaron (one home run for every 16 at-bats), and Dave Kingman (one home run for every 15 at-bats).

game with Brooklyn, the visiting Boston Braves directed a steady stream of racial insults at the former Negro League player. Reese, a southerner from Kentucky, walked over to Robinson and stood beside him. This small act of courage let everyone in Ebbets Field know that Reese would not tolerate the insults.[404] Reese repeated his support for Robinson when the Dodgers traveled to Cincinnati to play the Reds. When Robinson took his position at first base, many of the Cincinnati fans taunted him. Reese walked over to Robinson and put his arm around Robinson's shoulders. The crowd quieted. Without saying a word, Reese had again spoken loudly.[405]

Pee Wee Reese's Principle of Combating Racism

I will stand by my teammate, regardless of race or color.

If not for the courage shown by Reese, Robinson might not have lasted long with Brooklyn.[406] However, if not for the commitment of two other men, Branch Rickey and Happy Chandler, Robinson would never have even made it to Brooklyn and the big leagues. Before signing Robinson to a major league contract, Rickey, the Dodgers' general man-

---

[404] Mickey Mantle, *All My Octobers* (New York: Harper Collins Publishers, Inc., 1994), 30.

[405] Peter Golenbock, *Teammates* (New York: Harcourt Brace & Company, 1990), 28.

[406] Actor John Wayne once said that "courage is being scared to death and saddling up anyway." There is no doubt that the situation in Cincinnati left Reese scared. A native of Louisville, Kentucky, Reese was playing 100 miles from his hometown. Reese knew that some of the people yelling insults may have been his friends. "Pee Wee's legs felt heavy, but he knew what he had to do." Golenbock, *Teammates*, 26.

ager, visited with Chandler, then the commissioner of baseball. Meeting at Chandler's cabin in Kentucky, Rickey asked Chandler where he stood on the issue of Robinson playing for the Dodgers. In words destined to revolutionize major league baseball, Chandler responded, "Mr. Rickey, I'm going to have to meet my maker some day. If He asked me why I didn't let this boy play, and I answered, 'Because he's a Negro,' that might not be a sufficient answer. I will approve of the transfer of Robinson's contract from Montreal to Brooklyn, and we'll make a fight with you. So bring him on in."[407]

Happy Chandler's Principle of Racial Integration in Sports

I will approve of the transfer of Robinson's contract. We'll make a fight with you. So bring him on in.

A few years after Robinson's debut in the National League, Boston Celtics owner Walter Brown helped to break the color barrier in professional basketball when he drafted an African-American, Chuck Cooper. Brown's act was not widely applauded. Opposition came from a most surprising source—the Harlem Globetrotters. Globetrotters owner Abe Saperstein feared that if the NBA opened its rosters to African-Americans, the pool of talent available to the Globetrotters would be diluted.[408] In spite of Saperstein's opposition, Brown drafted Cooper. Other NBA teams soon followed suit.

If Congress had high expectations that the Civil Rights Act of 1964 might change racial attitudes in the United States, experience

---

[407] Peter Golenbock, *Bums: An Oral History of the Brooklyn Dodgers* (New York: G.P. Putnam's Sons, 1984), 171-172.

[408] Red Auerbach with Joe Fitzgerald, *On & Off The Court* (New York: Bantam Books, 1986), 198.

suggested otherwise. Elston Howard, who became the first African-American to wear New York Yankee pinstripes, established himself as an indispensable member of the Yankees early in his major league career. In his rookie year, 1955, Howard played in 97 games and hit .290 with 10 home runs. He eventually supplanted Yogi Berra as the Yankees' regular catcher and was the American League's Most Valuable Player in 1963.[409] Howard's accomplishments on the diamond carried little weight in other arenas. When he and his family decided to move to an upscale New Jersey neighborhood, they had to have the builder, a white man, purchase the property for them. It was well known that the owner of the property would not have sold it to an African-American family, New York Yankee ballplayer or not. When the Howards were set to move into the neighborhood, someone wrote the word "nigger" all over the house.[410]

Around the league, the experiences of African-American ballplayers were similar. Infielder Elijah "Pumpsie" Green, who broke the color barrier for the Boston Red Sox in 1959, once spoke of the isolation. "Twenty-four guys went one way and me another," said Green. "I didn't even ride on the same plane with the other players. But it wouldn't have been too smart for me to challenge it. Stars like [Ernie] Banks, Elston Howard, and others didn't say anything, so how could a rookie like me do it?"[411]

---

[409] Hitting .287 with 28 home runs and 85 runs batted in, Howard led the Yankees to the 1963 American League pennant. The Yankees then squared off against Sandy Koufax's Los Angeles Dodgers in the World Series. The Dodgers held Yankee batters to an anemic .171 average for the Series and won in four straight games, with Koufax winning two games and Don Drysdale and Johnny Podres winning one each. In the Series, Howard again paced the Yankees, collecting five hits in 15 at-bats for a .333 average.

[410] Tony Kubek and Terry Pluto, *Sixty One: The Team, The Record, The Men* (New York: Macmillan Publishing Company, Inc., 1987), 219.

[411] Edward Kiersh, *Where Have You Gone, Vince DiMaggio?* (New York: Bantam Books, 1983), 45.

Teammates often have an easier time treating athletes of different color, race or creed as equals than others in society. Former Washington Redskin center Trevor Matich once explained, "You'd have to make a concerted effort to be a racist in this kind of a setting. When you look at what we go through together, starting with the off-season and working hard and going into training camp and sweating and bleeding and playing hurt next to one another, and then getting into the season and playing games when your teammates are all you've got, and you're all they've got... it's hard to look at anything except character and performance, and that's it."[412]

> *The Trevor Matich Principle of Indifference to Racial Distinctions*
>
> *When your teammates are all you've got, it's hard to look at anything except character and performance.*

The New York Yankees looked at Elston Howard and saw only character and performance—and perhaps a little of their own weakness. Early in his career, Howard contributed a couple of game-winning hits. From then on, at least on the playing field, he was simply a teammate. During one game in 1955, outfielder Hank Bauer crawled on top of the Yankee dugout to confront a fan who was shouting racial insults at Howard. Bauer searched a long time, trying to identify the heckler. The fan, intimidated by Bauer's glare, remained silent. After the game, Bauer explained simply, "Ellie's my friend."[413] Ellie had other friends as well. During trips to spring training games in Florida, Howard, like Curt Flood, often had to eat his meals on the team bus while his teammates ate inside a restaurant. Mickey Mantle, then a budding superstar, would bring his dinner out to

---

[412] David Aldridge, *A Team's True Colors*, THE WASH. POST, December 16, 1995, A1, A18.

[413] Peter Golenbock, *Dynasty: The New York Yankees 1949-1964* (Englewood Cliffs, NJ: Prentice-Hall, Inc., 1975), 146.

the team bus so that Howard would not have to endure the indignity of eating alone.

It was one thing to silence an ignorant heckler or join Howard for a meal on the team bus, but quite another to effect structural changes in society. Bobby Richardson, another teammate of Elston Howard's from the 1950s and 1960s, once lamented, "It's hard for me to believe that I played in an era when black and white players weren't allowed to stay in the same hotel. When I think back on it, I'm embarrassed and ashamed that I couldn't do something about it."[414] It is not clear that even a prominent Yankee such as Bobby Richardson could have changed the racial climate significantly. A quip by former Brooklyn Dodger pitcher Joe Black illustrates the ingrained prejudice that Elston Howard and others encountered, especially during spring training in Southern cities.[415] "How you like the South?" Black once asked a sportswriter. "How do you like the South?" the sportswriter countered. "I can't tell you," Black answered, "they won't let me in."[416] As an institution, major league baseball helped to promote a more tolerant racial climate in the South and elsewhere. Early in 1954, months before the Supreme Court issued its historic school desegregation decision in *Brown v. Board of Education*,[417] the city council in Birmingham, Alabama eliminated a time-honored law that banned sports competitions between whites and African-Americans. Baseball provided the city council with incentive

---

[414] Kubek and Pluto, *Sixty One: The Team, The Record, The Men*, 214-15.

[415] Before embarking on his major league baseball career, Joe Black was a school teacher. Born in Plainfield, New Jersey, he reached the majors with the Brooklyn Dodgers in 1952. As a 28-year-old rookie for the Dodgers, he was an instant sensation, appearing in 56 games and posting a record of 15 wins, four losses and an earned run average of 2.15. Black spent parts of five more seasons in the major leagues but never again approached the success of his rookie year. He finished his career with a record of 30 wins and 12 losses.

[416] Golenbock, *Bums: An Oral History of the Brooklyn Dodgers*, 402.

[417] *Brown v. Board of Education*, 347 U.S. 483 (1954).

to repeal the law; the council wanted to entice the Brooklyn Dodgers to play a spring training game in Birmingham. As an interracial team, the Dodgers could not have played within the city limits as long as the law remained in effect.[418]

Football players, even those at the top of their profession, did not have it any easier than major league baseball players. When Don Perkins was a pile-driving fullback for the Dallas Cowboys in the 1960s, the Cowboys paid him handsomely for his talents. As a star on the Cowboys and with income that put him in the upper echelon of the National Football League's salary structure, Perkins was in a position to live comfortably in Dallas. Nonetheless, Perkins had to make do with substandard housing. "The Negroes on the Cowboys," Perkins said during the height of his football career, "can only find roach-infested houses." In the summer of 1968, while the Cowboys were at their pre-season camp in Thousand Oaks, California, some friends tried to find a suitable house in Dallas for Perkins and his family. Perkins reported that his friends were not having much luck. He told the press that the racial barriers in Dallas, even in 1968, made it difficult for African-American players to live in the city.[419]

If Joe Black had difficulty getting into the South in the 1950s and Don Perkins had trouble finding good housing in the 1960s, a generation later basketball superstar Michael Jordan would find it equally difficult to get into a prominent Illinois country club. By 1990, Jordan had become a solid amateur golfer, regularly scoring in the mid-to-high 70's for 18 holes. Through contacts in the community, he inquired about joining a predominantly Jewish country club near his home. The response came back negative; Jordan was not going to be invited to join the club. Membership, Jordan was informed, was closed.[420]

---

[418] George F. Will, *Bunts: Curt Flood, Camden Yards, Pete Rose and Other Reflections on Baseball* (New York: Scribner, 1998), 270.

[419] *Perkins: Dallas Life Not Easy*, THE WASH. POST, July 19, 1968, D3.

[420] Sam Smith, *The Jordan Rules* (New York: Simon and Schuster, 1992), 196.

The Civil Rights Act of 1964 prohibits discrimination on the grounds of race, color, religion or national origin in places of public accommodation whose operations affect interstate commerce.[421] The prohibition does not apply to discrimination or segregation at clubs that are private. Whether the country club to which Michael Jordan applied was in violation of the Civil Rights Act would depend on several factors. A court would want to know if the club was private—and thus not a place of "public accommodation." A private club is one that is self-governing, owned by its members and closed to the public. Under established law, a club that is open to all members of the public who are white is considered to be a place of public accommodation, even if the club calls itself private.[422] Once a club has been determined to be public, the law seeks to assess whether operation of the club affects commerce between the states. A court would look to see if the club serves customers from outside its own state, or sponsors activities or sells products that involve interstate commerce. If the country club that rejected Michael Jordan's application for membership sold food or golf gear that was manufactured in or transported from other states, that would be sufficient to prove that the club affected interstate commerce. Once any part of the club's activities were shown to involve interstate commerce, the entire club would be subject to the Civil Rights Act.[423]

The Civil Rights Act also prohibits discrimination on the basis of race in other contexts. In 1992, the National Collegiate Athletic Association (NCAA) adopted a measure known as Proposition 16. This measure established new, more rigorous academic requirements that student athletes had to meet in order to qualify for athletic scholarships. The stated intent of Proposition 16 was to improve the graduation rates among black

---

[421] Title II of the Civil Rights Act of 1964, 42 U.S.C. § 2000a *et seq.*

[422] *Daniel v. Paul*, 395 U.S. 298 (1969).

[423] *Daniel v. Paul*, at 305.

student athletes. The new requirements placed greater emphasis on standardized test scores than previous standards and required colleges to be more selective when recruiting athletes. Under Proposition 16, if a student had a 2.0 grade point average in high school, he or she had to score at least 1010 on the Scholastic Aptitude Test to be eligible for an athletic scholarship. In addition to losing eligibility for scholarships, students not meeting the minimum score were barred from participating in intercollegiate athletics during their freshman year of college.

In February 2000, two students, Kelly Pryor and Warren Spivey, Jr., challenged the legality of Proposition 16 in court. Pryor, an African-American, was recruited by San Jose State University to play soccer. Spivey, also African-American, agreed to play football at the University of Connecticut. Both signed letters of intent with their prospective schools. As a condition of the letters of intent, Pryor and Spivey had to meet the eligibility standards in Proposition 16. Neither attained the minimum SAT score, and they were therefore denied athletic scholarships. When Pryor and Spivey found themselves without scholarships, each sued the NCAA for violation of their civil rights. Upon review, the Court of Appeals found the NCAA's implementation of Proposition 16 troubling. In a decision issued in May 2002, the Court ruled that the NCAA's goal of improving the graduation rates for black student athletes amounted to "purposeful discrimination."[424]

There were other possible methods for increasing the graduation rate among black student athletes. The NCAA might have mandated special instructors or increased study aids for marginal students. Instead, it adopted a measure that made it more difficult for marginal students to participate in collegiate sports. The proposition produced exactly the results that the NCAA had predicted. Fewer marginal students qualified for athletic scholarships. The measure hit black student athletes especially

---

[424] *Pryor v. National Collegiate Athletic Association*, No. 01-3113 (3rd Cir. May 6, 2002).

hard. The court found that the NCAA intended, at least partially, to reduce the number of black athletes who could attend college on athletic scholarships. In the court's view, the NCAA had engaged in intentional, disparate treatment on account of race. The court held that the proposition was "presumptively invalid." Whatever the NCAA's motives may have been, Proposition 16 violated the Civil Rights Act.

When Washington, D.C. hosted the September 3, 2000 World Cup soccer qualifying match between the U.S. national team and Guatemala, "purposeful discrimination" was on display for the whole world to see. By design, fans who were rooting for Guatemala were restricted to seats in the upper deck at Robert F. Kennedy Stadium. The U.S. Soccer Federation limited the sale of seats closest to the playing field to registered members of local U.S. soccer affiliates. The Federation left no doubt about its purpose. The registered members would clearly comprise the most vocal supporters of the U.S. national team. "The goal for every home game," a spokesman said, "is to have a pro-American crowd and help us on the field in terms of real home-field advantage." It was, said one critic, "an idea that Guatemalan people would not like."[425] Guatemalans living in the United States did not challenge the seating arrangement, but the discriminatory policy would likely have caused concern in the courts. Natives of Guatemala, whether U.S. citizens or merely living in the United States on non-immigrant visas, share the same Constitutional protections as other individuals in the country.[426] Guatemalans have a constitutional right to gather in public places for social purposes. U.S. courts have held that public intolerance or animosity cannot form the basis for taking away a person's freedom of assembly. The right to gather in public places for social or

---

[425] Thomas Heath, *At RFK, Soccer Tickets Hit Home*, THE WASH. POST, August 12, 2000, D1.

[426] In *Hampton v. Mow Sun Wong*, 426 U.S. 88 (1976), the Supreme Court ruled that the state is powerless to treat aliens as a distinct class. *See also, Graham v. Richardson*, 403 U.S. 365 (1971).

political purposes cannot be suspended even if the actions of those assembling are annoying."[427] Further, the Civil Rights Act prohibits discrimination or segregation on the grounds of race, color, religion or national origin in the operation of a place of public accommodation—if the operations affect interstate commerce. RFK Stadium is a place of public accommodation, and its operations do affect interstate commerce. Therefore, constitutional protections should require that tickets to sporting events at RFK Stadium be sold on a non-discriminatory basis.

> ### *The Constitutional Principle of Freedom of Assembly*
>
> *Public intolerance cannot form the basis for taking away a person's freedom of assembly.*

Concerns about the discriminatory sale of soccer tickets arose again in August 2001 as the U.S. men's national team prepared to play Honduras in the six-nation final qualifying round for the 2002 World Cup competition. Again, the U.S. Soccer Federation limited the sale of seats closest to the playing field to U.S. partisans and soccer fans with "American-sounding names." Even the Honduran Ambassador to the United States, Hugo Noe Pino, was unable to purchase tickets in RFK Stadium's lower deck. The ambassador obtained tickets close to the playing field only by asking the wife of an aide to call for him. Happily, the name of the aide's wife sounded like it was American; she was allowed to buy lower deck seats. Sportswriter Tom Boswell could not let the discriminatory treatment of Hondurans pass without comment. He criticized the U.S. Soccer Federation for sticking "our soccer visitors in the Frank Howard home run seats. Way up." Boswell labeled the ticket policy "un-American." "One of the best aspects of American sports," he wrote, "is that, in many of our games, we still sell

---

[427] *Coates v. City of Cincinnati*, 402 U.S. 611(1971).

tickets on a first-come, first-served basis. We don't divide up by nationality or city or ethnicity." For Boswell, the benefits of a non-discriminatory ticket policy were obvious: the ballpark or the stadium becomes "a true melting pot." Boswell saw a dangerous precedent in the U.S. Soccer Federation's approach. "Blatantly selling tickets based on the ethnicity of the name of the buyer," he said, "is about as un-American as it gets."[428] Boswell was not the only one who saw a dangerous precedent. In the days following the September 1st match between Honduras and the United States, the U.S. Department of Justice announced that it would investigate the ticket policy. The announcement made it clear that federal civil rights laws apply to RFK Stadium. The Justice Department said the investigation would focus on whether sports and entertainment organizations had used national origin as a basis for restricting ticket sales.[429]

The Thomas Boswell Principle of Soccer Seating

It is un-American to stick soccer fans from foreign countries in the Frank Howard home run seats.

Not only was the discriminatory sale of tickets at RFK Stadium "un-American," it was also ineffective. Playing before a crowd of 54,282, Honduras prevailed by a score of 3-2. It was the first loss for the American team in a home qualifying match in more than 16 years. It was also the first time that a U.S. team had allowed three goals in a home qualifier since 1960. The discriminatory ticket policy may have prevented "a true melting pot" from emerging, but it failed to produce the home-field advantage that

---

[428] Thomas Boswell, *Unsportsmanlike Conduct for U.S. Soccer's Ticket Policy*, THE WASH. POST, August 31, 2001, D1, D5.

[429] David Cho, *U.S. Soccer Ticket Plan Comes Under Investigation*, THE WASH. POST, September 6, 2001, B1.

the Soccer Federation desired. Honduras's coach and players reported that
the atmosphere at the game was virtually the same as if they were playing at
home. U.S. midfielder Earnie Stewart estimated that the stadium crowd
was split "70-30, not for us." After the Honduran victory, United States
coach Bruce Arena questioned whether his team could ever get the benefit
of a home-field advantage playing in the nation's capital. "How can you do
it? We want to put on away games at home?," he asked.[430]

Arena may have no choice but to put on "away games at home." In
June 2002, Humberto Martinez of Sterling, Virginia filed a class-action
lawsuit against the U.S. Soccer Federation. Martinez, who was forced to
sit in the upper deck for the Honduras-U.S. match, claimed that the ticket
policy caused him pain, humiliation and embarrassment. In his lawsuit,
he sought $2 million in damages and an injunction against similar ticket
policies in the future.[431]

In June 1998, professional golfer Casey Martin became the first player in
history to participate in golf's U.S. Open while riding in a golf cart. Playing
at the Olympic Club in San Francisco, Martin was able to use a cart because
of a ruling issued four months earlier by U.S. Magistrate Thomas Coffin.
Martin is afflicted with Klippel-Trenaunay-Weber Syndrome. Klippel-
Trenaunay-Weber Syndrome is a degenerative circulatory disorder. It
obstructs the flow of blood from Martin's right leg back to his heart. The
disease causes pain, fatigue, and anxiety, and creates a risk of hemorrhaging
and blood clots. Martin is unable to walk great lengths without severe pain.
Walking also raises the risk that Martin might fracture his tibia.

The PGA Tour did not take Judge Coffin's decision quietly. Tour officials appealed the ruling to the U.S. Court of Appeals in San Francisco.
Again, Martin prevailed.[432] Still not content, the Tour took the appellate

---

[430] Steven Goff, *Arena Not Feeling Very Much at Home: U.S. Coach Questions D.C. as a Future Host*, THE WASH. POST, September 3, 2001, D1, D6.

[431] *USSF Faces Lawsuit*, THE WASH. POST, June 16, 2002, D2.

[432] *PGA Tour, Inc. v. Martin*, 204 F.3d 994 (2000).

court decision to the U.S. Supreme Court. Throughout the appeal process, Martin continued to compete in professional golf tournaments using a golf cart to advance from shot to shot. Other golfers had to walk— a situation that the PGA Tour believed created an advantage for Martin. Even with the use of a cart, Martin's performance was not particularly noteworthy. He finished in a tie for 23rd place at the 1998 Open with a four-day score of 291, one stroke behind his former Stanford University teammate, Tiger Woods. For the 2000 season, Martin ended the year in 179th place on the PGA's money list. The lackluster performance cost Martin his PGA Tour card and, for the 2001 season, Martin was relegated to playing on the "Buy.com" circuit, golf's minor league.

In January 2001, the Supreme Court heard oral arguments from Martin's lawyer and the lawyer for the PGA Tour. The arguments focused on whether the Americans with Disabilities Act, a law passed by Congress in 1990, required the PGA Tour to permit Martin to ride in a cart. Martin's lawyer argued that the law applied to PGA Tour competitions and that the Tour could not discriminate by denying Martin the use of a cart. The PGA Tour responded by arguing that, for purposes of golf tournaments, the law applied only to customers at the tournaments and to employees of the PGA Tour. Tour officials did not consider Martin to be either a customer or an employee of the PGA Tour.

By mid-May 2001, the Supreme Court was poised to issue its decision. In the intervening four months since the Court had heard arguments on the case, speculation on the outcome was running rampant. Publicly, Casey Martin professed to be pessimistic. He felt that the questions asked by the Supreme Court justices during the lawyers' arguments favored the PGA Tour. Others were equally sure that the PGA Tour would win the case. "Court Ruling May Signal Martin's Last Ride," a headline in the *Los Angeles Times* blared. The accompanying article predicted that Martin would lose the case. The article even reported that Tim Finchem, the Commissioner of the PGA Tour, had received word that the Supreme Court justices had already reached a decision in favor of the PGA Tour and that the Court was merely waiting to finish writing the decision before announcing the result. "The tour seems on the verge of closing out with a victory," the *Times* concluded. If the PGA Tour did win, the newspaper predicted, two things would happen right away: Casey Martin's golfing career would end, and the PGA Tour would have to face a storm of criticism from golfing fans, journalists and the public.[433]

As things turned out, Tim Finchem and the *Los Angeles Times* had it all wrong. Casey Martin's career did not end—and there was no storm of protest against the PGA Tour. The Supreme Court's decision, issued May 29, 2001, made it clear that Martin's pessimism was unfounded. By a vote of 7-2, the Court ruled that the law gave Martin the right to use a cart when he competed in professional tournaments.[434] For Martin, the key to victory lay in the actual words contained in the Americans with Disabilities Act:

> No individual shall be discriminated against on the basis of disability in the full and equal enjoyment of the goods, services, facilities, privileges, advantages, or accommodations of any place of public accommodation by any person who owns, leases, (or leases to), or operates a place of public accommodation.[435]

Martin was aided by the fact that when Congress wrote the Americans with Disabilities Act, it specifically mentioned golf courses as places of public accommodation that were subject to the law. The PGA Tour had rested its hopes on a part of the law that stated it was not necessary to make changes to accommodate disabled persons if the changes would fundamentally alter the nature of the goods, services, facilities, privileges, advantages, or accommodations. During the course of the legal proceedings, the Tour presented testimony from golfers Arnold Palmer and Jack

[433] *"Court Ruling May Signal Martin's Last Ride,"* LOS ANGELES TIMES, April 26, 2001, D3.

[434] *PGA Tour, Inc. v. Martin*, 121 S.Ct. 1879 (2001).

[435] Americans with Disabilities Act of 1990, 42 U.S.C. §12182(a).

Nicklaus stating that allowing players to use carts would fundamentally alter the nature of professional golf tournaments. Nicklaus testified that professional golfers are required to walk the courses on which they play because "physical fitness and fatigue are part of the game." However, another professional golfer, Eric Johnson, pointed out that golfers who walked a course enjoyed certain advantages over those who used a cart. Johnson testified that he preferred walking because it allowed him "to keep in rhythm, stay warmer when it is chilly, and develop a better sense of the elements and the course than riding a cart." Ultimately, the Supreme Court found that walking was peripheral—not fundamental— to professional golf tournaments. In reaching this conclusion, the Court observed that when a person walks on an 18-hole golf course, a distance of roughly five miles, he or she expends about 500 calories— "nutritionally... less than a Big Mac."[436]

Shortly after the Supreme Court issued its decision in favor of Casey Martin, a caddie who suffers from cerebral palsy requested permission from the U.S. Golf Association to use a cart when caddying in the U.S. Amateur Public Links Championship in San Antonio. The caddie, 38-year-old Lee Penterman, walks with a limp and has a gnarled right hand caused by his ailment. He is capable of walking eighteen holes with a golf bag but only with extreme fatigue. Notwithstanding Martin's favorable Supreme Court decision, the U.S. Golf Association denied Penterman's request. After receiving word of the denial, Penterman went out and caddied anyway for his friend, amateur golfer Ben Flam. With Penterman's help, Flam shot an even-par 71 in the opening round of the tournament. Penterman finished the round, tired but in good spirits. Afterwards, Flam criticized the Golf Association's decision. "I still think the ruling was unjust," Flam said. "He has a disability."[437]

---

[436] *PGA Tour, Inc. v. Martin*, 121 S.Ct. at 1896.

[437] *Caddie Denied Cart*, THE WASH. POST, July 10, 2001, D2.

Federal law, in the form of Title IX of the Education Amendments of 1972, also prohibits discrimination on the basis of sex in educational programs receiving financial aid from the Federal government.[438] Title IX applies directly to the sports programs of high schools and colleges. It presents colleges and universities with two options for balancing the opportunities available to men and women. Under the first approach, representing the more expansive interpretation, schools have the option of increasing expenditures for women's sports to the point where the funds budgeted for women are equal to the budgets for men's sports. That was the result that Congress anticipated when it adopted the law. A more detrimental approach, one probably not anticipated by many members of Congress, is for schools to reduce the budgets for men's sports, or eliminate certain men's sports entirely, as a way of achieving equality in the budgeting process. This approach, though not popular on college campuses and severely restrictive in its effect, is a handy device for achieving objective equality. It has resulted, for example, in Miami University of Ohio eliminating its men's wrestling, tennis and soccer teams. Several other colleges and universities have taken similar approaches toward meeting their obligations under Title IX.

In the case of Miami University of Ohio, male athletes whose teams were eliminated did not take the news quietly. In November 1999, a group of men athletes, all former members of the wrestling, tennis and soccer teams, sued the university for violation of the sex discrimination provisions of Title IX. The men claimed that school officials engaged in reverse discrimination

---

[438] The law states, in part, "No person in the United States shall, on the basis of sex, be excluded from participation in, be denied the benefits of, or be subjected to discrimination under any education program or activity receiving Federal financial assistance." There are a number of exceptions, such as for educational institutions of religious organizations and educational institutions that train individuals for military services. The law, which is popularly referred to simply as "Title IX," is contained in Section 901(a) of Title IX of the Education Amendments of 1972, Pub. L. 92-318, found at 20 United States Code § 1681. Title IX became law on July 1, 1972.

when they elected to discontinue the three teams in order to equalize the money spent on men's and women's sports. The lawsuit was filed in U.S. District Court in Cincinnati. The men athletes asked the court to order the university to reinstate the teams that were eliminated and pay team members monetary damages to compensate for their "shattered dreams" as well as the cost of transferring to other universities.[439]

When a college tries to comply with Title IX by eliminating men's athletic teams, the impact of Title IX is of dubious value. In other ways, however, the legacy of Title IX has been considerably more positive. Title IX provided the legal impetus for a successful lawsuit by a woman football player against Duke University. The woman, Heather Sue Mercer, had been an excellent high school place-kicker on a championship caliber team in Yorktown Heights, New York. She aspired to play football at Duke and possessed both the capability and credentials to back up her aspirations. Mercer had earned all-state honors in high school. Coaches who worked with her considered her place-kicking skills to be competitive with those of other kickers playing at the college level. Her credentials included the ability to kick field goals at distances of up to 48 yards. After enrolling at Duke, Mercer tried out for the football team as a "walk-on." She attended practices and kicked a 28-yard field goal that won an intrasquad game. Largely on the basis of that field goal, the Duke University head coach told Mercer that she had made the team. All along, however, Mercer suffered slights that came from being a woman. At one point, a coach told her that she could sit in the stands with her boyfriend during Duke's home games. In contrast, other walk-on kickers on the team sat on the field.[440] In 1996, the Duke coaching staff cut Mercer from the team.

---

[439] *Male Athletes Bring A Suit of Their Own*, THE WASH. POST, November 19, 1999, D2.

[440] Abigail Crouse, *Equal Athletic Opportunity: An Analysis of Mercer v. Duke University and a Proposal to Amend the Contact Sport Exception to Title IX*, 84 MINN. L. REV. 1655 (2000).

In player evaluations, Duke head coach Fred Goldsmith ranked Mercer's kicking skills behind those of other players. Goldsmith should have let Mercer's ability, or lack thereof, speak for itself. In words lacking in both diplomacy and flair, Goldsmith questioned Mercer, "Why do you insist on playing football? Why not try something like beauty pageants?" The words stung Mercer. They were words that Goldsmith surely did not say to other members of the football team. Mercer sued the university for violation of Title IX. In her lawsuit, she claimed that she was cut from the football team solely because she was a woman. Citing U.S. Department of Health, Education and Welfare regulations, the district court dismissed Mercer's lawsuit. The HEW regulation in question drew a clear distinction between participation by women in non-contact sports versus contact sports. Specifically, the policy stated that if a school:

> operates or sponsors a team in a particular sport for members of one sex but operates or sponsors no such team for members of the other sex, ...members of the excluded sex must be allowed to try out for the team *unless the sport involved is a contact sport.*[441]

The regulations defined contact sports as boxing, wrestling, rugby, ice hockey, football, and basketball.

Mercer appealed the district court ruling. On appeal, the court reversed the decision and held that there was a valid basis under Title IX for Mercer's lawsuit. The court of appeals carefully examined HEW's contact sport exception. The court concluded that a school could lawfully preclude women from trying out for men's football or any other men's team in a contact sport. However, the court said, once a school allows a woman to try out for a men's team in a contact sport, the school cannot later rely on the contact sport exception to discriminate against woman players.[442] With that ruling, Mercer's lawsuit was reinstated for consideration by the

---

[441] 34 Code of Federal Regulations §106.41(b) [emphasis added].

[442] *Mercer v. Duke University*, 190 F.3d 643 (4th Cir. 1999).

district court. A Federal jury heard the case and agreed that Mercer was the victim of unlawful discrimination. The jury found that university officials were aware of the discriminatory treatment of Mercer and did nothing about it. It was a blatant violation of Title IX. The jury ordered Duke to pay Mercer $2 million in damages.[443]

A more subtle form of discrimination occurred in Virginia. Public high schools in Virginia are classified in three groups, Group AAA, Group AA and Group A, based on the number of students enrolled in a school. The largest schools are in Group AAA, the smallest in Group A. The playing season for all of the boys' athletic teams, regardless of school size, came at identical times in the school year. Boys' basketball teams all started their seasons at the end of the scholastic football season. Boys' baseball teams all began their seasons in the spring. With this arrangement, small schools were able to schedule games against larger schools. In contrast, the schedule for girls' sports teams varied according to classification. Girls' teams from Group AAA schools played volleyball in the fall and basketball in the winter. Group AA and Group A schools played girls' basketball in the fall and girls' volleyball in the winter. The discrepancy in schedules limited the exposure of small schools to the top-flight competition often found in larger schools and necessitated more distant travel for road games.

If the boys' teams had been subjected to the same split schedule, girls' teams would have had little basis to complain. As it was, however, the differences in scheduling for boys' and girls' teams suggested unequal opportunity. As occurred in Heather Sue Mercer's case, gender was the distinguishing factor. In 1997, eleven girls in Virginia's Suffolk County filed a lawsuit against the governing body, the Virginia High School League. In July 2000, a Federal jury in Charlottesville, Virginia awarded the girls $187,000 in damages. The jury agreed that the difference in

---

[443] *Kicker Cut By Duke Gets $2 Million*, THE WASH. POST, October 13, 2000, A22.

scheduling policy, based solely on the sex of the players, violated the equal protection clause of the Constitution and the provisions of Title IX. [444]

> *The Virginia High School Principle of Title IX Equality*
>
> *Differences in the scheduling policies for high school sports, based solely on the gender of the players, constitute a violation of the equal protection clause of the Constitution and the provisions of Title IX.*

Title IX has had a dramatic effect on sports programs at all levels— from universities down to Little League. In 1995, sixteen women became members of the men's varsity wrestling team at California State University in Bakersfield.[445] If women are entitled under the law to have an opportunity to participate on men's teams at the collegiate level, there would seem to be little to prevent males from having equivalent access to traditionally female sports programs. In 1996, the national Little League organization, Little League Baseball, Inc., was forced to open its softball and hardball divisions to both boys and girls after losing lawsuits filed by boys demanding to play softball. In the 2000 Little League Softball World Series, previously an all-girl event, a team from San Cruz Valley, Arizona played five 16-year-old boys. It seemed unfair to many. Some teams threatened not to play the Arizona team. "These boys are huge," a parent from a Westfield, Massachusetts team said. "We're trying for equality for these girls and this is not equal." The boys enjoyed a distinct physical advantage. "They made catches in the outfield that no girls could have gotten to," said a member of the Westfield team.[446]

---

[443] Preston Williams, *Va. Girls Sports Will Be Seasonal*, THE WASH. POST, December 8, 2000, D8.

[444] *Look Who's Grappling*, SPORTS ILLUSTRATED, November 27, 1995, 13.

[446] *Boys Take Hit in Softball Game*, THE WASH. POST, August 17, 2000, D2.

Under Title IX, all programs receiving Federal aid must ensure gender equality with regard to equipment and supplies; scheduling and times of games; travel and per diem allowances; opportunities to receive coaching assignments and compensation; locker room facilities; medical and training facilities and services; publicity; and recruitment. Since its enactment in 1972, Title IX has led to many gains for women in academics as well as in sports. According to data accumulated by the University of Iowa, the number of women receiving medical degrees, law degrees, and doctoral degrees has increased by at least 19 percent since Title IX was adopted. In some cases, as with the Little League Softball World Series, there will be awkward moments resulting from Title IX's push toward equality. Even with these awkward moments, however, Title IX remains a law destined to produce significant, visible and irreversible benefits for society.

On August 27, 1989, during a game in which the New York Yankees were losing to the Baltimore Orioles at Yankee Stadium, fans at the Stadium began to yell: "George must go! George must go! George must go!" The chants were directed at meddlesome Yankee owner George Steinbrenner. Thereafter, fans frequently took up the same chant at other games. Anti-Steinbrenner banners also appeared at the stadium, but the Yankee Stadium security force would confiscate the banners at every opportunity. The common complaint among fans was that, under Steinbrenner's reign, the Yankee franchise was being destroyed and the Yankee tradition violated. When Steinbrenner's security guards continued to confiscate banners that criticized the Yankee owner, the American Civil Liberties Union threatened to sue the Yankees for violation of the First Amendment. The ACLU's threat prompted Steinbrenner to sponsor a "Banner Night" at Yankee Stadium. "Banner Night" took place on September 15, 1989. Fans brought more than 150 banners to the stadium, many of which continued the anti-Steinbrenner theme. One fan brought a banner that read: "Pardon US, George, Sell the Yankees." The banner was inspired by the presidential pardon given to Steinbrenner in

1989 relating to his conviction for illegal contributions to Richard Nixon's 1972 presidential re-election campaign.[447]

Even though the Yankees' "Banner Night" produced signs that undoubtedly caused Steinbrenner to blanch, the promotion most certainly brought additional fans to the ballpark. And, for at least one night, Steinbrenner did not run the risk of violating the fans' right to engage in free speech. The Hagerstown (Maryland) Suns of the Class A South Atlantic League ran a similarly unique fan promotion during the 1990s. In an apparent effort to promote family values, the Suns offered discount tickets for Sunday games to any fans who brought a church bulletin to the ballpark. The promotion also caught the attention of the ACLU. The ACLU challenged the Suns in court, claiming that the practice violated laws against religious discrimination in places of public accommodation. In response to the lawsuit, the team expanded the promotion to include any person bringing a bulletin from a civic or non-profit organization.[448]

During the 1973-1974 basketball season, a promotion held by the Denver Rockets basketball team of the American Basketball Association also came under fire, this time from the Colorado Civil Rights Commission. To attract a more balanced audience, the Rockets announced that all women attending a specified game would receive a free seat cushion. The Civil Rights Commission took exception to the practice and sued the Rockets and the team's coach and general manager, Alex Hannum. In the name of gender equality, the Commission sought to force the Rockets to make their fan promotions available to men as well as women. In the wake of the lawsuit, the Rockets' front office, ever attentive to equal opportunity and with tongues in cheek, distributed left-over seat cushions to men—but not

[447] Bill Madden and Moss Klein, *Damned Yankees: A No-Holds-Barred Account of Life with "Boss" Steinbrenner* (New York: Warner Books, Inc., 1990), 268.

[448] Lisa Winston, *Ticket Promo*, USA TODAY BASEBALL WEEKLY, Feb. 16-22, 2000, 29.

women—at a subsequent game.[449] Over time, the suit filed by the Civil Rights Commission lost whatever momentum it may have had and faded away.

It is not certain that the Colorado Civil Rights Commission would have won its lawsuit against the Rockets, even if the case had gone all the way to a hearing. A court might have displayed little patience with a lawsuit over seat cushions. Judicial impatience seems to have motivated, at least in part, a decision in which the Washington State Supreme Court affirmed the legality of ladies' night promotions staged by the Seattle Supersonics basketball team. In the early 1980s, a male basketball fan filed a class action suit in which he contested the Sonics' practice of allowing women fans to buy game tickets for half price on designated "ladies' nights." The fan accused the Sonics of sex discrimination. Accompanied by his wife and another married couple, the fan had gone to watch a game on ladies' night. The fan wanted to buy tickets having a face value of $5.00. With the ladies' discount, the four tickets would have cost $15.00—two regularly priced "men's" tickets at a total of $10.00 and two half-priced ladies' tickets at $5.00 total. The fan demanded that the ticket seller give him all four tickets at the reduced price. The ticket seller refused. The fan then paid the $15 tab, laying the foundation for his lawsuit.

The trial court dismissed the lawsuit. The fan, undeterred, appealed the decision. The appellate court reversed the trial court and ruled that ladies' nights were in violation of the Washington State equal rights amendment. The case then moved to the Supreme Court of Washington, which agreed with the trial court. The Supreme Court found that the fan had not proved discrimination against men as a class and did not demonstrate any injury to himself either. The Court noted that ladies' nights were simply one of many discount ticket promotions staged by the Sonics, and that other similar promotions included senior citizen discounts, as well as dis-

---

[449] Terry Pluto, *Loose Balls: The Short, Wild Life Of The American Basketball Association As Told By The Players, Coaches, And Movers And Shakers Who Made It Happen* (New York: Simon & Schuster, 1991), 273.

counts for students, members of the armed forces and low-income citizens. "There can be perceived in this scheme no intent to discriminate against men," the Court ruled. The Court stated that men "are included in every favored category except for 'ladies' night', and undoubtedly predominate in the military category."[450] In attempting to emphasize the discriminatory nature of ladies' night discounts, the fan offered the opinion of a male sociologist that special discounts for female fans reinforce the stereotype of women as unathletic, improvident and silly. "Ladies' Day," the sociologist had insisted, "is a silly day." The Washington Supreme Court examined the views of the sociologist and found them lacking. The Court pointed out that women attended the ladies' nights sponsored by the Sonics in great numbers, so "not all women have found that type of inducement offensive." More to the point, the Court noted that the sociologist had not shown that ladies' nights have an adverse effect on men—an assertion that the fan was obligated to prove in order to make his case.[451]

---

[450] *MacLean v. First Northwest Industries of America, Inc.*, 635 P.2d 683, 684 (1981).
[451] 635 P.2d at 685.

Chapter 16

Asylum and Other Immigration Issues Facing Foreign Athletes

Punter Darren Bennett took an unlikely path to the National Football League. A long-time Aussie Rules Football player and a full-time landscaper in his native Australia, Bennett visited the United States with his wife after winning two free airplane tickets in a long-ball kicking contest. While on his way to Sea World in San Diego, Bennett took a detour to talk to the San Diego Chargers football team. In need of a punter at the time, the Chargers gave Bennett a tryout.

Bennett began punting for the Chargers in 1994 and quickly established himself as a mainstay on the Chargers' roster. In the year 2000, after six years in the NFL, he was named to the Pro Football Hall of Fame All-Decade Team of the 1990s. Bennett remains a citizen of Australia. He returns home to his country at the end of every NFL season. He plays in the United States on a P-1 visa, which is reserved for athletes and others having an internationally recognized expertise. In 1998, after Bennett's fourth year in the NFL, the Immigration and Naturalization Service questioned the basis for Bennett's P-1 visa. The agency is not easily impressed by the stature of an NFL punter—even one who averages 47 yards per punt. The INS informed Bennett that he was at risk of being deported unless he was able to prove that his employment with the Chargers was not depriving a United States citizen of a spot on the Chargers' roster. In essence, Bennett had to demonstrate that he was uniquely qualified for his line of work. The INS suggested to Bennett that a letter from a sports-writer might bolster his case. Upon learning of Bennett's predicament, *Sports Illustrated* went one step further. The magazine assigned writer John Walters to profile Bennett's prowess as a punter. The result, an article styled as an open letter to the INS, appeared in *Sports Illustrated* in October 1998.[452] Bennett's P-1 visa was secure.

As Darren Bennett's story illustrates, one of the responsibilities of the Immigration and Naturalization Service is to ensure that citizens from other countries who work in the United States do not take jobs that could be performed by U.S. citizens. In performing this function, the INS over-sees an elaborate system of work-related visas. The visa system gives special consideration to persons of outstanding ability, whether in athletics or in other professions. A visa is a permit to apply to enter the United States. A stamp placed in a person's passport serves as an indication that the indi-vidual has been issued a visa. Issuance of a visa signifies that a consular official believes the alien is eligible to apply for temporary admission to the United States. U.S. immigration laws are designed to encourage ath-letes and other entertainers of special skills to come to the United States, both as workers on temporary visas and as permanent immigrants. A for-eign athlete of extraordinary skill who has achieved sustained national or international acclaim qualifies for what is termed an O-1 category visa. Such athletes are normally allowed entry to the United States with few obstacles, provided they intend to continue working as professional ath-letes. There is also a special category of visas, termed O-2, that is reserved for persons of foreign nationality who accompany athletes of national or international acclaim to the United States, such as coaches and trainers.

---

[452] John Walters, *Don't Kick Him Out*, SPORTS ILLUSTRATED, October 26, 1998, 59.

> **The Immigration and Naturalization Service Principle of Sustained Athletic Acclaim**
>
> *Foreign athletes of extraordinary skill who have achieved sustained national or international acclaim qualify for O-1 category visas.*

An athlete who falls short of the "sustained national or international acclaim" standard but who is capable of performing at an internationally recognized level may be admitted to the United States under a P-1 visa, as was Darren Bennett. To qualify for P-1 status, individual athletes of professional caliber must have a contract with a major U.S. sports league or team and two other credentials documenting their ability. These other credentials could be evidence of having previously played in a major professional sport in the United States, participation in collegiate sports, significant honors or awards in the sport, a written statement from a major U.S. sports league detailing the individual's international recognition—or an open letter from *Sports Illustrated*.

> **The Immigration and Naturalization Service Principle of International Athletes of Professional Caliber**
>
> *Athletes who fall short of the "sustained national or international acclaim" standard but who are capable of performing at an internationally recognized level may be admitted to the United States under P-1 visas.*

An athlete who does not qualify for either the O-1 or P-1 classification may come to the United States as a "temporary worker" under an H-2B visa. The H-2B visa category applies to professional sports teams and all types of other employers except for those in the agricultural or logging industries. H-2B visas are used in situations where unemployed persons capable of performing the work cannot be found in the United States. Unlike the O-1 or P-1 visas, the H-2B category requires that the employer submit documentation to show that there are no qualified U.S. workers available. Sports teams, like other employers, make this showing by submitting what is called a "labor certification application" to the U.S. Department of Labor. The facts stated on a labor certification application are unique to each employer or sports team. For this reason, when an H-2B worker changes employers, a new application for an H-2B visa must be filed.

The requirement to file a new H-2B visa application applies even to situations where athletes are traded from one team to another. In fact, there is a special Immigration and Naturalization Service rule that governs the trading of H-2B athletes in professional sports.[453] Under this rule, when an H-2B athlete is traded from one team to another, the player's existing employment authorization will continue automatically for 30 days after the player joins his new team. During this 30-day period, the player's new team must file an application with the Immigration Service for a new H-2B visa. If the player's new team does not file the application for an H-2B visa within 30 days of the trade, the player loses his authority to work in the United States.

Year after year, when professional baseball players are scheduled to report for spring training, there are invariably a few players who are late in joining their teams because of difficulty in obtaining their visas. In 1999, the Pittsburgh Pirates experienced particular difficulty in obtaining a visa for outfielder Jose Guillen, a native of the Dominican Republic. At the time, Guillen was listed as unmarried in the Pirates' media guide. When he filed for his visa, however, he informed the INS that he was married.[454] The INS raised questions about the validity of Guillen's marriage license.

---

[453] The INS rule pertaining to trades involving H-2B athletes is Section 214.2. This rule is found in Title 8 of the Code of Federal Regulations.

[454] *Spring Training Roundup*, THE WASH. POST, March 6, 1999, D5.

The INS finally cleared Guillen for a visa and he arrived at spring training eleven days late, but only after the Pirates appealed to the U.S. senators from Pennsylvania, Rick Santorum and Arlen Specter, for help.[455]

Sometimes even help from politicians may not be sufficient to sway the INS. In the spring of 2000, the D.C. United professional soccer team tried to obtain a visa for a highly regarded 19-year-old midfielder, Jose Alegria. Alegria, a native of Peru, had first come to the United States when he was eleven years old. Hopeful that Jose would be able to go to school in the United States, his parents had sent him to live with an uncle in Virginia. Alegria traveled to the U.S. under a temporary visitor visa. Visitor visas usually permit travelers to remain in the U.S. for six months or, in some cases, up to a year. When the visa expires, the traveler is expected to return to his native country. Alegria never returned, however. He remained in Virginia, attended public schools, and drew raves for his play on the soccer field. In 1999, when the 5-foot-8, 155-pound Alegria turned 18, he signed a contract with Major League Soccer and was assigned to play for D.C. United. Under guidance from D.C. United, Alegria returned to his birthplace in Lima, Peru in order to apply for a visa that would allow him to work in the United States. Alegria was told he would be able to return to the U.S. in two weeks.

Upon returning to Peru, however, Alegria ran into immigration trouble. The U.S. Embassy in Peru was unwilling to grant him a work permit. The difficulty lie in Alegria's years of unauthorized stay in the U.S. To receive a work visa to play for D.C. United, Alegria would have to demonstrate "nonimmigrant intent." Having lived in the U.S. for the better part of eight years, however, Alegria had all the appearances of a person who intended to stay in the United States permanently. Alegria had already violated the terms of his temporary visa once. The U.S. Embassy was reluctant to give him a second chance. In an effort to straighten out the

---

[455] *Spring Training Roundup*, THE WASH. POST, March 13, 1999, D3.

situation, a D.C. United official made two separate trips to Lima to plead with Embassy officials. Even with that effort, however, D.C. United was unable to convince the U.S. Embassy to issue a work visa. Peruvian soccer legend Teofilo "Nene" Cubillas, who scored ten goals for Peru during his World Cup career and served as Peru's minister of sport, intervened on behalf of Alegria. Several U.S. congressmen and State Department officials also wrote letters of support—all to no avail. For D.C. United, it was a frustrating experience. "We provided everything the law requires," a source close to the team said. 'We really thought we were going to pull it off. At this point, it's going to take someone with an awful lot of power to get it done."[456] Hearing nothing but bad news, Alegria gave up hope of ever again playing professionally in the United States.

Fortunately for Alegria, D.C. United eventually was able to find someone with "an awful lot of power." In September 2000, 19 months after Alegria had returned to Peru, the U.S. Embassy issued a work permit, and Alegria returned to the United States. For D.C. United, it was well worth the wait. Alegria played with the team during 2001 and, by the early months of the 2002 season, he had earned a starting position. "He's a clever, skillful little player," coach Ray Hudson said, "he's a keeper."[457]

Athletic skill can also provide a basis for foreign athletes to gain U.S. citizenship. Like other aliens of extraordinary ability in the sciences, arts, education and business, athletes possessing extraordinary ability are eligible to emigrate to the United States as priority workers. Such athletes must be recognized as having risen to the very top of their field. Generally, such players will have achieved All-Star status and be among the highest paid players in the game.

---

[456] Steven Goff, *Surgery Set for United's Pope*, THE WASH. POST, April 19, 2000, D1-D2.

[457] Steven Goff, *For Alegria, the Wait of the World: Midfielder Languished in Legal Limbo*, THE WASH. POST, April 20, 2002, D3.

The Immigration and Naturalization Service Principle of Citizenship for Athletes of Extraordinary Ability

1. Athletes possessing extraordinary ability are eligible to emigrate to the United States as priority workers.
2. Such athletes must be recognized as having risen to the very top of their field and must have achieved All-Star status or be among the highest paid performers in their sport.

Asylum is another avenue available to athletes who desire to gain U.S. citizenship. The Immigration and Naturalization Service receives 150,000 applications for asylum per year. The vast majority are denied. The class of persons eligible to apply for asylum in the United States is limited. An alien must be either physically present within the United States or in the process of applying for admission at a port of entry. An alien cannot apply for asylum at a United States Embassy in a foreign country. Tennis great Martina Navratilova, a native of Czechoslovakia, is one of many athletes who have been granted political asylum in the United States. For Navratilova, the process began on September 5, 1975 when, keeping one eye out for Czechoslovakian "enforcers," she walked into the office of the Immigration and Naturalization Service in New York's Manhattan borough. Eighteen years old at the time, Navratilova knew that her days of playing tennis—and perhaps her freedom—could be jeopardized if she returned to Czechoslovakia. When she entered the office of the Immigration Service, she did so at night under the cloak of darkness. She met with an INS official who assured her that she would almost certainly be granted a temporary resident permit. The temporary resident permit was the first step in gaining political asylum. In Navratilova's case, the decision to grant asylum was relatively routine. She was from a Communist country. More importantly, given her stature in the tennis world, the government of Czechoslovakia would not be inclined to tolerate behavior that hinted at political dissent.

Two decades after Navratilova received asylum, world-class Iraqi weightlifter Raed Ahmed went through the same process. Ahmed fled from the Iraqi team at the 1996 Olympics in Atlanta and then denounced his country's government. Clearly at odds with the regime of Saddam Hussein, Ahmed feared he would be executed if he returned to his homeland. Applying for asylum in the United States appeared to be the only option. Ahmed filed the asylum application with the Immigration Service, met with INS officials, and then waited nervously for a decision. "I was very sensitive, like a person waiting for exam results," Ahmed said. In August 1996, Ahmed received a letter from the director of the Immigration Service's asylum office in Arlington, Virginia informing him that his request for asylum had been granted. "It has been determined that you have established a well-founded fear of persecution were you to return to your country," read the letter.[458] As typically happens in asylum cases, Ahmed was granted indefinite asylum and, after one year, was permitted to apply for a "green card," which serves as the U.S. government's indicia of permanent residence.[459]

The foundation for U.S. policy on asylum is the United States' historic commitment to caring for people who face persecution in their homelands. When the U.S. grants asylum to athletes such as Martina

---

[458] *Iraqi Weightlifter, Fearing For His Life, Is Granted Asylum By INS*, THE WASH. POST, August 3, 1996, D9.

[459] The Immigration and Naturalization Service designates the "green card" as Form I-551. Officially, it is known as the Alien Registration Receipt Card. The form is the size of a standard state-issued driver's license. Over time, there have been many different versions of green cards. Most versions of green cards issued before 1978 were blue in color. In 1977, the INS adopted a green card that was white with a blue logo. The color of the green card was changed again in 1989. The green card contains the permanent resident's picture and one fingerprint, along with the person's name, alien registration number, date of birth and other data of significance to the INS.

Navratilova or Raed Ahmed, it is not because they are talented athletes. In both cases, the Immigration and Naturalization Service determined that the athletes had a well-founded fear of persecution in their home countries. Many aliens who are granted asylum come from countries afflicted by poor economic conditions. By itself, however, poverty is not sufficient to merit asylum. A person must be a "refugee" in order to receive asylum in the United States. Refugees are people who fear persecution in their homelands because of race, religion, nationality, membership in a particular social group, or political opinion.

Pitcher Orlando "El Duque" Hernandez, who won 14 games for the New York Yankees in 1998, including the second game of the World Series, easily satisfied the "fear of persecution" test. Hernandez had long been a star on Cuba's national team. His status in Cuba changed dramatically in 1995, after his half-brother, Livan, defected and was granted asylum in the United States. Livan, also a pitcher for Cuba's national team, walked away from the team during a trip to Monterrey, Mexico. He signed to play for the Florida Marlins and was one of the Marlins' heroes in the 1997 World Series, when Florida beat the American League champion Cleveland Indians, 4 games to 3. After Livan Hernandez defected, Cuban authorities feared that his brother would try to join him in the States. In 1996, Cuba banned Orlando Hernandez from playing for the national team. No longer able to play baseball, Hernandez struggled. For a short time, he worked in a psychiatric hospital, earning less than $10 a month.

In 1997, on the day after Christmas, Hernandez, his girlfriend, and six others sailed away from Cuba on a 20-foot sailboat made of scraps, carrying cans of Spam, some water and sugar. After ten hours on the open sea, Hernandez and his fellow sailors landed on Anguilla Cay, a small deserted island belonging to the Bahamas. Days later, a United States Coast Guard cutter, the *Baranoff*, picked up the stranded group and brought them to the Bahamas. Both before and after the group landed in the Bahamas, however, there were some anxious moments. At one point, the group feared that the Coast Guard was going to bring them back to Cuban soil. In broken English, El Duque tried to explain that he was the brother of the Marlins' World Series hero, Livan. El Duque's connections made little impression on the boarding officer for the *Baranoff*, Allen Bandrowsky, for whom the Marlins' triumph over the Indians was still fresh in memory. To the Coast Guard translator, Bandrowsky said, "Tell him I'm an Indians fan. He's not getting any sympathy from me."[460] The Coast Guard's policy on Cuban castaways saved Hernandez and his fellow travelers. The policy provided that castaways who were found on Bahamian soil should be taken to the Bahamas. What happened to them once they were in the Bahamas was up to Bahamian authorities. Once in the Bahamas, Hernandez and his fellow refugees were placed in a rat-infested detention center in Nassau. Upon settling in the detention center, Hernandez learned that the Bahamas had a repatriation agreement with Cuba, leading the pitcher to fear that the Bahamian government would return him to his native country.[461] However, due in large part to a hastily arranged press conference in Nassau, Hernandez quickly became a cause célèbre. In deference to Hernandez's stature and the publicity that his case generated, the Bahamian government ignored its repatriation agreement with Cuba and decided not to deport him.

The political mechanism in the United States soon produced the necessary approvals for asylum. On New Year's Eve, 1997, the U.S. Immigration Service processed a visa to permit Hernandez to come to the United States. Hernandez's girlfriend and a Cuban catcher, Alberto Hernandez, were also granted visas. After intervention by agent José Cubas, however, Hernandez decided to go first to Costa Rica, where Cubas had stockpiled Cuban ballplayers who were getting ready to play in

---

[460] Steve Fainaru and Ray Sanchez, *The Duke of Havana: Baseball, Cuba, and the Search for the American Dream* (New York: Villard Books, 2001), 211.

[461] Fainaru and Sanchez, *The Duke of Havana: Baseball, Cuba, and the Search for the American Dream*, 212.

the United States. On March 7, 1998, the Yankees met with Hernandez, who was considered to be a free agent, in Costa Rica and signed him to a four-year, $6.6 million contract.[462] Two weeks later, Hernandez was in the United States, a beneficiary of the asylum process.

Hernandez could have come directly to the United States after leaving the Bahamas but chose to go to Costa Rica instead. By remaining outside the U.S. until after he had signed a major league contract, Hernandez was able to command a more lucrative deal than otherwise would have been possible. If he had come directly to the United States, he would have been subject to baseball's annual draft of amateur players. In order to play baseball immediately, he would have had no option but to sign a contract with the team that drafted him; there would have been no competition for his talents. By going to Costa Rica, Hernandez avoided the amateur draft and was classified as a free agent. The ploy enabled Hernandez to entertain offers from all interested major league teams, resulting in a lively competition for his services.[463]

The high profile nature of Hernandez's case, together with the obvious interest of major league baseball, ensured that Hernandez would have a welcome reception in the United States whenever he arrived. Nonetheless, his side trip to Costa Rica raised the specter of immigration policies that often work against individuals seeking asylum. Under United States immigration law, aliens are not eligible for asylum in situations where they have permanently resettled in another country after leaving their homeland and before arriving in the United States. Newspaper reports indicated that Hernandez "established residence in Costa Rica."[464] Nonetheless,

---

[462] Buster Olney, *One Man's Journey to the Center of Baseball*, THE N.Y. TIMES, June 4, 1998, A1.

[463] Clyde Haberman, *Asylum Pitch: Persecution or a Curveball*, THE N.Y. TIMES, March 27, 1998, B1. In addition to the Yankees, the Cleveland Indians were known to be involved in the bidding for Hernandez. The Indians offered a package worth between $2 million and $3 million, far short of the Yankees' offer of $6.6 million.

[464] Olney, *One Man's Journey to the Center of Baseball*, A1.

Hernandez's stay in Costa Rica did not last long and did not constitute permanent resettlement. Any time a political refugee takes up residence in a third country before coming to the United States, however, there is a risk that the Immigration Service will use the individual's sojourn in the third country as a basis for denying asylum.

Khalid Khannouchi, a native of Morocco and one of the world's premier marathon runners, became a permanent resident of the United States by virtue of his 1996 marriage to Sandra Natal, a naturalized U.S. citizen from the Dominican Republic. Khannouchi first came to the United States to compete for Morocco at the World University Games in 1993. He moved to the United States shortly thereafter and began to earn a living by entering road races. After his marriage, Khannouchi became eligible to apply for conditional permanent residence in the U.S. The INS issued Khannouchi a conditional green card, good for a two-year period. Prior to expiration of the two-year conditional period, Khannouchi applied to become a full-fledged permanent resident, meaning that the INS would remove his conditional status.

The basic requirement for removal of conditional status is that the alien remain validly married. If a marriage ends in divorce before expiration of the two-year conditional period, an alien may still qualify for full-fledged permanent residence if it can be proved, to the satisfaction of the INS, that the marriage was truly the product of a loving relationship. The INS would not confer full-fledged permanent residence upon the alien spouse if it appears that the primary purpose of the marriage was to enable the alien spouse to become a U.S citizen.

Under U.S. immigration laws, the spouse of a U.S. citizen must normally wait three years after becoming a permanent resident before applying for U.S. citizenship. After that, there may be another 15 months before the spouse becomes a citizen. In 1999, Congresswoman Sue Kelly (R-N.Y.) was hoping to find a way for Khalid Khannouchi to compete for the U.S. in the 2000 summer Olympics. With that goal in mind, Kelly introduced special legislation intended to expedite Khannouchi's citizenship. Congress did not pass Congresswoman Kelly's proposed legislation, however.[465] In time, Khannouchi found a quicker route to citizenship. In March 2000, his wife started a job in Madrid with Elite Racing Inc., a U.S. road racing promotions company. Under section 319(d) of the Immigration and Nationality Act, Khalid Khannouchi became eligible for expedited citizenship as the spouse of an American citizen working abroad.[466]

Khannouchi was sworn in as a U.S. citizen on May 2, 2000. With the issue of citizenship resolved, Khannouchi became eligible to compete in the U.S. Olympic marathon trials held in mid-May. However, due to a conflicting commitment to run in another road race, Khannouchi was unable to participate in the Olympic trials. Having missed the trials, Khannouchi did not compete in the year 2000 Olympic marathon in Australia. Even if Khannouchi had qualified for the U.S. Olympic team, it is uncertain whether he would have been permitted to represent the United States in Australia. The Olympic Charter requires athletes who change citizenship to wait three years before competing in the Olympics. The International Olympic Committee has the authority to waive the three-year rule, but it generally requires the consent of the athlete's former nation.

When Khannouchi was sworn in as a naturalized citizen of the United States, it secured for him the right to remain in the U.S. for the rest of his life. Without the rights of citizenship, aliens who are in the United States on temporary visas have no guarantees that they will be able to remain in the U.S. perpetually. Even aliens who have received their green cards, and therefore hold the status of permanent residents, are subject to deportation if they should commit crimes involving "moral turpitude." Pitcher Pedro

---

[465] Athelia Knight, *Khannouchi Too Late, INS Says*, THE WASH. POST, March 8, 2000, D2.

[466] Jim Hage, *Record Marathoner Becomes U.S. Citizen*, THE WASH. POST, May 3, 2000, D1.

Astacio, once the ace of the Colorado Rockies' pitching staff, is a native of the Dominican Republic. During the 1999 baseball season, Colorado police arrested Astacio on charges of domestic violence after his wife reported that the pitcher had struck her during an argument. Astacio pleaded guilty to charges of assault and domestic violence and was sentenced to six months' probation. Under the immigration laws, the guilty plea was an admission that Astacio had committed a "crime of moral turpitude." Crimes of moral turpitude are grounds for deportation. Shortly after his guilty plea, the Immigration and Naturalization Service initiated steps to deport the pitcher. In March 2000, however, a judge allowed Astacio to withdraw his guilty plea. The judge found that Astacio had never been informed that a guilty plea to assault charges would raise the threat of deportation.[467] Lawyers later worked out an agreement under which Astacio pleaded guilty to a lesser charge of harassment, allowing him to avoid deportation.[468]

The Immigration and Naturalization Service Principle of Deportation for Crimes of Moral Turpitude

Under U.S. immigration laws, an individual from a foreign country who has not gained U.S. citizenship is subject to being deported if he or she is convicted of a crime involving moral turpitude.

For Major League Soccer players, possession of a green card or U.S. citizenship is particularly important. The league's rules limit each team to three foreign players. Players from outside the United States who seek to secure one of the three spots for foreign players face a highly competitive

---

[467] *Colorado Rockies: Last Year's Cellar-Dwellers Have A Slew of New Faces and a Fresh Style of Play*, SPORTS ILLUSTRATED, March 27, 2000, 154, 156.

[468] Mike Soraghan, *Astacio Case At Heart of Deportation Dispute*, DENVER POST, December 7, 2000, B1.

process. At the beginning of the 2001 Major League Soccer season, the D.C. United team had three foreign players, Raul Diaz Arce, Jaime Moreno and team captain Marco Etcheverry. In May 2001, D.C. United announced that it hoped to add 24-year-old Stephen Armstrong, a midfielder who held both British and South African citizenship, to its squad. The addition of Armstrong would result in D.C. United having to juggle its list of foreign players. Of the three foreign players on United's roster, Diaz Arce, a native of El Salvador and a star on D.C. United's championship teams in 1996 and 1997, was considered the most vulnerable.[469] He was the second leading scorer in Major League Soccer history, but his play had suffered considerably since 1997. In contrast, Armstrong, seven years younger than Diaz Arce, would infuse the team with greater speed and endurance.

For Diaz Arce, there were a couple of options. He had previously filed an application for permanent residence in the United States and was hopeful that he would soon receive his green card. Upon receiving his green card, he would no longer count as one of D.C. United's foreign players. In that way, the team could use one of its three foreign roster spots for Armstrong and still retain Diaz Arce on the team. Alternately, if Diaz Arce did not receive his green card before the team was ready to add Armstrong to the roster, the team would be forced to trade Diaz Arce or loan him to another club. As things turned out, Diaz Arce did not receive permanent residence in sufficient time. Armstrong joined D.C. United in early June 2001 and, simultaneously, D.C. United traded Diaz Arce to the Colorado Rapids.[470] In April 2002, D.C. United was able to take on another foreign player when the INS approved Marco Etcheverry, a native of Bolivia, for his green card and granted him permanent residence in the United

---

[469] Steven Goff, *Armstrong Says He's With MLS*, The Wash. Post, May 25, 2001, D3.

[470] Steven Goff, *United Trades Diaz Arce To Rapids*, The Wash. Post, June 13, 2001, D3.

States. Prior to obtaining his green card, Etcheverry was playing for D.C. United under a work visa that had to be renewed at periodic intervals. As a permanent resident, Etcheverry gained many of the same rights enjoyed by U.S. citizens. Equally important for D.C. United, the green card meant that Etcheverry would no longer be classified as a foreigner.[471]

As a citizen of both England and South Africa, Stephen Armstrong is one of many athletes who hold dual citizenship. Dallas Mavericks basketball player Shawn Bradley is another. Under international law, there are two fundamental principles of citizenship, the principle of *jus sanguinis*, or right of blood, and the principle of *jus solis*, the law of the place of birth. Under the principle of *jus sanguinis*, a person's citizenship is determined by the citizenship of the parents. Conversely, under the principle of *jus solis*, citizenship is based on a person's place of birth. Bradley was born in Germany to a parent holding U.S. citizenship. Therefore, Bradley became a U.S. citizen by virtue of *jus sanguinis*. However, under the principle of *jus solis*, Bradley was also eligible for German citizenship. In the summer of 2001, the government of Germany made Bradley a citizen. For the 7'6" center, it was the first step toward fulfilling a childhood dream. "One of my goals as a kid was to play in the Olympics," Bradley explained. "I doubt if I'll get invited for the next Dream Team," he said, "so I'm going to option 1A."[472] For Bradley, "option 1A" was to play for Germany in the Olympics. With his German citizenship in place, Bradley became eligible to play on Germany's Olympic basketball team. And if, by chance, Bradley was wrong, if he was invited to play for the Dream Team, he would be permitted to represent the United States in the Olympics because, like Stephen Armstrong, Bradley is a citizen of two countries.

---

[471] Steven Goff, *Etcheverry Gets His Green Card*, THE WASH. POST, April 12, 2002, D8.

[472] *Scorecard*, SPORTS ILLUSTRATED, August 20, 2001, 26.

The rosters of professional sports teams are dotted with athletes who have followed unlikely paths to the United States. Some escape from their homeland in makeshift sailboats, others seek refuge after international competitions, some knock on the doors of the Immigration Service late at night seeking asylum, others fall in love with U.S. citizens. Some come with the help of politicians, others with the help of *Sports Illustrated*. Their stories are diverse, their futures filled with uncertainty. Once in the United States, however, these athletes can be assured of a chance to play their games at the highest levels of sport—in an environment where talent dictates opportunity.

Chapter 17

Locker Room Secrets, Defamation and the "Mendoza Line"

When relief pitcher Jim Brosnan and his Cincinnati Redlegs teammates traveled to Milwaukee to play the Braves in 1960, they found an oversized sign hanging in the visiting team's clubhouse at Milwaukee County Stadium. The sign read:

> What you see here,
> What you say here,
> When you leave here,
> Let it stay here.

The sign was a none-too-subtle reminder that Brosnan had violated the "code." Brosnan incurred the wrath of the Braves and others in baseball when he wrote *The Long Season*, a diary of his experiences in 1959, a season in which he spent time with both the St. Louis Cardinals and the Redlegs. It was the first time a major leaguer had written an "inside" account of the events that take place during the baseball season without the help of a professional writer.

As a child, Brosnan's only adult ambition was to see a book that he had written make it onto the shelves of a library. *The Long Season* was the fulfillment of that boyhood dream. In fact, there are two books on library shelves with Brosnan's name on them. In 1961, he penned a sequel to *The*

Long Season, titled *Pennant Race*. Outfielder Gino Cimoli, Brosnan's team-mate in St. Louis, was particularly upset with *The Long Season*. In the book, Brosnan complained that, during one game, Cimoli had gotten a bad break on a fly ball and then nonchalantly chased after the ball, losing the game for the Cardinals. It was one of Brosnan's six losses during the 1959 season. Traded to Cincinnati in the middle of that season, Brosnan roomed with fellow Redlegs pitcher Howie Nunn. After Brosnan's book came out, Nunn, a friend of Cimoli, warned Brosnan, "You know if Cimoli ever sees you, he'll kill you because you embarrassed him in your book." Brosnan retorted, "I didn't know Cimoli learned how to read." Nunn laughed and later told Cimoli what Brosnan had said. Cimoli, of course, was even more angered.[473]

Brosnan's books were tame compared to Jim Bouton's *Ball Four*, published in 1970. Brosnan once explained that, in an effort to preserve the juvenile market, his editor at Harper & Row "vetoed sex and tried to put the kibosh on martinis!" Brosnan went along with the ban on sex but "poured more gin as the days and pages unfolded."[474] Clearly, the two pitchers, Brosnan and Bouton, were kindred spirits.[475] Bouton offered a typically humorous explanation for his book. "I always thought if I got to be famous or great," he said, "I'd write a book about it. Unfortunately, I

---

[473] Danny Peary, *We Played The Game: Sixty-Five Players Remember Baseball's Greatest Era, 1947-1964.* (New York: Hyperion, 1994), 511.

[474] Mike Shannon, ed., "The Spitball Interview: Jim Brosnan," in *The Best of Spitball: The Literary Baseball Magazine* (New York: Pocket Books, 1988), 156.

[475] The books by Brosnan and Bouton stand tall among the writings devoted to baseball. Both writers serve as a testament to the truth of a theory articulated by author and TV pitchman George Plimpton. Said Plimpton, "I have a theory: The larger the ball, the less the writing about the sport. There are superb books about golf, very good books about baseball, not many good books about football, and very few good books about basketball. There are no books about beach balls." Armand Eisen, *Play Ball! Quotes on America's Favorite Pastime* (Kansas City: Andrews and McMeel, 1995), 222.

can't wait any longer."[476] Both Brosnan and Bouton showed particular disdain for the coaches on major league teams. Brosnan maintained that "all coaches religiously carry fungo bats in the spring to ward off suggestions that they are not working."[477] Bouton had a different take on the duties of a coach. "The best qualification a coach can have," he said, "is being the manager's drinking buddy."[478] Bouton called long-time New York Yankee coach Frank Crosetti "a bit of a washerwoman and sometimes a pain in the ass." He labeled Seattle Pilot coaches Eddie O'Brien and Ron Plaza "officious types" who caused more trouble than they smoothed over. Bouton also displayed a special knack for humor. He recounted the time when, as a 150-pounder, he reasoned that if he gained a lot of weight, he'd be able to throw a better fastball. For six weeks, he ate five meals each day, "all very rich." The diet added 30 pounds to his frame and caused a permanent inflammation of his stomach. "The fastball went," he reported, "the stomach stayed."

Many failed to see the humor in *Ball Four*. Former teammates wrote Bouton letters complaining of betrayal. Fellow ballplayers refused to speak with him. Former Expos and Mets first baseman Rusty Staub said, "I hope it's damned good because it might be the last one he writes." In fact, *Ball Four* was not the last book that Jim Bouton would write. The outcry over *Ball Four* produced enough material for Bouton to write a sequel, titled *I'm Glad You Didn't Take It Personally*. Despite Bouton's obvious flair for writing, the baseball establishment was not amused. One observer said, "Bouton broke the code. He has suffered for it ever since."[479] Jim Bouton may have broken the code, but he didn't break any laws. And no one was ever able to discourage him from writing. He followed up *I'm Glad You*

---

[476] Jim Bouton, as related in Microsoft, *Complete Baseball Guide* (1995).

[477] Eisen, *Play Ball! Quotes on America's Favorite Pastime*, 257.

[478] Eisen, *Play Ball! Quotes on America's Favorite Pastime*, 246.

[479] Peter Golenbock, *Dynasty: The Yankees 1949-1964* (Englewood Cliffs, NJ: Prentice-Hall, Inc., 1975), 372.

Didn't Take It Personally with yet another book, *I Managed Good, But, Boy, Did They Play Bad.*

Jim Brosnan's contract with the Cincinnati Redlegs included a provision requiring him to obtain the team's permission before publishing any accounts of his experiences in professional baseball. If Brosnan was aware of the provision, he didn't let it deter him. His first book may have come as a surprise to team officials, but by the time Brosnan began his second book, the team knew exactly what he was doing. After the publication of *Pennant Race*, Cincinnati general manager Bill DeWitt pointed out to Brosnan the clause, common to all player contracts, which gave the team approval rights over anything a player wrote. Says Brosnan, "when I pointed out that writing was an avocation, he didn't press the issue. Instead, he traded me to the White Sox!"[480]

The baseball establishment has never been completely comfortable with players who turn to writing. Prior to the 1913 World Series between the Philadelphia Athletics and the New York Giants, pitcher Walter Johnson received lucrative offers, some for as much as $1,000, to sign his name to ghostwritten analyses of the World Series. American League president Ban Johnson, the leader of baseball's National Commission, did not approve of ballplayers using ghostwriters, however. Before the Series began, the National Commission announced that ballplayers would not be allowed to put their byline on ghostwritten articles. In issuing the ban, the National Commission was attempting to appease the Baseball Writers Association, at least some of whose members were disturbed by the practice of ballplayers passing themselves off as writers. Ban Johnson, a former sportswriter himself, issued a warning that any article appearing under a player's name would be closely scrutinized for "faking." Walter Johnson, having lost out on his fee for ghostwriting, then proceeded to wager heavy bets on the outcome of the Series. He placed his money on the Athletics.

---

[480] Shannon, *The Best of Spitball: The Literary Baseball Magazine*, 154.

When Philadelphia beat New York handily, 4 games to 1, Walter reportedly took home $5,000 in earnings from his gambling.[481]

If Gino Cimoli was incensed at Jim Brosnan for questioning Cimoli's ability to read, Brosnan's comment was nonetheless standard fare in dugout humor. Inspired by shortstop Mario Mendoza's anemic batting average, dugout humor reached a new level in 1979. That was the year that baseball coined the term "the Mendoza Line." Mendoza, a weak-hitting shortstop from Chihuahua, Mexico, broke into the major leagues in 1974 and played the next nine years with the Pittsburgh Pirates, Seattle Mariners and Texas Rangers. He retired from baseball in 1982, having compiled a lifetime batting average of .215. Mendoza possessed uncommon talent as a fielder. If judged solely on his ability with a bat, he would never have made it to the major leagues. Mendoza hit only four home runs during his career and, in five of his nine years, his batting average was below .200. In 1979, Mendoza played in 148 games for the Seattle Mariners and hit .198. Mendoza's struggles as a hitter were highlighted when Mariner teammate, first baseman Bruce Bochte, referred to a .200 average as "the Mendoza Line." The quip stuck. Ever since, the "Mendoza Line" has been synonymous with futility at the plate.

During his eighteen-year major league career, Lou Piniella was an above-average hitter. When he retired as a player in 1984, he took with him a .291 career average. Piniella played in four World Series with the New York Yankees, during which he hit .319. His crowning achievement came in the 1981 World Series, when he blistered Los Angeles Dodger pitchers for seven hits in 16 at-bats, good for a gaudy .438 batting average. Piniella also knew what it was like to struggle at the plate. His one bad year came in 1975—four years before the "Mendoza Line" would become a term of art. That year, playing in only 74 games, Piniella compiled

---

[481] Henry W. Thomas, *Walter Johnson: Baseball's Big Train* (Washington, D.C.: Phenom Press, 1995), 120.

Mendoza-like numbers. In 199 at-bats, he collected 39 hits, a woeful .196 clip. Fittingly, only Mario Mendoza stood between Piniella and the worst average in the majors. While Piniella was struggling, Mendoza was enduring an even more distressing season, hitting .180 in 56 games with the Pittsburgh Pirates.

Piniella went on to manage the Yankees, Cincinnati Reds and Seattle Mariners. The same qualities that made him an aggressive clutch hitter caused him to become, on occasion, a volatile manager. While managing Cincinnati, Piniella accused National League umpire Gary Darling of playing favorites. In a comment to *The Cincinnati Enquirer*, Piniella said, "I honestly feel Darling has a bias against us and won't give us a call all year." The National League fined Piniella $1,000 for his statement. The worst was yet to come, however. Before the week was out, Darling and the major league umpires had sued Piniella for $5 million for defamation of character. The suit accused Piniella of severely damaging the reputation of Darling and all other umpires. Four months later, Piniella and the umpires settled the lawsuit out of court.[482]

If Lou Piniella's remarks to *The Cincinnati Enquirer* damaged the reputation of umpire Gary Darling, Bruce Bochte's quip about the "Mendoza Line" certainly did little to enhance Mario Mendoza's reputation as a ballplayer. Darling was sufficiently offended to file a lawsuit. Mendoza may have been offended as well, but he did not sue—and for good reason. A statement is defamatory if it tends to injure a person's standing in his trade, profession or community. The law understands that there must be "breathing space" for imaginative expression and hyperbole. To allow room for imaginative expression and hyperbole, the law will usually not examine a statement of opinion to see if it is defamatory unless the statement relates to a matter that can be objectively verified. Additionally, if an opinion relates to a matter of public concern, the statement will not be

---

[482] Richard Goldstein, *You Be The Umpire* (New York: Dell Publishing, 1993), 300-301.

considered defamatory unless the statement is obviously false. Only then does the statement lose its protection under the freedom of speech provisions of the First Amendment. Under the law, both Gary Darling's performance as an umpire and Mario Mendoza's batting average would be considered "matters of public concern"—at least in the cities of Cincinnati and Seattle, respectively. To establish defamation, both Darling and Mendoza would have had to prove that the statements made about them were obviously false. For both, it would have been a most difficult burden.

The Lou Piniella Principles of Defamatory Statements

1. The law will not examine a statement of opinion to see if it is defamatory unless the statement relates to a matter that can be objectively verified.

2. If an opinion relates to a "matter of public concern," the statement will not be considered defamatory unless the statement is obviously false.

3. The conduct and performance of major league umpires is a "matter of public concern."

A case involving University of Kansas woman's basketball coach Marian Washington demonstrates the difficulties of proving defamation. Washington sued *Dick Vitale's College Basketball Preview* over its assessment that "the Jayhawks are loaded with talent… but coach Marian Washington usually finds a way to screw things up." Washington was offended. She alleged that the magazine had defamed her.[483] As with the performance of Gary Darling and the batting average of Mario Mendoza, Marian Washington's coaching ability was a matter of public concern. In the court's view, therefore, Washington had to prove that the statement in the magazine was both objectively verifiable and untrue. The court had difficulty with both prongs of the test. The *Preview* was stating an opinion

---

[483] *Fanfare*, THE WASH. POST, April 13, 1996, H2.

about a matter that was not verifiable. To win in court, Washington had to prove that the statement in the *Preview* was false. The court looked to see whether the statement was a plausible interpretation of Washington's coaching record. Based on the Jayhawks' performance, it appeared to be. Washington's squads had never been dominant. During her 22 years as the Kansas coach, her teams had never reached the NCAA "Final Four" tournament. Washington could not produce facts to show that the *Preview's* assessment was obviously false. The court ruled, therefore, that the *Preview* had not defamed her.[484]

The *Saturday Evening Post* was not so fortunate. In a defamation case that arose after a 1962 football game between the University of Georgia and the University of Alabama, the *Post* was ordered to pay University of Georgia coach Wally Butts $460,000. An article published in the *Post* accused Wally Butts and Alabama coach Paul "Bear" Bryant of conspiring to fix the game. The author, Frank Graham, Jr., wrote that, before the game, Butts had given Bear Bryant all of Georgia's plays and defensive patterns—"all the significant secrets Georgia's football team possessed." The article called Butts and Bryant "corrupt" men.[485] Several national magazines, including *Newsweek* and *Sports Illustrated*, had turned down the story because they doubted the accuracy of some of the alleged details. The *Saturday Evening Post* had no such qualms. After the article appeared in print, Wally Butts sued. A Georgia jury awarded him $60,000 in general damages and $3 million in punitive damages. The jury concluded that the article was clearly defamatory. Federal District Court Judge Lewis R. Morgan later reduced the punitive damages to $400,000.[486]

---

[484] *Marian E. Washington v. Joseph C. Smith, et al.*, 80 F.3d 555 (D.C. Cir. 1996).

[485] Frank Graham Jr., *The Story Of A College Football Fix*, THE SATURDAY EVENING POST, March 23, 1963, 80.

[486] James Kirby, *Fumble: Bear Bryant, Wally Butts & the Great College Football Scandal.* (New York: Dell Publishing, 1988), 160.

The law of defamation deals in verifiable facts—not opinions, not feelings, and not comments uttered in jest. When Jim Brosnan suggested that Gino Cimoli might be incapable of reading, he touched on a question of fact that could be verified one way or another. Brosnan's comment was clearly spoken in jest, however, and no court of law would ever concern itself with whether Brosnan had defamed Cimoli. In the same way, when Bruce Bochte fashioned the term "Mendoza Line," it was not particularly flattering to Mario Mendoza, but it passed as vintage clubhouse humor. When the element of humor underlies a seemingly derogatory comment, courts of law are not inclined to find defamation. As a derogatory comment passes from the realm of clubhouse humor to a statement of opinion, the comment comes closer to possible defamation but still falls short of a textbook defamation case. The opinion stated in *Dick Vitale's College Basketball Preview* may well have diminished Marian Washington's standing in college basketball circles, but it never went beyond a statement of opinion. It never reached the point of being a verifiable fact. Readers could choose to believe what the magazine had to say or to disregard it, but, either way, the statement did not lend itself to verification. It was pure opinion.

In July 2001, the St. Louis Cardinals baseball team named Mitchell Page to replace Mike Easler as the team's batting coach. The Cardinals then offered Easler a job as the organization's minor league hitting instructor.[487] From the Cardinals' perspective, the move made a lot of sense,

---

[487] The major league experiences of Mike Easler and Mitchell Page offer an interesting contrast. Easler, known as "The Hit Man" during his major league career, spent fourteen seasons in the big leagues and compiled a career .293 batting average with 118 home runs. Page enjoyed an excellent rookie season with the Oakland Athletics, hitting .307 with 21 home runs. He would go on to play eight years at the major league level. However, he never duplicated the success of his rookie season and, during the last four years of his career, was no more than a bench player and occasional designated hitter. For his career, Page hit .266 with 72 homers.

both for the team and for Easler. Easler, however, viewed the change solely in terms of injury to his standing in the profession. He sued the Cardinals for defamation and invasion of privacy. The 2001 Cardinals were a team that was stocked with stars. Long-time St. Louis and Kansas City manager Whitey Herzog was of the opinion that "on paper, if you take the teams in the National League, the Cardinals are the best team."[488] However, the team was beset by injuries and lackluster performances. In mid-July, the Cardinals were languishing in third place in the National League's Central Division, far behind the division-leading Chicago Cubs. Slugger Mark McGwire's batting average hovered around .200, almost dead-even with the Mendoza Line. Center fielder Jim Edmonds was batting .273 and having a respectable year, but catcher Mike Matheny, left fielder Ray Lankford, shortstop Edgar Renteria and power-hitting pinch hitter Bobby Bonilla were all struggling with batting averages below .240. Collectively, the team was hitting .264.

When the Cardinals replaced Easler as hitting coach, Easler said the team was making him a "scapegoat" for the club's hitting woes. He sued for more than $25,000 in damages. The lawsuit alleged that the Cardinals had wrongly discharged Easler and, in the process, defamed his character, slandered him, invaded his privacy, and disclosed facts that placed him in a false light. The Cardinals saw it differently. "We did everything more than right for him," St. Louis manager Tony La Russa said.[489] Underlying Easler's discharge were several circumstances that clouded the issues. For starters, there were questions as to whether Easler was sufficiently healthy to perform his job. A month before his release, he had been unable to accompany the team on a road trip to San Francisco because of a sinus infection that made airplane travel too painful. He also suffered from

---

[488] Bernie Miklasz, *Blown Lead At Wrigley Again Demonstrates Cardinals' Mediocrity*, St. Louis Post-Dispatch, July 28, 2001, 3 OT.

[489] Mike Eisenbath, *Former Coach Easler Files Suit Against Cardinals*, St. Louis Post-Dispatch, July 27, 2001, C1, C7.

arthritis in his neck and bronchitis and lost time due to those ailments. In addition, it was not clear whether the Cardinals actually fired Easler, demoted him, or simply offered him a new job that would afford more time for medical treatment.

The public statements suggest that the Cardinals did not defame Easler. The team said all the right words. In public pronouncements, the Cardinals denied that Easler had been fired. La Russa said that he hoped that Easler, by accepting the position of minor league hitting instructor, would have more time to take care of his health. Easler seemed as much concerned with perceptions as with anything the Cardinals had said publicly. He was, at times, ambivalent regarding the extent of the harm he had suffered. After being relieved of his job, he agreed that the decision was actually in his best interests. Two weeks later, however, he changed his stance. "They've got to stop treating coaches so bad," he said. "I have been severely wronged by an organization I put my faith in."[490] La Russa countered quickly. "He couldn't be more mistaken about the way coaches are treated by the St. Louis Cardinals," La Russa said. The manager also hinted that there was more to the story than Easler was revealing. "Litigating this thing," he said, "the entire truth is going to come out and he'll be worse off."[491]

The "entire truth" never had a chance to come out. Acting upon advice from Cardinals outfielder Bobby Bonilla, Easler abruptly changed course and withdrew his lawsuit less than a week after initiating the case. "I want to laugh again," Easler explained, and "I lost my laugh and my joy the last few weeks."[492] As in any other defamation lawsuit, however, if the case

---

[490] Eisenbath, *Former Coach Easler Files Suit Against Cardinals*, ST. LOUIS POST-DISPATCH, July 27, 2001, C7.

[491] Rick Hummel, *Freak Injury Sidelines Reliever Timlin; Jocketty Seeks Replacement*, ST. LOUIS POST-DISPATCH, July 28, 2001, 4 OT.

[492] Mike Eisenbath, *Easler Says He Opted To Move On; "I'm Bigger Than This," Former Cardinals Coach Proclaims In Ending Suit*, ST. LOUIS POST-DISPATCH, July 29, 2001, D11.

had gone to trial, the court would have had to determine whether, in relieving Easler, the Cardinals had merely expressed opinions as to his ability to perform his job or whether they had made statements that were obviously false and harmful to Easler's career.

The same issues may be the focal point of a lawsuit filed in 2002 against the father-son quarterbacking duo of Archie and Peyton Manning. Two years earlier, the father and son co-authored a book titled *Manning*. In the book, Peyton characterized Jamie Ann Naughright, one-time trainer for the University of Tennessee football team, as having a "vulgar mouth." Naughright disputed the accuracy of the allegation. She also contended that the statement forced her to leave her job at Florida Southern University. Naughright sued the Mannings for defamation and sought damages of more than $15,000.[493]

If it is difficult to verify whether Marian Washington tended to "screw things up," it may not be much easier to assess whether Jamie Ann Naughright has a "vulgar mouth." By talking to enough people who knew Naughright, however, a court could form an opinion as to whether she engaged in vulgarity. Even if the statements made by Peyton Manning are shown to be false, Naughright still must establish that Manning defamed her. She would have to show that the book caused harm to her reputation, character or standing in the community, or that the statements deprived her of income she would otherwise have gained. If a court finds that Naughright was defamed, Peyton's father, Archie, could be held liable for the defamation, even though Peyton made the statements. As co-author of the book, Archie assisted in the publication. Under the law of defamation, every person who assists in the publication of a defamatory statement is liable for the injury caused.

When Lou Piniella alleged that umpire Gary Darling was biased against the Cincinnati Reds, it was an opinion that could not be verified. In contrast, when the *Saturday Evening Post* reported that Wally Butts con-

---

[493] *The Blotter: Sued*, SPORTS ILLUSTRATED, June 10, 2002, 32.

spired with Bear Bryant to fix a football game, it presented as factual a series of events that were shown to be false. It was a classic case of printed words causing injury to a person's standing in his profession. It was the essence of defamation. When a defamatory statement is in writing, it is termed libel. When the defamation is spoken, it is called slander. Either way, the result tends to be the same: there is a damage to a person's reputation, character or career.

Chapter 18

Property: Partitioning the "Field of Dreams"

In the years following his retirement from baseball, former Kansas City and New York infielder-outfielder Hector Lopez kept his Yankee uniform in the trunk of his car. Lopez explained, "I keep this close to me all the time. Every time I open the trunk I say to myself, 'I used to play ball for the greatest team.' "[494]

Carl Taylor, an outfielder with the Kansas City Royals in the early 1970s, had no such fondness for his uniform. One night in 1972, Taylor removed himself from a game against the Baltimore Orioles, went to the Royals' clubhouse and burned his uniform and equipment in front of his locker. When

---

[494] Edward Kiersh, *Where Have You Gone, Vince DiMaggio?* (New York: Bantam Books, 1983), 63-64. Lopez has a credible argument when he says he used to play for "the greatest team." He was with the New York Yankees from 1959 to 1966. During that period, the Yankees won the American League pennant five times and the World Series twice.

reporters entered the clubhouse after the game, they were confronted with thick smoke and the charred remnants of Taylor's equipment.[495]

Except for cleated shoes, major league baseball clubs provide their players with complete playing uniforms. The uniforms are like any other property that belongs to a team. Players are expected to return the uniforms at the end of each season, and the uniforms remain in the team's possession and ownership. Except in unusual cases, professional sports teams do not allow players to keep their uniforms. Nor do they authorize the players to burn their uniforms. If a player should take his uniform, as Hector Lopez did, or destroy a uniform, as Carl Taylor did, the team has a right to compensation.

Major league uniforms were not always considered to be the property of the team. In years past, some teams required the players to buy their own uniforms. In such cases, the uniforms became the players' property. Arthur "Bugs" Raymond pitched for the New York Giants for five seasons, beginning in 1907. In spite of an uncontrollable addiction to alcohol, Raymond had a respectable career in the big leagues, including one standout season, 1909, when he won 18 games and posted an earned run average of 2.47. In 1911, Raymond's last season in the majors, he put together a record of 6 wins and 4 losses. In mid-season of that year, Raymond came to the park two hours late for a game in St. Louis. For Giants manager John McGraw, it was the last straw. "Bugs," McGraw told Raymond, "you're through in baseball. Here's your uniform. See Mr. Foster, and he'll

---

[495] Taylor is the half-brother of former Baltimore Orioles slugger Boog Powell. Unlike Powell, Taylor never achieved stardom in baseball. He did excel for the Pittsburgh Pirates in 1969, however, when he hit .348 in 104 games. Taylor, a first baseman and outfielder, had difficulty breaking into a Pirates lineup that featured Roberto Clemente, Matty Alou and Willie Stargell in the outfield and Al Oliver at first base. His career in Pittsburgh suffered when he accused the Pirates' management of keeping him on the bench because of politics. In the wake of his complaint, the Pirates dubbed him the "Senator." After his stint with the Pirates, Taylor spent parts of three seasons, 1971 to 1973, in Kansas City, during which both his batting average and his playing time dwindled.

give you a ticket back to New York." Although through in baseball, Raymond was not through in New York. When McGraw and the Giants returned to the Polo Grounds after their road trip, they found Bugs Raymond's uniform hanging in the window of a saloon near the stadium. Affixed to the uniform was a sign that read, "Bugs Raymond Tending Bar Here."[496]

The law divides property and possessions into two broad categories, real and personal. Real property, also known as real estate, stays in one place. Personal property is any property that is not fixed to real property. Hector Lopez' Yankee uniform is personal property; it is moveable. Yankee Stadium is real property; it is not moveable. The law records ownership of personal property in a different way than it does for real property. With personal property, the adage "possession is nine-tenths of the law" often holds true. An item of personal property that is in the possession of an individual is assumed to be the property of that person, unless someone else is able to prove ownership.

During the 1970s, the Baltimore Claws basketball team endured a very brief and entirely unsuccessful existence in the American Basketball Association. The team consisted of the remnants of the Memphis Tams, which had lost both money and its fan base in Memphis and closed down at the end of the 1974-1975 season. The Claws' ownership in Baltimore claimed to have $1.25 million that it intended to use to operate the team. The money never materialized. As the team prepared to open the 1975-1976 season in Baltimore, it had a veteran coach, Joe Mullaney, under contract. It had a bunch of players led by aging star Mel Daniels and a talented but troubled former Clemson star, Skip Wise. Like Mullaney, Daniels and most of the other players had come from Memphis. Unlike Mullaney, neither Daniels nor any of the other former Memphis players

---

[496] Lawrence S. Ritter, *The Glory of Their Times: The Story of the Early Days of Baseball Told by the Men Who Played It* (New York: William Morrow and Company, Inc., 1992), 97.

were actually under contract. Mullaney implored the Baltimore owners to send contracts to his players. Despite the owners' assurances that there were sufficient operating funds, the franchise faced budgetary problems from the very start. The owners never did sign the players to contracts. Plagued by indecisiveness and a shortage of funds, the team ceased its existence even before it played its first game. The team did not have enough money to pay either Mullaney or the players. When the team announced that it was folding, the players showed up at the team's offices in the hope of getting their paychecks. The Claws' front office personnel told the players that the team could not pay them but, in lieu of pay, the players could take any equipment that was in the Claws' offices. The players walked out with the team's typewriters and telephones and all kinds of other office equipment. In this way, ownership of the office equipment was transferred to the players.[497]

With the escalating value of sports memorabilia, ownership of personal property used in collegiate and professional sports events often becomes a matter of dispute. When Baltimore Orioles third baseman Cal Ripken played in his 2,131st consecutive game on September 5, 1995, it was an historic moment for Ripken, the Orioles and major league baseball. Ripken broke Lou Gehrig's record of 2,130 consecutive games, once considered the least likely baseball record to be broken. Of all the baseball memorabilia that celebrates Ripken's career, one of the most highly prized souvenirs is a copy of the lineup card for the record-breaking game. When Orioles manager Phil Regan filled out the player lineup before the game, he made five duplicate copies of the lineup card.[498] He kept one of the

---

[497] Terry Pluto, *Loose Balls: The Short, Wild Life Of The American Basketball Association As Told By The Players, Coaches, And Movers And Shakers Who Made It Happen* (New York: Simon & Schuster, 1991), 393-94.

[498] Major league managers, or on some teams the bench coaches, usually make two copies of the lineup cards for each game. Realizing the historic nature of Ripken's 2,131st game, Regan made extra copies of the lineup card for that game.

duplicates for himself. In 1998, Regan tried to auction his copy of the lineup card, along with the pen he used to fill out the card. The card had been valued at $30,000 and the pen at $9,000. Though Regan had possession of these items, the Orioles claimed ownership.

The Orioles and the team's owner, Peter Angelos, sued Regan. The Orioles argued that Regan had been an employee of the team. As an employee, the Orioles said, Regan was acting within the scope of his employment when he wrote out the lineup card. The team argued that all of the duplicate lineup cards belonged to the club—and not to the manager or anyone else. The court agreed and issued an injunction forbidding Regan from selling the lineup card. Ultimately, Angelos and Regan reached a settlement in which they agreed to split the revenue from sale of the lineup card. The lineup card, pen and other memorabilia were sold for more than $40,000.[499]

The Baltimore Orioles' Principles of Ownership of Lineup Cards

1. Possession is not nine-tenths of the law.
2. When a manager, acting within the scope of his employment, fills out a lineup card, the lineup card is the property of the team.

The value of the Ripken lineup card paled in comparison to the baseball that slugger Barry Bonds hit for his 73rd home run of the 2001 season. On October 7, the San Francisco Giants' last game of the season, Bonds faced 36-year-old Los Angeles Dodgers knuckleballer Dennis Springer in the first inning with two out and the bases empty. With the count at three balls and two strikes, Bonds hit a shot just beyond the Arcade seats atop Pac Bell Park's right-field wall for his final home run of the season. The value of the historic ball was pegged at more than one million dollars. Thirty-seven-year-old fan Alex Popov, in the right place at the

---

[499] *Orioles, Regan Settle Lineup Card Dispute*, THE WASH. POST, April 20, 2000, D6.

right time, caught the ball cleanly on the fly—a fact confirmed by video footage recorded by San Francisco TV station KNTV. However, nearby fans immediately wrestled Popov to the ground and a vicious scuffle for the ball followed. After a few minutes, Patrick Hayashi emerged from the mob with the ball in his pocket. Both Popov and Hayaski claimed ownership of the baseball. Popov hired a lawyer and asked the court to grant a restraining order that would prohibit Hayashi from selling the ball. Hayashi immediately hired a public relations agent. The agent went on record proclaiming Hayashi as the legitimate owner. In the agent's view, Hayashi was simply "the recipient of the ball coming out of the mad mob." University of Tulsa law professor Paul Finkelman, the author of *Fugitive Baseballs: Abandoned Property*, was among those who didn't think Hayashi was the rightful owner. "If Popov caught the ball," Finkelman said, "it's his ball." Finkelman reasoned, "If you say what happened is okay, then you're arguing you can punch, kick and scratch someone to get something that isn't yours."[500]

When Hank Aaron hit the last home run of his storied major league career, a similar dispute arose. From his rookie season in 1954 until 1974, Aaron wore a Braves uniform, first in Milwaukee and later in Atlanta. In 1975, Aaron returned to Milwaukee for the first of his two seasons with the Brewers. On July 20, 1976, playing at home for the Brewers, Aaron hit the 755th home run of his major league career. It would turn out to be the last home run he ever hit. Richard Arndt, who worked for the Brewers' stadium grounds crew, retrieved Aaron's home run. Arndt asked the Brewers to allow him to personally present the ball to Aaron. The team refused his request. The next day, the Brewers fired Arndt, apparently in a dispute over ownership of the home run ball. Arndt kept the ball for twenty-two years, preserving it in a safe deposit box. On one occasion, he brought the ball to a card show at which Aaron was signing autographs.

---

[500] *The Battle for Bonds's Ball*, SPORTS ILLUSTRATED, October 22, 2001, 32.

Arndt asked Aaron to sign the baseball, without telling the home run king that it was his last home run ball. Aaron signed the baseball, and Arndt returned it to the safe deposit box.[501]

Sometimes courts have to decide whether season tickets to sporting events are the personal property of the ticket holders. In one bankruptcy case, the U.S. Court of Appeals for the Ninth Circuit, located in San Francisco, had to determine whether the season tickets to Phoenix Suns' games held by a bankrupt basketball fan, as well as the right to renew those tickets for later seasons, were personal property that could be sold to pay off the fan's debts. After reviewing the conditions attached to the season tickets, the appeals court ruled that neither the tickets nor the right of renewal constituted "property." The court said that the tickets were, instead, a "privilege" granted by the Suns and that the Suns had reserved the right to revoke that privilege. In the court's view, therefore, unlike tangible personal property such as autographed baseballs and Cal Ripken lineup cards, neither the season tickets nor the right of renewal could be sold to others in bankruptcy proceedings.[502]

When former New York Yankee player and manager Billy Martin died in 1989, he left little personal property of any value. He did, however, leave a house near Binghamton, New York. According to the deed for his property, Martin and his wife owned the house and the land on which it was situated as "tenants by the entirety." A tenancy by the entirety is a form of joint ownership by a husband and wife which, upon the death of one spouse, results in the property being owned solely by the surviving partner. This "right of survivorship" is inherent in the tenancy by the entirety form of ownership. A tenancy by the entirety is based on the notion that husband and wife are one person—or at least one legal entity. Because a surviving spouse continues to have full ownership, property

---

[501] *Aaron's 755th for Sale*, THE WASH. POST, September 24, 1998, C2.

[502] *In re William Harrell; Robert Abele v. Phoenix Suns L.P.*, 73 F.3d 218 (9th Cir. 1996).

owned as tenants by the entirety will not usually be passed to heirs by a will. The property is also immune from any claims that may be brought by creditors of the spouse who passed away. In Billy Martin's case, although Martin owed more than $80,000 in federal income taxes at his death, his Binghamton house could not be sold to satisfy the debt.

The Billy Martin Principle of Tenancy By the Entirety

When a married couple holds real property as tenants by the entirety, the property will be immune from attack by creditors seeking to satisfy the personal debts of one of the spouses.

The tenancy by the entirety form of ownership is unique to a husband and wife. When slugging New York Yankee first baseman Jason Giambi and his brother Jeremy both played for the Oakland A's, the two shared the same house. They could have bought a house together, but the law would not permit them to own the house as tenants by the entirety. They could, however, own a house as "tenants in common"—a form of joint ownership in which each owner holds an undivided interest in the property. With a tenancy in common, if one of the owners should die, the surviving owner is generally not entitled to sole ownership of the property. Instead, when one owner dies, that owner's one-half interest in the property passes to the owner's heirs or estate. The legal form in which real property is deeded to its owners, whether as tenants by the entirety, tenants in common, or some other form, will determine how, and if, the property is passed to others.

When a married couple undergoes a divorce, a tenancy by the entirety is severed. Divorce typically changes a tenancy by the entirety into a tenancy in common. When a divorce takes place, the husband and wife become the same, from the standpoint of property ownership, as the Giambi brothers. After a divorce, even though the former marital residence may still be jointly owned, there is no right of survivorship. Instead, each of the joint owners can convey his or her one-half interest to designated heirs.

When a married person puts property into a tenancy by the entirety, the law may find that the person has made a "gift" to his or her spouse. That happened to former Washington Redskins quarterback Joe Theismann. Theismann married in May 1991. Before his marriage, Theismann had purchased a farm in Loudoun County, Virginia. The farm was worth more than $800,000. After his marriage, Theismann made a deed that transferred ownership of the farm to himself and his wife as tenants by the entirety. A few years later, Theismann and his wife divorced. During the divorce proceedings, ownership of the farm became an issue. The divorce court ruled that, when he created a tenancy by the entirety, Theismann had made a gift of joint ownership in the farm to his wife. The court found that Theismann had "donative intent" when he put his wife's name on the property.[503] As a result, at the time of divorce, Theismann's wife was entitled to a significant share of the couple's marital estate. If Theismann had kept the farm in his own name, there would have been no donative intent and no gift. The farm would have remained as Theismann's sole property.

For purposes of property law, Virginia, where Joe Theismann purchased his farm, is a "common law" jurisdiction. Other states are "community property" jurisdictions. In total, there are nine community property states in the country: Arizona, California, Idaho, Louisiana, Nevada, New Mexico, Texas, Wisconsin and Washington. In a common law system, each partner in a marriage generally owns whatever he or she earns or receives as a gift. In a community property jurisdiction, one-half of the earnings of each spouse is considered to be the property of the other spouse. The consequences of community property laws can be far-reaching. In the case of *MacLean v. First Northwest Industries of America, Inc.*, the Supreme Court of the State of Washington found that a basketball

---

[503] *Theismann v. Theismann*, 22 Va. App. 557 (1996).

fan's failure to understand the impact of the community property laws in Washington led to a fatal flaw in legal theory.[504] In that case, the fan, a man, attempted to persuade a judge that the Seattle Supersonics were discriminating against men when the team sold discount tickets to women on ladies' night.[505] As part of his argument, the fan stated that paying less for his wife's ticket made him feel "like her keeper." The Court took issue with the fan's argument. First, the Court suggested that, under the community property laws of the State of Washington, the money used to purchase tickets for the fan and his wife came equally from the husband's assets and the wife's assets. Second, the fan had not argued that he used his own separate property to buy the tickets.[506] The Court concluded, therefore, that the husband and wife each provided exactly half of the money used to acquire the tickets. This being the case, the husband could not be considered the wife's "keeper." In keeping with the property theory in a community property state, the wife had paid for half of her ticket and half of her husband's ticket. The fan would have had a stronger legal argument if he had lived in a common law jurisdiction, where the money earned by a married man and wife remain the separate property of each, unless there has been a Theismann-type gift.

When a married couple splits up, there is often a need to divide up jointly owned property. Divorce is not the only time the need arises, however. Disputes over property arise in many circumstances. One of the more prominent disputes involved the Iowa farmland that served as the backdrop for the 1989 Kevin Costner movie, "Field of Dreams." When filming the movie, the producers carved Ray Kinsella's magical baseball diamond out of farmland located in Dyersville, Iowa. Most of the baseball diamond was situated on property owned by a man named Don Lansing and his family. However, the producers wanted to locate the field west of

---

[504] 635 P.2d 683 (1981).

505 This case is discussed from a different perspective in Chapter 15.

[506] *MacLean v. First Northwest Industries of America, Inc.*, 635 P. 2d. at 685.

Lansing's farmhouse to take advantage of the Iowa sunsets. Lansing's property didn't extend far enough to the west, so the producers had to use a small tract of land belonging to one of Lansing's neighbors. The producers signed two contracts, one with Lansing and one with his neighbors, Al and Rita Ameskamp. The infield, right field and part of center field were on Lansing's property. Left field and part of center field were on land owned by the Ameskamps.

The commercial success of the movie unexpectedly turned the Iowa baseball diamond into a tourist attraction. Local amateur teams came to play on the field. Unfortunately, the Ameskamps and Lansing had different ideas on how the field should be used. The Ameskamps turned the management of their property over to an investment banker and proposed to install batting cages and an 1,800-square-foot souvenir stand on their land. Lansing objected. To demonstrate his dissatisfaction with the Ameskamps' approach, Lansing began to ban local baseball teams from using his portion of the field.[507]

Property owners have the right to enjoy the uninterrupted use of their property. They have the right to be free of trespassers. A trespass is an intentional and unauthorized intrusion on the property of another person. If an airplane flies over the "field of dreams," it is not trespass. The airplane has not caused any inconvenience to the landowner and has not violated the landowner's rights. When a baseball flies over Lansing's property, the law reaches a different result. Visitors to the baseball diamond may not legally step onto Lansing's property without permission. If a local Dyersville baseball player runs onto the property to chase down a baseball, it is trespass. Under the law of trespass, all of the property owned by Lansing, including the infield, right field and part of center field, is "off limits" to the Ameskamps and their guests.

---

[507] *'Field of Dreams': Field of Squabbles*, THE WASH. POST, July 28, 1996, D15.

The "Field of Dreams" Principle of Trespass

The law does not permit individuals to step on private property—to play baseball or for any other reason—unless the property owner consents.

Even in the case of insignificant intrusions, such as when uninvited batters hit ground balls onto the infield property or when a player chases a foul ball and steps on the infield dirt, the Lansings would have suffered a trespass. If a player merely swings his Louisville slugger across the property line and into Lansing's property, the law would view it as a trespass. In March 1999, a 39-year-old plumber trespassed on the Seattle Mariners' new baseball diamond at Safeco Field. The plumber, a man named Nolan West, was installing plumbing for the beer taps in preparation for the July 1999 opening of the ballpark. After finishing his work one day, West took a baseball and bat and wandered down to the playing field. Wearing his plumber's uniform and a hard hat, West stood at home plate, tossed the baseball in the air and hit it. With the enthusiasm of a young rookie, West ran around the bases at Safeco and topped off his round-tripper with a headfirst slide into home plate. Unlike most trespassers, West made no effort to conceal the trespass. To the contrary, he had a friend videotape his trip around the bases. West then delivered the videotape to a Seattle television station, which played it on the air. Upon learning of West's exploits on the bases, his employer, Polar Beer Systems of Santee, California, promptly fired him. The trespass was not without cost to the Mariners. When West hit his "homer," there was a protective tarp covering the infield. In running the bases, West damaged the tarp, which required a couple of hundred dollars to repair.[508]

---

[508] *Bat, Ball and Videotape Cost Eager Plumber His Stadium Job*, THE WASH. POST, March 20, 1999, D2.

When a trespass occurs, the property owner is usually not responsible for any harm that the trespasser may suffer. Stated another way, the law does not require property owners to safeguard those who come on their land without permission. In the early 1970s, 6'11' Moses Malone, a high school basketball star in Petersburg, Virginia, was pursued by more than 200 colleges and by pro scouts as well. The recruiting frenzy began when Malone scored 32 points in his first game with the high school varsity. With each succeeding year in high school, Malone gained more attention, especially after he earned the highest possible rating at Garfinkel's Five-Star basketball summer camp following his junior year. At the same time college coaches were attempting to woo Malone, Bucky Buckwalter, the general manager of the Utah Stars of the American Basketball Association, was trying to persuade the phenom to skip college and head straight to the pros. Buckwalter's efforts did not go unnoticed. He drew the ire of those college coaches who were in the running for Malone's services. To avoid detection on his trips to the Malone house, Buckwalter would sneak through a field and approach the house out of sight of the college coaches. On one such surreptitious visit, a dog that the Malone family had bought to protect their house bit Buckwalter.[509] Buckwalter, of course, had no one to blame but himself. He was a trespasser; the land owners had no obligation to look out for his safety.

The conflict that developed between the Ameskamps and the Lansings over the "field of dreams" has a parallel in the law—in situations where a parcel of land is inherited by two or more individuals. If one of the heirs wanted to have sole ownership over a distinct portion of the land, he or she could ask the local court to "partition" the property. Partitioning is a legal mechanism used to terminate joint ownership of property. In a partitioning case, the court might divide the property into shares, assigning

---

[509] Pluto, *Loose Balls: The Short, Wild Life Of The American Basketball Association As Told By The Players, Coaches, And Movers And Shakers Who Made It Happen*, 323.

separate portions to each heir. More commonly, however, instead of physically dividing up the property, the court will order the property to be sold and the proceeds divided among the owners. If the property includes a house or building, sale of the property is usually the only equitable way to resolve the issue.

Whenever property disputes arise, and regardless of whether the disputes involve a storied setting such as the "field of dreams," an expensive farm in rural Virginia or more modest estates, there are useful, if not completely satisfactory, remedies available under the law.

Chapter 19

Copyrights, Trademarks and Patents in Sports

Until the 1997-98 season, the Washington Wizards professional basketball team went by the nickname of "Bullets," a remnant from the team's playing days in Baltimore. Reacting to the negative implications of the word "bullets," the team decided to change its name. To stimulate fan interest, the team held a "Rename the Bullets" contest. Four possible nicknames, Ravens, Wizards, Glory and Justice, drew the greatest support from voters. There was also some sentiment for using the name, "Washington Monuments." The team withdrew the "Monuments" from consideration, however, after it discovered a particularly daunting obstacle—the National Park Service already held a copyright on "Washington Monuments."[510]

The team ultimately settled on "Wizards" as its nickname. Almost immediately, there were unexpected protests. The Harlem Wizards, a globe-traveling basketball team that entertained audiences with both tricks and ball-handling skills, alleged trademark infringement. The Harlem team filed a lawsuit seeking to force the NBA team to select another nickname. The lawsuit expressed concern that, if the Harlem Wizards were forced to share their nickname with the NBA team, the

---

[510] *Fanfare*, THE WASH. POST, December 17, 1995, D2.

Harlem team would be harmed by the confusion created among its fans and the general public. The owner of baseball's Fort Wayne Wizards, a minor league farm team of the Minnesota Twins, also objected. The Fort Wayne Wizards claimed copyright protection for the name. A spokesman for the Fort Wayne Wizards said that the baseball team was also considering a lawsuit against the National Basketball Association for infringement. "That name is our property and we'll protect it just like any other piece of property that we have," the Wizards from Fort Wayne announced.[511]

In fact, the name "Wizards" is different from other property that the Fort Wayne baseball team owns. The team protects its baseball bats and other equipment by locking them up. It protects its baseball field by installing a fence. In contrast, the name "Wizards" is intangible; it cannot be locked up. In the eyes of the law, team nicknames and logos are "intellectual property." What a fence is to real property, trademarks, copyrights and patents are to intellectual property. They help to protect against unwanted intrusions. Copyright protection, however, does not necessarily convey rights to exclusive use of a name. For years, teams in different sports have used the same nickname without any apparent harm to the teams' identities and without creating confusion among fans. Before baseball's San Francisco Giants relocated to the west coast from New York, the New York Giants professional baseball team and the New York Giants professional football team coexisted with the same name in the same city. In response to the Harlem Wizards' lawsuit against the Washington Wizards, the presiding judge looked to see whether the shared use of the same name would lead to confusion among consumers. The judge determined that there would be little confusion among sports fans because there was little similarity in the logos for the two teams and the teams provided different types of entertainment to different audiences.[512] For this reason, the NBA team

---

[511] Richard Justice, *Identity Crisis*, THE WASH. POST, February 24, 1996, H4.

[512] *Harlem Wizards Entertainment Basketball, Inc. v. NBA Properties, Inc.*, 952 F. Supp. 1084 (1997).

was allowed to use its chosen nickname. The same considerations would have applied in the case of the Fort Wayne Wizards. When the law allows two basketball teams to share the same nickname, the thought of a professional basketball team and a minor league baseball team sharing the same name would have raised little difficulty, especially for two teams located in the distant cities of Washington, D.C. and Fort Wayne, Indiana.

In 1977, at age 38, former New York Yankee pitcher Jim Bouton found himself pitching out of the bullpen for the Class A Portland (Oregon) Mavericks. Bouton was thirteen years removed from his heyday with the New York Yankees and seven years past his last major league appearance. Pitching in Portland, Bouton hoped, would be a small step in his climb back to the big leagues. The Portland Mavericks were anything but major league. They traveled to games in an old red seatless school bus. During trips, the players slept on mattresses spread over the floor of the bus. Bouton found that his young teammates persisted in chewing tobacco, even though it made them sick. "Why do you do that?" Bouton would ask, as player after player dribbled tobacco juice on his uniform. The answer, Bouton knew, was simple—big leaguers chew tobacco.

Bouton spent countless hours in the Mavericks' bullpen with the team's pitching coach, Rob Nelson. One day, Nelson commented that young ballplayers needed a product that looked like chewing tobacco but tasted better. Nelson's innocent remark proved to be the inspiration for "Big League Chew"—thin strips of chewing gum that came in a pouch. Bouton and Nelson set to work. While Nelson cooked up samples of the product in his kitchen, Bouton tackled legal matters. His first step was to protect the name "Big League Chew" by applying for a trademark. A trademark is a word, name, symbol or design that identifies the brand or source of goods. Only terms that are distinctive can be trademarked. For this reason, a generic term can never be trademarked. Bouton could not have obtained a trademark for the terms "bubble gum" or "chewing gum." They are generic terms. However, "Big League Chew" was distinctive and fit easily under the requirements for a trademark.

The basis for legal protection of trademarks is a federal law known as the Lanham Act. Under the Lanham Act, a trademark is a property right. In creating a trademark, a person selects a word or design that represents his business or product. Legal rights in a trademark can arise when a person actually uses a trademark in connection with the sale of particular goods. Jim Bouton could have created a trademark in "Big League Chew" merely by making the gum and selling it under that name.[513] It is beneficial, however, to take the extra step of registering a trademark with the U.S. Patent and Trademark Office, as Bouton did with "Big League Chew."[514] Registration of a trademark puts the public on notice that the owner of the trademark claims exclusive rights to the mark. Once a person is recognized as the owner of a trademark, whether simply through use of the trademark in connection with a product or through registration and commercial use of the mark, the owner can take legal action to prevent others from using or profiting from the trademark. Under the Lanham Act, it is also possible to obtain what is called a "service mark." A service mark is any mark used in the sale or advertising of services to distinguish them from the services of others. Like a trademark, a service mark is a property right. Trademarks promote products; service marks promote services. A single mark can be registered as both a trademark and a service mark.[515]

---

[513] In that case, Bouton could have printed the characters "TM" after the name "Big League Chew" to let the public know that he claimed ownership of the trademark. It would not have been necessary to use the "TM", however. Merely using "Big League Chew" on the packages of the chewing gum would have been sufficient to confer ownership of the mark.

[514] To indicate a trademark that is registered, owners of the trademark place the symbol ® after the mark. The ® may not be used until the mark has been registered with the U.S. Patent and Trademark Office. Failure to use the ® in connection with a trademark or service mark that has been registered could make it difficult later for the owner of the mark to successfully sue to prevent others from infringing the mark.

[515] An unregistered service mark is indicated by placing "SM" after the mark. As with a trademark, the symbol ® after a service mark indicates that the mark is registered.

Virtually all professional sports teams have obtained trademarks on their team logos and other distinctive team insignias. The trademarks entitle teams to claim royalty fees whenever another enterprise seeks to use the team logos. Marvin Miller, former Executive Director of the Major League Baseball Players Association, recounts the time that Coca-Cola wanted to print pictures of major league baseball players on the inside of Coca-Cola bottle caps. Coca-Cola planned to portray the players wearing their team hats. To do so, however, the soft drink company had to obtain permission from the baseball owners to reproduce the logos that appeared on the ballplayers' caps. To Coca-Cola's dismay, the team owners demanded hefty royalties for use of the logos. The fees were far more than Coca-Cola wanted to pay. Negotiations were at a standstill until the Players Association proposed that the logos be airbrushed from the players' caps.[516] From Coca-Cola's perspective, with the team logos removed, the player portraits became less desirable. Coca-Cola agreed, however, that removing the team logos was the only way to resolve the impasse. Coca-Cola signed the agreement with the Players Association, the team logos were removed from the pictures and, in a figurative sense, so were the owners.[517]

---

[516] Marvin Miller, *A Whole Different Ball Game: The Sport and Business of Baseball* (New York: Simon and Schuster, 1991), 147.

[517] In exchange for the right to reproduce the players' pictures, Coca-Cola paid the Players Association $66,000. The significance of the agreement is documented by Roger Abrams, a professor of sports law and labor law. Abrams reports that when Marvin Miller took over as Executive Director of the Players Association, the Association's assets consisted of a filing cabinet and $5,400 in its bank account. The $66,000 paid by Coca-Cola was the first time that major league ballplayers were able to capitalize, as a group, on the public's fascination with the game. The contract was the beginning of a licensing program that has produced millions of dollars in revenue for the players. Equally important, the agreement provided sorely needed operating funds for an association that was then still in its infancy. Roger I. Abrams, *Legal Bases: Baseball and the Law* (Philadelphia, PA: Temple University Press, 1998), 74.

In the 1970s, a company named Dallas Cap & Emblem Manufacturing wanted to sell embroidered patches patterned after the logos used by teams in the National Hockey League. The patches looked much like the symbols that appeared on the players' jerseys. At first, Dallas Cap & Emblem Manufacturing tried to follow the law. It asked the National Hockey League for a license to reproduce the teams' emblems. When the NHL would not agree, the company went outside the law. It simply started to manufacture and sell the patches to sporting goods stores. In all, the company made and sold more than 24,000 patches. The National Hockey League had registered the team emblems as service marks, not as trademarks. From the standpoint of the law, however, the manner of registration did not matter. Whether the emblems were treated as service marks or trademarks, the result was the same. The National Hockey League and the individual teams had obtained ownership of the emblems. The NHL sued Dallas Cap & Emblem Manufacturing for infringement. The court ruled that the company had violated the Lanham Act and ordered it to stop unauthorized use of the hockey logos.[518]

Trademarks and service marks serve different purposes than do copyrights. Trademarks and service marks grant perpetual ownership. Copyrights do not. In defense of its infringement of the hockey service marks, Dallas Cap & Emblem Manufacturing argued that the only way the NHL teams could protect their team logos was through copyrights. The court was not persuaded. The court decision pointed out that a copyright serves a completely different purpose than does a trademark or a service mark. While the Lanham Act provides the legal basis for trademarks and service marks, the foundation for copyrights lies in Article I of the United States Constitution.[519] The purpose of a copyright is to encourage creativity. Copyrights do not convey perpetual

---

[518] *Boston Professional Hockey Association, Inc. et al. v. Dallas Cap & Emblem Mfg., Inc.*, 510 F.2d 1004 (1975).

[519] Article I, Section 8, Clause 8 of the Constitution gives the U.S. Congress the authority "to promote the Progress of Science and useful Arts by securing for limited Times to Authors and Inventors the exclusive Right to their respective Writings and Discoveries." The prevailing federal law on copyright protection is the Copyright Act of 1976.

ownership. Rather, copyright protection lasts for the life of the author plus 70 years. After a copyright expires, the copyrighted work becomes part of the public domain and can be copied and used without fear of lawsuits.

The National Hockey League Principle of Perpetual Ownership

Trademarks and service marks grant perpetual ownership; copyrights do not.

When the Brooklyn Dodgers closed down Ebbets Field in 1957 and moved to Los Angeles, many of the team's ardent fans in Brooklyn took to rooting against the Dodgers. The team lost more than part of its fan base, however. It also jeopardized its right to exclusive use of the "Brooklyn Dodgers" trademark. The Dodgers trademark became an issue in 1988 when a group of former Dodger fans opened "The Brooklyn Dodger Sports Bar and Restaurant" in Brooklyn. In honor of shortstop Pee Wee Reese, the restaurant featured "Dodger Pee-Wee" pasta. The menu also offered two specialty hamburgers, "The Duke," in celebration of center fielder Edwin "Duke" Snider, and "The Furillo," commemorating the play of strong-armed right fielder Carl Furillo. Originally, the restaurant owners had planned to name the restaurant, "Ebbets Field." However, when the restaurant was still in the planning stages, the owners discovered that there already existed a restaurant named "Ebbets Field" in the Long Island suburb of Hicksville. The owners then searched Federal trademark registrations for the name "Brooklyn Dodger." They found that there was no registration of the "Brooklyn Dodger" mark and shortly thereafter opened the restaurant for business. For the restaurant's exterior signs, the owners intentionally used a script that was similar to the writing on the Dodger uniforms of old. The script was in Dodger blue. Three thousand miles away in California, the Los Angeles Dodgers were not amused. The team sued the restaurant for trademark infringement and asked the court to enjoin the restaurant from capitalizing on the Brooklyn Dodgers' name.

The restaurant owners were neither apologetic nor concerned. They opened two more restaurants under the same name in other neighborhoods of Brooklyn. When the case went to trial, the court looked at several factors, all in an effort to determine if the restaurant owners had infringed the Dodgers' trademark. The court's primary concern was whether operation of the restaurants would cause confusion among potential customers. The court took note of the fact that the Dodgers baseball club had never operated restaurants and was unlikely to enter the sports bar and restaurant business in the future. In the court's view, the club's activities, which focused on fielding a major league baseball team, were distinctly different than the activities involved in running restaurants. If the Dodgers had remained in Brooklyn, the court might have found that the restaurant owners were trying to capitalize on the team's reputation and good will among fans. With the team 3,000 miles away, however, the court found that there was little likelihood that the restaurant's customers would think the baseball club was the operator of the restaurant services. There was, the court held, little likelihood of product confusion. It ruled that the restaurant owners were free to operate as "The Brooklyn Dodger Sports Bar and Restaurant."[520] The court left untouched the issue of whether former Brooklyn stars Pee Wee Reese, Duke Snider or Carl Furillo might have had the right to remove "Dodger Pee-Wee" pasta, "The Duke" or "The Furillo" from the restaurant menu.

Trademark protection, once established, can be lost if the trademark is not actively used. Under the Lanham Act, a mark is abandoned when the owner of the mark has discontinued its use and there is no apparent intent to resume use of the mark. In the Dodgers case, the court found that the

---

[520] *Major League Baseball Properties and Los Angeles Dodgers, Inc. v. Sed Non Olet Denarius, Ltd. d/b/a The Brooklyn Dodger Sports Bar & Restaurant*, 817 F.Supp. 1103 (S.D.N.Y. 1993).

baseball team had failed to use the "Brooklyn Dodgers" trademark for any significant commercial purpose between 1958 and 1981. In the court's view, by failing to use the trademark for such an extended period, the Dodgers' organization had abandoned the mark.

In 1996, the term "cheeseheads" became the subject of a copyright dispute in Wisconsin. The origin of the dispute dates back to the 1987 baseball season. The Milwaukee Brewers started that season by winning their first 13 games.[521] The Brewers' thirteenth win came on April 20th in Chicago against the White Sox. At the game, White Sox fans ridiculed the Brewer fans in attendance by calling them "cheeseheads." The nickname struck a chord with Amerik Wojciechowski, an ardent Brewers' fan who was at Comiskey Park for the game.[522] Upon returning home, Wojciechowski constructed a triangular-shaped hat out of cardboard and decorated the hat to resemble a wedge of cheese. The next day, carrying his homemade "cheesehead" hat, he returned to Chicago to watch the Brewers play the White Sox again. This time the Brewers lost. However, Wojciechowski gained notoriety when the *Chicago Sun Times* printed a picture of him wearing his cheesehead hat on the front page of the sports section. Sensing that the cheesehead hats would be a popular item, Wojciechowski manufactured and sold some 3,000 hats similar to the one pictured in the *Sun Times*.[523]

In May 1987, a Wisconsin outfit known as "S&R" also began manufacturing cheesehead hats. The company got the idea after seeing the cardboard cheesehead hats developed by Wojciechowski. S&R changed its name to Foamation. Foamation sold cheesehead hats for several years without placing a copyright notice on the hats or filing for copyright

---

[521] Propelled by their auspicious start, the Brewers finished with a season record of 91 wins and 71 loses, finishing in third place in the American League East behind the Detroit Tigers (98 wins, 64 loses) and the Toronto Blue Jays (96-66).

[522] According to the U.S. District Court for the Eastern District of Wisconsin, which would later rule on the copyright dispute, the pronunciation of Mr. Wojciechowski's name was similar to the phrase, "Where's your house key?"

[523] Wojciechowski had three phrases silkscreened onto his hats: "Curd Herd," "It Ain't Easy Being Cheesy" and "Cheesehead or Dead."

protection.[524] In 1995, another company, Scofield Souvenir & Post Card Company, explored the idea of manufacturing cheesehead hats. Scofield could find no evidence of a copyright registration for cheesehead hats and decided to enter the market. Scofield called its hats "Cheese Tops." With Scofield's sales of Cheese Tops mounting, Foamation began advising Scofield's customers that Foamation held a copyright on the cheesehead hat. Foamation also threatened Scofield's customers with civil lawsuits for copyright infringement. In its notices, Foamation claimed that it held copyright protection dating back to January 1987. Scofield, in turn, charged that Foamation was wrongfully claiming copyright protection. The dispute ended up in court.

The court determined that Foamation was guilty of misrepresenting several critical facts. While Foamation claimed that its owner was the "author" of the cheese wedge hat, the court found that the actual author was Amerik Wojciechowski. The court also found that Foamation did not place any copyright notices on its cheese wedge hats until 1996 and, even then, the notices were not legible.[525] The court determined that Foamation had failed to assert a copyright interest in the cheesehead hats. Without proper copyright notice, the court ruled, the cheesehead hat remained in the public domain—and within the rights of Scofield or anyone else to sell to the public.

The Foamation Principle of Copyright Notice

Unless proper notice of a copyright is given, the product name remains in the public domain.

---

[524] In February 1996, Foamation finally did apply for copyright protection.

[525] A copyright notice, or "copyright bug," as it is sometimes called, consists of the mark ©, followed by the year of publication and the name of the author or owner of the copyright. An illegible notice, the court said, is the same as no notice.

On broadcasts of collegiate or professional athletic events, there is invariably an announcement warning the audience that the telecast is "a copyrighted presentation" and that any rebroadcast or retransmission of the pictures and events without express written consent is prohibited. In 1996, the National Basketball Association tested, in federal court, the limits of the copyright protection the NBA held over its games. Working in concert with Sports Team Analysis and Tracking Systems Inc. ("STATS"), Motorola, Inc. had developed a radio-based information service to provide sports fans with instantaneous updates on the progress of NBA games. Subscribers to the service used a small device capable of receiving "paging" signals. The device electronically displayed the outline of a basketball court and could be tuned to any NBA game in progress. The pager became available to the public in January 1996 and sold for about $200. It showed the score of each game being reported and indicated the quarter, the time remaining in the game and which team scored the last basket. The data was updated every two to three minutes.[526] There was a lag of approximately three minutes between events in the games and the time the information was reported on the pager screen. The data was assembled by "reporters" working for STATS, who either attended the games in person, watched broadcasts on television or listened to the games on radio.

The NBA charged that the reporting of game information violated copyright restrictions. It accused Motorola of distributing descriptions of live NBA games and broadcasts without permission. The NBA also claimed that Motorola was unlawfully intercepting "private broadcasts" of games. After an initial decision in favor of the NBA, the case went to appeal. The appeals court cleared Motorola and STATS of any wrongdoing. The court said that Motorola and STATS were only reproducing and reporting facts from the games—and not descriptions of the games. The court also found that Motorola and STATS were using their own resources

---

[526] *NBA Files Lawsuit Against Motorola Over Sports Paging Service*, LAND MOBILE RADIO NEWS, March 15, 1996, 1-2.

to collect the game data, their own networks to relay the information and their own radio transmission systems to distribute it. These activities, the court declared, did not amount to misappropriation of the NBA's legal right to control the broadcast of its games. The court also held that basketball games do not fall within the protection of the Federal copyright laws because they are not "original works of authorship." The court distinguished between the actual games being played in NBA arenas and the transmission of play-by-play descriptions to audiences over television and radio. The TV and radio broadcasts are original works of authorship, the court said, and were entitled to copyright protection—but not the games themselves.[527]

The Motorola Principle of Distributing News of NBA Games in Progress

Using radio to report facts from basketball games in progress is not a violation of the copyright restriction, as long as the "play-by-play" descriptions of the games are not being transmitted.

The outcome of the NBA's lawsuit would have been different if STATS had attempted to transmit play-by-play descriptions of the basketball games. Years ago, a Pittsburgh radio station, station KQV, broadcast play-by-play descriptions of Pittsburgh Pirate games to its listeners without obtaining authority from the Pirates. The radio station positioned its employees at key vantage points outside Forbes Fields, then the home of Pirates baseball. The station employees would provide information about the games to KQV's announcers. The Pirates brought suit in Federal court to stop the unauthorized broadcasts. In a 1938 decision, the court ruled

---

[527] *National Basketball Association v. Motorola, Inc.*, 105 F.3d 841 (1997).

that the Pirates baseball organization had a property right in the play-by-play descriptions of its games because the club created the games and controlled access to Forbes Field. The court stated that KQV had misappropriated the Pirates' property rights and ordered KQV to cease its broadcasts.[528] A similar case arose in 1954, with similar results. An independent news gatherer named Martin Fass began the practice of listening to radio and TV broadcasts of New York Giants games during the 1953 and 1954 seasons and sending simultaneous teletype reports of the games to radio stations across the country for immediate broadcast. Fass did not have the approval of the New York Giants for his teletype transmissions. As did the Pirates in 1938, the Giants sued. After examining the issues, the court ruled in favor of the Giants and forbade Fass from transmitting his accounts of the play-by-play.[529]

In addition to developing "Big League Chew," Jim Bouton was also the founder of "Big League Cards." For a small fee, Bouton's company would print baseball cards for babies, Little Leaguers and anyone else who ever aspired to see his or her photograph on a baseball card. In his post-baseball days, Bouton's company produced a card for Bouton himself. On the back, the card noted that Bouton was a writer, speaker, and inventor—and had a "garage full of ideas that have bombed."[530]

Danny Litwhiler, baseball inventor *extraordinaire*, had a garage full of ideas that did not "bomb." Litwhiler played eleven seasons in the major leagues as an outfielder and sometime third baseman. From 1940 to 1951,

---

[528] *Pittsburgh Athletic Club v. KQV Broadcasting Co.*, 24 F. Supp. 490 (W.D. Pa. 1938).

[529] *National Exhibition Co. v. Fass*, 143 N.Y.S. 2d 767 (Sup. Ct. 1955).

[530] As the narrative on Bouton's Big League card makes clear, not all of his ideas bombed. In full, the narrative reads, "The former Yankee pitcher and author of *Ball Four* is now an inventor. Jim's better known products include: Big League Chew shredded bubble gum, Big League personalized baseball cards, Big League Ice Cream with autographed bat-shaped sticks, Collect-A-Books and Table-To-Go picnic trays. Jim also has a

he played for four teams. His best season came in 1941 when, as a member of the Philadelphia Phillies, he feasted on National League pitching. Playing in 151 games, he compiled a .305 batting average, with 18 home runs and 66 runs batted in. For his career, he hit .281. After his playing days, Litwhiler was the baseball coach at Michigan State University. In 1974, Litwhiler read about policemen using a radar "gun" to detect motorists who were driving too fast. Litwhiler questioned whether the same concept would allow him to gauge how fast a baseball was traveling. After some inquiry, Litwhiler concluded that radar devices would be able to measure the speed of baseballs in flight. He took his idea to JUGS, a manufacturer of pitching machines. The company adapted the radar gun for use in timing the speed of pitches. Since 1974, the speed gun has become an indispensable piece of equipment for pitching coaches and baseball scouts everywhere.[531]

Other inventions in Litwhiler's "garage" include a "fly swatter" catcher's mitt, a wooden bat specially designed to teach proper bunting technique, and an unbreakable mirror capable of withstanding the impact of major league fastballs and designed to allow pitchers to watch their arm motion while pitching.[532] As an inventor, Danny Litwhiler was undoubtedly well-steeped in the concept of a patent. A patent is a document issued by

---

[531] Speed guns track the flight of a baseball by transmitting a radio signal that reflects off the baseball and returns. Due to the transmission of radio signals, users of speed guns must obtain a license from the Federal Communications Commission before using the device. In 1993, the FCC caught the Norfolk (Virginia) Tides, the Triple-A farm team of the New York Mets, in a violation of the licensing requirement. The Tides used a radar gun as part of a fan promotion in which the team clocked the speed of pitches thrown by spectators at a game. An engineer employed by the FCC attended the game and determined that the Tides had not obtained a license to use the device. The FCC assessed an $8,000 fine against the team. Federal Communications Commission, *Notice of Apparent Liability*, issued May 12, 1993.

[532] Dan Gutman, *The Way Baseball Works* (New York: Simon and Schuster, 1996), 42-43.

the United States Patent and Trademark Office that grants total control, for a limited period of time, over the use and development of an invention. With a patent, the creator of an invention gains the right to prevent others from selling the invention or profiting from its use without the creator's permission. To qualify for a patent, a device must be something that is new and represents a surprising or unexpected development. For machines or devices invented for use in connection with sports, a patent lasts for twenty years after the date on which the inventor filed the patent application. After the patent expires, others may produce and sell the patented device without having to pay royalties to the inventor.

The process of obtaining a patent can be quite difficult. As the American Basketball Association learned during its brief history, the law carefully controls the situations in which a patent may be obtained. George Mikan, the first commissioner of the American Basketball Association, came up with the idea of developing the red, white and blue basketball that was used in all ABA games. Mikan thought the colors would make the ball more visible to fans and heighten spectator interest. Owners, coaches and players all opposed using a tri-colored ball. Alex Hannum, a coach in the NBA during the ABA's first season, said the ball looked like a beach ball. The ball, Hannum said, belonged on the nose of a seal. ABA players complained that the colors made the ball hard to grip. Mikan insisted that he would quit as commissioner unless the ABA used the "beach ball." The Indiana Pacers had so many players complaining about the new ball that the team threatened to fine any player who said anything derogatory about the ball. Despite all the objections, the ball proved to be a distinctive marketing tool. Basketball fans came to associate the tri-colored ball with the ABA. Eventually, the players adjusted to playing with it and one player, Roger Brown, even used the colors to his advantage. Brown would spin the ball before making a move. The sight of the spinning colors seemed to mesmerize the players guarding him and often allowed Brown to get an extra step. Mike Storen, once the general manager of the Kentucky Colonels and later commissioner of the league, tried to patent the red, white and blue color scheme on the basketball. However, Storen's efforts failed. According to the law, a patent is not available for a color scheme, only for a logo. So Storen combined the red, white and blue ball with the ABA's logo and was successful in obtaining a patent on the logo with colors.[533]

For the first twenty years of use, inventors holding a patent enjoy a legal monopoly over the rights to manufacture and sell their products. Without the rights conveyed by patent, or the analogous rights of exclusive use conveyed by trademarks and service marks, there would be little incentive for creative individuals to introduce their ideas, concepts and inventions to the public. The protections inherent in trademarks, service marks, patents and copyrights help to stimulate the development of new ideas. The same legal protections enable the public to get a glimpse of the ideas and devices, useful or not, that rest in Jim Bouton's garage and in Danny Litwhiler's garage—and, in fact, help to fill their garages with ideas in the first place.

---

[533] Terry Pluto, *Loose Balls: The Short, Wild Life of the American Basketball Association As Told By the Players, Coaches, and Movers and Shakers Who Made It Happen* (New York: Simon & Schuster Inc., 1991), 48.

Snapshot Summary of Patent, Copyright, Trademark and Service Mark Protections

	PATENT	COPYRIGHT	TRADE-MARK	SERVICE MARK
Subject Matter	Machine or device	Literary, musical or pictorial works	Word, phrase, logo or symbol promoting a product	Word, phrase, logo or symbol promoting a service
Filing Requirement	Must file with U.S. Patent and Trademark Office	Registration with U.S. Copyright Office is optional	Registration with U.S. Patent and Trademark Office is optional	Registration with U.S. Patent and Trademark Office is optional
When Protection Begins	After approval of patent	When the work assumes a tangible form	When the mark is first used in commerce	When the mark is first used in commerce
Duration of Protection	20 years after application date	Life of author plus 70 years	Perpetual as long as not abandoned	Perpetual as long as not abandoned
Symbol	None	© (Use of symbol is optional)	™ (Use of symbol is optional)	SM (Use of symbol is optional)

Chapter 20

Shoeless Joe's Will and Related Points of Law

Billy Martin, the New York Yankee second baseman from 1950 to 1957 and the Yankee manager for five separate stints under owner George Steinbrenner, died on Christmas Day, 1989 in an accident near Binghamton, New York. Martin's pickup truck, bearing the license plate number VR3569, skidded off an icy road, struck a four-foot-deep concrete culvert, and landed on its side. The tragedy brought instant rewards for several zealous fans. Martin's license plate number was readily visible in the pictures accompanying newspaper accounts of his death. Yankee fans played the number 3569 in the state lottery shortly after Martin's death. It proved to be a winner. The lottery winners owed their good fortune directly to Martin.

Martin's son and daughter did not fare as well as Martin's fans. In his will, Martin had given his collection of guns to his son and a Yankee pendant to his daughter. At his death, however, Martin's overall estate was valued at less than $100,000, and, according to the Internal Revenue Service, he owed more than $80,000 in back taxes. In a lawsuit filed in Broome County, New York, Martin's children claimed ownership of the gun collection and pendant. The court declined to award the property to the children. In the court's view, the guns and pendant were part of Martin's estate and could be used, if necessary, to satisfy Martin's debts. The lesson was readily apparent. If Martin wanted to be sure that his children received the property designated for them in his will, he should have given the items to them as gifts while he was still living.

At Martin's death, he was described alternately as pugnacious, kind and irascible, often by the same person. He was said to have a special affinity for children but, at the same time, would sneak out through the back door of spring training clubhouses to avoid signing autographs.[534] Even if Martin purposely avoided signing autographs, he undoubtedly penned his signature more times during his career than did legendary Chicago White Sox outfielder "Shoeless Joe" Jackson. Jackson was unable to write. He could sign his name only with a laborious effort. When signing for fans, he would typically scribble an "X". Jackson died in 1951. At his death, his will was one of the few documents in existence that bore his full signature. The will itself became an item of value, appraised at more than $100,000. In 1993, Jackson's will became the focal point of a lawsuit. Jackson's widow, Katie, had named the American Cancer Society and the American Heart Association as the primary beneficiaries of her estate. As Katie's beneficiaries, the two organizations believed they were entitled to possession of Shoeless Joe's will when Katie died. The charities sued to gain possession of the will.

The Supreme Court of South Carolina ruled against the charities. The court distinguished Shoeless Joe's will from other personal assets. People may own gun collections and pendants; they may not own will papers—at least in South Carolina. The court concluded that Katie Jackson never

---

[534] Tony Kornheiser, *Billy Martin's Own Kind of Game*, THE WASH. POST, December 27, 1989, D1, D12.

owned her husband's will and, for that reason, she was unable to pass the will to others. The court classified Shoeless Joe's will as a public record that belonged to the state.[535]

> *The Shoeless Joe Jackson Principle of the Ownership of Will Documents*
>
> *The signed copy of a testamentary will is a public record and is not the property of the decedent's heirs or any other person.*

When lawyers for the American Cancer Society and the American Heart Association tried to claim ownership of Jackson's will, they argued that, as with personal property, people are able to own, use, enjoy and dispose of their wills any way they see fit. The charities might also have added that people can change their wills any way they like and as often as they desire. Jack Kent Cooke, former owner of the Los Angeles Lakers and the Washington Redskins, certainly treated his will as if it were personal property. He changed it often, and in quixotic ways.

The testamentary gifts designated in a will can be changed in one of two ways, either by destroying the will and signing a new one or by keeping the will intact but signing an amendment to the will. An amendment to a will is called a codicil. Jack Kent Cooke had a special affinity for codicils. In all, he signed eight different codicils to his will. And, as a newspaper account wryly noted, unfortunately for Cooke's widow, Marlene, Cooke died after signing Codicil No. 8 and before he could get around to Codicil No. 9.[536] Cooke's Codicil No. 7 directed that his wife be given $5 million in cash over four years and income of nearly $1 million per year for the rest of her life. Codicil No. 8, which Cooke apparently wrote in a

[535] *Say It Ain't Sold*, SPORTS ILLUSTRATED, October 13, 1997, 18; *American Heart Association v. County of Greenville*, 489 S.E.2d 921 (1997).

[536] Ann Gerhart, *Widow's Weeds; Jack Kent Cooke Never Exactly Promised Marlene A Rose Garden. But This?*, THE WASH. POST, May 29, 1997, B1.

fit of pique, eliminated Marlene entirely from Cooke's estate. Marlene was stunned by the reversal. She attributed Cooke's change in heart to "a mistake."[537] When a will is signed or revised, there are legal formalities that must be observed. The purpose of these formalities is to avoid "mistakes." Cooke's Codicil No. 8 left little doubt as to his intent. The codicil was in Cooke's own handwriting. He had signed and dated it. Cooke had observed the necessary formalities.

When people sign wills and similar legal documents, it is commonplace for a notary public to become involved. Rarely, however, does a notary public play an active role in sporting events. The infamous 1983 "pine tar" game between the New York Yankees and the Kansas City Royals stands as a notable exception. Fittingly, it was Billy Martin who precipitated the pine tar incident.[538] On or off the playing field, Martin was no stranger to controversy.[539] After eight innings of the Yankees-Royals contest on July 24, 1983, New York was clinging to a 4-3 lead. With the Royals at bat and two outs in the top of the ninth, third baseman George Brett hit a

---

[537] Jack Kent Cooke's estate was valued at between $500 million and $825 million. In response to Codicil No. 8, Marlene Cooke challenged the will in a lawsuit. Marlene sought to obtain one-third of her husband's estate. Ultimately, she agreed to a settlement. It was reported that, under the settlement, Ms. Cooke accepted $20 million in return for agreeing to drop her challenge to the will.

[538] The "pine tar" incident actually had its origins in a comment that Yankee third base coach Don Zimmer made to Martin shortly before the game. Zimmer noticed the excessive pine tar on Brett's bat and said to Martin, "Look at all that pine tar on his bat. That's illegal." Martin instructed Zimmer not to say anything to the umpires. "We'll protest it when the time is right," Martin told Zimmer. Don Zimmer with Bill Madden, *Zim: A Baseball Life* (New York: Contemporary Books, 2001), 168.

[539] Willie Randolph, a smooth-fielding Yankee second baseman who played under Martin, served as a pallbearer at Martin's funeral. While praising Martin at the funeral, Randolph spoke of his special relationship with his former manager. "He taught me how to carry myself on and off the field," Randolph told those attending the funeral. Then, recognizing the need to qualify his statement, Randolph quickly added, "Well, not off the field."

two-run homer to put Kansas City ahead. After Brett's hit, Martin stormed from the Yankee dugout in protest. He argued that Brett had coated his bat with too much pine tar. The umpires agreed and called Brett out, nullifying his home run and ending the game.

Brett and the Royals were livid. American League president Lee MacPhail reviewed the ruling. MacPhail decided that Brett was entitled to have his home run count, meaning that the ninth inning would have to be replayed. The teams resumed play on August 18, beginning with the point at which Brett touched home plate. With the scoreboard showing Kansas City ahead 5-4 and two outs in the top of the ninth, Hal McRae, who followed Brett in the Royals' lineup, stepped to the plate. The Yankees immediately appealed Brett's run, arguing that the third baseman had not touched all of the bases after his home run. Martin instructed the Yankee infielders to touch first and second bases with the ball in the hope of having Brett declared out. The umpires immediately signaled that Brett had touched both bases. The leading run was allowed to stand. Never one to shrink from an argument, Martin protested the game. On the surface, his protest seemed reasonable. Due to the complexities of scheduling, the American League had to change umpires for August 18. Umpire Joe Brinkman and his crew had worked the game on July 24. Dave Phillips' crew umpired on August 18. Martin argued that it was impossible for the substitute umpires to confirm that Brett had touched every base during his home run trot. Not to be outwitted, Dave Phillips produced a letter signed by all of the umpires in Brinkman's crew. The letter stated that both Brett and U. L. Washington, who was on base for Brett's homer, had touched all the bases. Adding to the impact, Brinkman's crew had gone to the extra step of having their signatures witnessed by a notary public. The notarized letter quieted the Yankee manager, and Kansas City proceeded to retire the Yankees without a run in the bottom of the ninth to end the game.

The responsibilities of a notary public include certifying that another person's signature is authentic. The notary's certification gives the signature credibility in a "foreign jurisdiction." For umpire Dave Phillips and his crew, Yankee Stadium on August 18, 1983 qualified as a foreign jurisdiction. If the umpires working the game on July 24 had merely signed the letter, without the notary's certification, Martin could have contested the signatures. Armed with the notary's certification, however, Dave Phillips and his crew had the upper hand. After the umpires disposed of Martin's protest, it took nine minutes and 41 seconds to complete the last inning. The Royals won, 5-4. With an assist from the notary public, the pine tar game went into the record books.[540]

Before certifying a person's signature, a notary public must verify the identity of the person. In addition, the law requires the notary public to observe the person as he or she signs the document. If the public notary did not personally know the umpires in Joe Brinkman's crew, the umpires would have had to provide their driver's licenses or other identification. Alternatively, if the notary public knew Joe Brinkman but none of the other umpires, Brinkman could have taken an oath affirming the identity of his fellow umpires.

On July 23, 1970, Jan Kalsu, the wife of 6'3", 250-pound Buffalo Bills guard James Robert (Bob) Kalsu, gave birth to a baby boy. She named the boy Robert Todd Kalsu. The baby had been conceived just before his father, an officer in the U.S. Army Reserves, left the States for a one-year tour in Vietnam. Kalsu was assigned to Firebase Ripcord, a hilltop not far from the demilitarized zone that formed the border between North Vietnam and South Vietnam. Firebase Ripcord was home to two U.S. artillery batteries. When Robert Todd was born, Jan Kalsu remarked, "Bob is going to jump off that mountain when he finds he has a boy!" Bob Kalsu never had an opportunity to jump off the mountain. Unbeknownst to his wife, he had been killed two days earlier in an enemy mortar attack. Kalsu was one of the few National Football League players to serve in

---

[540] David Nemec, *The Rules of Baseball* (New York: Lyons & Burford Publishers, 1994), 13-14.

Vietnam and the only professional athlete killed in the War. Jan Kalsu was still recovering in the hospital when she learned of her husband's death. An Army lieutenant delivered the news at her bedside. Immediately after learning of her husband's death, Jan Kalsu asked the attendants for a new birth certificate for her baby. She quickly filled out the new birth certificate, changing the baby's name from Robert Todd Kalsu to James Robert Kalsu, Jr. The hospital discarded the original birth certificate.[541]

Filling out a second birth certificate at the hospital, as Jan Kalsu did, is not the usual way to go about changing a person's name. There are three common ways of legally changing one's name. A person may change his or her name when getting married. An individual who is being sworn in as a U.S. citizen may also request to change his or her name as part of the naturalization process. A third option is to go to a court, fill out a petition for change of name, signed the petition and pay the court's fee.

World B. Free, once a flamboyant shooting guard with the Philadelphia 76ers, had a penchant for telling stories, some true, some not. Authenticity seemed to count little for Free. "Need anything else?" he once asked a group of reporters. "If you do," he assured them, "I'll make something up." Free even made up his own name. Named "Lloyd Free" at birth, he legally changed his name to "World B. Free" on December 8, 1981. "Everybody had a nickname in the ghetto," Free explained. "My game is my nickname—World."[542]

Free wanted to adopt his ghetto nickname because it was more consistent with his personality. Others change their names out of necessity. As a child, former Red Sox shortstop Johnny Pesky lived in Oregon. His father, whose last name was "Paveskovich," was an immigrant from Yugoslavia. Pesky's classmates in school were not accustomed to Yugoslavian names and had little patience with trying to pronounce "Paveskovich." Early in

---

[541] William Nack, *A Name on the Wall*, SPORTS ILLUSTRATED, July 23, 2001, 60.

[542] Paul Gutierrez, *World B. Free, NBA Gunner*, SPORTS ILLUSTRATED, March 8, 1999, 10.

344 • *Clubhouse Lawyer*

life, therefore, John Paveskovich became known to classmates and teachers
as Johnny Pesky. Pesky graduated from the playing fields of Oregon to the
major leagues. For a period of ten years in the 1940s and early 1950s, he
was a slick-fielding shortstop and crafty hitter. He compiled a lifetime batting average of .307. Like many professional baseball players of his era,
Pesky spent most of World War II on active military duty. He missed three
years, from 1943 to 1945, returning in time to help lead the Red Sox into
the 1946 World Series against the St. Louis Cardinals. In the seventh
game of that Series, the Cardinals scored the winning run when outfielder
Enos Slaughter scored from first base on a ball that dropped in front of
Boston center fielder Leon Culberson. With the thought of stealing second base, Slaughter was running on the pitch and never stopped. Pesky
took the relay from Culberson, but his throw to home was too late to
catch Slaughter. Pesky has gone down in history as the man who hesitated
before throwing the ball to home plate. In fact, Pesky chose to shoulder
the blame. "I'm the goat," Pesky said after the game. "It's my fault. I'm to
blame. I had the ball in my hand. I hesitated and gave Slaughter six
steps.... I couldn't hear anybody. There was too much yelling. It looked
like an ordinary single."[543]

Major league box scores could not accommodate "Paveskovich" any
better than could Pesky's school pals. In 1947, John Paveskovich walked
into a Massachusetts court, paid $75, and officially changed his last name
to Pesky. Pesky went to a court near his home, filled out a petition for
change of name, signed the petition and paid his fee. Upon receiving a
person's petition for change of name, a judge checks to see that it contains
the required information, including the date and place of the petitioner's
birth and the names of the petitioner's parents. When satisfied that the
petition is complete and that the name change is being requested for lawful purposes, the judge signs an order granting the new name. In this way,

---

[543] Dan Shaughnessy, *The Curse of the Bambino* (New York: Penguin Books, 1991),
68-69.

John Paveskovich became John Pesky, and Lloyd Free became World B. Free. Court orders granting name changes are brief and to the point. When former UCLA and Los Angeles Laker star Lew Alcindor changed his name to Kareem Abdul-Jabbar, the court order read simply, "said petitioner's name be, and the same is hereby changed from FERDINAND LEWIS ALCINDOR to KAREEM ABDUL-JABBAR by which said last-mentioned name he shall be hereafter known and called."[544]

In most cases, courts will grant a petition for change of name regardless of the reasons for the change. A court can deny a name change, however, if there is a good reason such as the name change leading to a fraud on the public. A court may also deny a name change if the name is bizarre, unduly lengthy, ridiculous or contrary to good taste, or if the name change would harm the interests of the petitioner's spouse or children. In one case, a man named Walter Knight asked to change his name to Sundiata Simba. The court declined Knight's petition because he was in prison at the time and had a lengthy list of criminal convictions under his birth name. When the court denied his request, Knight appealed. The appeals court ruled that Knight was entitled to change his name. As precedent, the court cited Kareem Abdul-Jabbar's change in name. "In this day," the court stated, "when a Lew Alcindor elects to be known as Kareem Abdul-Jabbar, and Cassius Clay opts for Muhammed Ali, the desire of Walter Knight to reflect his African heritage by adopting the name Sundiata Simba should not be dismissed lightly."[545]

When a person changes his name, he does not necessarily lose all rights to the use of his former name. Years after Lew Alcindor became Kareem Abdul-Jabbar, General Motors used the name "Lew Alcindor" in a television commercial aired during the 1993 National Collegiate Athletic

---

[544] *Kareem Abdul-Jabbar v. General Motors Corporation*, 85 F.3d 407, 409 (9th Cir. 1996).

[545] *In the Matter of the Application for Change of Name of Walter Knight*, 537 P.2d 1085, 1086 (1975).

Association men's basketball tournament. The advertisement compared the performance of the Oldsmobile Eighty-Eight to Alcindor's performance during his championship years at UCLA. The ad never mentioned the name "Kareem Abdul-Jabbar." Nonetheless, Jabbar sued. He complained that the advertisement was attempting to capitalize on his accomplishments. The court ruled that Jabbar enjoyed a "right of publicity" that extended to his former name. If the car company had used the name "Lew Alcindor" in connection with a newsworthy event, a public affairs program, a sports broadcast or a political campaign, it would not have been necessary to obtain Jabbar's approval. However, the court said, when the name is used for commercial purposes, it must obtain prior approval. In the view of the court, the advertisement touting Lew Alcindor's accomplishments had injured Jabbar's right of publicity.[546]

> ### The Kareem Abdul-Jabbar Principle of Name Changes
>
> *When a person changes his name, he retains control over the use of his former name for commercial purposes.*

While Jabbar's right of publicity was injured by General Motors' TV commercial, Jabbar suffered an even greater loss when he granted power of attorney to his former agent, Tom Collins, in 1980. A power of attorney is a written document in which a person authorizes another individual, referred to as the "attorney-in-fact," to act on behalf of the person granting the power. When signing a power of attorney, an individual may grant the attorney-in-fact either a full or limited power of attorney. A full power of attorney authorizes the attorney-in-fact to perform any act on behalf of the signer, designated as the "principal," in all facets of the principal's life. A limited power of attorney identifies specific functions that the attorney-in-fact may perform. The power of attorney that Jabbar gave to Collins

---

[546] *Kareem Abdul-Jabbar v. General Motors Corporation*, 85 F.3d at 416.

allowed the agent to budget and control all of Jabbar's business expenditures. The document stated, in part:

> You [Collins] are irrevocably appointed as the true attorney-in-fact for the Corporation [Jabbar] during the term of this Agreement and empowered by it to do the following: endorse, sign, and deposit all checks payable to it, on its behalf, subject to the division of monies in the manner provided for herein ....[547]

With the benefit of the power of attorney, Collins was able to exercise near total authority over Jabbar's finances. The document itself was not defective; there was nothing wrong with the words used or with Jabbar signing it. Jabbar's mistake was in giving power of attorney to the wrong person. Ultimately, he sued Collins for $50,000,000. In the lawsuit, Jabbar alleged that Collins provided poor financial advice and business judgment and invested the basketball player's money in questionable investments, such as a limousine leasing corporation and a cattle feed venture. In turn, Collins sued Jabbar for more than $300,000. Collins argued that Jabbar owed him that much in fees and commissions. The two parties, Collins and Jabbar, ended up settling their dispute outside of the courtroom. After the settlement, the National Basketball Players Association decertified Collins as an agent. Among other things, the NBPA found that Collins had ignored his client's request to put his money in safe investments.

---

[547] Martin J. Greenberg and James T. Gray, *Sports Law Practice* (Charlottesville, VA: LEXIS Law Publishing, 1998), I, 985.

Chapter 21

Violations of the Rules of Sport

Before beginning his professional baseball career in the Texas Rangers organization, Baltimore Orioles manager Mike Hargrove played baseball at Northwest Oklahoma State University. Each year, Hargrove's college coach would announce to his team that there were three rules to be observed by all players: no profanity, no fighting and no heckling the opposing team. Before one game, Hargrove asked the coach if he would mind lifting the third rule. Hargrove explained to his coach that he was concerned the team was becoming too passive on the field. In response to Hargrove's plea, the coach reluctantly agreed to dispense with the rule on heckling. The results were immediate. Hargrove began heckling members of the opposing team and, by the third inning, he found himself immersed in a full-scale brawl at first base. The coach quickly put rule number three back in place. Both Hargrove and his coach learned a lesson from the experience: no matter how distasteful, some rules are necessary.

Hargrove's college team, with its three rules, may have been unique. Other teams have many more rules, often for very practical reasons. During his ten-year major league career, pitcher Clyde Wright earned exactly 100 victories. After closing out his major league career with the Texas Rangers in 1975, Wright took his 100 wins to Japan to play for the famed Yomiuri Giants. In Japan, one out of every two people profess to be fans of the Yomiuri Giants. Wright quickly found that he was not destined to be among them. In one game, with the score knotted at 1-1, Wright allowed two consecutive batters to reach base. The Giants' manager, Shigeo Nagashima, one of the most beloved figures in Japanese sports, called for a relief pitcher. Wright was irate. When Nagashima came to the mound, Wright refused to give him the ball. The pitcher stalked off the mound, threw the ball against the dugout wall and retired to the club-house. In the sanctity of the clubhouse, Wright ripped off his uniform, shredded it, and threw it into the team's bath. Though the team's English-speaking interpreter didn't catch all of Wright's words, he did hear Wright proclaim Japanese baseball as the "stupidest damn baseball I've ever seen."

Wright's outburst accomplished two things. First, it led Japan's sports-writers to nickname the pitcher "Crazy Wright." Second, it resulted in the Giants issuing a list of "*Gaijin* Ten Commandments" that every American player signed by the Giants in the future would have to obey. The Ten Commandments inspired by Crazy Wright were as follows:

Obey all orders issued by the manager.

Do not criticize the strategy of the manager.

Take good care of your uniform.

Do not scream and yell in the dugout or destroy objects in the clubhouse.

Do not reveal team secrets to other foreign players.

Do not severely tease your teammates.

In the event of injury, follow the treatment prescribed by the team.

Be on time.

Do not return home during the season.

Do not disturb the harmony of the team.[548]

Unfortunately for professional athletes in the United States, the rules of the game are not so easily codified. Some rules are written. Many are

---

[548] Robert Whiting, *You've Gotta Have "Wa"*, in The Armchair Book of Baseball II: An All-Star Lineup Celebrates America's National Pastime (New York: Charles Scribner's Sons, 1987), 410.

not. The unwritten rules often command greater deference than the written ones. Ahead of the Cleveland Cavaliers,110-83, and with only seconds remaining in their March 20, 1999 contest, the Washington Wizards violated an unwritten rule. One of the team's guards threw up a three-point shot. The shot was good, the final buzzer sounded, and the Wizards walked off the court with a convincing 30-point win. Wizards' coach Bernie Bickerstaff immediately sought out Cavaliers' assistant Sidney Lowe. Referring to the Wizards' meaningless final shot, Bickerstaff told Lowe, "We want to apologize for that. We're not about that."[549]

Long before Bernie Bickerstaff ascended to a coaching position in the National Basketball Association, there was pitcher Al "Red" Worthington. Worthington's baseball team, the New York Giants, would commonly hide a "spy" beyond the center field fence during games at New York's Polo Grounds. When the Giants were at bat, the spy would pick up the opposing catcher's hand signals and relay the signals to a Giant player sitting in the bullpen. By alternately flipping a ball or remaining motionless, the bullpen player would pass the stolen sign to the team's batters. The spy was coach Herman Franks, a former catcher and an expert at deciphering the codes of other catchers.[550] Accounts differ as to how Franks relayed the signals. In some versions, he hid in the center field clubhouse, picked

[549] Steve Wyche, *Wizards Get Biggest Win This Season*, THE WASH. POST, March 21, 1999, D1, D8.

[550] In six major league seasons, Franks played with four National League teams, never appearing in more than 65 games in a season. After his days as a "spy" for the Giants, Franks served as a manager for seven years, four with the San Francisco Giants and three with the Chicago Cubs. His first year as Giants' manager was Japanese pitching star Masanori Murakami's only full season with San Francisco. Murakami spoke little English. Teammates were quick to help Murakami with the fine points of American baseball customs. They instructed him that, out of respect for the manager, he should say, "take a hike, Fatso," whenever Franks came to the mound to take him out of a game.

up the catcher's signals with a telescope and used a wired buzzer to relay the signals to the bullpen.[551] By another account, Franks, hiding behind the center field scoreboard, used binoculars to pick up the catcher's signs and relayed the signals using a walkie-talkie radio.[552] Either way, the practice was offensive to the Giants' opponents. It also offended at least one member of the Giants' team, Al Worthington. Worthington was so troubled by the use of a spy that he asked the Giants to trade him.[553]

"Stealing signs is nothing to be proud of," said former outfielder Bobby Thomson, a member of Leo Durocher's Giants. Thomson is best remembered for hitting the "Shot Heard 'Round the World, the ninth-inning home run that clinched the 1951 pennant for the Giants. Fifty years afterwards, the *Wall Street Journal* asked him if his dramatic home run came off a stolen signal. Thomson was noncommittal. "I'd have to say more no than yes," he responded.[554]

In sports, one expects a sense of proportion. Basketball teams that are ahead by 27 points don't prove anything by needlessly expanding their lead to 30. And if sports are based on the fundamental premise that the best team should win, then teams should not be using spies to steal an opponent's signs. A federal appeals judge once observed, "rules are rules, and fidelity to the rules is required."[555] Bernie Bickerstaff and Al Worthington would no doubt agree. Beyond fidelity to the rules, there

---

[551] Thomas Boswell, *The Miracle of Coogan's Bluff Tarnished*, THE WASH. POST, February 1, 2001, D1.

[552] Peter Golenbock, *Bums: An Oral History of the Brooklyn Dodgers* (New York: G.P. Putnam's Sons, 1984), 344.

[553] Durocher managed the Giants from mid-1948 through the end of the 1955 season. The Giants never did act on Worthington's trade request during Durocher's tenure with the team. Worthington stayed with the Giants for six years, from 1953 until March 1960, when he was traded to the Boston Red Sox.

[554] Boswell, *The Miracle of Coogan's Bluff Tarnished*, D3.

[555] *Reuters Limited v. Federal Communications Commission*, 781 F.2d 946 (D.C. Cir. 1986).

must also be consistency. In one of the more notable gaffes in sports history, referees working a 1990 college football game between Colorado and Missouri lost track of the downs in the closing minutes. Trailing 31-26, Colorado had the ball near the Missouri goal line. With time running out, the Colorado quarterback spiked the ball on first down. Colorado then ran two consecutive running plays but failed to reach paydirt. On fourth down, the Colorado quarterback inexplicably spiked the ball again, which stopped the clock. Then, on what was the "fifth down," the Colorado quarterback kept the ball and plunged over the goal line for the winning score. None of the game officials detected the extra down. The game went into the books as a victory for Colorado.[556]

The officials' miscue continues to rankle Missouri football fans—and with good reason. It was a blatant failure by the referees to enforce the rules. If the officials had made a similar error in favor of Missouri, they would at least have had the virtue of being consistent. All game long, however, the officials allowed the Missouri team only four downs for each offensive series. In addition to being unfaithful to the rules, the officials were grossly inconsistent.

In May 1999, American League baseball president Gene Budig suspended C.J. Nitkowski, a pitcher for the Detroit Tigers, for two games and fined him $500 for "throwing close and inside to batter Kenny

---

[556] Errors by officials do not always produce such a serendipitous ending. When the Detroit Tigers played the Boston Red Sox in a September 2000 game, Tigers pitcher C.J. Nitkowski faced Red Sox shortstop Nomar Garciaparra with the score tied 3-3 in the eighth inning. The potential lead run, in the person of Boston outfielder Carl Everett, was on first base. With the count at three balls and two strikes, Nitkowski threw what should have been ball four. Home plate umpire Rick Reed, having lost track of the count, failed to award Garciaparra first base. The Red Sox raised a mild protest, but Garciaparra remained at the plate. Presented with a second opportunity to retire Garciaparra, Nitkowski gave the hard-hitting shortstop a pitch he could handle, and Garciaparra lined the ball safely to right field, driving in Everett and propelling the Red Sox to victory. *Ball Four, Take Your Hacks*, USA TODAY BASEBALL WEEKLY, September 20-26, 2000, 3.

Lofton" in a game against the Cleveland Indians. Nitkowski objected to the penalty. His pitch didn't hit Lofton. It merely came too close for Lofton's liking. Earlier in the game, after Tiger first baseman Tony Clark and Cleveland right fielder Manny Ramirez had both been hit with pitches, home plate umpire Chuck Meriwether had warned the two teams about throwing at opposing hitters. After Nitkowski's pitch to Lofton, players from both teams streamed onto the playing field, and minor scuffles broke out.

Nine days after the Cleveland game, with Meriwether again behind the plate, Red Sox hurler Tom Gordon hit Tiger second baseman Damion Easley during a game at Fenway Park. In the Red Sox game, as in the earlier contest between Detroit and Cleveland, Meriwether had warned the teams about throwing at batters. Budig did not fine or suspend Gordon. Nitkowski made no effort to hide his displeasure. He wrote a letter to Budig. Nitkowski explained that he was not trying to hit Lofton. And, in a passage worthy of legal scholars, Nitkowski pointed out that Budig was being wildly inconsistent:

> Tom Gordon receives his warning from the same umpire I did in Cleveland. He proceeds to hit one of our batters and no action was taken against him. I don't think I need to remind you that I did not hit anyone in Cleveland. Inconsistency like this should be intolerable in our game and the fact that Chuck did not have the courage to throw out a star like Tom Gordon irritates me to no end. To be quite honest, I feel that Tom should not have been thrown out, it was obviously unintentional, as was mine, but if I get ejected, and subsequently fined and suspended, then so should he.[557]

---

[557] On the issue of whether Gordon should have been thrown out of the game, Damion Easley might have taken a different view. Red Sox pitchers hit Easley three times during the game. In addition to Gordon, Pat Rapp and Mark Portugal also plunked the second baseman with pitches.

> ### *The C.J. Nitkowski Principle of Intolerable Inconsistency*
>
> *Inconsistency in an umpire's decisions should be intolerable in our game.*

Two years after the sequence of events that C.J. Nitkowski found offensive, a weekend series between the New York Mets and the St. Louis Cardinals demonstrated that inconsistent umpiring was not confined to the American League. In two contests played on the last weekend of April 2001, St. Louis pitchers hit four Met batters. When the two teams squared off on April 27, Cardinals starter Matt Morris hit Mets second baseman Edgardo Alfonzo on the elbow in the first inning. Morris then hit outfielder Tsuyoshi Shinjo in the second inning. At that point, home plate umpire Lance Barksdale issued warnings to both teams. In the eighth inning, with St. Louis ahead 9-0, Cardinal relief pitcher Jason Karnuth hit Met catcher Todd Pratt. The umpires allowed Karnuth to remain in the game. The next day, Cardinal outfielder J.D. Drew homered off the Mets' Turk Wendell in the seventh inning. Shortly thereafter, Wendell threw a pitch that went behind the back of St. Louis catcher Mike Matheny but did not hit him. Home plate umpire Ron Kulpa threw Wendell out of the game and issued a warning to both teams. In the eleventh inning, Cardinal reliever Mike James plunked the Mets' Todd Zeile in the back with a pitch. James was not ejected. Immediately after the series ended, Steve Phillips, general manager of the Mets, filed a complaint with the commissioner's office regarding the umpires' actions.[558] Again the complaint focused on intolerable inconsistency. "There were guys hit," Mets

---

[558] *Mets Complain*, THE WASH. POST, May 1, 2001, D4.

manager Bobby Valentine said with unconventional grammar but unassailable logic, "and one not hit. And the guy who didn't hit him got thrown out of the game."⁵⁵⁹

Years earlier, baseball commissioner Bowie Kuhn fined New York Yankee outfielder Bobby Murcer $250 for telling reporters that neither Kuhn nor American League president Joe Cronin had the "guts" to stop Cleveland pitcher Gaylord Perry from throwing spitballs. Murcer's allegations came immediately after a June 1973 game in which Perry pitched the Indians to victory over the Yankees. "I don't think I deserved the fine," said Murcer, "but I can't deny that I made the statement. They don't allow us to use an illegal bat. I don't think it's right for a pitcher to use an illegal pitch."⁵⁶⁰

> *The Bobby Murcer Principle of Fair Play*
>
> *If they don't let batters use an illegal bat, they shouldn't let pitchers use an illegal pitch.*

---

[559] "The guy who didn't hit him" professed to be bewildered by his ejection from the game. "Why would I hit the guy?" Wendell asked rhetorically. "I was 1-1 on the guy, two sliders away, I'm trying to throw a fastball in. It gets away from me and moves a little bit too much and it goes behind the guy. It happens." Not surprisingly, however, umpires seem to feel particularly adept at distinguishing between pitches that are aimed at batters with a "purpose"and pitches that accidentally go astray. After Morris hit Shinjo in the Friday night game, Barksdale approached Met starter Kevin Appier as Appier took the field in the bottom half of the inning. The umpire said to Appier, "you know there's been a warning." Appier replied, "I know that. It's got to be obviously intentional, right? I mean, I'm going to be working inside." Barksdale answered, "Oh yeah. I'll be able to tell the difference."

[560] *Murcer Sticks by His Guns Though Kuhn Nicks Wallet*, THE WASH. POST, June 30, 1973, D2.

C.J. Nitkowski, in 1999, and Bobby Murcer, in 1973, were both look-ing for the same thing—consistency.[561] In sports, consistent treatment holds a special value. One cannot justify awarding Colorado five downs to score when Missouri had the benefit of only four. Similarly, it is difficult to reconcile the fact that C.J. Nitkowski received a suspension for pitching close to a batter while Tom Gordon hit a batter and was not suspended. On a more fundamental level, if Eddie Stanky, a white man, can play sec-ond base for the Brooklyn Dodgers, why not Jackie Robinson? Consistent treatment lies at the heart of fair play. And, as Happy Chandler pointed out, making decisions based on consistent treatment may also help to improve a person's stock when the time comes to meet his "maker."

At the same time, inconsistency lies at the very heart of sports. One-time Baltimore Orioles farmhand Steve Dalkowski could throw a baseball more than 100 miles an hour. In contrast, Oriole reliever Stu Miller rarely threw more than 80 mph. Dalkowski never played in a major league game; Miller's major league career lasted sixteen years. Inconsistency in ability and results is fundamental to the game. In 1953, Dick Teed, a 27-year-old rookie catcher, appeared in one game for the Brooklyn Dodgers. Teed came up from the minors as a backup to Roy Campanella after Rube Walker, the Dodgers' second string catcher, suffered a bruised thumb. "Everything seemed different in the big leagues—magnified," Teed recalled. "The lights were brighter, the crowds were larger. I even thought the sound of the

---

[561] As Murcer no doubt recognized, some of his own Yankee teammates tended to stretch the rule governing use of foreign substances. The year that Murcer first came up to the big leagues, 1965, was Whitey Ford's last year as a front-line starter for the Yankees. According to former American League umpire Ron Luciano, Ford applied an unusual concoction of turpentine, baby oil and resin to baseballs. Ford would store the mixture in a tube of roll-on deodorant and then put it on his hands and uniform shirt between innings. After one game, catcher Yogi Berra noticed the turpentine tube lying on the top shelf of Ford's locker. Berra naively assumed the tube contained deodorant. He removed the container from Ford's locker and spread the turpentine mixture under his arms. Immediately, Berra's arms stuck to his sides. Unable to move his arms, Berra had to get Yankee trainer Gus Mauch to cut some of the hair away from his armpits. Ron Luciano and David Fisher, *Remembrance of Swings Past* (New York: Bantam Books, 1988), 105

pitches hitting Campy's glove was louder."[562] Teed would later learn that there was a reason why the pitches sounded louder when they hit Campanella's glove. Campanella always wore a stiff new glove when catching—it made the pitches seem that much faster to opposing batters.[563]

In distinct contrast to rookie Dick Teed, Roy Campanella was a wily veteran. Wily veterans accumulate an inventory of tricks to go along with their natural talents. Some of the tricks are perfectly consistent with the rules of sport. If Roy Campanella wanted to break in a new catcher's glove for every game, that was his prerogative. Though his use of a new glove for each game may have helped to intimidate opposing batters, there was nothing illegal about it. Other tricks present more perplexing situations. The "in the neighborhood" play is a case in point. Former New York Yankee second baseman Bobby Richardson participated in 999 double plays during his 12-year major league career. Undoubtedly, there were times when Richardson, serving as the pivot man on a double play, failed to touch second base before relaying the ball to first. Whether the second baseman actually touches second base on a double play is a matter for the umpires to decide. Often, as long as the second baseman is "in the neighborhood" of second base, he gets credit for touching the bag. For Richardson, there were no moral or legal implications involved. The second baseman's job was simply to make the play as best he could. It was the umpire's job to determine if the runner advancing to second was safe or out.

---

[562] Ira Berkow, "Boy of Summer, Briefly" in *Pitchers Do Get Lonely And Other Sports Stories* (New York: Atheneum, 1988), 159.

[563] Long-time Baltimore Orioles pitcher Mike Flanagan says that, for pitchers, there is nothing worse than when a pitch hits the catcher's mitt and the only sound it makes is a muffled "plop." Flanagan used to complain about the well-worn glove used by Danny Graham, a catcher for the 1980-81 Orioles. "Throw that glove away," Flanagan would scold Graham, "I'll buy you a new one." For his part, Graham never expected to be catching a pitcher like Flanagan anyway. After joining the Orioles in 1980, he told Tom Boswell, "A few months ago, I figured I was going to end up 60 years old, driving a taxi and telling AAA stories. Now, I may still be 60 and driving a taxi, but I'll be telling big league stories." Thomas Boswell, Graham Is Reborn, THE WASH. POST, July 26, 1980, F1.

The Bobby Richardson Principle of the "In the Neighborhood" Play

I only make the play; it's the umpire's job to make the call.

If an umpire appears to give the second basemen too much latitude on an "in-the-neighborhood" play, the consequences can be severe. Former Pittsburgh Pirate infielder Gene Freese was the lead out on a double play ball hit in the ninth inning of a 1956 game between the Pirates and the St. Louis Cardinals. After umpire Augie Donatelli called Freese out, Freese erupted. He charged after Donatelli and was thrown out of the game. Pirate fans hurled beer cans toward the field in protest. A spectator occupying a front row seat was injured. The Pirates lost the game, 6-3, and Freese lost $50—the amount he was fined after National League president Warren Giles found him guilty of "inciting a riot."[564]

When the New York Knicks of the Phil Jackson-Bill Bradley-Walt Frazier era were pursuing NBA championships in the 1970s, New York often found itself matched against quicker teams. The Knicks developed tactics for slowing down running teams, not all of which were legal. One tactic was to let air out of the balls used in games. Knick players carried inflating needles in their uniforms while playing. When the opportunity arose, the Knicks would insert the needle into a game ball to produce a "softer" ball. A softer ball bounced less crisply and was slower on the dribble. The nice word for the Knicks' practice, according to one commentator, was "gamesmanship."[565]

---

[564] *Pirates' Freese Fined, Is Assessed $50 by Giles for 'Inciting' Fans to Riot,* THE N.Y. TIMES, May 26, 1956, 21.

[565] Sam Smith, *The Jordan Rules* (New York: Simon and Schuster, 1992), 176.

There is a fine line between gamesmanship and cheating. "Gamesmanship" involves the use of somewhat unorthodox methods and tactics without actually breaking the rules of the game. Roy Campanella and Bobby Richardson broke no rules. Former New York Yankee pitcher "Bullet Bob" Turley was a master at reading the motions of opposing pitchers. From his vantage point in the Yankee dugout, Turley would identify whether a pitcher was throwing a fastball or a curve. He would then tip off Yankee batters by whistling. Mickey Mantle, in particular, profited from Turley's unique talent. "My whistle was the kind that could penetrate the loudest crowd noise," Turley explained. "Mickey and I would always start by assuming the pitcher would throw a curve. If I didn't whistle, Mickey knew it was a breaking pitch. If I did, he got set for a fastball."[566] For Turley, there were always "little clues." Sometimes he would retreat to the Yankee clubhouse and watch an opposing pitcher's motion on television. Usually, Turley found, a pitcher could be counted upon to tip his pitches, either by the way he fingered the ball before winding up or by the way he held his glove.[567]

The "law of sport" distinguishes between Leo Durocher and Bob Turley. Turley stole pitches. Durocher stole signals. Turley relied on ingenuity and a loud whistle. Durocher relied on a scoreboard spy and a radio. Even Al Worthington shouldn't have had any qualms with Bob Turley's tactics. Durocher's tactics offended notions of fair play; Turley's did not. In a game of skill, Turley relied on observation and insight.

Like Turley, Hall-of-Famer Ty Cobb relied on observation and insight when playing the game. An excellent bunter, Cobb got a lot of help from

---

[566] Tony Kubek and Terry Pluto, *Sixty One: The Team, The Record, The Men* (New York: Macmillan Publishing Company, Inc., 1987), 151.

[567] Over time, opposing pitchers caught on to the purpose of Turley's whistle. Most did not appreciate the help Turley was giving to his teammates. An opposing pitcher once threatened to "bean" Yankee batters whenever Turley whistled. The threat led the cagey Yogi Berra to assure the opposing pitcher, "If he whistles, I ain't listening."

the grounds crew responsible for maintaining his home field in Detroit. The grounds crew would make a special effort to water the area in front of home plate, so that Cobb's bunts would die well before either the first baseman or third baseman could reach them. Around the league, the area near home plate at the Detroit ballpark was dubbed "Cobb's Lake."[568] A lake in front of home plate is legal; a drop of water on a pitched ball is not. Major league rules prohibit a pitcher from applying a foreign substance of any kind to a game ball, spitting on the ball, or spitting on either of the pitcher's hands or his glove. What constitutes a "foreign substance" is open to interpretation. Former Los Angeles Dodgers pitcher Don Sutton, an accomplished spitball artist, was once asked if he applied foreign substances to the ball. Without conceding anything, Sutton answered, "Vaseline is made right here in the USA."[569] Though outlawed by major league baseball in 1920, spitballs remain a part of the game. The pitch has been justified on many grounds, usually by practitioners of the trade. Pitchers have argued that it takes considerable talent to throw a good spitball. Even fictional relief pitcher "Junkman" Durham, a character in David James Duncan's novel, *The Brothers K*, has come to the defense of the spitball. Perhaps speaking for many spitball pitchers, Durham argues, "The spit that's gone 'fore it reaches an ump is what we in the trade call incidental percipitation. An' I say, if it's incidental, it's *legal*."[570]

Before Junkman Durham, there was Lew Burdette. Burdette helped pitch the Milwaukee Braves to the World Series in 1957 and 1958. By rule, pitchers cannot deliver a spitball, a shine ball, a mud ball or an emery ball. There are no exceptions, even for "incidental percipitation." The rules, however, did not stop Burdette. During his highly successful

---

[568] Dan Gutman, *The Way Baseball Works* (New York: Simon and Schuster, 1996), 155.

[569] Microsoft, COMPLETE BASEBALL GUIDE (1995).

[570] David James Duncan, *The Brothers K* (New York: Bantam Books, 1996), 282.

18-year career,[571] Burdette was widely accused of throwing a spitball, but rarely caught. Former teammate Gene Conley once confirmed that Burdette used to "load up" the baseball. "Sure he threw spitters," said Conley. "Everybody knew it but they could never catch him at it. He would drive the third-base coaches crazy, loading up the ball so that they could see him doing it and then wiping it off.... Then he'd turn around and grin at them. He knew how to agitate."[572]

Just as a pitcher isn't supposed to add a foreign substance to a baseball, a batter is prohibited from tampering with his bats. A bat must be one piece of solid wood. The rules say so. For every Lew Burdette, however, there is a Graig Nettles. As a member of the New York Yankees during the 1970s, Nettles was known to load his bats with rubber Super Balls. On September 7, 1974, Nettles hit a home run in the first game of a double-header and another one early in the nightcap. When Nettles came to the plate in the fifth inning of the second game, he hit a ball to left field. The blow caused Nettles' bat to split open. Out flew six Super Balls.[573] Nettles recalled, "Bill Freehan was catching, and he dashed all over the place collecting the evidence." Added Nettles, "I guess Bill thought they'd put me before a firing squad."

Nettles knew better. When a batter uses an illegal bat, he is automatically out. He loses his time at bat, but nothing more. There is no suspension and no firing squad. "What the hell," Nettles said to Freehan, "I was out anyway."[574] Former Baltimore Orioles manager Earl Weaver once played on a minor league team that had corked every one of its bats. Using

[571] Burdette finished his career with 203 wins, 144 losses, and an earned run average of 3.66.

[572] Donald Honig, *Baseball Between The Lines* (New York: Coward, McCann and Geoghegan, Inc., 1976), 198.

[573] Gutman, *The Way Baseball Works*, 122. When reporting the incident, *Time* magazine observed that "Nettles was the first man to bounce out to the third baseman, the shortstop, and the second baseman all at once."

[574] Thomas Boswell, *How Life Imitates the World Series* (New York: Penguin Books, 1982), 166.

the corked bats, Weaver hit six home runs in a single month. To Weaver's dismay, the umpires soon caught on. One day, Weaver related, "The umpires raided our clubhouse like they were the Untouchables. They destroyed the bats in public, right on the field. I wanted to cry."[575]

The rules of sport are the starting point for any analysis of what's right and wrong, of where gamesmanship ends and cheating begins. As Junkman Durham suggested, some violations are incidental. The law of sport strives to achieve good sportsmanship. Players are obliged by their contracts to give their best effort on the playing field and to conform to team rules. In 1995, the Seattle Seahawks fined free safety and defensive captain Eugene Robinson, quarterback Rick Mirer and defensive tackle Cortez Kennedy $1,000 each for violation of team rules. During the third quarter of a pre-season game in San Francisco, the three players were caught eating hot dogs while standing on the Seahawks' sideline. The three had seen action in the first half of the game and were not slated to return. If not for the presence of network television cameras, they might have been able to consume the hot dogs without drawing attention. The cameras, however, caught the players "trying furtively to eat the hot dogs." Furtive or not, it was a violation of the rules. Mirer and Kennedy were embarrassed; Robinson apologetic. "It makes us look like we're undisciplined," Robinson said. "It was just uncalled for. I hold myself fully accountable."[576]

In 1999, the Washington Redskins had reason to believe that the team's punter, Matt Turk, also violated team rules, if not the terms of his contract. Turk, who three times was named to the National Football Conference Pro Bowl team, sustained a broken finger on his left hand. The cause of the injury was a matter of dispute. Turk claimed to have hurt his finger during the Redskins' game against the Arizona Cardinals on October 17, 1999. Redskins officials suspected that the punter had actu-

---

[575] Boswell, *How Life Imitates the World Series*, 167.

[576] *3 Seahawks Fined for Hot-Dogging*, THE WASH. POST, August 29, 1995, E6.

ally hurt himself playing basketball on the day after the game. After Turk reported the injury, the Redskins studied film of the Arizona game and could not identify any play in which Turk might have sustained the injury. Physicians also advised the team that the break was sufficiently severe that Turk would have realized he was hurt as soon as the injury occurred.[577] The broken finger sidelined Turk for one game. Throughout the controversy, the punter insisted that the injury was football-related. The Redskins considered fining Turk, but ultimately all he received was a stern lecture from teammate Irving Fryar.[578] However, the incident caused hard feelings on both sides and signaled the end of Turk's career with the Redskins. After the season, Washington traded him to the Miami Dophins for a future draft pick.[579]

When San Francisco Giants second baseman Jeff Kent suffered a broken wrist in March 2002, the team was not in any position to trade him. Kent, the National League's most valuable player for the 2000 season, was vital to the Giants' pennant hopes for 2002. Nonetheless, the circumstances surrounding the injury gave the team reason to examine its legal options. On March 2, the day after he was injured, Kent told team officials and reporters that he had fallen off his pickup truck while washing it and had attempted to break the fall with his wrist. As Kent knew well, there is nothing in his player contract that prohibits him from washing his truck. There is, however, language that prohibits him from engaging in dangerous activities. Even as Kent held to the story about washing his truck, Giants general manager Brian Sabean cited "mounting evidence" from eyewitnesses that Kent had fallen off his motorcycle while popping

---

[577] Mark Maske, *Redskins May Fine M. Turk For Injury; Punter's Availability Vs. Cowboys In Doubt*, THE WASH. POST, October 22, 1999, D1.

[578] Mark Maske, *Redskins Notebook: Punter Turk Won't Be Fined By Team For Injuring Finger*, THE WASH. POST, November 24, 1999, D3.

[579] Mark Maske, *Redskins Trade M. Turk; Punter Shipped To Dolphins For 2001 Draft Pick*, THE WASH. POST, March 9, 2000, D5.

wheelies. As in Matt Turk's case, there was widespread suspicion that the injury was the result of a contractually prohibited activity. Sabean left no doubt that he considered popping wheelies to be a violation of Kent's contract. If the Giants were able to prove the injury had resulted from a motorcycle accident, the team could have attempted to void Kent's $6 million contract for the 2002 season or dock his pay, at the rate of $33,000 per day, for each day of the regular season that he was unable to play.[580]

In 1995, there was suspicion that University of Virginia head athletic trainer Joe Gieck had engaged in a different sort of prohibited activity. On the final play of a football game between Virginia Tech and Virginia, Tech cornerback Antonio Banks returned an interception 65 yards for a touchdown to seal his team's 36-29 victory. University of Virginia fans were clearly disappointed—and none more than Gieck. Television replays showed Gieck moving onto the field and sticking out his left leg in an apparent attempt to trip Banks as he ran down the sideline past the Virginia bench. Gieck denied trying to trip Banks, but left no doubt as to where his sympathies lay. "I thought about tackling him," Gieck admitted, "[but] I'm not going to break my leg." Despite Gieck's denial, the evidence was enough to warrant an investigation by Virginia Athletic Director Terry Holland. Holland prohibited Gieck from representing the University of Virginia at other athletic events until the investigation was completed.[581]

Gieck's actions upset notions of fair play. Other rule violations do not. In the Yankee-Kansas City "pine tar game," George Brett used an illegal

---

[580] Henry Schulman, *Cycle Crash Evidence Surfaces; Club Investigates Kent's Injury*, SAN FRANCISCO CHRONICLE, March 20, 2002, C1.

[581] *U-Va. Athletic Director Probes Tripping Incident*, THE WASH. POST, November 20, 1995, C2.

bat. According to the rules, he was allowed to use pine tar on his bat handle "for not more than 18 inches from its end."[582] Brett's bat did not conform; the pine tar extended 19 inches from the handle. The law of sport distinguishes between Graig Nettles and George Brett, however. Nettles hit while using a bat filled with Super Balls. Brett hit with a bat having an extra inch of pine tar. The extra inch of pine tar was incidental to Brett's performance. It neither improved his grip on the bat nor propelled the ball farther.

In distinct contrast to pine tar on a baseball bat, an extra inch of blade on a goalie's hockey stick might well affect the outcome of a game. In 1995, the San Jose Sharks hockey team suspected that the stick used by New Jersey Devils goaltender Martin Brodeur was illegal. During the middle of a game between the Sharks and Devils, the Sharks asked officials to measure the width of the blade on Brodeur's stick. Officials found the blade was too wide and assessed a penalty on the Devils.[583] If a hockey team must send a player to the penalty box for two minutes when its goalie uses a stick blade that is too wide, then it makes sense to penalize baseball pitchers who load the ball with spit or Vaseline. Neither Martin Brodeur's wide blade nor Don Sutton's Vaseline pitches were incidental. Both had the potential to affect the outcome of a game. By contrast, an extra inch of pine tar on a baseball bat won't alter the score of a game. The penalties assessed for each violation reflect the differences in the gravity of the offenses. A pitcher found to have applied a foreign substance to a baseball is ejected from the game. A batter found to have used a corked or "doctored" bat is automatically out. A batter using a bat illegally coated with pine tar is not out. The player loses the bat but not any hits that were produced with the bat.

---

[582] Rule 1.10(c) of the Official Baseball Rules.

[583] L. Brooks, *Angry Lemaire: I Didn't Stick Blame on Aide*, NEW YORK POST, November 4, 1995, 41.

Football has been called a game of inches. Sometimes it becomes a game of quarter-inches. In the 1996 Citrus Bowl, Ohio State suffered a bitter defeat at the hands of the University of Tennessee, 20 to 14. After the game, Ohio State partisans entered the Tennessee locker room and took one of the football shoes worn by the Vols' wide receiver Joey Kent. The cleats measured three-fourths of an inch—a quarter of an inch longer than the regulations allowed. Ohio State coach John Cooper and his staff noticed Kent's cleats during pre-game warmups. They even complained to the officials who worked the game. College football rules state that a five-yard penalty shall be imposed for use of illegal equipment, but the officials never assessed a penalty against Tennessee. One referee told the Ohio State coaches that the officials didn't have a ruler.[584]

After all the tricks and after all the gamesmanship, the law of sport demands fair play. The gamesmanship and the tricks should not harm the competitive chances of either team. Fair play should be preserved. The essence of sport is that teams in competition should have the same opportunity to win; the playing field should be "level." Using the level playing field as a measure, "Cobb's Lake" was not as offensive as Leo Durocher's spying. When a visiting team came to Detroit to play Cobb's Tigers, they could expect the area in front of home plate to be soaked. Visiting teams had the same opportunity to perfect the art of bunting as did the Tigers. In contrast, teams playing Durocher's Giants in the Polo Grounds did not have the same opportunity to steal signals. The playing field at the Polo Grounds was not level; the spirit of fair play was violated.

Some violations are neither obvious nor offensive to fair play. When George Brett applied pine tar 19 inches from his bat handle, he may not even have known that the bat was illegal. Similarly, when University of Washington football coach Rick Neuheisel challenged high school football star Domynic Shaw to an informal game of three-point shooting on a basketball court, Neuheisel was probably unaware that the three-point contest

---

[584] *Tennessee's Cleats Under Scrutiny*, THE WASH. POST, January 7, 1996, D11.

violated the National Collegiate Athletic Association's recruiting rules. According to NCAA rules, such a game, no matter how informal, constitutes an illegal tryout.[585] As in life, however, ignorance of the rules is no excuse. Nor is ignorance of sporting customs. In a 1999 soccer match in London pitting Sheffield United against Arsenal in the English F.A. Cup competition, the Arsenal squad was victorious, 2-1. Arsenal's decisive goal came on a play that Arsene Wenger, coach of the Arsenal team, said "sport-wise, was not right." Arsenal's Marc Overmars scored the winning goal in the 76th minute on a pass from teammate Nwankwo Kanu, a Nigerian who was new to English football. When a player went down during play with an injury, a Sheffield United player intentionally kicked the ball out of bounds, stopping action so that the injured player could receive medical attention. Arsenal player Ray Parlour threw the ball in toward United's goalkeeper to permit United to resume play. Oblivious to Parlour's purpose, his teammate Kanu intercepted the throw and passed to Overmars, who easily shot the ball past the unsuspecting United goalkeeper. Officials counted the goal. United protested furiously. Arsenal took no pride in the victory. Arsenal coach Arsene Wenger said, "It was an unfortunate accident…. We wanted to give the ball back but, unfortunately, it happened like that. The maximum I can do is offer to play the game again." The Cup committee accepted Wenger's offer to replay the game. A committee spokesman explained, "it is obviously an unprecedented situation but one we could not ignore. Everybody in football will welcome Wenger's sporting gesture and he should be congratulated for it."[586]

"Sport-wise," it is not right when basketball teams deflate a basketball during a game to slow down the opposition, as did the Knicks during the 1970s. It is said that, as a result of his experiences playing for the Knicks, Los Angeles Lakers coach Phil Jackson always tests the game balls before an

---

[585] *Neuheisel in Trouble*, THE WASH. POST, February 14, 1999, D13.

[586] *In Grand Gesture, Arsenal Offers to Play It Again*, THE WASH. POST, February 14, 1999, D2.

NBA contest to make sure they are properly inflated. When Jackson coached the Chicago Bulls of the Michael Jordan era, opposing teams would under-inflate the game balls to slow down Jordan and his teammates. Jackson used to find that, during Earvin "Magic" Johnson's playing days, the Lakers would inflate the balls to 15 to 17 pounds per square inch—well over the 7½ to 8½ pounds dictated by league rules. Johnson, who dribbled the ball high, liked a livelier basketball. The livelier ball also produced long rebounds and allowed the Lakers to run the fast break with abandon.[587]

In sports, as in life, some of the tactics used in competition are not fair and some are not legal. The expectation is that game officials will detect and impose penalties for the most blatant injustices. Martin Brodeur, fond of using extra wide goalie sticks, has also been known to whack opposing hockey players with his stick. On one such occasion, after Brodeur whacked Pittsburgh Penguin player Matthew Barnaby, the officials gave Brodeur a match penalty, forcing him to sit out the game. The goalie then had to endure the indignity of explaining to his four-year-old son why he had to spend time in the penalty box. Brodeur explained his misconduct in a way that a four-year-old could understand. He said simply that the referee had given him a "time-out," just as Brodeur would give his son a "time-out" when the boy didn't play nicely with his brothers. "Answering to my sons," Brodeur says, "is the hardest thing I have to do."[588]

The rules of sport are intended to eliminate intolerable inconsistencies The goal is to produce a level playing field for all participants. For the sake of a level playing field, Arsenal coach Arsene Wenger offered to have his team play Sheffield United over again. For every Arsene Wenger, however, there are others who prefer to tilt the playing field in their favor. "Incidental percipitation" tilts the playing field a little. Placing spies in the center field stands tilts it a lot. Too much pine tar on a bat tilts it not at all. Baseball authority Thomas Boswell sees three different levels of "gamesmanship" in

---

[587] Smith, *The Jordan Rules*, 176.

[588] Michael Farber, *Exorcised!*, SPORTS ILLUSTRATED, May 1, 2000, 60.

sports. According to Boswell, the first and most harmless level involves tricks that may work to the advantage of one team but present conditions with which both teams have to contend, such as when the home team waters the base paths to slow down opposing base runners. Boswell's second level would include Lew Burdette and Junkman Durham—athletes who apply "incidental percipitation" or stretch other rules in ways that can be detected and regulated by the umpires or referees. The third level, in Boswell's view, consists of the most contemptible offenses—those which render both umps and foes defenseless, as did Leo Durocher's use of a spy. The distinguishing characteristic of Boswell's third level is that it involves "team-wide dishonesty," not the isolated actions of a single player. When Leo Durocher's Giants used binoculars and electronic devices to steal the signs of opposing catchers, it became team-wide dishonesty Former New York Giant outfielder Monte Irvin once confirmed that the entire Giants team was aware that the team employed a center field spy. According to Irvin, Leo Durocher "asked each player if he wanted the sign." About half the players did. Irvin was one of those who preferred to play by the rules. Durocher was incredulous. "You mean to tell me," Durocher said, "if a big fat fastball is coming, you don't want to know?"

Former major league pitcher Ross Grimsley, a starter for the Baltimore Orioles from 1974 to 1977, once found himself in a difficult situation on the mound. The bases were loaded, and Grimsley's usual repertoire of pitches wasn't working. Orioles manager Earl Weaver visited the mound with the only advice he could muster. "If you know how to cheat," he said to Grimsley, "this would be a good time to start."[589] Professional sports are rife with situations that represent a good time to cheat. There is no universal standard that can be used to judge such conduct. For some, such as Leo Durocher, cheating is simply a part of the game. Others draw a line

[589] Boswell, *The Miracle of Coogan's Bluff Tarnished*, D1.

between gamesmanship and cheating. Still others distinguish conduct on the basis of whether it involves the isolated actions of an individual player or entails more reprehensible team-wide dishonesty.

In a different context, former Pittsburgh Pirates and Washington Senators pitcher Bennie Daniels once said, "I've done plenty of good, and I haven't done anything that keeps me from looking in the mirror."[590] In the end, Bennie Daniels' "mirror test" may be the most useful standard for judging gamesmanship in sports. Win or lose, players will always have to feel comfortable when they look in a mirror. If the actions of golfer Greg Chalmers at the Professional Golf Association's Kemper Open in May 2001 are any indication, there is little that will keep Chalmers from looking in the mirror. After completing his final round at the Kemper, Chalmers disqualified himself for violating a PGA rule that he didn't even know existed. In the opening round of the tournament, Chalmers had hit a shot that didn't go as planned. In frustration, he made an offhand remark about the club he had used to a caddie working for a fellow player. Unbeknownst to Chalmers, his remark was a violation of U.S. Golf Association Rule 8.1, which prohibits a golfer from giving advice to

---

[590] In the late 1970s, Daniels was sentenced to three years in prison for misappropriating $100,000 in public funds while serving as a youth counselor under the California Comprehensive Employment and Training Act. Daniels would enroll youth trainees in the program and then, after their training program had ended, keep their names on the program roster and collect wages in their names. He used the money to give Training Act jobs—and pay—to deserving teenagers who didn't qualify for the program. Said Daniels, "I brought kids into the program illegally, under false pretenses, but you'd see some of them benefit themselves, and so you'd want to help another." As a pitcher, Daniels finished his major league career with a lackluster 45-76 won and lost record but had the distinction of pitching the last game in the history of Brooklyn's Ebbets Field, the last game in Washington's Griffith Stadium and the first game ever in Robert F. Kennedy Stadium. He also started the only opening day game that John F. Kennedy ever attended as President. Thomas Boswell, "Hard Time in Chino," in *Game-Day Sports Writings 1970-1990* (New York: Penguin Books, 1990), 354-361.

another golfer during the course of tournament play. Chalmers did not learn of the rule until three days later, when he struck up a conversation with a fellow player. The player told Chalmers about a situation that had arisen in another tournament, when two caddies had engaged in a forbidden conversation regarding club selection. Upon learning that he may have unwittingly violated Rule 8.1, Chalmers immediately consulted with a PGA rules official. "I had to know right then and there," Chalmers explained.

Chalmers paid dearly for his honesty. If not for the rule violation, he would have earned $94,500 for his play in the Kemper. Before the Kemper, Chalmers had won $532,761 in tournament play during the 2001 season. He was, therefore, in a better position than many golfers to forfeit $94,500. Chalmers' comments suggested, however, that he would have done the same thing even if he had not been so prosperous. "What I try to do," he said, " is play like [the money] doesn't matter. I try to make a decision on what I should do no matter where I'm running in the field. I guess you have got to make a choice to try to play within the rules."[591]

One suspects that if Chalmers had been a baseball player, he would have resisted the urge to know when a fat fastball was coming and that Monte Irvin, if he had been a golfer, wouldn't have thought twice about disqualifying himself for a rules violation, no matter what the price. In their own way, the actions of Greg Chalmers and Monte Irvin each helped to preserve fair play and consistency in sports.

---

[591] *Chalmers Pays Willingly for Honesty*, THE WASH. POST, May 31, 2001, D2.

Chapter 22

Litigation: Lousy Food and Lawsuits

At 270 pounds, Dion Rayford, a former defensive end for the University of Kansas, is a bit fussy about his food consumption. Rayford is also a person who is inclined to remedy perceived injustices in his own way. Early in the morning of November 17, 1999, Rayford placed an order at the drive-through window of a Taco Bell Restaurant in Lawrence, Kansas. When handed his food, Rayford found that a chalupa was missing. First he got angry. Then he decided to get even. With the thought of attacking the Taco Bell attendant, Rayford climbed into the drive-through window. It was a big mistake—especially so because Rayford is a big man. The window, which measured 14 inches by 46 inches, was not designed to accommodate defensive ends. Rayford got stuck. As a Lawrence police sergeant recounted the unlawful entry, "when you take a big guy and put him through a small space, something's got to give."[592] In this case, it was Rayford who gave.

A more common approach for resolving disputes or remedying injustices is simply to file a lawsuit. In the world of sports, lawsuits abound. The foundation of any lawsuit brought to remedy injuries is the notion that each person is responsible for the foreseeable consequences of his or

---

[592] *Drop the Chalupa!*, THE WASH. POST, November 19, 1999, D2.

372

her own actions. In any lawsuit in tort for unintentional injuries, the injured person must allege that the person responsible for the injury owed a duty of care. Dion Rayford might have been injured when he became stuck in the Taco Bell window, but he would have been hard-pressed to make out a credible claim in a lawsuit. Taco Bell owed no duty of care to football players or anyone else who might try to climb into its drive-through window.

The essence of the duty of care is the simple notion that the person owing the duty of care must take precautions to prevent harm to others. The State of Virginia Supreme Court has found that the operator of a skating rink owes a duty of care to protect its patrons against harm from a "known troublemaker." Jonathan Thompson, a teenager, suffered a fractured skull at the hands of a known troublemaker, Travis Bateman. Bateman struck Thompson in the back of his head while both were at the Skate America roller skating rink in Hanover County, Virginia. Bateman was familiar to the Skate America managers. He had been ejected from the skating rink in the past. More troubling, Bateman shouldn't even have been at the rink on the day he hit Thompson. As a result of Bateman's past conduct, Skate America had banned him from its facilities. Despite the ban, Bateman was allowed to enter the rink on the day he attacked Jonathan Thompson. After finishing skating, Bateman encountered Thompson, who was waiting at the rink for a ride home. Without provocation, Bateman struck Thompson and fractured his skull. The Virginia Supreme Court took note of Bateman's reputation for criminal conduct and determined that the rink's managers should have foreseen that he might injure an unwary patron. The court ruled that Skate America had a duty to protect its customers from known miscreants. The justices took pains to point out that Skate America could easily have taken steps to make sure that Bateman did not enter the rink.[593]

---

[593] *Thompson v. Skate America, Inc.*, 261 Va. 121, 540 S.E.2d 123 (2001).

374 • *Clubhouse Lawyer*

Another decision handed down by the Virginia Supreme Court on the same day as the Skate America ruling makes it clear that golf courses—at least golf courses in Virginia—are not liable for criminal acts committed by strangers. The case involved the Glenwood Golf Club, a public course in Richmond, Virginia. Michael Dudas was playing golf at Glenwood when he was accosted by two unknown male trespassers near the thirteenth green. The trespassers pulled a gun, took Dudas' money and shot him in the leg. The golfer sued the golf club for $2,350,000. He argued that the owners had an obligation to protect him from criminal acts committed by others. Dudas uncovered evidence showing that, in the month before he was robbed, there had been two robberies on the golf course, including one with gunfire. One of the earlier robberies had also taken place on the thirteenth hole. The plaintiff urged the court to find that, in view of the earlier acts of violence, Glenwood was obligated to warn its patrons there was a possibility they might encounter criminal behavior. The court found otherwise, however. It ruled that golf clubs in Virginia, like other owners of land, are under no duty to protect patrons and visitors from unanticipated criminal acts.[594] In making its decision, the court was no doubt influenced by the fact that if the golf course were to post warnings of the earlier criminal conduct, many prospective golfers would find other places to play. In the court's view, it was not realistic to expect golf courses to go out of their way to warn customers of prior robberies. Additionally, the court took into consideration the "magnitude of the burden" that the golf course would face in trying to provide security over an entire 18-hole layout.

Actions by a Canadian movie producer created a bit of a scare for some Montreal Expos fans who attended an Expos' game at Olympic Stadium on April 29, 2001. For no apparent reason, during the middle of the game, smoke began billowing out from a spot behind the Stadium's right

---

[594] *Dudas v. Glenwood Golf Club, Inc.*, 261 Va. 133, 540 S.E.2d 129 (2001).

field fence. Upon investigation, the smoke was found to be coming from an area in the bowels of the Stadium that was being rented to a Canadian movie company. The movie company had stored some of its special effects equipment in the rented area. The special effects equipment included a smoke-making machine. Without considering the consequences, the movie company began testing the smoke machine while the game was in progress.[595] If individuals had been injured in the process of fleeing the smoke, a variety of legal issues could have arisen. One area of inquiry would have been whether the movie company owed a duty of care to the fans at Olympic Stadium and, if so, whether it breached that duty of care. A second inquiry would have focused on the liability, if any, of the stadium owners for permitting smoke-making machinery to be kept in the facility.

The duty of care can be an imposing obstacle to prospective lawsuits. In 1951, 37-year-old heavyweight boxer Jersey Joe Walcott knocked out Ezzard Charles in the seventh round of their championship boxing match. With the knockout, Walcott became the oldest man ever to win the heavyweight title. His victory was one of the most stunning upsets in boxing history. The bout was too much for one fan. While watching the match on television, 50-year-old Francis Goss of Pennsauken, New Jersey suffered a fatal heart attack. Goss collapsed within a minute after Walcott's knockout blow and never recovered. The coroner attributed Goss' death to excitement caused by the fight.[596] The suddenness of the tragedy left Goss' friends and relatives in shock. One can only speculate that Goss would have survived the fight if not for the stunning nature of Walcott's win. Nonetheless, the death would not have formed an appropriate basis for a

---

[595] *Hey, We're Playing a Ballgame Here*, USA TODAY BASEBALL WEEKLY, April 25-May 1, 2001, 3.

[596] *Excitement Kills Fan: Television Viewer Dies After Seeing Walcott Win By Knockout*, THE N.Y. TIMES, July 20, 1951, 17.

lawsuit. Neither Jersey Joe Walcott nor the fight's promoters owed a duty of care to Goss.

The Jersey Joe Walcott Principle of the Duty of Care

Unless a person owes a duty of care to another, there can be no legal liability for injury or harm incurred.

When a duty of care exists and the duty is violated, it amounts to negligence on the part of the person owing the duty of care. Negligence is the failure to use the care that a reasonably prudent and careful person would exercise under similar circumstances. A negligent act can be as simple— and as catastrophic—as leaving a barn door open when it is supposed to be closed. The failure to secure a barn door was the basis for a lawsuit filed in October 2000 in Michigan. The suit was filed by the New North Star Stable, owner of a race horse named "Black Raider." New North Star Stable was housing Black Raider at the Howard Niles stable. During the early morning hours of October 31, 1997, Black Raider got loose. The horse wandered onto a public highway. At approximately 2:30 a.m., the horse was hit by a Ford Escort. The impact killed the horse. New North Star Stable maintained that the Niles stable was guilty of negligence. It sued Niles for more than $25,000. The suit alleged that the Howard Niles stable owed a duty to ensure that Black Raider was securely in its stall— and that the stable failed to perform that duty.[597]

When a 60-car freight train derailed and set off a fire inside the Howard Street train tunnel in Baltimore on the afternoon of July 18, 2001, it brought traffic in the vicinity of Baltimore's popular Inner Harbor to a standstill. The train had begun its trip in North Carolina and

---

[597] *Horse's Death Leads to Lawsuit*, THE DETROIT NEWS, October 11, 2000, www.detnews.com/2000.

was headed for New Jersey. The fire apparently burst the city's water lines, causing geysers to shoot 20 feet in the air. Nine of the train's cars were carrying hazardous materials, including propylene glycol, which is used in de-icing fluids, and hydrochloric acid. Police crews closed off all of the major roads into the city while firefighters battled the intense underground fire and suffocating smoke for the better part of five days. The accident also caused havoc at neighboring Oriole Park at Camden Yards. The fire started just as the Orioles were preparing for a night game against the Texas Rangers. After the fire broke out, a cloud of thick smoke settled over the ballpark. The Orioles hastily canceled the game. Panicked players sprinted for their cars in full uniform. For three straight days, the Orioles had to cancel their games. Fearing that the combination of fire and hydrochloric acid would produce dangerous vapors, city officials would not allow the Orioles to resume play at Camden Yards until all of the cars carrying hazardous materials were secured and the fire contained.

The Orioles lost two home dates against the Texas Rangers and one against the Anaheim Angels. For each postponed game, the estimated cost to the Orioles was $1 million.[598] With the financial impact of the derailment mounting, the Orioles hinted that they were examining the possibility of taking legal action against CSX Corp., the owner of the train, tunnel and tracks.[599] Any such action would inevitably be based on a legal theory similar to the allegations of negligence in the lawsuit over the death of Black Raider. The Orioles would have claimed, first, that CSX Transportation owed a duty to the city of Baltimore in general—and to the Orioles specifically—to operate its trains and maintain its tunnel and

---

[598] Manuel Roig-Franzia and Michael E. Ruane, *Firefighters Pull Out 36 Burned Freight Cars: Intense Smoke Slows Job of Extracting Wreckage*, THE WASH. POST, July 21, 2001, A1, A6.

[599] Josh Barr, *Orioles Postponed Again: Team Might Pursue Legal Options to Recoup Losses*, THE WASH. POST, July 21, 2001, D1, D7.

tracks in a safe manner; and, second, that CSX negligently violated its duty of care.

Beyond the duty of care, there is also a matter of foreseeability. The law distinguishes between proximate and remote effects. Proximate effects can be anticipated. Remote effects are not foreseeable and, for that reason, cannot be anticipated. Before a court awards monetary compensation for damages, it must find that the conduct of the defendant was the proximate cause of the injury suffered by the plaintiff. Even people who owe a duty of care to others cannot be held liable for consequences of their acts that are too remote and therefore not foreseeable. The distinction between proximate and remote results becomes particularly significant in a situation such as the train derailment in Baltimore. If the Orioles were to take their case to court, they would likely argue that CSX could have foreseen that a derailment in the vicinity of Camden Yards would cause injury to the baseball franchise. The Orioles' argument would have two principal components: *first*, that CSX could have foreseen that a derailment might cause an uncontrollable fire; and, *second*, that CSX could have foreseen that any such fire had the potential to heat railroad cars carrying chemicals, thereby creating the possibility of dangerous vapors in the vicinity of the ballpark.[600]

---

[600] Shortly after the accident, there was speculation that the water lines in the vicinity of the Howard Street tunnel may have burst and flooded the tunnel, eroding the ground underneath the train tracks and causing the derailment. CSX would have had no role in maintaining the water lines. Thus, significant questions existed regarding the extent of CSX's responsibility for the derailment. A week after the derailment, CSX agreed to pay the City of Baltimore for the overtime expenses of police, fire and rescue crews that responded to the emergency. City officials placed the overtime costs at $1.3 million. CSX was quick to note that the agreement to pay the overtime costs was not an admission of liability. "There is no acknowledgment of blame here," a CSX spokesman said. "We're doing it because it's the right thing to do." Matthew Mosk, *CSX Pays Baltimore's Overtime Bill; City Puts Tab at $1.3 Million*, THE WASH. POST, July 26, 2001, B2.

When St. John's University was competing in the 1999 men's National Collegiate Athletic Association basketball tournament, the Red Storm's 6'6" guard and leading scorer, Ron Artest, became sick to his stomach two days before St. John's was to play the University of Maryland. While staying with his teammates at a Knoxville, Tennessee hotel, Artest ate some food that did not agree with him. Afterwards, while resting in his hotel room, Artest made a hurried trip to the bathroom when his stomach began acting up. In his haste, Artest banged his right foot against the bottom of his bed—leaving him with both an upset stomach and an injured foot. "I ate some lousy food," Artest said. "It was bad, and my foot hurt after that. But I'm 99.9 percent sure it will be okay."[601] In the game against Maryland, Artest did not have one of his better performances, scoring only 8 points in 39 minutes of action.

When restaurants serve "lousy food," people get sick. Illness is a proximate result of the bad food. When basketball players eat bad food and injure their feet running to the bathroom, it may affect their play. However, even if Artest's injured foot contributed to his low point total, neither Artest's foot injury nor his below average output against Maryland was foreseeable. The bad food was not a proximate cause of either. Only Artest knows if his injured foot hindered his play.[602] What is clear is that the restaurant had an obligation to serve Artest something other than "lousy food." The restaurant or its food suppliers may have been liable for the bad food and making Artest sick, but neither would have been liable for Artest's foot injury and any consequences flowing from that foot injury.

---

[601] C. Jemal Horton and Neil H. Greenberger, *Gators' Shannon Has Ticket to Final Four*, THE WASH. POST, March 18, 1999, D6.

[602] Artest averaged 14.8 points per game during the regular season. Against Maryland, he collected seven rebounds and handed out four assists, so his limited point production did not accurately reflect his overall contribution. Beginning midway through the first half of the game, St. John's ran off a streak of 23 consecutive points and routed Maryland, 76-62. The victory earned St. John's a spot among the final eight teams in the tournament.

> ## *The Ron Artest Principle of Foreseeability*
>
> *People are legally liable for the foreseeable consequences of their actions but not for consequences that could not reasonably have been foreseen*

The recruiting experiences of George Mason University basketball coach Jim Larranaga also illustrate the distinction between proximate and remote effects. Early in his coaching career, Larranaga served as an assistant to Terry Holland at the University of Virginia. Larranaga once traveled to upstate New York to recruit 6'9" high school basketball star Tom Sheehey for the Virginia Cavaliers. Larranaga flew in a Lear jet to meet Sheehey at his home. Sheehey was to accompany Larranaga back to Virginia for a campus visit. After arriving at the local airport near Sheehey's home, Larranaga took a taxi to the Sheehey residence. Larranaga and Sheehey exchanged pleasantries, and the two got into the taxi to go back to the airport. When the cab driver put the taxi into gear, Sheehey's dog ran in pursuit. The taxi hit the dog. Larranaga and Sheehey hopped quickly from the cab. When Sheehey picked up the dog and attempted to comfort him, the dog bit Sheehey, inflicting a wound.[603] If not for the taxi driver hitting the dog, Sheehey would not have been bit. The injury to the dog was a proximate result of the taxi driver's act of driving. The injury to Sheehey was considerably more remote—and not something for which the taxi driver would have been liable.

---

[603] A resourceful recruiter, Larranaga assured Sheehey that the hospital at the University of Virginia was staffed by the best doctors in the country. Larranaga promised Sheehey that he would receive excellent medical attention if he attended the university. Whether swayed by Larranaga's line of argument or attracted by other factors, Sheehey did enroll at Virginia. For four years, from 1983 to 1987, he was a prominent member of the Cavaliers' varsity basketball squad and was co-captain of the team in his senior year. Sheehey's hand healed without significant complications.

Not all injuries are physical, in the sense of Ron Artest's foot injury or Tom Sheehey's dog bite. Some injuries are financial. Some come in the form of opportunities lost. Just as the duty of care lies at the foundation of lawsuits based on physical injury, the notion of a duty owed to another person underlies lawsuits based on financial injury or lost opportunities. In his book, *Ball Four*, Jim Bouton related an incident in which fans in the Seattle Pilots' radio audience were chosen at random to win a cash prize if a Seattle player hit a home run in a selected inning. The prize included a $25,000 bonus if the home run was a grand slam. In one game, Bouton's teammate, pitcher Fred Talbot, hit a grand slam home run in the designated inning, winning $27,500 for a fan in Gladstone, Oregon. With Bouton as the inspiration, the Seattle bullpen crew conspired to send Talbot a telegram that was purportedly from the fan. The telegram read, "Thank you very much for making our lives so happy, Mr. Talbert. We feel we must share our good fortune with you. A check for $5,000 will be sent to you when the money arrives."[604] Bouton intentionally misspelled Talbot's name to add realism. It was, Bouton revealed, simply another "clever touch."

"Mr. Talbert," of course, never received his check for $5,000. Talbot had no recourse, other than to direct angry comments at Bouton. Even if the telegram had been authentic, there would have been no guarantees. If the telegram were legitimate, it would have constituted a promise, not a contract. Under the law, promises are not equivalent to contracts. In a contract, one person agrees to perform an act or forego something in exchange for a benefit given by another. There is mutual benefit. A promise, on the other hand, is given freely—without expectation of a reciprocal benefit. Contracts are enforceable under the law. Promises are not. If the Seattle Pilots' fan had actually sent the "Talbert" telegram and then failed to pay $5,000 as promised, Fred Talbot would have had no recourse under

---

[604] Jim Bouton, *Ball Four: My Life and Hard Times Throwing the Knuckleball in the Big Leagues* (Cleveland, Ohio: The World Publishing Company, 1970), 252.

the law. The fan may have felt a moral obligation to pay Talbot, but there would have been no contractual duty to pay. And, without a legal duty, there would have been no basis for a lawsuit.

The absence of a legal duty often does not deter individuals from filing lawsuits. Fred Talbot lost out on the $5,000 that he expected to receive. There is no doubt that Talbot felt deprived. In fact, as Bouton tells the tale, after receiving the bogus telegram, Talbot made plans to buy a motorboat. Talbot could have sued the fan for his $5,000. Or perhaps he might have elected to sue Bouton to obtain the money. In either case, the lawsuit would have been frivolous. Neither the fan nor Bouton owed a duty to pay Talbot $5,000.

The Fred Talbot Principles of Reliance on Promises

1. A mere promise, even if made in good faith, is not enforceable under the law.
2. Only a contract that involves mutual commitments by both parties is legally enforceable

---

Fred Talbot may well have felt embarrassed and humiliated by the fake telegram.[605] People have sued for less. During a football game between the New York Giants and the San Diego Chargers, fans at Giants Stadium

---

[605] The episode of the "Talbert" telegram evidences some similarities to a classic "pot of gold" case from the 1920s. In the pot of gold case, townspeople in Cotton Valley, Louisiana convinced a rather gullible maiden that her relatives had buried a pot of gold on the grounds of a certain house. The townsfolk then proceeded to bury a pot containing rocks and dirt on the property. The maiden spent several months digging and, one day, happened upon the pot of rocks. She transported the pot, unopened, to a local bank. With great fanfare, the bank scheduled a ceremony for the opening of the pot. At the ceremony, the maiden opened the pot with great anticipation, only to find the rocks—and no gold. She sued for disappointment and mental suffering and ultimately prevailed in court. *Nickerson v. Hodges*, 84 So. 37 (1920).

hurled a barrage of snowballs from the stands. The snowballs injured fifteen people and caused police to eject 175 spectators from the stadium. One person charged with throwing snowballs, Jeffrey Lange, sued the New Jersey Sports and Exposition Authority, which operates the stadium, and other New Jersey State officials for "ruining his life." Lange's lawyer charged that the state had invaded Lange's privacy and defamed him by stirring media hysteria about his role in the snowball-throwing melee. Lange's lawsuit accused the state of holding Lange up to ridicule, public humiliation and public scorn by singling him out. Lange lost his job shortly after the snowball incident. In his lawsuit, he asked the court to compensate him for loss of income and emotional anguish. The New Jersey Sports and Exposition Authority replied in decidedly terse fashion. "We would consider this a frivolous suit," said a spokesman.[606]

In a twist on the traditional notion of duty of care, a New York Jets football fan once sued the team after he had lost his season tickets to Jets' home games. The fan had purchased season tickets for three seats during the 1989-1990 season. When the fan discovered that he had misplaced the tickets, he asked the Jets to issue replacement tickets. The Jets refused. However, team officials told the fan that if he again paid the face value of the tickets, they would give him tickets for the same seats. The Jets also advised the fan that if the original tickets turned up later, the team would issue a refund. The fan paid again for two of the season tickets and then sued the Jets for double billing and unjust enrichment. After considering the arguments of both sides, the court ruled in favor of the Jets. The court found that the fan's transactions with the team involved two separate contracts, the first for purchase of the original season tickets and the second for purchase of the replacement tickets. In each case, the court said, to fulfill the terms of the contract, there was a condition: the fan had to present the tickets to the Jets when seeking admission to the games. With respect

---

[606] *Fanfare*, THE WASH. POST, March 15, 1996, C2.

to the first contract, the fan was unable to fulfill the condition because he had lost the tickets. In the court's analysis, the fan was obligated to take care of the tickets. He failed in that obligation. The court noted that, in the past, there had been instances where fans had lied about losing their tickets in an effort to get extra tickets without charge. In light of the Jets' prior experiences, the court found that the team's policy regarding the replacement of lost tickets was a necessary precaution to ensure the safety and well-being of fans during games.[607]

In order for a contract to be enforceable under the law, the parties to the agreement must have been capable of making an affirmative decision to be bound by the terms of the agreement. After his junior year at Oregon State, basketball player Lonnie Shelton came to St. Louis to discuss signing a pro contract with the ABA's Spirits of St. Louis. While Shelton's agents were talking to the St. Louis management, Shelton went for a ride with 6'10" free spirit Marvin Barnes, then a center/forward with the St. Louis team. The two toured the city in Barnes' Rolls Royce. After being out with Barnes for a few hours, Shelton came back and signed a five-year contract with St. Louis at a salary of $150,000 per year. When Shelton returned to Oregon State, fans and school officials were livid at the prospect of Shelton leaving college. Stories began circulating that Marvin Barnes had gotten Shelton drunk and that the inebriated Shelton had been coerced into signing the contract. Shelton began having severe misgivings about turning pro. A variety of lawsuits were filed against the Spirits team and Shelton's agents.

With the controversy building, the Spirits decided not to enforce the contract. Shelton then asked the NCAA to be reinstated for his senior season of college ball. When the NCAA refused his request, Shelton sued. In response to the lawsuit, a Federal district court in Oregon issued an order requiring Oregon State to reinstate Shelton. Pending the outcome of an

---

[607] *Ganey v. New York Jets Football Club*, 550 N.Y.S.2d 566 (N.Y. City Civ. Ct. 1990).

appeal filed by the NCAA, the 6'8" center rejoined the Oregon State team for his senior season and led his squad to an 18-9 record for the year. After the season ended, the court of appeals reversed the earlier court order and upheld the NCAA's initial finding that Shelton was ineligible to play. In a final touch to the Shelton saga, the NCAA, bolstered by its victory at the appeals court, stripped Oregon State of all fifteen victories during the 1975-1976 season in which Shelton had played. Leaving no stone unturned, the NCAA also ordered Oregon State to erase Shelton's senior season statistics from the school's record books.[608] By the time the NCAA got around to taking away Oregon State's victories, Shelton had already graduated to the professional ranks and was on the way to establishing himself as a key contributor for the New York Knicks.[609]

Several questions remained regarding whether Shelton's contract with the Spirits of St. Louis was valid and whether Shelton possessed sufficient capacity, at the time he signed the contract, to know what he was doing. In many states, a person who is intoxicated by alcohol or use of drugs is considered incompetent to sign a contract. These states allow a person who does sign a contract while intoxicated to disavow the contract. A smaller number of states allow a person who is intoxicated to get out of a contract only if the other party to the contract knows of the intoxication. In Lonnie Shelton's case, if the Spirits of St. Louis had tried to enforce the contract, the details regarding Shelton's activities while in the company of Marvin Barnes would have played a big role in determining whether the

---

[608] Shelton averaged 17.8 points per game and 7.7 rebounds in his senior season. *Oregon State Forfeits Victories With Shelton*, THE N.Y. TIMES, November 10, 1976, A24.

[609] Less than ten games into his rookie season in the NBA, Shelton was being hailed as "a bright light for the Knicks." The *New York Times* reported that when facing the Denver Nuggets in his first starting assignment at center, Shelton "played 27 minutes, made eight of 13 field goals, mostly on power moves inside, and led New York with 10 rebounds, eight of them off the defensive board." *Nets Down Braves; Knicks Are Beaten: Nuggets Win Before 17,808 by 119-110*, THE N.Y. TIMES, November 4, 1976, 53, 57.

contract was valid. Rod Thorn, the coach of the Spirits at the time, was of the opinion that the contract was valid. "The kid wanted to sign," said Thorn, "he had excellent representation and he was going to get what, for that time, was huge money." Harry Weltman, the president of the Spirits, was of the same opinion. Weltman recalled that Shelton "went out with Marvin Barnes. Maybe they had a drink and maybe they didn't. They were only gone two or three hours and I don't know where they went or what they did." For his part, Marvin Barnes urged Shelton to sign. Barnes told Shelton, "Man, you're getting $150,000 a year, a house for your mother, a car. Boy, you better sign that damn contract. It's not as much as I'm making, but you're not as good as me."[610] Barnes proved persuasive, Shelton signed and the lawsuits followed soon after.

A case that arose in Carlstadt, New Jersey provided a classic example of the duty owed in a contractual setting. In 1995, a 22-year-old fan of the University of Notre Dame football team contracted with a Carlstadt tattoo parlor to have the words "Fighting Irish" inscribed on his arm. Upon completion of the job, the Notre Dame fan discovered, to his dismay, that the tattoo artist had left out the "t" in "Fighting." The inscription read, "Fighing Irish." The fan sued the tattoo parlor for damages. [611]Though one might dispute the extent of the damages, it was an easy case to prove.[612] The fan had contracted to have "Fighting" spelled with eight

---

[606] Terry Pluto, *Loose Balls: The Short, Wild Life of the American Basketball Association As Told by the Players, Coaches, and Movers and Shakers Who Made It Happen*, (New York: Simon & Schuster, 1990), 377.

[611] *Dye-Hard Fan*, THE WASH. POST, January 1, 1996, C3.

[6612] There is no doubt, however, that misspellings in tattoos can be expensive mistakes. In another case, also from New Jersey, a tattoo parlor paid $7,000 in settlement to a victim of a misspelled word in a tattoo. The customer contracted with the tattoo artist for a picture of a knife being inserted into a person's back and the words "Why Not, Everyone Else Does" inscribed underneath. The word "Else" came out as "Elese." Neil Genzlinger, *Proof That New Jersey Is a Bit Wacky*, THE N.Y. TIMES, December 30, 2001, 1.

characters. The tattoo artist's work fell one character short. From an evidentiary standpoint, it was a simple case as well. The plaintiff needed only to bare his arm to prove his case.

A Tattoo Artist's Principle of Contract Performance

When performing a duty owed under the terms of a contract, it is important to dot all of the i's and cross all the t's.

The Notre Dame fan suffered only damage to his arm. His damage, though lasting, might be viewed as inconsequential. As a case involving the University of Tennessee football team demonstrates, the stakes get higher when invasion of privacy is alleged. In June 1991, Tennessee dismissed assistant football coach Jack Sells. When the 1991-92 collegiate football season started, Sells found a way to help a friend, Ron Zook, who was the defensive coordinator for the University of Florida. A few days before Tennessee was to play Florida, Sells took some diagrams of Tennessee's football plays to a Kinko's copy center and directed the attendant to fax the papers to Zook. At that point, Sells had a valid oral contract with Kinko's. Kinko's agreed to fax the papers for Sells, and Sells agreed to pay for the service. Sells did not ask the Kinko's attendant to read the papers. As events unfolded, a Kinko's employee examined Sells' papers, recognized that the diagrams were football plays used by Tennessee, and alerted the Tennessee athletic department.[613] The incident soon became public knowledge. Unhappy Tennessee football fans harassed Sells. Sells placed the blame squarely on Kinko's. He sued the company for $3 million dollars. Sells alleged that Kinko's had violated his privacy and damaged his reputation. The lawsuit was resolved when Sells and Kinko's settled out of court.[614] From the perspective of Tennessee football fans,

---

[613] The plays never reached Zook. Florida, however, did not need them in any event, beating Tennessee handily, 35-18.

[614] *Coach Settles Suit With Kinko's*, THE WASH. POST, July 29, 1995, D2.

Sells was certainly guilty of "unclean hands." Playbooks are usually considered to be the property of football teams and not of individual players or coaches. Tennessee regulations most likely required coaches to return all playbooks at the end of their employment. From Sells' perspective, he hired Kinko's only to fax his papers, not to read or intercept them. Kinko's did not fulfill its part of the agreement.

When the Washington Wizards selected 6'11" high school senior Kwame Brown with the first pick in the June 2001 draft of amateur basketball players, there was widespread recognition, if not concern, that even the most promising high school players lacked the maturity, physical strength and technique to tangle with the likes of Los Angeles Lakers center Shaquille O'Neal. One interested observer, Southwest Missouri Coach Barry Hinson said that asking a high school player to guard the 7'1" O'Neal was "like sending a Chihuahua to guard Marmaduke," an apt reference to Brad Anderson's fearsome Great Dane cartoon character.[615] Former NBA star Spencer Haywood was among those expressing concern with talented high school players skipping college to play in the pros. "It's all my fault," Haywood told the *New York Times*. "They need to fix the system. It's out of control."[616] Whether it was all Haywood's fault is debatable, but there is no denying the role he played in opening up professional basketball to high school students. As a college sophomore, Haywood sued the National Basketball Association for the right to play professionally. In 1968, fresh out of high school, he had represented the United States on the Olympic basketball team. He then played at Detroit University. At the time, the NBA had a rule that no team could sign a college-age player earlier than four years from the graduation date of his high school class. Shortly after Haywood turned 21 years old, but within four

---

[615] Ken Denlinger and Ross Siler, *School's Out for NBA's Latest*, THE WASH. POST, July 5, 2001, D1, D3.

[616] Denlinger and Siler, *School's Out for NBA's Latest*, THE WASH. POST, July 5, 2001, D1, D3.

years from his high school graduation date, the Seattle Supersonics signed Haywood to a professional contract, blatantly disregarding the NBA rule. The NBA commissioner immediately threatened to disallow the contract and impose sanctions on the Supersonics.

With his professional career jeopardized, Haywood filed an antitrust action against the league. The court hearing Haywood's case granted a preliminary injunction, allowing Haywood to play for Seattle temporarily. In its ruling, the court declared that Haywood would suffer substantial harm to his playing ability and career potential if precluded from playing with the Supersonics. The NBA appealed the court's decision. On appeal, the injunction was overturned. At that point, it looked as if Haywood would have to wait until the four-year anniversary of his high school graduation to resume his NBA career. However, Haywood took the case to the Supreme Court. For the Seattle Supersonics, Haywood's reinstatement was especially important because, without his rebounding and scoring, the Sonics stood little chance of qualifying for the 1971 NBA playoffs. In a ruling on March 1, 1971, just twenty-two days before the playoffs were scheduled to begin, Supreme Court Justice William Douglas ordered the NBA to permit Haywood to play on a temporary basis until all the legal issues were decided.[617] Less than two weeks later, a Federal district court in Los Angeles declared that the NBA's ban on signing college underclassmen was illegal. The court granted summary judgment for Haywood, clearing the way for him to play permanently in the NBA.[618] Even with Haywood's services available for the remainder of the season, however, Seattle fell short of qualifying for the playoffs. Haywood and his teammates closed out the season with 38 wins and 44 losses, placing them fourth out of five teams in their division and well behind the pace-setting Los Angeles Lakers.

---

[617] *Haywood v. National Basketball Association*, 401 U.S. 1204 (1971).

[618] *N.B.A. Rule Found Invalid By Judge*, THE N.Y. TIMES, March 13, 1971, 19.

There is no lack of frivolous lawsuits in sports. A manufacturer of radar guns once took offense when NBC broadcasters handling the telecast of a World Series game questioned the accuracy of speed guns used at ballparks. In an impromptu comment on the subject, one of the announcers declared, "Some speed guns have clocked trees going forty-five miles per hour." The radar gun manufacturer sued for libel even though the announcer had not referred to the manufacturer by name.[619] The father of a youth league baseball player once sued the coach of his son's team for $2,000 because the team had performed poorly during the season. The father reasoned that the team might have played better if the coach had been more capable. In turn, if the team had played better, it might have earned a trip to play in a tournament in Florida.[620] In the father's estimation, the value of the trip to Florida was $2,000—the amount specified as damages in the lawsuit. However, the mere prospect of a trip to Florida cannot be transformed into a duty. The coach was not under a legally enforceable duty to ensure that his team earned a spot in the tournament. Without a legal duty, there was no basis for the lawsuit.

Just as there is no legal compulsion for coaches to ensure that their players earn trips to post-season tournaments, there is no obligation for coaches to put players into playoff games. In 1996, a Texas high school student sued his school's baseball coach for having benched him. The player, Kyle Rutherford, also played quarterback for the school's football team. After the football team endured a losing season, Rutherford had blamed the coach for costing him a college scholarship. In the school's senior prom "Memory Book," Rutherford had written, "To Coach Hooks, I leave a $40,000 debt. I figure you cost me that much with your 3-7 [football] season." In response, the coach benched Rutherford for a key playoff game during the baseball season. Rutherford filed suit in Federal

---

[619] Ron Luciano and David Fisher, *Remembrance of Swings Past* (New York: Bantam Books, 1988), 299-300.

[620] *Scorecard*, SPORTS ILLUSTRATED, January 24, 2000, 34.

court alleging that the coach had violated his constitutional rights. Rutherford asked the court to compensate him for the humiliation of having to explain why he did not see action in the playoff game. Lawyers for the school district had a quick response. "There is no constitutional right to play," they said.[621]

Kyle Rutherford had no legal recourse when Coach Hooks benched him. Unless there is evidence of unlawful discrimination or denial of a student's civil rights, the law cares little if an athlete has to watch from the sidelines. The stakes are heightened, however, when a person's right to employment is jeopardized. The former groundskeepers for the Washington Redskins' practice facility in Chantilly, Virginia sued Redskins owner Daniel Snyder for allegedly interfering with their ability to obtain employment. Snyder bought the Redskins franchise in July 1999. Shortly thereafter, he fired John Jenkins Sr. and John Jenkins Jr., a father and son groundskeeping team that had taken care of the Redskins' practice fields for 30 years. In explaining his decision, Snyder resorted to hyperbole. He told *Sports Illustrated*, "At Redskins Park the fields were in bad shape. There were three guys trying to kill the players with their crappy fields ...."[622] The Jenkinses sued Snyder for mental anxiety, emotional distress, embarrassment and humiliation. They alleged that Snyder's comments hindered their prospects for finding similar jobs. The Jenkinses could easily prove they weren't "trying to kill the players." In fact, the very nature of Snyder's statement suggested that he was simply exaggerating for effect—at least that is the way the court interpreted the statement. A Federal district court judge ruled in favor of the Redskins' owner and dismissed the lawsuit. The judge concluded that the "hyperbolic nature" of Snyder's statement "negates any serious accusation of unfitness or wrongdoing."[623]

---

[621] *Benching Provokes Uncivil Response*, THE WASH. POST, August 24, 1997, D2.

[622] Thomas Heath, *Snyder Sued by Former Groundskeepers*, THE WASH. POST, September 22, 2000, D9.

[623] Mark Maske, *Lawsuit Against Snyder Dismissed*, THE WASH. POST, February 8, 2001, D4.

In the early 1950s, Cincinnati Redlegs fans contrived a plan to place the entire Redlegs lineup on the National League All-Star team. At the time, as is the current practice, fans filled out ballots to select the players who would form the starting lineups for the All-Star game. Redlegs fans voted early and often, overwhelming the ballot box. When the balloting ended, seven Cincinnati ballplayers emerged as the leading vote-getters at their respective positions. In addition to Frank Robinson and other legitimate Cincinnati all-stars, Redlegs outfielders Gus Bell and Wally Post were elected to the starting team, out-polling the tandem of Willie Mays and Hank Aaron. Ford Frick, then commissioner of Major League Baseball, overruled the election results and named Mays and Aaron to start in the outfield. Predictably, Frick's decision angered the Cincinnati fans. They dragged Frick in effigy around the city, accusing the commissioner of using "Soviet tactics," and threatening to bring a lawsuit against him.[624]

Frick would not back down, nor should he have. Mays and Aaron belonged in the starting lineup. And, as a tactical weapon, dragging Frick in effigy around the city was likely to be more effective than bringing a lawsuit. Even if the Cincinnati fans had been able to demonstrate that Ford Frick owed them some sort of legally enforceable duty, they would have been hard-pressed to measure damages, financial or otherwise. There were certainly no damages that could have been documented in a lawsuit. To the contrary, with Aaron and Mays in the starting lineup, fans in Cincinnati and throughout the country had the benefit of seeing bona fide National League all-stars in the outfield.

In 1909, fans in Detroit and Pittsburgh were nearly deprived of the opportunity to see one of the most gifted players of all time, Ty Cobb, play in the World Series. Like Dion Rayford, Cobb was inclined to remedy perceived injustices in his own way. Propelled by Cobb's .377 batting average and 107 runs batted in, the Tigers won the American League pennant and squared off against the Pirates in the Series. For the opening game in

---

[624] Daniel Okrent, *Midsummer Snooze*, SPORTS ILLUSTRATED, July 12, 1999, 74.

Pittsburgh, Cobb's teammates traveled by train from Michigan, through Ohio and on to Pittsburgh. Cobb took a more circuitous route—one that circumvented Ohio.

Cobb's travels had little to do with geography, and a lot to do with his peculiarly antisocial behavior. A month before the World Series, when the Tigers were playing in Cleveland, Cobb had returned to his hotel at 1:30 a.m. after an evening of dinner and drinking. The night elevator operator informed Cobb that the elevators had been taken out of service at midnight. "Get going up," Cobb commanded the operator. The operator put the elevator back in service but stopped at the wrong floor. His patience wearing thin, Cobb slapped the operator. The operator returned the elevator to the lobby, where the night watchman berated Cobb for causing a disturbance. Cobb shouted at the watchman. Fisticuffs followed. Cobb pulled out a pocketknife and began cutting the watchman. After Cobb was restrained, the watchman swore out an arrest warrant, charging aggravated assault with intent to kill.

The day after the incident, Cleveland police went to the ballpark to detain Cobb for questioning, but they were not quick enough. The Tigers' train had already left for a game in St. Louis, and Cobb was on it. He was officially declared a fugitive. As the World Series approached, Cleveland police threatened to stop the Tigers' World Series train when it steamed through Ohio and pull Cobb off. "Ohio is blocked to me," Cobb wrote.[625] So, instead of traveling to Game 1 of the World Series with his teammates, Cobb took a series of trains from Detroit to Ontario, Canada, and then south to Buffalo, New York and on to Pittsburgh. The need to bypass Ohio more than doubled Cobb's travel time, leaving him little opportunity to rest. The risks did not end once Cobb arrived in Pittsburgh. There was a chance that Pennsylvania police might arrest Cobb and extradite him to Ohio. With Cobb facing distractions on several different fronts, Detroit and the Pirates split the first two games in Pittsburgh. The Series then returned to Detroit for games three, four and five. Cobb repeated the arduous trip

---

[625] Al Stump, *Cobb* (Chapel Hill, NC: Algonquin Books of Chapel Hill, 1996), 172.

through Canada. The Tigers ended up losing the Series in seven games. Cobb collected only six hits in 26 at bats, a humbling .231 batting average. The extended travel had taken a toll.

After the Series, Cobb returned to Cleveland, turned himself in, and was released on $500 bond. The Tigers hired two Ohio attorneys to represent Cobb. One of the attorneys was an influential former mayor of Cleveland. With Cobb facing the threat of jail time, his attorneys were able to work out a plea agreement with the prosecutors. Helped by a friendly judge, an influential lawyer, and money from the Tigers' owners, Cobb avoided trial by pleading guilty to simple assault and battery. The court fined him $100.

The process of working out a plea bargain entails off-the-record negotiations between lawyers for the defendant and a government prosecutor. Typically, negotiations focus on the strength of the testimony to be given by prospective witnesses and the defendant's prior criminal record. The lack of witnesses willing to testify may have been a factor in Cobb's case. It was widely rumored that, in advance of the hearing, the owners of the Tigers paid a settlement fee of $10,000 to the hotel watchman.[626] With the money in hand, Cobb's victim would have been understandably reluctant to testify.

The outcome of judicial proceedings, like the outcome of baseball games, turns on "intangibles." Cobb was fortunate to have a friendly judge, lawyers who knew their way around the Cleveland courts—and enough money to pay his legal fees. "We bought this one," Cobb would later say.[627] Throughout Cobb's ordeal, his teammates extended little sympathy. They recognized that Cobb could easily have avoided all of his troubles. If he had simply walked the stairs to his hotel room in Cleveland,

---

[626] Stump, *Cobb*, 172.

[627] Stump, *Cobb*, 181.

there would have been no encounter with the night watchman and no encounter with the law.

Lawsuits arise for many reasons. They may stem from lousy food, lousy coaching or lousy personalities. Regardless of the cause, however, the demands of the law are strict. For lawsuits based on torts, there must have been a duty of care, a violation of that duty, and harmful consequences. For lawsuits based on contracts, there must have been a contractual commitment, a breach of the commitment, and costs or damages resulting from the breach.

About the Author

Fred Day is an inveterate sports fan who, to this day, has difficulty accepting the fact that the New York Yankees lost the 1960 World Series. He possesses a solid background in baseball history and holds a master's degree in political economics from the State University of New York at Albany and a law degree from George Washington University in Washington, D.C. He is the author of three books in the field of FCC law and telecommunications, *Policies and Practices in the Regulation of Private Radio Communications Systems* (1994), *Private Land Mobile and Private Microwave Radio Decisions: A Chronology and Summary* (1994) and *Regulation of Wireless Communications Systems* (1997). Day maintains a law practice in Falls Church, Virginia, where he resides with his wife and his two sports-minded dogs.

Principles of Sports, Law and Life

The Ban Johnson Principles of Spitting on Umpires
1.   There isn't room in the game for players who spit on umpires.
2.   Players who do spit on umpires will be fined and suspended.

The Julius Erving Principles of Trading "Franchise" Players
1.   When sports fans buy season tickets, they are buying the right to watch a team, and not individual players.
2.   Teams are free to trade established stars, no matter how popular, for a good reason, a bad reason, or any reason at all.

The Arthur Ashe Principle of Contract Finality
Once you put your name on a contract, don't complain.

Pat Boone's Principles of Signing Checks
1.   There is no way to prove a check was blank when you signed it.
2.   Never, ever put your signature on a blank check.

The Rick Barry Principles of Contract Interpretation
1.   Don't rely on oral assurances from Pat Boone or anyone else.
2.   Don't forget to read Paragraph 6.
3.   If your contract requires you to play in Washington, get in your car and drive to Washington.

The Tony Barone Principle of Bantering with Prospective Draft Picks
A Director of Player Personnel should not joke about things that players might think are "for real."

The Charlie Flowers Principle of "Soiled Hands"
If a player agrees to play for two different teams in the same season, the team with the "cleaner hands" will probably prevail.

The Lou Lamoriello Principle of Signed Contracts
Whether a player signs a fax copy of a contract or the original document, the contract is valid and must be honored.

The Babe Ruth Principle of Comparative Salary Levels
If a person has a better year than the President, he or she deserves to get paid more than the President.

The Elliot Maddox Principles of Assumption of the Risk
1.   Players have the right and obligation not to expose themselves to dangerous conditions.
2.   If players willingly expose themselves to dangerous conditions, they assume the risk of injuries that may result.

The Bob Rush Principles of Assumption of the Risk
1.   Spectators at baseball games cannot be expected to keep their eyes on baseballs being thrown in the bullpen at the same time that a game is in progress.
2.   Spectators do not necessarily assume the risk of injury if they get hit by a baseball thrown from the bullpen while a game is in progress.

The Gerald R. Ford Principle of Assumption of the Risk
When a golfer's tendency to hit errant shots has been well documented in the newspapers, spectators should be ready to duck.

The May Lee Principle of Recovery in Negligence Cases
In order for a plaintiff to recover for injuries in a negligence case, four conditions must exist: (1) the defendant must have owed a duty of care to the plaintiff; (2) the defendant must have violated its duty of care; (3) the plaintiff must have suffered injury, damages or loss; and (4) the injury, damages or loss must have been caused by the defendant's actions or failure to act.

The Eddie George Principle of the Duty of Care
If a person is under a duty to safeguard the Heisman Trophy or any other object of value and causes damage to the valuable object while it is in his or her possession, the duty of care has been violated and a tort committed.

The Randy Myers Principles of Reasonable Apprehension
1. If a spectator leaves his seat in the ballpark, walks onto the playing field and appears to be reaching for a weapon, the spectator has created a reasonable apprehension of harmful contact.
2. So long as the actions of the spectator are intentional and create a well-founded fear of peril, it is an assault.
3. For an assault to occur, there need not be actual contact between the assailant and the victim; a reasonable apprehension of harmful contact is sufficient.

The Scott Kamieniecki Principles of Offensive Contact
1. For a battery to occur, there must be intentional contact that is harmful or offensive.
2. If the intentional contact leaves a person with a "sheepish grin," it is probably not a battery.

The Yogi Berra Principle of Criminal Law
It's not a crime when nobody does nothin' to nobody.

The Judge Lee Dreyfus Principle of Proper Perspective on Athletic Competitions
It is important for athletes to retain a proper perspective on the role of recreational sports in the grand scheme of things.

The Roger Clemens Principles of Proving Intent
1.   In the heat of competition, a baseball bat may be mistaken for a baseball.
2.   When a person's actions are susceptible to two contradictory interpretations, proving intent is difficult.

The Shoeless Joe Jackson Principle of False Accusations
When you play your heart out, it is not right for people to accuse you of a crime.

The Judge Motley Principles of Equal Access to Clubhouses
1.   It is unconstitutional to expect women reporters to stand in a tunnel outside a clubhouse when men reporters are standing inside the clubhouse.
2.   Professional sports cannot adopt policies that have the effect of creating "an all-male preserve."

The Jane Gross Principles of Equal Access to the Sportswriting Profession
1.   Professional sports need reporting by women sportswriters.
2.   Women sportswriters ask different questions.

The Heather Nabozny Principle of Promotions in the Field of Sports
Promotions should be based strictly on ability.

The Arthur Ashe Principle of Protecting One's Privacy
No person should be placed in the position of having to lie to protect his or her privacy.

The Warren Spahn Principle of Biographical Distortion
The right of privacy protects athletes and other celebrities against "distortions and fanciful passages" in print, no matter how flattering the writing may be.

The Corey Hirsch Principle of the Right of Publicity
I have the right to determine whether I want to be pictured as the losing goalie on a postage stamp.

The Uncle Robbie Principle of Straight Shooting
If I am expecting a baseball, don't throw me a grapefruit.

The Tony La Russa Principle of Acceptable Ruses
There is nothing wrong with ruses that don't involve telling a lie.

The Baltimore Orioles' Principle of Detrimental Reliance
Misrepresentations become legally significant when others rely on them to their detriment.

The Jon Clark Principle of Voiding Contracts
When a person is induced to enter into a contract because of misrepresentation by the other party, the contract can be voided if the misrepresentation is material.

The Bob Locker Principle of Acceptable Deception in Contract Negotiations
It's okay when people engage in a little deception during contract negotiations but when they tell outright lies, they have crossed the line.

404   •   *Clubhouse Lawyer*

The Ron Weaver Principle of the Emergence of Truth
Sometimes the truth emerges at the most inopportune moments.

The Art Ditmar Principle of Contract Negotiations
If I agree to play for $14,500 in Kansas City, that doesn't mean I agree to play for the same salary in New York.

The Sandy Koufax and Don Drysdale Principle of Contract Negotiations
Two front-line players can most effectively create clout in contract negotiations when they jointly negotiate their contracts.

The John Curtis Principle of Friendship In Professional Baseball
You need your friends in this business.

The Pat Riley Principle of Trades
Players who refuse to report to a new team after a trade should be sued for violation of contract.

The Curt Flood Principle of Leaving the Game on One's Own Terms
A ballplayer has a right to go out like a man and not like a bottle cap.

The Peter Seitz Principles of Free Agency
1.   The parties to an agreement are free to create an "endless contract" but must do so by clear and explicit words.
2.   The contract that Andy Messersmith signed in 1974 gave the Los Angeles Dodgers the option of renewing his contract for one year.
3.   A one-year option clause means exactly that—an option for one year and not a perpetual renewal.

Bob Feller's Principle of the Purpose of Baseball
Baseball was made for kids.

Walter Johnson's Principle of "Dog Eat Dog"
The employer tries to starve out the laborer, and the laborer tries to ruin the employer's business.

The Jim Delahanty Principle of the Unionization of Labor
When our job security is threatened by the unilateral actions of baseball management, it's time to get together and form a union.

The Robert Murphy Principle of the Economic Contribution of the Players
It is the ballplayers who make possible big dividends and high salaries for stockholders and club executives.

The Rip Sewell Principle of the Unlimited Earning Power of Ballplayers
A player has no limit on what he can earn in this game.

The Robert Murphy Principle of the Effects of Unionization
By forming a united labor organization, players can turn apples into an orchard.

The National Labor Relations Act's Principles of Workers' Rights
1.   Workers have the right to organize into unions.
2.   Employers must negotiate with labor unions, in good faith, regarding hours, wages and other "terms and conditions" of employment.
3   Workers have the right to engage in peaceful strikes.

The National Labor Relations Board's Principle of Interstate Commerce
When an industry such as baseball results in millions of dollars in goods and services crossing the boundaries between the states, that industry is engaged in interstate commerce.

The Mackay Radio & Telegraph Principle of Replacement Workers
Under the National Labor Relations Act, when a company's workers have gone out on strike, the employer has the right to hire replacement workers to carry on the company's business.

Jim Lachey's Principle of the Distinction Between "Team Doctors" and "Company Doctors"
1.   A team doctor looks out for the best interests of the athletes in his or her care.
2.   A company doctor does whatever it takes to get athletes back on the field.

Marty Barrett's Principle of the Duty of Care Owed by Physicians
A team doctor has multiple obligations to athletes in his or her care:
1.   the obligation to render a proper diagnosis.
2.   the obligation to provide proper treatment and/or surgery.
3.   the obligation to adequately inform the patient about the nature of the injury and the alternatives for treatment.

Pee Wee Reese's Principle of Combating Racism
I will stand by my teammate, regardless of race or color.

Happy Chandler's Principle of Racial Integration in Sports
I will approve of the transfer of Robinson's contract. We'll make a fight with you. So bring him on in.

The Trevor Matich Principle of Indifference to Racial Distinctions
When your teammates are all you've got, it's hard to look at anything except character and performance.

The Constitutional Principle of Freedom of Assembly
Public intolerance cannot form the basis for taking away a person's freedom of assembly.

The Thomas Boswell Principle of Soccer Seating
It is un-American to stick soccer fans from foreign countries in the Frank Howard home run seats.

The Virginia High School Principle of Title IX Equality
Differences in the scheduling policies for high school sports, based solely on the gender of the players, is a violation of the equal protection clause of the Constitution and the provisions of Title IX.

The Immigration and Naturalization Service Principle of Sustained Athletic Acclaim
Foreign athletes of extraordinary skill who have achieved sustained national or international acclaim qualify for O-1 category visas.

The Immigration and Naturalization Service Principle of International Athletes of Professional Caliber
Athletes who fall short of the "sustained national or international acclaim" standard but who are capable of performing at an internationally recognized level may be admitted to the United States under P-1 visas.

The Immigration and Naturalization Principle of Citizenship for Athletes of Extraordinary Ability
1. Athletes possessing extraordinary ability are eligible to emigrate to the United States as priority workers.
2. Such athletes must be recognized as having risen to the very top of their field and must have achieved All-Star status or be among the highest paid performers in their sport.

The Immigration and Naturalization Service Principle of Eligibility for Asylum

To qualify for asylum in the United States, a person must be able to demonstrate that he or she has a well-founded fear of being persecuted because of race, religion, nationality, membership in a particular social group, or political opinion.

The Immigration and Naturalization Service Principle of Deportation for Crimes of Moral Turpitude

Under U.S. immigration laws, an individual from a foreign country who has not gained U.S. citizenship is subject to being deported if he or she is convicted of a crime involving moral turpitude.

The Lou Piniella Principles of Defamatory Statements

1. The law will not examine a statement of opinion to see if it is defamatory unless the statement relates to a matter that can be objectively verified.
2. If an opinion relates to a "matter of public concern," the statement will not be considered defamatory unless the statement is obviously false.
3. The conduct and performance of major league umpires is a "matter of public concern."

The Baltimore Orioles' Principles of Ownership of Lineup Cards

1. Possession is not nine-tenths of the law.
2. When a manager, acting within the scope of his employment, fills out a lineup card, the lineup card is the property of the team.

The Billy Martin Principle of Tenancy By the Entirety

If a person creates a tenancy by the entirety with his or her spouse, the property will be immune from attack by creditors seeking to satisfy the personal debts of one of the spouses.

The "Field of Dreams" Principle of Trespass
The law does not permit individuals to step on private property—to play baseball or for any other reason—unless the property owner consents.

The National Hockey League Principle of Perpetual Ownership
Trademarks and service marks grant perpetual ownership; copyrights do not.

The Foamation Principle of Copyright Notice
Unless proper notice of a copyright is given, the product name remains in the public domain.

The Motorola Principle of Distributing News of NBA Games in Progress
Using radio to report facts from basketball games in progress is not a violation of the copyright restriction, as long as actual descriptions of the games are not being transmitted.

The Shoeless Joe Jackson Principle of the Ownership of Will Documents
The signed copy of a testamentary will is a public record and is not the property of the decedent's heirs or any other person.

The Kareem Abdul-Jabbar Principle of Name Changes
When a person changes his name, he retains control over the use of his former name for commercial purposes.

The C.J. Nitkowski Principle of Intolerable Inconsistency
Inconsistency in an umpire's decisions should be intolerable in our game.

The Bobby Murcer Principle of Fair Play
If they don't let batters use an illegal bat, they shouldn't let pitchers use an illegal pitch.

The Bobby Richardson Principle of the "In the Neighborhood" Play
I only make the play; it's the umpire's job to make the call.

The Jersey Joe Walcott Principle of the Duty of Care
Unless a person owes a duty of care to another, there can be no legal liability for harm incurred.

The Ron Artest Principle of Foreseeability
People are legally liable for the foreseeable consequences of their actions but not for consequences that could not reasonably have been foreseen.

The Fred Talbot Principles of Reliance on Promises
1. A mere promise, even if made in good faith, is not enforceable under the law.
2. Only a contract, entailing mutual commitments by both parties, is legally enforceable.

A Tattoo Artist's Principle of Contract Performance
When performing a duty owed under the terms of a contract, it is important to dot all of the i's and cross all the t's.

The Kinko's Principle of Contract Performance
In a contract setting, one should do what is required to fulfill the terms of the contract—no less and no more.

Table of Cases Cited

American Heart Association v. County of Greenville, 489 S.E.2d 921 (1997).

Atlanta Braves, Inc. v. Leslie, 378 S.E.2d 133 (Ga. App. 1989).

Boston Professional Hockey Association, Inc. et al. v. Dallas Cap & Emblem Mfg., Inc., 510 F.2d 1004 (1975).

Coates v. City of Cincinnati, 402 U.S. 611(1971).

Diversified Group Inc. v. Sahn, 696 N.Y.S.2d 133 (A.D. 1 Dept. 1999).

Dudas v. Glenwood Golf Club, Inc., 261 Va. 133, 540 S.E.2d 129 (2001).

Federal Baseball Club of Baltimore, Inc. v. National League of Professional Baseball Clubs, et al., 259 U.S. 200 (1922).

Finley v. Kuhn, 569 F.2d 527 (7th Cir. 1978).

Flood v. Kuhn, 407 U.S. 258 (1972).

Graham v. Richardson, 403 U.S. 365, 376 (1971).

Hackbart v. Cincinnati Bengals, Inc., 601 F.2d 516 (10th Cir. 1979).

Hampton v. Mow Sun Wong, 426 U.S. 88, 100-01 (1976).

Harlem Wizards Entertainment Basketball, Inc. v. NBA Properties, Inc., 952 F. Supp. 1084 (1997).

Harrell, In re William; Robert Abele v. Phoenix Suns L.P., 73 F.3d 218 (9th Cir. 1996).

Haywood v. National Basketball Association, 401 U.S. 1204 (1971).

Jim Bouton Corporation v. Wm. Wrigley Jr. Company and Amurol Products Company, decided July 7, 1989 (Southern District of New York).

Kareem Abdul-Jabbar v. General Motors Corporation, 85 F.3d 407, 409 (9th Cir. 1996).

Knapp v. Northwestern University, 942 F.Supp 1191 (1996).

Knapp v. Northwestern University, 101 F.3d 473 (7th Cir. 1996), *cert. denied*, 520 U.S. 1274 (1997).

Kreuger v. San Francisco Forty Niners, 234 Cal. Rptr. 579 (Cal. App. 1987).

Lee v. National League Baseball Club of Milwaukee, 89 N.W.2d 811 (1958).

Lefkowitz v. Great Minneapolis Surplus Store, Inc., 86 N.W.2d 689 (1957).

Los Angeles Memorial Coliseum v. National Football League, 726 F.2d 1381 (1984).

Los Angeles Rams Football Club v. Cannon, 185 F.Supp. 717 (S.D. Cal. 1960).

Lucy v. Zehmer, 84 S.E.2d 516 (1954).

Ludtke v. Kuhn, 461 F.Supp 86, 90 (1978).

MacLean v. First Northwest Industries of America, Inc., 635 P.2d 683, 684 (1981).

Maddox v. City of New York, 487 N.E.2d 553 (N.Y. 1985).

Major League Baseball Properties and Los Angeles Dodgers, Inc. v. Sed Non Olet Denarius, Ltd. d/b/a The Brooklyn Dodger Sports Bar & Restaurant, 817 F.Supp. 1103 (S.D.N.Y. 1993).

Manning v. Grimsley, 643 F.2d 20 (1st Cir. 1981).

Mayor and City of Baltimore v. Baltimore Football Club Inc., 624 F.Supp. 278 (D.Md. 1985).

Maytnier v. Rush and Chicago National League Ball Club, Inc., 225 N.E.2d 83 (1967).

McDonnell Douglas Corp. v. Green, 411 U.S. 792 (1973).

Mercer v. Duke University, 190 F.3d 643 (4th Cir. 1999).

National Basketball Association v. Motorola, Inc., 105 F.3d 841 (1997).

National Exhibition Co. v. Fass, 143 N.Y.S. 2d 767 (Sup. Ct. 1955).

National Labor Relations Board v. Mackay Radio & Telegraph, 304 U.S. 333 (1938).

New York Football Giants, Inc. v. Los Angeles Chargers Football Club, Inc., 291 F.2d 471 (5th Circuit 1961).

Nickerson v. Hodges, 84 So. 37 (1920).

Niemiec v. Seattle Rainier Baseball Club, Inc., 67 F. Supp. 705 (W.D. Wash. 1946).

Northwest Greyhound Kennel Association v. State, 506 P.2d 878 (1973).

O'Brien v. Pabst Sales Co., 124 F.2d 167 (1942)

PGA Tour, Inc. v. Martin, 204 F.3d 994, 121 S.Ct. 1879 (2001).

Piazza v. Major League Baseball, 831 F.Supp. 420 (E.D. Penn. 1993).

Pittsburgh Athletic Club v. KQV Broadcasting Co., 24 F. Supp. 490 (W.D. Pa. 1938).

Postema v. National League of Professional Baseball Clubs, 799 F.Supp 1475 (1992).

Pryor v. National Collegiate Athletic Association, No. 01-3113 (3rd Cir. May 6, 2002).

Rabiner v. Rosenberg, 28 N.Y.S.2d 533 (1941).

Reuters Limited v. Federal Communications Commission, 781 F.2d 946 (D.C. Cir. 1986).

Riley v. Chicago Cougars Hockey Club, Inc., 427 N.E.2d 290 (Ill. App. 1981).

Robertson v. National Basketball Association, 389 F. Supp. 867 (S.D.N.Y. 1975).

Rose v. Morris, 104 S.E.2d 485 (1958).

Sielicki v. New York Yankees, 388 So.2d 25 (1980).

Spahn v. Julian Messner, Inc., 250 N.Y.S.2d 529 (1964).

State v. Spann, 623 S.W.2d 272 (Tenn. Sup. Ct. 1981).

Strauss v. Long Island Sports, Inc., d/b/a New York Nets, 401 N.Y. Supp. 2d 233 (1978).

Sundra v. St. Louis American League Baseball Club, 87 F. Supp. 471 (E.D. Miss. 1949).

Talcott v. National Exhibition Co., 128 N.Y.S. 1059 (1911).

Theismann v. Theismann, 22 Va. App. 557 (1996).

Thompson v. Skate America, Inc., 261 Va. 121, 540 S.E.2d 123 (2001).

Tomjanovich v. California Sports, Inc., No. H-78-243 (S.D. Tex. 1979).

Uhlaender v. Henricksen, 316 F.Supp. 1277 (1970).

Washington v. Joseph C. Smith, et al., 80 F.3d 555 (D.C. Cir. 1996).
Wisconsin v. Milwaukee Braves Inc., 144 N.W.2d 1, cert. denied, 385 U.S. 900 (1966).

Bibliography: Books

Abrams, Roger I. *Legal Bases: Baseball and the Law.* Philadelphia, Pennsylvania: Temple University Press, 1998.

Angell, Roger. *Late Innings: A Baseball Companion.* New York: Ballantine Books, 1983.

Ashe, Arthur R. *A Hard Road to Glory: A History of the African-American Athlete Since 1946.* New York: Amistad, 1993.

Ashe, Arthur R. and Frank Deford. *Arthur Ashe: Portrait in Motion.* New York: Carroll & Graf Publishers, Inc., 1993.

Ashe, Arthur R. and Arnold Rampersad. *Days of Grace: A Memoir.* New York: Ballantine Books, 1993.

Asinof, Eliot. *Eight Men Out.* New York: Henry Holt and Company, 1988.

Auerbach, Arnold "Red" and Joe Fitzgerald. *On & Off The Court.* New York: Bantam Books, 1986.

Berkow, Ira. *Pitchers Do Get Lonely and Other Sports Stories.* New York: Atheneum, 1988.

Berra, Yogi and Dave Kaplan. *When You Come to a Fork in the Road, Take It!* New York: Hyperion, 2001.

Berry, Robert C. and Glenn M. Wong. *Law and Business Of The Sports Industries: Common Issues in Amateur and Professional Sports.* 2nd ed. 2 vols. Westport, CT: Greenwood Publishing Group, Inc., 1993.

Betancourt, Marian. *Playing Like a Girl.* New York: Contemporary Books, 2001.

Boswell, Thomas. *Game-Day Sports Writings 1970-1990.* New York: Penguin Books, 1990.

Boswell, Thomas. *How Life Imitates the World Series.* New York: Penguin Books, 1983.

Boyd, Brendan C. and Fred C. Harris. *The Great American Baseball Card Flipping, Trading, and Bubble Gum Book*. Boston: Little, Brown and Company, 1973.

Bouton, Jim. *Ball Four: My Life and Hard Times Throwing the Knuckleball in the Big Leagues*. Cleveland, Ohio: The World Publishing Company, 1970.

Caren, Eric C. *Baseball Extra: A Newspaper History of the Glorious Game From Its Beginning to the Present*. Edison, New Jersey: Castle Books, 2000.

Collins, Bud and Zander Hollander, eds. *Bud Collins' Tennis Encyclopedia*. Detroit, Michigan: Visible Ink Press, 1997.

Cramer, Richard Ben. *Joe DiMaggio: The Hero's Life*. New York: Simon & Schuster, 2000.

Deford, Frank. *The World's Tallest Midget: The Best of Frank Deford*. Boston: Little, Brown and Company, 1987.

Dressler, Joshua. *Understanding Criminal Law*. New York: Matthew Bender & Co., Inc., 1995.

Eisen, Armand. *Play Ball! Quotes on America's Favorite Pastime*. Kansas City: Andrews and McMeel, 1995.

Elias, Stephen. *Patent, Copyright & Trademark*. Berkeley, California: Nolo Press, 1999.

Fainaru, Steve and Ray Sánchez. *The Duke of Havana: Baseball, Cuba and the Search for the American Dream*. New York: Villard Books, 2001.

Fleming, G.H. *The Dizziest Season: The Gashouse Gang Chases the Pennant*. New York: William Morrow and Company, Inc., 1984.

Duncan, David James. *The Brothers K*. New York: Bantam Books, 1996.

Gallen, David, ed. *The Baseball Chronicles*. New York: Carroll & Graf Publishers, Inc., 1991.

Goldstein, Richard. *You Be The Umpire*. New York: Dell Publishing, 1993.

Golenbock, Peter. *Bums: An Oral History of the Brooklyn Dodgers*. New York: G.P. Putnam's Sons, 1984.

Golenbock, Peter. *Dynasty: The New York Yankees, 1949-1964.* Englewood Cliffs, NJ: Prentice-Hall, Inc., 1975.

Golenbock, Peter. *Teammates.* New York: Harcourt Brace & Company, 1990.

Golenbock, Peter. *Wild, High and Tight: The Life and Death of Billy Martin.* New York: St. Martin's Press, 1994.

Greenberg, Martin J. and James T. Gray. *Sports Law Practice.* 2nd ed. 2 vols. Charlottesville, Virginia: Lexis Law Publishing, 1998.

Gregory, Robert. *Diz: The Story of Dizzy Dean and Baseball During the Great Depression.* New York: Viking Penguin, 1992.

Gutman, Dan. *The Way Baseball Works.* New York: Simon & Schuster, 1996.

Halberstam, David. *October 1964.* New York: Villard Books, 1994.

Harris, Mark. *Bang The Drum Slowly.* Lincoln, Nebraska: University of Nebraska Press, 1984.

Helyar, John. *Lords of the Realm: The Real History of Baseball.* New York: Ballantine Books, 1994.

Honig, Donald. *Baseball Between the Lines.* New York: Coward, McCann and Geoghegan, Inc., 1976.

Kalinsky, George and Phil Berger. *The New York Knicks: The Official 50th Anniversary Celebration.* New York: Macmillan Books, 1997.

Kiersh, Edward. *Where Have You Gone, Vince DiMaggio?* New York: Bantam Books, 1983.

Kirby, James. *Fumble: Bear Bryant, Wally Butts & the Great College Football Scandal.* New York: Dell Publishing, 1988.

Kubek, Tony and Terry Pluto. *Sixty-One: The Team, The Record, The Men.* New York: Macmillan Publishing Company, Inc., 1987.

Lowenfish, Lee. *The Imperfect Diamond: A History of Baseball's Labor Wars.* New York: Da Capo Press, Inc., 1991.

Luciano, Ron and David Fisher. *Remembrance of Swings Past.* New York: Bantam Books, 1988.

Madden, Bill and Moss Klein. *Damned Yankees: A No-Holds-Barred Account of Life with "Boss" Steinbrenner.* New York: Warner Books, Inc., 1990.

Majerus, Rick. *My Life on a Napkin: Pillow Mints, Playground Dreams, and Coaching the Runnin' Utes.* New York: Hyperion, 2000.

Malamud, Bernard. *The Natural.* New York: Avon Books, 1980.

Maraniss, David. *When Pride Still Mattered: A Life of Vince Lombardi.* New York: Simon and Schuster, 1999.

Mantle, Mickey. *All My Octobers: My Memories of 12 World Series When The Yankees Ruled Baseball.* New York: Harpers Collins Publishers, Inc., 1994.

Marazzi, Rich and Len Fiorito. *Aaron to Zuverink: A Nostalgic Look At The Baseball Players Of The Fifties.* New York: Stein and Day, 1982.

McCabe, Neal and Constance McCabe. *Baseball's Golden Age: The Photographs of Charles M. Conlon.* New York: Harry N. Abrams, Inc., 1997.

Miller, Marvin. *A Whole Different Ball Game: The Sport and Business of Baseball.* New York: Simon and Schuster, 1991.

Nemec, David. *The Rules of Baseball.* New York: Lyons & Burford, Publishers, 1994.

Peary, Danny. *We Played the Game: Sixty-Five Players Remember Baseball's Greatest Era, 1947-1964.* New York: Hyperion, 1994.

Perea, Juan F. and Richard Delgado, Angela P. Harris and Stephanie M. Wildman. *Race and Races: Cases and Resources for a Diverse America.* St. Paul, MN: West Group, 2000.

Pietrusza, David; Matthew Silverman and Michael Gershman, eds. *Baseball: The Biographical Encyclopedia.* Kingston, New York: Total Sports Publishing, 2000.

Pluto, Terry. *Loose Balls: The Short, Wild Life of the American Basketball Association As Told by the Players, Coaches, and Movers and Shakers Who Made It Happen.* New York: Simon & Schuster, 1990.

Posner, Richard A., ed. *The Essential Holmes: Selections from the Letters, Speeches, Judicial Opinions, and Other Writings of Oliver Wendell Holmes, Jr.* Chicago, Illinois: University of Chicago Press, 1996.

Ritter, Lawrence S. *The Glory of Their Times: The Story of the Early Days of Baseball Told by the Men Who Played It.* New York: William Morrow and Company, Inc., 1992.

Rosin, Skip. *One Step From Glory: On the Fringe of Professional Sports.* New York: Simon and Schuster, 1979.

Salin, Tony. *Baseball's Forgotten Heroes: One Fan's Search for the Game's Most Interesting Overlooked Players.* Lincolnwood, Illinois: Masters Press, 1999.

Schubert, George W.; Rodney K. Smith and Jesse C. Trentadue. *Sports Law.* St. Paul, Minnesota: West Publishing Co., 1986.

Mike Shannon, ed. *The Best of Spitball: The Literary Baseball Magazine.* New York: Pocket Books, 1988.

Shaughnessy, Dan. *The Curse of the Bambino.* New York: Penguin Books, 1991.

Simon, Scott. *Home and Away: Memoir of a Fan.* New York: Hyperion, 2000.

Smith, Sam. *The Jordan Rules.* New York: Simon and Schuster, 1992.

Stump, Al. *Cobb.* Chapel Hill, NC: Algonquin Books of Chapel Hill, 1996.

Swirsky, Seth. *Baseball Letters: A Fan's Correspondence with His Heroes.* New York: Kodansha America, Inc., 1996.

Swirsky, Seth. *Every Pitcher Tells A Story: Letters Gathered by a Devoted Baseball Fan.* New York: Times Books, 1999.

Thomas, Henry W. *Walter Johnson: Baseball's Big Train.* Washington, D.C.: Phenom Press, 1995.

Thompson, Chuck. *Ain't the Beer Cold.* South Bend, Indiana: Diamond Communications, Inc., 1996.

Thorn, John, ed. *The Armchair Book of Baseball II: An All-Star Lineup Celebrates America's National Pastime.* New York: Charles Scribner's Sons, 1987.

Will, George F. *Bunts: Curt Flood, Camden Yards, Pete Rose and Other Reflections on Baseball.* New York: Scribner, 1998.

Wolff, Rick, ed. dir. *The Baseball Encyclopedia.* New York: Macmillan Publishing Company, 1990.

Zimmer, Don with Bill Madden. *Zim: A Baseball Life.* New York: Contemporary Books, 2001.

Bibliography: Magazine and Newspaper Articles

Chapter 1
Spit's Long Trajectory: Back to 1913, THE WASH. POST, October 5, 1996, D5.

Chapter 2
Sports in Brief: Williamses Sued, THE WASH. POST, April 23, 2002, D2.

The Blotter: Sidelined, SPORTS ILLUSTRATED, June 3, 2002, 22.

Josh Barr, *Esherick Is Under Spotlight*, THE WASH. POST, January 9, 1999, D3.

Ken Denlinger, *Esherick Weathers Georgetown's Storm*, THE WASH. POST, March 3, 1999, D4.

Josh Barr, *Promises to Keep*, THE WASH. POST, September 3, 2001, D3.

Franz Lidz, *Up and Down in Beverly Hills*, SPORTS ILLUSTRATED, April 17, 2000, 63.

Promising Prospects, SPORTS ILLUSTRATED, July 3, 2000, 41.

Brooke A. Masters, *Sweet Car Deal For Redskins Takes Sour Turn*, THE WASH. POST, January 8, 1999, D3.

U-Va. Fans Make Their Case, THE WASH. POST, January 24, 1999, D8.

Mark Bechtel, *Catching Up With Tom Heinsohn, Celtics Forward*, SPORTS ILLUSTRATED, February 8, 1999, 12.

MacLean Waits For an Offer From Celtics, THE WASH. POST, October 7, 1995, D1-D3.

Joe LaPointe, *Pucks About to Drop Again*, THE N.Y. TIMES, September 10, 1995, Sec. 8, 5.

Alex Yannis, *Devils Win Lemieux Case*, THE N.Y. TIMES, September 30, 1995, Sec. 1, 29.

Dave Sheinin, *Youth Serves O's With Win*, THE WASH. POST, Aug. 8, 2000, D6.

Chapter 3
Injured Boy Awarded $1.05 Million, THE WASH. POST, April 7, 2000, D9.
Citing Safety, CART Won't Race: G-Forces Are a Problem in Texas, THE WASH. POST, April 30, 2001, D4.
Sued, SPORTS ILLUSTRATED, May 21, 2001, 24.
CART, Track Reach Settlement on Races, THE WASH. POST, October 17, 2001, D2.
National League Notes, USA TODAY BASEBALL WEEKLY, February 24- March 2, 1999, 12.
Monte Reel and Micah Pollack, *A Boxer's Dream, Now a Nightmare: 'Bee' Scottland Died Doing What He Loved*, THE WASH. POST, July 8, 2001, D1, D11.
William Gildea and Micah Pollack, *Sen. McCain Asks For Investigation Of Scottland Fight*, THE WASH. POST, July 11, 2001, D1.
Jack McCallum and Kostya P. Kennedy, *The Windup, The Pitch, The Suit*, SPORTS ILLUSTRATED, January 15, 1996, 30.
Fanfare, THE WASH. POST, February 22, 1996, D2.
L. Jon Wertheim, *No Penalty*, SPORTS ILLUSTRATED, April 1, 2002, 63.
L. Jon Wertheim, *Special Report: How She Died*, SPORTS ILLUSTRATED, April 1, 2002, 60.
Albin Krebs, *Notes on People*, THE N.Y. TIMES, June 21, 1978, C2.
Paying Through The Nose, USA TODAY, July 20, 1995, 1C.
Ann Gerhart, *Dreams of the Well-Pressed Woman*, THE WASH. POST, June 16, 2001, C1, C2.
Randy Kennedy, *Yankee Stadium Closed As Beam Falls Onto Seats*, THE N.Y. TIMES, April 14, 1998, A1.
Blaine Harden, Letter From New York: *One Steel Beam May Not Be Enough to Wreck the House That Ruth Built*, THE N.Y. TIMES, April 16, 1998, A2.

George's Heisman Has a Chip on Its Block, THE WASH. POST, Dec. 15, 1995, B2.

Chuck Shepherd and Jim Sweeney, *News of the Weird*, WASHINGTON (D.C.) CITY PAPER, February 16, 1996, 16.

Jeff White, *After Coliseum Debacle, Talk Turns Toward Refund Policy*, RICHMOND TIMES-DISPATCH, November 30, 2001, A1, A9.

Jeremy Redmon, *Mayor Says City Should Refund Ticket Costs for Slippery Show*, RICHMOND TIMES-DISPATCH, November 30, 2001, A1, A8.

Chapter 4

Cubs Pitcher Is Attacked By Spectator, THE WASH. POST, September 29, 1995, D1, D8.

Filip Bondy, *Yankees Stripped of Victory*, THE N.Y. TIMES, Jul. 29, 1991, C1, C3.

Fan Sentenced, THE WASH. POST, April 9, 2000, D11.

Phils Must Pay, THE WASH. POST, November 28, 1995, E3.

Animal Farm, SPORTS ILLUSTRATED, November 20, 1995, 16.

Woman Wins Suit Against Heat, THE N.Y. TIMES, Feb. 15, 1997, 31.

Dave Kindred, *Blind Ambition*, THE SPORTING NEWS, July 5, 1999.

Adam Knapp, *After 2 Years, Beaning Lawsuit Still Unresolved*, THE WICHITA EAGLE, May 4, 2001, 3C.

Chapter 5

McCandlish Phillips, *Yankee Is Linked to Fight In Café: But Bauer Denies That He Took a Swing at Fan in Copacabana 'Incident'*, THE N.Y. TIMES, May 17, 1957, 50.

Arthur Daley, *Crime and Punishment*, THE N.Y. TIMES, August 25, 1965, 42.

Leonard Koppett, *Marichal Says He Used the Bat To Hit Roseboro in Self-Defense*, THE N.Y. TIMES, August 24, 1965, 20.

Gerald Eskenazi, *Latest Giants-Dodgers Brawl Brings a Few Others to Mind*, THE N.Y. TIMES, August 23, 1965, 24.

Flagrant Foul, SPORTS ILLUSTRATED, February 21, 2000, 22.

Thomas Heath, *Bruins' McSorley Charged; Faces Up to 18 Months in Prison*, THE WASH. POST, March 8, 2000, D1.

Thomas Heath and DeNeen L. Brown, *McSorley Gets Probation For Slash: NHL Defenseman Avoids Jail Time*, THE WASH. POST, October 7, 2000, D1 .

Ump-Pushing Softballer Ordered to Cool Off in Jail, THE WASH. POST, September 24, 1998, C2.

Fern Shen and Christine Spolar, *Three Lives Once Full of Great Hope: Young Officers' Deaths Shake Naval Academy*, THE WASH. POST, December 3, 1993, A1.

Jane Gross, *Winfield Charges Will Be Dropped*, THE N.Y. TIMES, August 6, 1983, 29.

Winfield Gets An Apology, THE N.Y. TIMES, August 9, 1983, B9.

Tom Verducci, *Roger & Out*, SPORTS ILLUSTRATED, October 30, 2000, 40.

Kathy Orton, *Club Pro Quells Armed Man*, THE WASH. POST, June 21, 2001, D9.

Baby, You Can Drive My Car, THE WASH. POST, June 7, 2001, D7.

Rick Kuhn Sentenced to 10 Years, THE N.Y. TIMES, February 6, 1982, 17.

Peter D. Vroom, *Cicotte And Jackson's Confessions Admitted*, THE CHICAGO EVENING POST, July 25, 1921, 1.

Chicago 'Black Sox' Acquitted, SAN FRANCISCO CHRONICLE, August 3, 1921, 1.

Court's Ruling Just the Ticket For Keeping Scalpers in Check, THE NATIONAL LAW JOURNAL, June 12, 1995, A27.

John Donovan, *Your Cheatin' Horse: Some People In Sports Just Can't Play By The Rules*, CNNSI, www.sports illustrated.cnn.com, January 19, 2001.

Kevin Lynch, *Horse Trainers Call New State Doping Law Unfair*, THE DETROIT NEWS, October 11, 2000.

Courts, THE WASH. POST, July 20, 2001, D2.

Chapter 6
Christine Brennan, *Tagliabue To Probe Harassment: Woman Reporter Accuses Patriots*, THE WASH. POST, September 28, 1990, B5.

Polygraph Test Reportedly Clears Mowatt, THE WASH. POST, October 7, 1990, C5.

Dave Butz, *Respect Should Keep Women Out of Men's Locker Rooms*, THE WASH. POST, October 7, 1990, C5.

Miss Arlington's Tour: The Girl Pitcher to Twirl Against Professional Teams, THE PHILADELPHIA PRESS, July 1, 1898, 10.

Mariett M. Buggie, *Girl Tosser Wins Game, Also Fans: Chews Gum and Pitchers All-Star Team to Standstill*, THE CLEVELAND LEADER, October 3, 1907, 1.

J.A. Adande, *'Boys Will Be Boys' Sad Excuse For Fouling Her Out, She Says: Female 1st Baseman Bids Insults Goodbye*, THE WASH. POST, June 25, 1991, E5.

Little League Has Female Trail Blazer: Canadian Girl Starts In the World Series, THE WASH. POST, August 22, 1990, D6.

Ray Glier, *After Making the Team, She Is Making History*, THE WASH. POST, August 31, 2001, A3.

Mark Beech, *Julie Krone, Star Jockey*, SPORTS ILLUSTRATED, May 21, 2001, 12.

Rheaume Plays First Game, THE WASH. POST, December 14, 1992, C4.

Rachel Alexander, *Cammi Granato Providing Color*, THE WASH. POST, February 3, 1999, D10.

Mark Bechtel, *IRL's Leading Lady: Fisher Is Making Her Mark*, SPORTS ILLUSTRATED, June 4, 2001, 100.

Tom Verducci, *Woman's Place Is on the Field*, SPORTS ILLUSTRATED, February 8, 1999, 117.

Award Reduced, THE WASH. POST, April 2, 1999, D6.

Chapter 7

Jeff Pearlman, *Big Hit*, SPORTS ILLUSTRATED, May 28, 2001, 34.

Mark Maske, *AL President Orders Belle to Get Counseling*, THE WASH. POST, May 17, 1996, C1.

Five U-Mass. Players File Suit, THE WASH. POST, Dec. 15, 1995, B4.

Mark Asher and David Nakamura, *Simpkins's Tab $8,000, Says NCAA*,

THE WASH. POST, February 21, 1996, F1.

Dean William Prosser, *Privacy,* 48 Cal.L.Rev. 383, 289.

Stamp of Disapproval, SPORTS ILLUSTRATED, April 17, 1995, 12.

Louis Effrat, *Ditmar, 15-Game Winner, Had No Luck and Little Help, Says Stengel,* THE N.Y. TIMES, October 11, 1960.

Sued, SPORTS ILLUSTRATED, January 15, 2001, 26.

A Chocolate Ear Flap, THE WASH. POST, September 14, 1997, D2.

Sports in Brief, THE WASH POST, July 7, 2000, D2.

Tim Wendel, *Pass Time With This Litany Of Baseball Love Letters,* USA TODAY BASEBALL WEEKLY, November 6-12, 1996, 26.

Tossed Out, from Scorecard, Mark Mravic, ed., SPORTS ILLUSTRATED, April 24, 2000, 28.

Chapter 8

La Russa's Deception, THE WASH. POST, October 4, 2000, D5.

D'Vera Cohn, *TV Golf, Botching the Birdies: Sharp-Eared Viewers Hear False Notes in 'Ambient Sound',* THE WASH. POST, September 2, 2000, C1.

Rachel Alexander Nichols, *Roddick Recovers,* THE WASH. POST, June 7, 2001, D3.

S.L. Price, *Andy Roddick's Breakthrough: New American in Paris,* SPORTS ILLUSTRATED, June 11, 2001, 93.

The Tall Tale of Bob Kurland, SPORTS ILLUSTRATED, November 6, 1995, 18.

J.A. Adande, *Respert Shooting For The Big Time; Michigan State's Top Scorer Impresses Scouts With Range, But Height Is A Shortcoming,* THE WASH. POST, June 24, 1995, C3.

Jason La Canfora, *Spurgeon Up, Brea Down,* THE WASH. POST, Aug. 15, 2000, D4.

Peter Slevin and Dave Sheinin, *An Age-Old Numbers Game: Amid Visa Crackdown, Many Dominican Players Aren't as Young as Thought,* THE WASH. POST, March 2, 2002, D1, D3.

Sheldon, Pitcher, Wins Award As Bombers' Leading Rookie, THE N.Y. TIMES, April 6, 1961, 41.

Charles Nobles, *Yanks Agree to Terms With Defector*, THE N.Y. TIMES, February 14, 2001, D2.

Ian Thomsen and Luis Fernando Llosa, *One for the Ages*, SPORTS ILLUSTRATED, September 3, 2001, 63.

Sally Jenkins, *Let the Little Kids Play—Without The League*, THE WASH. POST, September 1, 2001, D1, D5.

Almonte's Father Could Face Charges, THE WASH. POST, September 5, 2001, D2.

Dave Sheinin, *Rogers Is Caught in Age Game*, THE WASH. POST, March 2, 2002, D3.

Jack McCallum and Kostya Kennedy, *Pre-Games Stretch*, SPORTS ILLUSTRATED, April 15, 1996, 20.

Josh Barr and Robert E. Pierre, *O'Leary Resigns as Coach at Notre Dame: Falsified Credentials Lead to Downfall*, The Wash. Post, December 15, 2001, D1.

Olympian Effort for Naught, RICHMOND TIMES-DISPATCH, November 23, 1995, D1, D3.

Frankly, This Imposter Wasn't Very Truthful, USA TODAY BASEBALL WEEKLY, Sept. 20-26, 2000, 3.

Woods Imposter Gets 200 to Life, THE WASH. POST, April 29, 2001, D2.

Picture This, SPORTS ILLUSTRATED, May 28, 2001, 28.

Texas Considers Suing Imposter, THE WASH. POST, January 3, 1996, F4.

Imposter Pleads Guilty, THE WASH. POST, March 16, 1996, B7.

Chapter 9
Secret Agent, SPORTS ILLUSTRATED, February 15, 1999, 28.

Bob Woolf, Athletes' Agent, Dies, THE WASH. POST, December 1, 1993, B2.

Chapter 10
William Gildea, *Difficult Goodbye For Surhoff, And the Orioles*, THE WASH. POST, August 1, 2000, D1, D6.

Dave Sheinin, *Covering the Bases*, THE WASH. POST, July 14, 2002, D7.

Dave Sheinin, *Orioles: Belle's Career Is Over,* THE WASH. POST, March 9, 2001, D1.

Tim Kurkjian, *Swing Shift,* SPORTS ILLUSTRATED, January 23, 1995, 70, 74.

Dave Sheinin, *O's Ship Clark to Cards and Surhoff to Braves In Deals for Reserves and Minor Leaguers,* THE WASH. POST, August 31, 2000, D1.

Gabriel Files Suit Disputing Ram Contract, THE WASH. POST, May 10, 1973, D4.

Gabriel Suit Dismissed, THE WASH. POST, May 31, 1973, D5.

Phil Taylor, *Hell, No, They Won't Go,* SPORTS ILLUSTRATED, March 2, 1998, 80.

Dave Brady, *Rams Escape Fine In Draft Deal Oversight,* THE WASH. POST, March 9, 1973, D2.

Chapter 11

Thomas Boswell, *Quite Simply, a Hero,* THE WASH. POST, January 22, 1997, D3.

Antitrust Exemption Is Partly Revoked, THE N.Y. TIMES, October 28, 1998, D7.

Chapter 12

John Drebinger, *Defeat by Indians Reduces Yankee Lead Over Idle Red Sox to 2½ Games: Old Mates Mourn Bonham,* THE N.Y. TIMES, September 16, 1949, 39.

Tiny' Bonham Dies; Baseball Star, 36, THE N.Y. TIMES, September 16, 1949, 27.

Walter Johnson, *Baseball Slavery: The Great American Principle of Dog Eat Dog,* BASEBALL Magazine, July 1911.

Guild Threatens Strike by Pirates: No Giants Game Tomorrow Night Unless Club Agrees to Bargaining Election, THE N.Y. TIMES, June 6, 1946, 26.

Roscoe McGowen, *Dodgers Vanquish Pirates by 5-3 As Higbe and Melton Excel in Box,* THE N.Y. TIMES, June 6, 1946, 26.

Dave Sheinin, *Union Challenges Contraction Bid*, THE WASH. POST, December 5, 2001, D3.

Bill Shaikin, *Strike 2? Major Leagues Plan to Cut Pair of Teams*, L.A. TIMES, November 7, 2001, 1.

Bill Shaikin, *Players' Union Files Grievance*, L.A. TIMES, November 9, 2001, 1.

Chapter 13

Jeffrey Gordon, *Baseball's Antitrust Exemption and Franchise Relocation: Can A Team Move?*, FORDHAM URBAN LAW JOURNAL, XXVI (1999), 1201.

Bill Shaikin, *Players' Union Files Grievance*, L.A. TIMES, November 9, 2001, 1.

Bill Shaikin, *Strike 2? Major Leagues Plan to Cut Pair of Teams*, L.A. TIMES, November 7, 2001, 1.

Mark Asher, *Setback for Contraction: Courts' Rulings Strain Timetable for '02 Season*, THE WASH. POST, December 1, 2001, D5.

Thomas Boswell, *Ventura Works High and Tight to Selig*, THE WASH. POST, December 7, 2001, D1, D5.

Dave Sheinin and Mark Asher, *Twins Are Ordered to Stay Put*, THE WASH. POST, January 23, 2002, D2.

MLB Contraction Reset for 2003, MLB Press Release, February 5, 2002.

Chapter 14

Roosevelt Would Oust Football's Brutal Features, THE PHILADELPHIA INQUIRER, October 10, 1905, 1.

Ken Denlinger, *A Prescription For Pain? Trust Is Tenuous Between Athletes, Team Doctors*, THE WASH. POST, October 31, 1995, E1.

Dave Sheinin, *O's, Segui Have Dispute About His Wrist Injury*, THE WASH. POST, May 8, 2002, D5.

Tarik El-Bashir and Dave Sheinin, *Injured Segui Returns to O's Lineup*, THE WASH. POST, May 9, 2002, D8.

Preston Williams, *Surgery Set for Segui, Out 10-12 Weeks*, THE WASH. POST, May 18, 2002, D5.

J. Nocera, *Special Report: Bitter Medicine*, SPORTS ILLUSTRATED, November 6, 1995, 81.

Around the Majors, THE WASH. POST, October 26, 1995, D7.

The Heart of the Matter, SPORTS ILLUSTRATED, November 27, 1995, 26.

Judge Rules Recruit Can Play Despite Heart Attack, THE. WASH. POST, September 11, 1996, B3.

Tikkanen Rarin' to Go, THE WASH. POST, December 17, 1995, D10.

Thomas Boswell, *On His Way Out, Belle Takes A Swing At Introspection*, THE WASH. POST, March 7, 2001, D1.

Chapter 15

David Aldridge, *A Team's True Colors*, THE WASH. POST, December 16, 1995, A1, A18.

Perkins: Dallas Life Not Easy, THE WASH. POST, July 19, 1968, D3.

Thomas Heath, *At RFK, Soccer Tickets Hit Home*, THE WASH. POST, August 12, 2000, D1.

Thomas Boswell, *Unsportsmanlike Conduct for U.S. Soccer's Ticket Policy*, THE WASH. POST, August 31, 2001, D1, D5.

David Cho, *U.S. Soccer Ticket Plan Comes Under Investigation*, THE WASH. POST, September 6, 2001, B1.

Steven Goff, *Arena Not Feeling Very Much at Home: U.S. Coach Questions D.C. as a Future Host*, THE WASH. POST, September 3, 2001, D1, D6.

USSF Faces Lawsuit, THE WASH. POST, June 16, 2002, D2.

Court Ruling May Signal Martin's Last Ride," LOS ANGELES TIMES, April 26, 2001, D3.

Caddie Denied Cart, THE WASH. POST, July 10, 2001, D2.

Male Athletes Bring A Suit of Their Own, THE WASH. POST, November 19, 1999, D2.

Abigail Crouse, *Equal Athletic Opportunity: An Analysis of Mercer v. Duke University and a Proposal to Amend the Contact Sport Exception to Title IX*, 84 MINN. L. REV. 1655 (2000).

Kicker Cut By Duke Gets $2 Million, THE WASH. POST, October 13, 2000, A22.

Preston Williams, *Va. Girls Sports Will Be Seasonal*, THE WASH. POST, December 8, 2000, D8.

Look Who's Grappling, SPORTS ILLUSTRATED, November 27, 1995, 13.

Boys Take Hit in Softball Game, THE WASH. POST, August 17, 2000, D2.

Lisa Winston, *Ticket Promo*, USA TODAY BASEBALL WEEKLY, February 16-22, 2000, 29.

Chapter 16

John Walters, *Don't Kick Him Out*, SPORTS ILLUSTRATED, October 26, 1998, 59.

Spring Training Roundup, THE WASH. POST, March 6, 1999, D5.

Spring Training Roundup, THE WASH. POST, March 13, 1999, D3.

Steven Goff, *Surgery Set for United's Pope*, THE WASH. POST, April 19, 2000, D1-D2.

Steven Goff, *For Alegria, the Wait of the World: Midfielder Languished in Legal Limbo*, THE WASH. POST, April 20, 2002, D3.

Iraqi Weightlifter, Fearing For His Life, Is Granted Asylum By INS, THE WASH. POST, August 3, 1996, D9.

Buster Olney, *One Man's Journey to the Center of Baseball*, THE N.Y. TIMES, June 4, 1998, A1.

Clyde Haberman, *Asylum Pitch: Persecution or a Curveball*, THE N.Y. TIMES, March 27, 1998, B1.

Athelia Knight, *Khannouchi Too Late, INS Says*, THE WASH. POST, March 8, 2000, D2.

Jim Hage, *Record Marathoner Becomes U.S. Citizen*, THE WASH. POST, May 3, 2000, D1.

Colorado Rockies: Last Year's Cellar-Dwellers Have A Slew of New Faces and a Fresh Style of Play, SPORTS ILLUSTRATED, March 27, 2000, 154, 156.

Mike Soraghan, *Astacio Case At Heart of Deportation Dispute*, DENVER POST, December 7, 2000, B1.

Steven Goff, *Armstrong Says He's With MLS*, The Wash. Post, May 25, 2001, D3.

Steven Goff, *United Trades Diaz Arce To Rapids*, The Wash. Post, June 13, 2001, D3.

Steven Goff, *Etcheverry Gets His Green Card*, THE WASH. POST, April 12, 2002, D8.

Scorecard, SPORTS ILLUSTRATED, August 20, 2001, 26.

Chapter 17

Fanfare, THE WASH. POST, April 13, 1996, H2.

Frank Graham Jr., *The Story Of A College Football Fix*, THE SATURDAY EVENING POST, March 23, 1963, 80.

Bernie Miklasz, *Blown Lead At Wrigley Again Demonstrates Cardinals' Mediocrity*, ST. LOUIS POST-DISPATCH, July 28, 2001, 3 OT.

Mike Eisenbath, *Former Coach Easler Files Suit Against Cardinals*, ST. LOUIS POST-DISPATCH, July 27, 2001, C1.

Rick Hummel, *Freak Injury Sidelines Reliever Timlin; Jocketty Seeks Replacement*, ST. LOUIS POST-DISPATCH, July 28, 2001, 4 OT.

Mike Eisenbath, *Easler Says He Opted To Move On; "I'm Bigger Than This," Former Cardinals Coach Proclaims In Ending Suit*, ST. LOUIS POST-DISPATCH, July 29, 2001, D11.

The Blotter: Sued, SPORTS ILLUSTRATED, June 10, 2002, 32.

Chapter 18

Orioles, Regan Settle Lineup Card Dispute, THE WASH. POST, April 20, 2000, D6.

Aaron's 755th for Sale, THE WASH. POST, September 24, 1998, C2.

The Battle for Bonds's Ball, SPORTS ILLUSTRATED, October 22, 2001, 32.

'Field of Dreams': Field of Squabbles, THE WASH. POST, July 28, 1996, D15.

Bat, Ball and Videotape Cost Eager Plumber His Stadium Job, THE WASH. POST, March 20, 1999, D2.

Chapter 19

Fanfare, THE WASH. POST, December 17, 1995, D2.

Richard Justice, *Identity Crisis*, THE WASH. POST, February 24, 1996, H4.

NBA Files Lawsuit Against Motorola Over Sports Paging Service, LAND MOBILE RADIO NEWS, March 15, 1996, 1-2.

Chapter 20

Tony Kornheiser, *Billy Martin's Own Kind of Game*, THE WASH. POST, December 27, 1989, D1, D12.

Say It Ain't Sold, SPORTS ILLUSTRATED, October 13, 1997, 18.

Ann Gerhart, *Widow's Weeds; Jack Kent Cooke Never Exactly Promised Marlene A Rose Garden. But This?*, THE WASH. POST, May 29, 1997, B1.

William Nack, *A Name on the Wall*, SPORTS ILLUSTRATED, July 23, 2001, 60.

Paul Gutierrez, *World B. Free, NBA Gunner*, SPORTS ILLUSTRATED, March 8, 1999, 10.

Chapter 21

Steve Wyche, *Wizards Get Biggest Win This Season*, THE WASH. POST, March 21, 1999, D1, D8.

Thomas Boswell, *The Miracle of Coogan's Bluff Tarnished*, THE WASH. POST, February 1, 2001, D1.

Ball Four, Take Your Hacks, USA TODAY BASEBALL WEEKLY, September 20-26, 2000, 3.

Mets Complain, THE WASH. POST, May 1, 2001, D4.

Murcer Sticks by His Guns Though Kuhn Nicks Wallet, THE WASH. POST, June 30, 1973, D2.

Thomas Boswell, *Graham Is Reborn*, THE WASH. POST, July 26, 1980, F1.

Pirates' Freeze Fined, Is Assessed $50 by Giles for 'Inciting' Fans to Riot, The N.Y. Times, May 26, 1956, 21.

3 Seahawks Fined for Hot-Dogging, THE WASH. POST, August 29, 1995, E6.

Mark Maske, *Redskins May Fine M. Turk For Injury; Punter's Availability Vs. Cowboys In Doubt,* THE WASH. POST, October 22, 1999, D1.

Mark Maske, *Redskins Notebook: Punter Turk Won't Be Fined By Team For Injuring Finger,* THE WASH. POST, November 24, 1999, D3.

Mark Maske, *Redskins Trade M. Turk; Punter Shipped To Dolphins For 2001 Draft Pick,* THE WASH. POST, March 9, 2000, D5.

Henry Schulman, *Cycle Crash Evidence Surfaces; Club Investigates Kent's Injury,* SAN FRANCISCO CHRONICLE, March 20, 2002, C1.

U-Va. Athletic Director Probes Tripping Incident, THE WASH. POST, November 20, 1995, C2.

L. Brooks, *Angry Lemaire: I Didn't Stick Blame on Aide,* NEW YORK POST, November 4, 1995, 41.

Tennessee's Cleats Under Scrutiny, THE WASH. POST, January 7, 1996, D11.

Neuheisel in Trouble, THE WASH. POST, February 14, 1999, D13.

In Grand Gesture, Arsenal Offers to Play It Again, THE WASH. POST, February 14, 1999, D2.

Michael Farber, *Exorcised!,* SPORTS ILLUSTRATED, May 1, 2000, 60.

Chapter 22

Drop the Chalupa!, THE WASH. POST, November 19, 1999, D2.

Hey, We're Playing a Ballgame Here, USA TODAY BASEBALL WEEKLY, April 25-May 1, 2001, 3.

Excitement Kills Fan: Television Viewer Dies After Seeing Walcott Win By Knockout, THE N.Y. TIMES, July 20, 1951, 17.

Horse's Death Leads to Lawsuit, THE DETROIT NEWS, October 11, 2000, www.detnews.com..

Manuel Roig-Franzia and Michael E. Ruane, *Firefighters Pull Out 36 Burned Freight Cars: Intense Smoke Slows Job of Extracting Wreckage,* THE WASH. POST, July 21, 2001, A1.

Josh Barr, *Orioles Postponed Again: Team Might Pursue Legal Options to Recoup Losses*, THE WASH. POST, July 21, 2001, D1.

Matthew Mosk, *CSX Pays Baltimore's Overtime Bill; City Puts Tab at $1.3 Million*, THE WASH. POST, July 26, 2001, B2.

C. Jemal Horton and Neil H. Greenberger, *Gators' Shannon Has Ticket to Final Four*, THE WASH. POST, March 18, 1999, D6.

Oregon State Forfeits Victories With Shelton, THE N.Y. TIMES, November 10, 1976, A24.

Nets Down Braves; Knicks Are Beaten: Nuggets Win Before 17,808 by 119-110, THE N.Y. TIMES, November 4, 1976, 53.

Dye-Hard Fan, THE WASH. POST, January 1, 1996, C3.

Coach Settles Suit With Kinko's, THE WASH. POST, July 29, 1995, D2.

Fanfare, THE WASH. POST, March 15, 1996, C2.

Ken Denlinger and Ross Siler, *School's Out for NBA's Latest*, THE WASH. POST, July 5, 2001, D1.

N.B.A. Rule Found Invalid By Judge, THE N.Y. TIMES, March 13, 1971, 19.

Scorecard, SPORTS ILLUSTRATED, January 24, 2000, 34.

Benching Provokes Uncivil Response, THE WASH. POST, August 24, 1997, D2.

Thomas Heath, *Snyder Sued by Former Groundskeepers*, THE WASH. POST, September 22, 2000, D9.

Mark Maske, *Lawsuit Against Snyder Dismissed*, THE WASH. POST, February 8, 2001, D4.

Daniel Okrent, *Midsummer Snooze*, SPORTS ILLUSTRATED, July 12, 1999, 74.

Index of Athletes and Other Sports Figures

A

Aaron, Hank, 251, 311, 392
Abdul-Jabbar, Kareem, 345-346, 409, 411
Adcock, Joe, 87-88
Agramonte, Marcus, 156
Ahmed, Raed, 283-284
Ainge, Danny, 42
Alcindor, Ferdinand Lewis (Lew), 345
Alegria, Jose, 280
Alfonzo, Edgardo, 354
Ali, Muhammed, 345
Allen, Dick, 185, 199
Allen, George, 186
Allen, Ray, 171-172
Almonte, Danny, 154-156
Alomar, Roberto, 1-2, 5
Alou, Matty, 307
Anderson, Brady, 46, 58
Anderson, Matt, 18
Angelos, Peter, 167, 230, 310
Ankiel, Rick, 145
Appier, Kevin, 355
Arena, Bruce, 263
Arlington, Lizzie, 118
Arndt, Richard, 311
Artest, Ron, 379, 381, 410

Armstrong, Stephen, 290-291
Ashe, Arthur, 11-12, 36, 131-133, 399, 403, 415
Astacio, Pedro, 288
Attanasio, Tony, 174
Auerbach, Arnold (Red), 32

B

Badger, Brad, 34
Banks, Antonio, 364
Banks, Ernie, 254
Barajas, Rod, 95
Barksdale, Lance, 354
Barnaby, Matthew, 368
Barnes, Marvin, 172, 384-386
Barone, Tony, 26, 28-29, 31, 400
Barrett, Marty, 238, 240, 246, 248, 406
Barry, Rick, 19, 21-22, 203-204, 399
Bauer, Hank, 84-85, 87, 255
Bavasi, Buzzy, 14-15
Beard, Butch, 15
Belardi, Wayne, 168
Belle, Albert, 126-129, 248
Bell, Gus, 249, 392
Bennett, Darren, 276-278
Benswanger, William, 217
Bere, Jason, 99
Bernero, Adam, 44-45
Berra, Lawrence P. (Yogi), 3, 84, 228, 254, 402
Bickerstaff, Bernie, 350-351
Bird, Larry, 172
Black, Joe, 256-257
Black, Lloyd, 195, 208
Blackmun, Harry, 200
Blue, Vida, 189-190
Bochte, Bruce, 297-298, 301

Bonds, Barry,310
Bonham, Ernie (Tiny), 211
Bonilla, Bobby, 302-303
Boone, Pat, 12, 14, 17, 20, 399
Boras, Scott, 167
Bordagaray, Stanley (Frenchy), 2
Bordick, Mike, 151
Boswell, Thomas, 205, 235, 248, 262, 351, 357, 361, 368, 370, 407, 428-430, 433
Bouton, Jim, 160, 181-182, 190, 294-295, 322-323, 332, 335, 381, 411
Bowden, Tommy, 23-24, 27
Boyd, Brendan, 138
Boyer, Cletis, 168
Bradley, Bill, 359
Bradley, Shawn, 291
Brashear, Donald, 90
Brea, Leslie, 151, 156
Breadon, Sam, 10
Brennan, Christine, 114-115, 424
Brennan, William, 201
Brett, George, 340, 364-366
Brickhouse, Jack, 163
Brinkman, Joe, 341-342
Brodeur, Martin, 365, 368
Brooks, Garth, 52, 55
Brosnan, Jim, 293-294, 296-297, 301
Brown, Ellie, 109
Brown, Hubie, 109
Brown, Kwame, 388
Brown, Larry, 74-75
Brown, Jimmy, 218
Brown, John Y., 113
Brown, Roger, 334
Brown, Walter, 39, 253
Browne, Byron, 185
Browning, Bob, 185

Bruton, Bill, 22
Bryant, Paul (Bear), 300
Buckner, Bill, 140
Buckwalter, Bucky, 318
Budig, Gene, 352
Burdette, Lew, 132, 360-361, 369
Busch, August (Gussie), 199
Bush, George W., 226
Butkus, Dick, 243
Butts, Wally, 300, 417
Butz, Dave, 115, 425

C

Cain, Bob, 9
Camby, Marcus, 128-129, 131-133
Campanella, Roy, 356-357, 359
Cannon, Billy, 36
Cecil, Brittanie, 59
Cerv, Bob, 178, 182
Chalmers, Greg, 370-371
Chandler, Happy, 212-213, 252, 356, 406
Charles, Ezzard, 375
Christensen, Ben, 77, 89
Ciccarelli, Dino, 91
Cicotte, Eddie, 102
Cimoli, Gino, 294, 297, 301
Clark, Charles (Boobie), 80
Clark, Jon, 157-159, 166, 403
Clark, Tony, 353
Clark, Will, 18, 183
Clemens, Roger, 97-98, 402
Clemente, Roberto, 11-12, 307
Claxton, Speedy, 26, 31
Cobb, Ty, 214, 227, 359, 392
Coleman, Rip, 168

Collins, Tom, 346
Colon, Bartolo, 156
Comiskey, Charles, 103, 178
Conley, Christopher, 67, 69
Conley, Gene, 361
Conyers, John, 210, 233
Cooke, Jack Kent, 340-341, 433
Cooper, Irving Ben, 200
Cooper, John, 366
Costner, Kevin, 315
Craig, Kelly, 119
Craig, Roger, 116
Crawford, Gerry, 2
Cronin, Joe, 355
Crosby, Roscoe, 23
Crosetti, Frank, 295
Croteau, Julie, 118, 121
Crowe, Jack, 120
Cubas, José, 285
Cubillas, Teofilo (Nene), 281
Cuccurullo, Cookie, 211
Culberson, Leon, 344
Curry, Ronald, 37
Curtis, John, 185, 404

D

Dalkowski, Steve, 356
Daly, Bill, 91
Dampier, Louie, 109
Daniels, Bennie, 370
Daniels, Mel, 308
Darling, Gary, 298-299, 304
Davis, Al, 230
Dean, Jay Hanna (Dizzy), 10-11
Dean, Paul, 11

Delahanty, Jim, 214-215, 405
DeWitt, Bill, 8, 296
Diaz Arce, Raul, 290
Ditmar, Art, 134-135, 168-170, 228, 404
Donatelli, Augie, 358
Douglas, Sherman, 40
Douglas, William, 389
Doyle, Carrie, 130
Drew, J.D., 354
Drossos, Angelo, 188
Drysdale, Don, 173, 254, 404
Dumars, Joe, 149
Duncan, Tim, 172
Duquette, Dan, 170
Durocher, Leo, 351, 359, 366, 369
Dykes, Jimmy, 178

E

Early, Peggy Ann, 121
Easler, Mike, 301
Easley, Damion, 353
Edmonds, Jim, 302
Embrey, Wayne, 174
Esherick, Craig, 19
Erving, Julius (Dr. J.), 6, 187
Etcheverry, Marco, 290
Everett, Carl, 352
Evers, Johnny, 66

F

Fehr, Donald, 205, 225
Feller, Bob, 213, 404
Fernandez, Tony, 6
Ferrara, Al, 202

Fidrych, Mark, 172
Finchem, Tim, 264-265
Fingers, Rollie, 189
Finkelman, Paul, 311
Finley, Charles O., 169, 189
Fisher, "Pop", 35
Fisher, Sarah, 123
Flam, Ben, 266
Flanagan, Mike, 161, 357
Flood, Curt, 18, 185, 198, 201-202, 205, 207-208, 222, 250-251, 255, 257, 404, 420
Flowers, Charlie, 35-36, 400
Floyd, Cliff, 37-39, 179
Ford, Gerald R., 60, 400
Ford, Whitey, 84, 146, 149, 356
Foreman, Earl, 20, 44, 188
Forsberg, Peter, 130, 141
Fortugno, Tim, 181-182, 184
Franks, Herman, 350
Frazier, Walt, 359
Free, World B., 344, 346, 433
Freehan, Bill, 361
Freese, Gene, 358
Fricano, Marion, 229
Frick, Ford, 213, 392
Frisch, Frankie, 217
Fryar, Irving, 363
Fryman, Woody, 152
Fulton, Leroy, 162-163
Furcal, Rafael, 156
Furillo, Carl, 326-327

G

Gabriel, Roman, 184
Gabrielson, Len, 8

Garciaparra, Nomar, 352
Garth, Brooks, 52, 55
Gaedel, Eddie, 8-10
Gaetti, Gary, 8
George, Eddie, 66, 401
George, Phyllis, 113
Gervin, George (Ice), 187
Giambi, Jason, 313
Giambi, Jeremy, 313
Gieck, Joe, 364
Gilbert, Buddy, 249-251
Giles, Warren, 86, 358
Gill, Eddie, 26, 31
Gilmore, Artis, 109
Goldsmith, Fred, 120, 269
Gomez, Ruben, 87-88
Gonzales, Rene, 47
Gonzalez, Luis, 208
Gordon, Joe, 178
Gordon, Tom, 353, 356
Graff, Milt, 168
Graham, Danny, 358
Granato, Cammi, 123, 425
Granato, Tony, 123
Grange, Red, 172
Green, Elijah (Pumpsie), 254
Gregg, John, 237
Grimsley, Ross, 79, 369
Grizzard, Alton, 93
Gross, Jane, 97, 112, 402, 424
Guerrero, Wilton, 179
Guillen, Jose, 279
Gwynn, Tony, 6

H

Haas, Eddie, 56
Hackbart, Dale, 80, 83
Hadl, John, 184
Haller, Bill, 241
Hampton, Mike, 75
Hanlon, Ned, 197
Hannum, Alex, 21-22, 273, 334
Hargrove, Mike, 243, 248, 348
Harper, Alvin, 34
Harrelson, Ken, 172
Harridge, Will, 9
Harris, Fred, 138
Harrison, Roric, 182
Havlicek, John, 172
Hayes, J. William, 173
Haywood, Spencer, 388
Hazle, Bob (Hurricane), 21
Healy, Fran, 148
Heinsohn, Tom, 39, 421
Helling, Rick, 225
Hernandez, Alberto,285
Hernandez, Livan, 284
Hernandez, Orlando (El Duque), 284
Herzog, Whitey, 302
Heymann, Philip, 114
Higbe, Kirby, 217
Hill, Grant, 172
Hines, Henry, 11-12, 16
Hinson, Barry, 388
Hirsch, Corey, 130, 141, 403
Hirschbeck, John, 2
Hobbs, Roy, 35

Hoerner, Joe, 185
Holland, Terry, 364, 380
Holmes, Brent, 90-91
Holmes, Oliver Wendell, 197, 230
Holyfield, Evander, 6, 137-138
Howard, Elston,254-256
Howard, Frank, 261, 407
Hubbard, Trenidad, 179
Hudson, Ray, 281
Huizenga, Rob, 240
Hunter, Billy, 168
Hurley, Ed, 3, 8
Hurst, Bruce, 6
Hutchinson, Fred, 249

I

Iba, Henry, 149
Irsay, Robert, 232
Irvin, Monte, 369, 371
Issel, Dan, 109

J

Jackson, Phil, 367
Jackson, Reggie, 110-112
Jackson, Shoeless Joe, 102-103, 339, 402, 409
James, Mike, 354
Jenkins, John, Jr., 392
Jenkins, John, Sr., 392
Johnson, Arnold, 229
Johnson, Ban, 2, 214, 296, 399, 438
Johnson, Charles, 167
Johnson, Earvin (Magic), 369
Johnson, Eric, 266
Johnson, Jerry, 185

Johnson, Randy, 95
Johnson, Vance, 130-131
Johnson, Walter, 214-215, 296-297, 405, 419, 428
Jones, Andruw, 1
Jones, Chris, 52
Jones, George Khalid, 53
Jordan, Michael, 29, 257-258, 368

K

Kaiser, Don, 56
Kalsu, James Robert, 344
Kamieniecki, Scott, 70, 72, 75, 401
Kamm, Willie, 176
Kanu, Nwankwo, 367
Karnuth, Jason, 354
Kemnitz, Brent, 78
Kennedy, Cortez, 362
Kennedy, John F., 371
Kent, Jeff, 363
Kent, Joey, 366
Khannouchi, Khalid, 287-288
Khannouchi, Sandra, 287
Kiam, Victor, 114-115
Kile, Darryl, 145
Kindred, Dave, 78-79, 423
Kingman, Dave, 251
Klem, Bill, 3
Knapp, Nick, 244-245
Knepper, Bob, 116-117
Knutsen, Espen, 59
Kohl, Herb, 171
Koufax, Sandy, 173, 254, 404
Kreuger, Charles, 240, 246, 248
Krone, Julie, 121, 425
Kucks, Johnny, 84

Kuhn, Bowie, 110-112, 115, 189, 199, 207, 355
Kuhn, Rick, 100-101, 424
Kulpa, Ron, 354
Kunnert, Kevin, 82
Kurland, Bob, 148-150, 166, 426
Kutyna, Marty, 198

L

Lachey, Jim, 237, 406
Lamoriello, Lou, 41, 400
Lanier, Hal, 116
Lankford, Ray, 47, 302
Larranaga, Jim, 380
La Russa, Tony, 144-145, 302, 403
Lary, Frank, 162-163
Lazzell, John, 98
Lemieux, Claude, 40-41, 43
Levinski, Don, 179
Lieberman-Cline, Nancy, 122
Light, Greg, 161-162, 166
Limon, Tony, 90
Littlefield, Dick, 186
Littles, Gene, 109-110
Litwhiler, Danny, 332-333, 335
Lloyd, Graeme, 179
Locker, Bob, 159-160, 166, 174, 403
Lofton, Kenny, 353
Lombardi, Vince, 170-171, 174, 418
Lonborg, Jim, 173
Lopat, Eddie, 134
Lopez, Hector, 306-308
Lowe, Sidney, 350
Luciano, Ron, 14, 148, 161, 356, 390
Ludtke, Melissa, 110-112, 114, 116, 124
Lunar, Fernando, 179

Lupien, Tony, 192, 194
Lupoli, Johnny, 57-58

M

McAdoo, Bob, 43, 113
McCain, John, 55
McCarver, Tim, 185
McCollum, Rudolph C., 64
McCormick, Frank, 193
McCormick, Mike, 173
McDaniels, Jim, 41
McDermott, Mickey, 168
McEnroe, John, 17
McEnroe, Patrick, 17
McGraw, John, 152, 307
McGriff, Fred (Crime Dog), 6, 180, 183, 238
McGwire, Mark, 136-137, 302
McMahan, Jack, 168
McNamara, John, 140
McNamara, Tank, 37
McSorley, Marty, 90
Mack, Connie, 18, 229
Mack, Roy, 229
MacLean, Don, 39-40
MacPhail, Lee, 341
Maddox, Elliot, 400
Maddux, Greg, 145
Madlock, Bill, 2
Majerus, Rick, 44
Malone, Moses, 318
Maloof, Gavin, 29
Maloof, Joe, 29-30
Manning, Archie, 304
Manning, Peyton, 304
Mantle, Mickey, 84, 145, 147-148, 228, 252, 255, 359

Marichal, Juan, 85, 87, 91
Marion, Marty, 9
Maris, Roger, 168, 241-242, 248, 251
Marshall, Thurgood, 201, 208, 251
Martin, Ashley, 120
Martin, Billy, 84, 96, 110, 146, 312-313, 337-338, 340, 408, 417, 433
Martin, Casey, 263-266
Martinez, Humberto, 263
Massa, Gordon, 57
Matheny, Mike, 302, 354
Mathewson, Christy, 66, 152
Matich, Trevor, 255, 406
May, Rudy, 97
Mays, Willie, 86, 392
Mazeroski, Bill, 134
Melton, Rube, 217
Mendoza, Mario, 297-299, 301
Mercer, Heather Sue, 120, 268, 270
Meredith, Don, 10
Meriwether, Chuck, 353
Merkle, Fred, 66
Messersmith, Andy, 205, 404
Meyers, John Tortes (Chief), 152
Mikan, George, 203, 334
Miller, Marvin, 203, 324
Miller, Stu, 356
Mirer, Rick, 362
Molina, Anthony, 77-78, 89
Molina, Gabe, 179
Montanez, Willie, 185
Moorad, Jeffrey, 169
Morales, Andy, 153-154
Mordecai, Mike, 179
Moreno, Jaime, 290
Morgan, Tom, 168
Morris, Matt, 354

Motley, Constance Baker, 112
Mouton, James, 71
Mowatt, Zeke, 114-115
Mullaney, Joe, 308
Munson, Thurman, 172
Murcer, Bobby, 355-356, 410
Murakami, Masanori, 350
Murphy, Brian, 170
Murphy, Robert, 215, 218-219, 405
Murray, Calvin, 95
Musial, Stan, 181
Myers, Randy, 71-73, 83, 401

N

Nabozny, Heather, 124, 402
Nagashima, Shigeo, 349
Nash, John, 40, 186
Navratilova, Martina, 282
Nelson, Rob, 322
Nelson, Willie, 33
Nettles, Graig, 361, 365
Neuheisel, Rick, 366
Newell, Pete, 174
Nicklaus, Jack, 265
Niemiec, Al, 194-195
Nitkowski, C.J., 352, 354, 356, 409
Noren, Irv, 168
Nunn, Howie, 294

O

O'Brien, Davey, 127-129
O'Brien, Eddie, 295
O'Leary, George, 158
Oliver, Al, 307

Olson, Lisa, 114
O'Neal, Shaquille, 389
O'Neill, Kerryn, 93
Ortiz-Del Valle, Sandra, 124
Overmars, Marc, 367
Owens, Brig, 113
Oxelson, Canh,164

P

Page, Mitchell, 301
Palmer, Arnold, 265
Palmer, Jim, 1-2, 5
Pappas, Arthur, 238
Parlour, Ray, 367
Paulino, Rolando, 154
Pavano, Carl, 179
Pennock, Herb, 193
Penterman, Lee, 266
Peppler, Pat, 171
Perez, Odalis, 156
Perkins, Don, 257
Perry, Gaylord, 355
Perryman, Robert, 114
Pesky, Johnny, 343-344
Phillips, Dave, 341-342
Phillips, Steve, 354
Phillips, Taylor, 56
Piazza, Mike, 97
Piazza, Vincent, 231
Pierce, Billy, 163
Piniella, Lou, 297-298, 304, 408
Pinson, Vada, 249
Plaza, Ron, 295
Plimpton, George, 294
Podres, Johnny, 254

Pollock, Bill, 192
Portugal, Mark, 353
Post, Wally, 392
Postema, Pam, 116
Powell, Boog, 307
Pratt, Todd, 354
Pryor, Kelly, 259
Pyle, Charles C. (Cash and Carry), 172

Q

Quinn, John, 22-24

R

Ramirez, Manny, 169-170, 353
Randolph, Willie, 340
Rapp, Pat, 353
Raschi, Vic, 211
Rayford, Dion, 372-373, 392
Raymond, Arthur (Bugs), 307
Reed, Jody, 239
Regan, Phil, 159-160, 309
Renteria, Edgar, 302
Reynolds, Allie, 211
Reese, Harold (Pew Wee), 14, 254, 326, 327, 406
Respert, Shawn, 149-150
Rheaume, Manon, 122
Richardson, Bobby, 256, 357, 359, 410
Richardson, Dot, 119
Richardson, Luke, 91
Rickey, Branch, 252
Riley, Pat, 186, 404
Ringo, Jim, 170-171
Ripken, Cal, 309, 312
Rivera, Luis, 179

Rivera, Mariano, 208
Rizzuto, Phil, 148
Roberts, Curt, 168
Robertson, Oscar, 126, 128, 207
Robinson, Eugene, 362
Robinson, Frank, 1-2, 5, 249, 392
Robinson, Jackie, 125, 132, 186, 251, 356
Robinson, Wilbert (Uncle Robbie), 142
Roddick, Andy, 147-148, 426
Rodriguez, Aurelio, 138
Rogers, Ed, 156
Rogers, Omar, 156
Roland, Johnny, 4
Roosevelt, Theodore, Jr., 236
Roosevelt, Theodore, Sr., 236
Roseboro, John, 86, 88, 91
Rosenbloom, Carroll, 184
Rojas, Cookie, 185, 199
Rucker, Dana, 53
Rudi, Joe, 189
Rujano, Miguel, 121
Rush, Bob, 56-58, 400
Rush, Rick, 140
Russell, Bill, 33
Ruth, George Herman (Babe), 46
Rutherford, Kyle, 390-391

S

Sabean, Brian, 363
Salazar, Eliseo, 123
Santiago, Benito, 6
Saucier, Frank, 8
Schmidt, Willard, 198
Schultz, Joe, 196
Scottland, Beethavean (Bee), 53

Seabrooke, Glen, 237
Segui, David, 242-244
Seitz, Peter, 206, 208, 404
Selig, Bud, 227, 234-235
Sells, Jack, 387
Sewell, Truett (Rip), 218
Shantz, Bobby, 168
Shaw, Domynic, 366
Sheehey, Tom, 380-381
Sheffield, Gary, 6
Sheldon, Rollie, 152, 154
Shelton, Lonnie, 384-385
Shinjo, Tsuyoshi, 354
Short, Ed, 160
Simmons, Francis, 16
Simon, Scott, 163
Simpkins, Duane, 129-131, 133
Simpson, O.J., 73
Sipin, John, 49-50
Skiff, Bill, 195
Skowron, Bill (Moose), 228
Slaughter, Enos, 181-182, 190, 344
Smalley, Roy, 97
Snider, Edwin (Duke), 14, 327
Snyder, Daniel, 391
Sojo, Luis, 70, 72
Sotomayor, Sonia Maria, 224
Spahn, Warren, 132-134, 141, 403
Spiers, Bill, 75, 83
Spilger, Michael, 24-25
Spivey, Jr., Warren, 259
Stanky, Eddie, 356
Stanley, Fred, 111
Stapleton, Dave, 140
Stargell, Willie, 307
Staub, Rusty, 295

Steinbrenner, George, 50, 272, 337
Stengel, Casey, 85, 132, 134, 146, 178, 228
Sterling, Donald, 24-26
Stewart, Earnie, 263
Storen, Mike, 17, 188-189, 334
Stovall, George, 2, 5
Street, Charles (Gabby), 142
Sullivan, Jerry, 121
Sundra, Steve, 196
Surhoff, B.J., 178, 182-183
Sutton, Don, 360, 365
Suzuki, Ichiro, 125-126
Swift, Stromille, 27
Swirsky, Seth, 136, 139-140

T

Talbot, Fred, 381-382, 410
Tapscott, Ed, 149
Tagliabue, Paul, 114
Tanner, Chuck, 116
Taylor, Carl, 306-307
Taylor, Joe, 198
Taylor, Sammy, 56
Taylor, Zack, 8
Teed, Dick, 356-357
Temple, Johnny, 249
Terracciano, Neil, 106
Terry, Ralph, 31-32, 134
Theismann, Joe, 314
Thomasson, Gary, 185, 190
Thompson, Chuck, 134-135
Thompson, John, 18
Thomson, Bobby, 351
Thorn, Rod, 386
Thrift, Syd, 152

Tikkanen, Esa, 245
Timpson, Michael, 114
Tirendi, Vincent, 231
Tomjanovich, Rudy, 82, 90
Tomsic, Tony, 126
Topping, Dan, 84
Trebelhorn, Tom, 116
Turk, Matt, 362, 364
Turley, Bob, 359
Twist, Tony, 138, 141
Tyson, Mike, 6, 137

U

Uhlaender, Ted, 128
Umbricht, Jim, 249
Unitas, Johnny, 139

V

Valentine, Bobby, 37-38, 355
Vargas, Claudio, 179
Veeck, Bill, 8-9, 52, 148, 229-230, 232
Ventura, Jesse, 234
Violette, Richard, 25-26
Vitale, Dick, 299, 301

W

Waddell, Rube, 18
Wagner, Honus, 217
Walcott, Jersey Joe, 376-377, 410
Walker, Rube, 356
Walters, John, 277, 431
Walton, Bill, 243
Washington, Kermit, 82, 90
Washington, Marian, 299, 301, 304

Washington, U.L., 341
Wayne, John, 252
Wayne, Justin, 179
Weaver, Earl, 1, 361, 369
Weaver, Ron, 165-166, 404
Webber, Chris, 29
Weiss, Alta, 118
Weiss, George, 146, 148, 169
Wellstone, Paul, 210
Wendell, Turk, 354
Wenger, Arsene, 367-368
Werblin, Sonny, 113
West, Nolan, 317
Westphal, Paul, 26, 32-33
White, Byron, 200
White, Roy, 111
Wieand, Franklin Delano Roosevelt (Ted), 198
Wilkens, Lenny, 30
Williams, Claude (Lefty), 102
Williams, Gus, 30
Williams, Richard, 17
Williams, Serena, 17
Williams, Ted, 201-202, 208
Williams, Venus, 17
Wilson, Earl, 172-173
Wilson, Hack, 5
Winfield, David, 95, 96, 98
Wise, Skip, 308
Witt, Brendan, 92
Wojciechowski, Amerik, 328-329
Womack, Dooley, 182
Woods, Tiger, 140, 164, 264
Woolf, Bob, 172-173, 427
Worthington, Al (Red), 350
Wright, Clyde, 348

Y

Yasser, Ray, 132
Yastrzemski, Carl, 172
York, Gary, 44

Z

Zeile, Todd, 354
Zimmer, Don, 340
Zook, Ron, 387
Zupo, Frank (Noodles), 3

Index of Terms

A

acceptance of offer, 9, 14, 37-38, 40
agents, 24, 167, 171-172, 174-175, 207, 384
American Baseball Guild, 216, 219
Americans with Disabilities Act, 264-265
antitrust exemption, 192, 195, 197-198, 208, 210, 230-231, 233-234, 428-429
antitrust laws, 195, 197-198, 200, 208, 210, 220, 229-232, 234
arbitration, 161, 174, 208, 216, 226
artistic creation, 141
assault, 71-73, 76, 83, 90-91, 289, 393-394, 401
assumption of risk, 46, 51-53, 60, 62, 69, 400
asylum, 276, 282-287, 292, 408, 431

B

Ball Four, 160, 181, 294-295, 332, 352, 381, 416, 433
battery, 72-75, 79-80, 83, 89-90, 394, 401
bird sounds, broadcast of, 147, 148, 331
Black Sox scandal, 102
Bowman Gum Company, 202

C

cheeseheads, 328
Civil Rights Act of 1964, 249, 251, 253, 258
class action suit, 6, 274
Cobb's Lake, 360, 366

Coca-Cola, 324
codicil, 339-340
collective bargaining agreement, 31, 205-206, 225
common law, 14-15, 314-315
consideration, 9-10, 14, 16, 22-24, 26, 81, 225, 269, 277, 320, 374
Constitution of the United States, 126, 325
  First Amendment, 141, 272, 299
  Fourteenth Amendment, 112
contraction, 209-210, 225-228, 233-235, 429
contracts, 8-11, 14-15, 17-18, 31, 36, 38-40, 43-44, 139, 167, 172-173, 175,
    180, 182, 184, 202-203, 206-207, 244, 296, 309, 316, 362, 381, 383, 395,
    400, 403-404
  blank, 13-16, 399
  Brownies, 9-10
  implied, 37-39
  legal capacity to sign, 10
  meeting of the minds, 15
  on fax paper, 44
  on napkins, 45
  oral, 30, 253, 256, 264, 351, 387, 399, 416
  prohibition against eating crackers, 18
  prohibition of dangerous activities, 18
  voiding, 403
  written, 5, 13, 17, 20-22, 28, 31, 34, 39, 44-45, 114, 155, 195, 197, 214, 230,
    243, 278, 293, 330, 346, 349-350, 390
Copacabana, 84-85, 423
copyright bug, 329
copyrighted presentation, 330
copyrights, 320-321, 325, 335, 409
Curt Flood Act of 1998, 208

D

defamation, 293, 298-305
Department of Justice, 262
Dick Vitale's College Basketball Preview, 299, 301

doctors, 54, 59, 106, 236-238, 240-247, 380, 406, 429
   company doctors, 237, 244-246, 406
     duty of care, 63, 66-67, 373, 375-376, 378, 381, 383, 395, 401, 406, 410
     team doctors, 237-238, 240, 243, 406, 429
duty of care, 63, 66-67, 373, 375-376, 378, 381, 383, 395, 401, 406, 410

E

Education Amendments of 1972, 267
expedited citizenship, 288

F

false identity, 165
Federal Baseball Club of Baltimore decision, 198, 200-201, 230
Field of Dreams, 306, 315-316, 318-319, 409, 433
Flood v. Kuhn, 200-201, 411
foreseeability, 378, 410
free agent, 29, 189-190, 204, 206-207, 286
frivolous lawsuits, 390

G

gamesmanship, 148, 358-359, 362, 366, 368, 370
Great Depression, 10-11, 219, 417
green card, 283, 287, 289-291, 432
   conditional green card, 287

H

Immigration and Naturalization Service, 276-277, 279, 282-284, 289, 407-408
interstate commerce, 104, 197, 201, 220-223, 258, 261, 405

J

joyriding, 99-100

L

labor strikes, 217-218, 224
Ladies' Nights, 274-275
Landrum-Griffin Act, 220
Lanham Act, 323, 325, 327
larceny, 100
level playing field, 366, 368
lineup cards, 309-310, 312, 408
Little League Baseball, Inc., 271
Little League Softball World Series, 271-272
luxury tax, 224

M

Major League Baseball Players Association, 138-139, 205, 212-213, 215, 221-223, 233, 324
malice, 94
manslaughter, 94-95
Mendoza Line, 293, 297-298, 301-302
Merkle's bonehead, 66
Milwaukee County Stadium, 62, 293
misrepresentation, 142-144, 148-151, 153, 157, 160, 162-163, 166, 403
moral turpitude, 288-289, 408
Morgan State University, 15-16
Motorola, 330-331, 409, 412, 433
murder, 94-95
Murphy money, 219

N

NAACP Legal Defense Fund, 251
name changes, 345, 409
National Association for the Advancement of Colored People, 251

National Basketball Association, 6, 16, 19, 29, 31, 43, 111, 124, 149, 186, 203, 207, 221, 321, 330-331, 347, 350, 388-389, 411-413
National Basketball Players Association, 207, 221, 347
National Collegiate Athletic Association, 120, 127, 129, 236, 258-259, 367, 379, 413
National Football League Players Association, 221
National Hockey League Players Association, 221
National Labor Relations Act, 220, 223, 405-406
National Labor Relations Act of 1935, 220
National Labor Relations Board, 211, 220-224, 226, 405, 412
negligence, 63-64, 79-81, 376-377, 401
Norfolk Tides, 333
Norris-LaGuardia Act, 220
notary public, 340-342
no-trade clause, 180, 184

O

O-1 visa, 279
O-2 visa, 277
offer, 9, 12-14, 16-17, 24-31, 36-40, 44, 141, 159, 211, 286, 301, 367, 421

P

P-1 visa, 276-278
Patent and Trademark Office, 323, 334
patents, 320-321, 335
Pennant Race, 86, 180, 294, 296
pension fund, 212, 219
pine tar, 340-342, 364-366, 368
pine tar game, 340, 342, 364
playbooks, 388
plea bargain, 394
precedent, 3, 5-6, 62, 200-201, 262, 345
privacy, 72, 112, 115, 125-133, 135-138, 140-141, 302, 383, 387, 403, 426
privacy, right of, 126-127, 129-133, 136, 138, 141, 403

promises, 20, 23, 30-31, 381, 410, 421
property, 87, 99-100, 108, 171, 181-182, 201-202, 208, 232, 254, 306-309, 311-319, 321, 323, 332, 337-339, 382, 388, 408-409
  gifts of, 339, 340
  partitioning, 306, 318
  personal, 34, 85, 100, 140, 155, 198, 205, 247, 308-309, 312, 338-339, 408
  real, 22, 24, 26-28, 30-31, 35, 41, 147-148, 152, 164, 213, 217, 229, 248, 260, 308, 313, 321, 400, 417
proximate results, 379
public gaze, 127-129, 132, 135
publicity, right of, 136-138, 140-141, 346, 403
puffing, 150, 157-158

R

reasonable apprehension, 72, 76, 401
relocation of franchises, 229-331
remote results, 378
replacement players, 214, 217, 224
replacement workers, 406
reserve clause, 203-205, 207
Robert F. Kennedy Stadium, 260, 370

S

salary arbitration, 161, 174
salary cap, 223
Saturday Evening Post, 300, 432
scalping, 100, 104, 108
self-defense, 86-88, 94, 423
service marks, 323, 325, 335, 409
sex discrimination, 267, 274
sexual harassment, 115
speed guns, 333, 390
spitballs, 355, 360

Sports Illustrated, 18, 24, 26, 31, 34, 39, 52, 58-60, 77, 90, 97-98, 110-112, 121, 123-124, 126, 131, 136, 141, 148-149, 154, 157, 164, 172, 181, 186, 199, 238, 244, 271, 277-278, 289, 291-292, 300, 304, 311, 339, 343, 368, 390-392, 421-428, 430-435
standard of proof, 73, 95
statutory law, 15
Super Balls, 361, 365

T

Taft-Hartley Amendments of 1947, 220
team-wide dishonesty, 369-370
tenants by the entirety, 312-314
tenants in common, 313
Texas Motor Speedway, 51
The Long Season, 293-294
Title IX, 267-272, 407, 431
Topps Chewing Gum, 139, 202
torts, 70-72, 83, 395
trademarks, 320-321, 323-325, 335, 409
trades, 7, 178-179, 182, 185-186, 189-191, 279, 290, 404, 432
  legal elements of, 183
  refusal to accept, 186
trespass, 316-318, 409

U

umpires, 3, 5, 66, 86, 116-117, 222-223, 298, 340-342, 354-355, 357, 362, 369, 399, 408, 438
unclean hands, 36-37, 388

V

Veterans Act, 193-196
Virginia School League, 270

W

Wagner Act, 220-221, 223
wills, 339-340
Wimbledon, 64-65
"Wilkens Clause,", 30-31
workmen's compensation, 247-248
Wrigley Field, 56, 71

Y

Yankee Stadium, 63-64, 70, 228, 272, 308, 342, 422